ALL HALLOWS EVE ON RIVERSIDE DRIVE

The coven had met on Samhain to perform a great work, opening a Rift between our world and the next . . . but before the rite could be completed, they were interrupted. The High Priest died of the shock, and the gap between worlds was never closed.

Annalise Brown thought she had found a good deal on an apartment. No one told her how the previous tenant had died.

THE GUARDIANS

Other books by Lynn Abbey

DAUGHTER OF THE BRIGHT MOON

THE BLACK FLAME

THE GUARDIANS

LYNN ABBEY

FANTASY
ACE BOOKS, NEW YORK

THE GUARDIANS

An Ace Book

Published by arrangement with the author.

ISBN:0-441-30589-X

First Ace Printing: October 1982
Published simultaneously in Canada

Manufactured in the United States of America
Ace Books, 200 Madison Avenue, New York, New York 10016

The Guardians

a novel

From the Grimoires and Spellbooks of Lady Camulac

High Priestess of the High Coven at Caer Maen

Be it known that this world and the Otherworld are separated by the frailest curtain.

Be it known also that those Spirits which dwell in the Otherworld envy our worlds of life and death and are ever-vigilant in seeking escape from their abode to ours.

* * *

Ye have heard that the Summerland is the abiding place where we will await Our Next Journey through Life. Know Ye that while this is true and the Summerland is death-partner to us, neither is it the Otherworld. It is not within our province to defend the Summerland, nor does the Summerland rise to our defense. Yet the two are linked in Common Cause to forbid the Otherworld any exit from its barren and eternal exile.

It is said that the Otherworld is filled with the errors of Life and Death. It is said that Spirits which cannot be redeemed live but once and are cast by the Gods into the Otherworld where they dwell in exile knowing neither life nor death. All this is said, but it is not Known.

Yet because the Otherworld purges the Great Chain of Being, so must all souls feel its power as they pass between

Life and Death. For those who may be redeemed there need be no fear; for those beyond redemption there is no hope.

* * *

That Gods have ordained since the Beginning of Time that it shall be given to a very few initiates to know the Otherworld and guard its boundaries from the circles of a High Coven.

It was said that all Passage shall take place at Certain Times and Places; that these Times and Places shall be Guarded by a High Coven chosen and honed to the task and much esteemed by the Gods they serve. Of each High Circle there shall be chosen Priest and Priestess who shall hold dominion over these Times and Places from the Gods Themselves until death or accident shall overtake them.

SO MOTE IT BE

* * *

In the beginning of Time there was but one Time and one Place—but it is the way of man to grow. There are many places where Rifts of the Great Curtain exist and are guarded. It is given to us to know that we were twelve High Circles before the coming of the Romans. That our sister circles continue to exist is certain but we now hold the names of only four: Caer Maen, Gretna, Dorking and Chemin des Aix. But the Time shall never change and it is Samhain.

All the years of our lives shall be measured from Samhain, the years of your death as well, for there is naught in Living or Dying that is not ordained on that date.

SO MOTE IT BE

* * *

(additional notes)

For eleven months we have watched the disturbances that can be no less than the opening of another place of passage through the Curtain. Daffid has sickened and departed though his name was not thought to have been called; it is the same at the other covens known to us. We have linked hearts and spirits to find this Rift and have seen it in the city of New York, America, where no High Coven has existed.

We have passed the autumn equinox without sensing the control or mastery which we believe guards those many Rifts we know exist but whose traditions and spells have always been closed to us. A second unattended Samhain is too great a risk. By our powers as High Priestesses the Lady Deonore of Gretna and I have brought forth a talisman and sent it with our children so that a High Coven might be established at this new place.

Be it known, henceforth, that there is a new Place. There are now thirteen sisters of this rite: Thirteen Places of which we can name five—Caer Maen, Gretna, Dorking, Chemin des Aix and Riverside. But there is yet one Time and that Time is Samhain.

Lady Ravenna
In her own hand this 21st of September 1928

Chapter One

The oak grove was a good distance from a road that was itself only a set of rutted tracks through half-abandoned Hudson Valley farmland. Golden, red and brown leaves covered the path and also covered the endemic rabbit and gopher holes. Arthur Andrews walked in silent, intense caution. He had reached that age where he was a distinguished gentleman, but one fall would transform him into a crippled old man.

Steel clouds banked up from the western horizon to provide high-contrast light for the few remaining leaves on the tree branches. The clouds had gathered since he had left the car. He glanced at them occasionally, wishing he'd brought a raincoat, or at least his cane.

His concentration of the half-hidden network of roots and fallen branches had been so complete that the grove, its trees still golden-clad, took him by surprise. Though it was late October and the cloudy rawness could easily mean snow, Arthur paused before entering the oak circle. He patted a linen handkerchief across his brow and removed his shapeless tweed hat. The breeze caught wisps of his white hair and lifted them into a wild halo. Unmindful of the grinding stiffness in his back and legs, Arthur walked forward and swept the leaves from a granite boulder at the center of the grove, revealing its polished, carved surface.

"Ah, Gwen, is it still peaceful here, or have the skiers and hikers come through to disturb you? I couldn't get here all summer. Arthritis. Dr. Court would have the car keys if he thought I'd walked this far without his permission which, of course, he'd never give me. I've fretted all year, my love," he paused in his soliloquy to his dead wife, crumpling the hat from one hand to the other. "At home it was so different. Traditions were stronger. There were always children; none of us here ever had children." His voice softened. "Perhaps we could have known that was a sign long ago; we were not the ones to hold this place forever. Today I mean to give it back. I shall count myself fortunate if They listen and I make it back to the car without disaster.

"You understand, don't you? You always understood things before I did. Have you been expecting me?"

He set the hat on the stone then looked up to the treetops. He slowed his breathing, letting his eyes focus themselves where they would, and waited. Breezes riffled through his hair, blew the hat to the ground and brought a shower of leaves to flutter against him.

"Do you hear me?" he asked and the breezes stilled. "For fifty years I've come here to hear Your counsels. I've given my life to guard this world from the Other. Only one life, one lifetime—but let it end? My Morwedd, my Gwen, is gone and I'm tired. I've failed, I know—there're none in the coven to take up our responsibilities. For five years I've pushed on without her. I've tried to bring new blood into the circle but they have no strength. I fear for them and You."

A wind started in the treetops, spiraled down clattering among the branches and raising a pillar of leaves momentarily from the ground. Arthur, who called himself Anerien when he spoke to the Gods, hesitated. The wind died as suddenly as it had sprung up. He knew Their ways well enough to know it was time to rest his case. If They heard, They would answer. If They hadn't heard, he should not have asked, and that was an answer as well.

His mind wandered. In the final quarter of the twentieth century it was more than slightly ludicrous to stand bareheaded in an oak grove expecting Gods or Goddesses who had been worshipped when man still lived in caves to answer his questions. It was ludicrous to have lived a double life: Arthur Andrews, corporate lawyer of impeccable connections and Anerien, High Priest of a coven that traced itself back to those same caves. It was ludicrous to be seventy-eight, but at seventy-eight he at least no longer had to worry about being ludicrous.

He had no cause for complaint with the life that had fallen

to him. The grimoires promised that those who served the Gods as Guardians of the Rifts between life and death would not go unrewarded. His life had been comfortable though never ostentacious. Luck usually travelled with him and Gwen. There had been disappointments, major ones sometimes, but everything had fallen within the limits of understanding. The Gods had never abandoned him.

The maelstrom of thought died away and he waited, confident that there would be a sign: a tailor-made sign that would cut through his doubts to reveal the wishes of his dieties. The wind picked up again. A pair of crows wheeled over the grove and took position in the trees. He felt comfort; there were witnesses. One of the crows hopped through the branches stopping before a cluster a bright gold leaves. The bird snapped the twig with its beak and lifted off from the branch. It dropped the leaves as it flew. Arthur stood firm when the twig struck his cheek and fell to his feet.

The Gods were, and yet were not, subtle. They could produce a talisman so innocuous that one could tuck it in one's lapel, which Arthur did, but also swat him in the face with it. A tiny drop of blood marked his handkerchief where he had daubed it against his cheek.

A few drops of rain splattered to the leaf-covered ground. The crows took noisy flight. The dark grey clouds had spread until they left only a narrow band of yellowish light on the eastern horizon. He tossed the question: what do I do with it? to his unconscious mind and tugged the hat over his wild hair. Finding a twisted branch of a walking stick hidden in the leaves, he started back to the car.

He was drenched. His feet were stiff and numb. His fingers had knotted around the staff like lichen by the time the ancient Mercedes appeared through the trees and shrubs. The last few hundred feet were the steepest of the trek. He resisted the impulse to hurry and reached the car with the same methodical slowness that had marked the entire journey.

The worn leather seats still released the aroma of freshly cured leather whenever they got wet. Arthur inhaled the narcotic smell and let the tension drain from his body into the car and out to the mud-channeled road beneath.

"Burn it."

The answer to his question rose out of the depth of his mind once the muscles in his neck had relaxed enough to release it. With the words came the semblence of a ritual. He would burn the twig at the altar, consign its vapors to the currents of the air and enjoin them to find another coven gathering on the most sacred of the old pagan festivals. Let Riverside be dissolved. Let the burden settle on some native circle. Let it settle on some priest more worthy than he was.

His smile became a chilled shudder. Premonition or simply the dampness? A thousand, maybe only five hundred years before he would not have let the doubts settle. He would have ignored the storm and gone straight back to the grove for clarification. As it was, Arthur concluded in favor of dampness. He started the engine and set the defroster for full blast.

Behind the wheel of the car twenty years of arthritic timidity dropped away. He was sixty again, retiring from Wall Street with a generous pension, planning vacations with Gwen and looking forward to a freedom not allowed to pagans since Constantine had seen *"in hoc signe vincet"* written in the clouds. Even the emptiness of her death was easier to bear on the little country roads. She was easier to imagine sitting beside him, seeing beauty in the dreary landscape, than by her memorial in the grove.

Arthur conversed with her memory until they reached Yonkers and there was no more beauty to be wrung out of the wet cement. The traffic had become a stream of angry, aggressive drivers. He gripped the wheel with both hands and gently cursed his growing forgetfulness. He had remembered Samhain, but he'd completely forgotten that it was also Sunday. The Thruway was a crush of weekenders hurrying home, their manners unimproved by the miserable weather.

The car crept along, eating up the time Arthur had allotted for ceremonial preparations. His stomach churned fitfully, reminding him that he had left the chops in the freezer and would have to brave the crowds at the delicatessen if he wished to eat. But good luck did not desert him completely; the Monday parking space right in front of the building was being vacated as he approached it. A woman in a subcompact thought to out-maneuver him, darting in from behind while he set the Mercedes into reverse, but plastic and aluminum was outclassed by German steel. What the Gods have granted, let no man, woman nor automobile deny.

Sam, the doorman of the Riverside building and master of the mahogany doors since V-J day, held the door open for him.

"Evening, Mr. Andrews. Bad night out, isn't it?"

"Oh, not so bad, Sam. Keeps the hooligans off the streets."

The lobby was a clanking, hissing chamber of radiator pipes whose activity spelled the certain end of Indian Summer.

"Now that's true enough, Mr. Andrews. Is your car set for the morning or would you like Sam Junior to move it for you?"

Sam Junior was the soft-spoken son of the doorman, now on scholarship at nearby Columbia University. The young man braved the rigors of alternate-side-parking, undercutting the services offered by the management's dark and vermin-infested garage.

"No, Sam, it's good until Tuesday."

"Tuesday's Election Day, Mr. Andrews. You're set until Thursday."

"Ah, I'd forgotten that holiday, too."

They nodded to each other. Arthur, his cane tapping in rhythm with the pipes, headed for the closet-sized elevator. The old steel cables whined and shook as if each upward foot might be their last, but they had sounded the same on the day they were installed fifty years before. Rent-control had kept a stable, but aging, community within the building until the last few years when many had died or finally moved away. Arthur wouldn't move out, but the new, young, status-conscious residents were a colder, less neighborly lot.

He'd lost count of the times in the past year when the management had received anonymous letters about the parties he gave. Copies of the letters had been slipped under the door. He suspected the young couple across the hall who openly envied his river view, but unless the smoke from the talisman settled around their shoulders they would never occupy number 647. The letters always arrived after the Great Pagan festivals, but the couple had never detected the pattern; somehow they had concluded he was running a dope ring. Arthur was alternately amused and confused.

The kitchen, which branched off the apartment's pullman corridor, was still very much Gwen. Her plants still wound around the window, the ceramics she had collected on their vacations sat on the sill and the three enormous canisters she used to store loose tea that Edith, her sister, sent them from Cornwall still sat on the counter. The canisters were kept full, reminding him of his hunger and the hours since his last cup—and of the letter he had yet to write to Edith.

He put the kettle on and went down to the bedroom to change out of his damp clothes. Attired in a proper cashmere dressing robe and with a cup of fragrant dark tea steaming at the corner of his writing table, Arthur sat back to compose the letter. He was immediately caught up in a demon's dance being broadcast in a concert tribute to Hallowe'en. The point of his pen conducted the frantic music and did not settle back to the paper, unmoving, until well after the next piece had started.

"Edith," he wrote, embellishing her name with absent-minded swirls.

Edith had been three when he and Gwen had left England for America, and a more unlikely candidate for High Priestess of the Great Coven of Caer Maen had never been spawned in all that group's history. Gwen, the eldest, had been the logical choice to take over, but when the Rift had broken across the ocean everyone's future had been altered. Ravenna had married off her daughter and sent the pair to America. She then set about the thankless task of refining the wild and stubborn Edith to the responsibilities almost certain to fall to her.

That the transformation had been successful was a potent sign of the Gods' abiding power. Edith had matured into a

High Priestess uniquely suited to the task of guiding Caer Maen through World War II and all that had come after it.

"I've delayed the better part of six months in writing this," Arthur wrote. "If you'd gotten phone lines in, my word—I'd have called and gotten this out at once the day after I'd made up my mind. As it is, well, I've waited until there's no time left at all.

"I've gone back to the grove and gotten a token from Them. This can only mean that, after five years, They've heard and agreed to release me from this responsibility. If ever there were a place fit for the Otherworldly Ones to blast their way into our world it has got to be this accursed city. Half a century we've guarded this place and done our duties but these last few years, especially, have convinced me that for all the good we've done we might just as well stayed in Cornwall.

"You said it was just my bitterness when Gwen died, and that I'd get over it in time. But, you see, I haven't. And neither has anyone else in the coven—what's left of it. I lost two more this past June. They moved out West for the climate and to get away from here. I might have gone with them. And the newer people—well, the less said the better. Aside from Rowen and Glasfryn there'll only be three others here tonight who've parted the curtain before.

"Maybe I've grown careless. I've certainly grown fearful. It seems half the people I meet in the shops think they're witches, pagans and the Gods know what all else. They'd dance around a jar of peanut butter and call it Beltane! I shall not mind at all if my own name is called from beyond the Rift tonight; I certainly don't belong here anymore. If the Curtain is properly sealed behind me and the Otherworld contained for yet one more year I'll be content. At any road, it's to be my last Samhain at Riverside."

He stopped again and stared at the unevenly scrawled lines, written in haste and scarcely legible. His hand trembled. Putting down the pen he shook the blood back to his suddenly numbed fingertips. Sudden loss of feeling in the extremities: a danger sign for any of the numerous slings and arrows the aged were particularly susceptible to, but more likely the result of holding the pen too tight for too long. He missed Gwen, longed to join her in the idyllic Summerland where the Wiccans believed the soul rested and awaited rebirth, but he would have to die first, and despite what he had written, that thought did not sit lightly within him.

No occult cartographer had learned what perils lay between this world and the next, but they deemed it likely, because of the Others, who held sway in the limbo between all worlds and touched each soul in its journey, that the first moment would be terrifying. For someone like Arthur, who had felt the obscene and malignant lust of those evil, non-human spirits in every Samhain ritual, the journey across the Hellish limbo would be conscious, exquisite terror.

Edith would know of the terrors. She might even understand the longing he had to be done with this life. True, when he had been in his fifties, himself, such thoughts had been far from his mind, but at Caer Maen there was always death and rebirth. Edith would have to understand, there was nothing more he could say. He signed his name adding the runic form of Anerien beneath it and the intricate sigil of the High Coven of Riverside beneath that. He had gotten the proper number of stamps from the half-round table in the hall when Sam buzzed up from the lobby to announce that he had visitors.

"They're early," Arthur grumbled in reply, not caring if they heard him downstairs or not. "Send them up. I suppose."

He looked at his watch—seven-thirty, a full hour before Rowen was due to help him prepare the livingroom, and hour and a half before any of the others were expected. Another sign of his coven's failure to adopt proper attitudes and traditions. Unlatching the door he hurried back to the bedroom to change again.

Chapter Two

"I see you haven't started yet."

"No, I wasn't expecting you so soon—you're an hour early," Arthur grumbled, entering the livingroom to find Rowen already rearranging the furniture. He tightened the sash on his black ceremonial robe and helped to move the plush love-seat closer to the walls.

"But, it's eight-thirty." The frail, tiny woman with skin like parchment looked first at her watch then at the bookcase clock that chimed seven-thirty as she watched it. "Oh, Anerien, you've forgotten to reset your clocks."

She went to the shelf and fussed with the clock while Arthur, in stony silence, removed a Lalique statue of a beautiful, mysterious woman from a locked cabinet. He had forgotten the secular ritual of spring ahead; fall back. Rowen's reminder, no matter how gently or casually phrased, only empasized the vicissitudes of his own aging.

He studied Rowen. She had always been frail and of uncertain health and despite this one of the strongest members of the coven: the logical choice to be his ritual partner after Gwen died. They were High Priest and Priestess by virtue of individual power and experience—but they had never established the rapport that would allow them to exceed their individual strengths.

Arthur had never known exactly how old Rowen was, nor for that matter much else about her private life. The rigid, traditional and isolationist strictures that the High Covens followed had suited Rowen perfectly. Some twenty years back he had heard her name was Marjory Sutton; he had never learned her married name, if she had one, nor knew for certain if Glasfryn was indeed her husband. The High Coven was very much like a revolutionary cell; the members knew no more about each other than was necessary to do their work.

"What shall I do with this?" Rowen held up the oak sprig she had found on the writing table.

"Give it here, it goes on the altar. I'll be needing it during the ritual tonight."

Rowen did as requested, her pale skin a mirror of sudden concern. "You're planning to change the Samhain ritual?"

"I think so," Arthur explained with his back to her, carefully rearranging the candles, plates and other ritual paraphernalia until it complimented his mood and purpose. "After the invocation and opening, I think. I had an inspiration up at the grove this afternoon." He had prepared an explanation and hoped she would be satisfied with a less than truthful one.

"You went up to the grove in all this rain? You really shouldn't do that, you know. We're none of us getting any younger."

"No argument, but it had to be done, and I'm the one who had to do it." He brushed imaginary dust from his hands and stepped back from the altar.

"Well, yes, I suppose. It makes me a bit nervous, though. Are you expecting this one to go bad? Are the Gods?" she whispered.

There was no taboo against discussing those ceremonies where something had gone wrong but the unpleasant, often terrifying experiences did not lend themselves to normal conversation. Any pride a High Coven witch might feel about the privelege of sending the dead on their way and receiving those about to be reborn was easily tempered by the palpable terrors of the Otherworld through which the exchange was made.

Yet there were times when the fears and anxieties could not be borne in silence. When Arthur made no move to answer her questions, Rowen moved closer to him and asked in a scarcely audible voice:

"Are *They*?"

"No, the token is for my peace of mind, my own partings as it were. I found no untoward omen in the grove." Arthur placed his hand on hers as he spoke and once again pushed a chill from his mind.

Rowen was satisfied with his explanations and assurances. Retrieving a canvas satchel from the hall she went into the bedroom herself.

In times past the High Covens had worked their rituals naked, or skyclad, but they had succumbed to the mores of the Victorian era and wore long-sleeved robes of rich and original design. The silver and gilt medallions worked into Arthur's black robe had been copied from the margins of the Caer Maen Book of Shadows where they had been drawn by Gwen's grandmother in 1869. The crimson bird-of-paradise embroideries on Rowen's deep-green bishop-sleeved gown, however, were strictly of her own devising.

Arthur poured the last of the tea into two cups and they sat in Gwen's cheerful kitchen sipping and waiting for the others. Glasfryn, the dark-eyed, dark-haired gentleman who had worked with Rowen when Gwen was still alive was the first to ring the doorbell bringing with him a sack of homemade rolls to place before the altar. As was his custom he selected the wine from a closet wine-cellar, decanted it carefully and studied its color against the light. He was a connoisseur and considered a vintage Bordeaux the only wine strong enough for the dangers of Samhain.

It was an extravagant waste now that most members could not distinguish Lafite Rothschild from last Thursday up in the Finger Lakes. When the wine was at the altar and Glasfryn in the bedroom donning his robes Arthur took his tea into the livingroom where he shut the doors and sat alone by the altar.

"I've lied to Rowen," he whispered after a moment. The candles were as yet unlit and light from the electric bulbs robbed the altar of its mystery. "There is something ajar this evening. What should I have done that I have not?" He looked into the coolly beautiful statue on the altar, but if in the past that serene face had brought him insight or solace it did not do so now.

He set himself to meditation, testing the undefinable currents of what occultists often call the "ether." Faith alone guided him on these unscientific ramblings and often it was enough to restore calm. The discordance which had led him to meditation in the first place persisted even after he should have broken through to self-unity. He relaxed and tried again.

Arthur's powers of concentration were sufficient to block out the street noises, the echoes of the pipes clanking through the building and the wind-driven rain beating against the windows, but they were no match for the sound of his own coven trooping down the corridor. He could imagine Rowen telling them to be quiet; that he was acting strangely and needed peace. And they would try, even the uninitiated among them, but they would still whisper loudly.

His imagination cost him his meditating ability. One knee gave out with a painful snap as he stood up. Stepping gingerly he tested his balance and sighed as the joint accepted his weight without disaster.

The presence of uninitiated witches at a High Coven Samhain was unheard of. Neither he nor Rowen had remembered to place the initiation paraphrenalia on the altar. He rummaged quickly through hidy-holes until he had the lengths of silk cord and the purely symbolic thrice-knotted scourge. The young pair's true initiation would be their first glimpse of the Otherworld; a public flogging might be less traumatic, but there was no other way.

The tree-stump looked cluttered; Arthur grimaced at it. His oak leaves were all but lost amid the candles, censers and goblets. Everything was necessary and it was too late to bring another table in to set beside the altar. Nothing was unequivocably wrong, yet Arthur was nervous: irritated instead of confident. His hands shook when he opened the French doors to admit his coven.

"Is that the altar?"

A bewildered young man not out of his teens, not known to Arthur and therefore one of the uninitiated, stopped short in the doorway; he shed fear as a skunk sheds scent. Arthur wondered what he had been told about the coven. Whatever it probably wasn't enough or accurate. Everyone faced the Otherworld from a different perspective. Would he have accepted the High Coven responsibilities if Samhain had been *his* first rite?

"Go on in, it won't eat you," Sunniva, a plain blonde woman in her late twenties complained to the neophyte before Arthur found the words to console him.

"What's your name?" Arthur asked when the young man finally sat down. He tried to set aside his own anxieties to reassure the youth.

"Uh . . . Jim, Jim Staski."

"Tonight you will choose another name, Jim. Perhaps you'd like to sit a moment and find one that suits you."

"A secret name? I'd never thought of that."

"Not so much secret—though in the Burning Times we needed secrecy. We choose new names now when we choose the Wiccan Gods to remind ourselves that this is a separate, self-chosen path. It is your decision how profound a division you make in your own life."

The youth sat obediently at the edge of the sofa. "Sir," he said softly, "I'll be called Fleet, if that's acceptable."

Arthur nodded. He was past questioning how the younger ones found their names so long as the names worked within the Circle. He watched the rest as they entered the room. His gaze paused on a dark, curly-haired woman who was also a stranger to him. She was apparently intended as Fleet's partner, though it was obvious she'd never set eyes on him before. Though scarcely the type to intend disrespect, she was garbed in a choir robe brilliantly embellished with Christian Chi-Rho embroideries. Rowen's attention was riveted on the symbol; her lips were pale lines of anger across her face. Arthur intervened.

"And who are you?" he asked the young woman.

"May I be just plain Sara?"

It was impossible to tell if the tremor in her voice was due to awe or a profound desire to be anywhere but where she was.

"Well, Sara, we welcome you, and we won't ask you to do anything disrespectful to your past—but, I think you'll find it inappropriate to wear clothing celebrating the Christian Messiah at our rituals. I'm sure that Rowen can find you one of my wife's gowns to wear." Arthur looked from the embarrassed girl to Rowan who was visibly torn between her desire to be rid of the offensive symbol and her dislike of giving Gwen's robes to a stranger. "I think something plain and in a dark shade would be right, don't you?" Arthur met Rowen's stare calmly.

Rowen did not relax as she guided the young woman with icy gestures, refusing to touch either the robe or the woman within it. Hangers clattered noisily in the bedroom then Rowen emerged alone and vibrating with displeasure.

"Try not to be so harsh with her. We were all frightened once and we still make mistakes. Any failings they have will be revealed soon enough without our help. Remember too, they have not had the training we take for granted," Arthur whispered a generous conciliation and was rewarded with a bitter, injured stare.

The mood between himself and the High Priestess was now thoroughly shattered. Arthur felt himself slipping into despair. He wondered what else could go wrong and regretted the thought almost at once.

"Stella and Uidred won't be here," Branwen said to no-one in particular. And that pair had been through Samhain before and might have stabilized the circle.

"Did they give you a reason," Arthur demanded.

"Fear, they said. Stella was still having nightmares from last year. And Uidred, well, I talked with him a few hours ago and he just said he couldn't face it again."

Branwen avoided the questioning glances of the others by focusing only on Arthur's face. Their eyes were locked in a futile, empty communication of the unspoken.

"Nightmares?" A woman whose forehead bore a Hindu marriage-mark though she herself seemed more Scandanavian than Indian broke the silence.

"Sir," Fleet said in an empty, forlorn tone, "I'm not sure anymore. I've been looking for something for a long time, my sister knows that," he looked at Branwen who nodded. "The others were too light, too filled with flowers and sunshine—and that's not me. But, I'm not looking for fear and nightmares."

Arthur had no answer for them. He lowered his eyes and contemplated the dynamics of his coven. Glasfryn sat back in the easy chair, waiting, concealing his thoughts from everyone. Would he close the Rift with Rowen in the future? How long had he coveted the first-among-equals position? Rowen, still sulking, her dislike for the younger members apparent in every pore of that parchment skin. Branwen, who had brought her brother to join them. Devi and Yama who fancied themselves as a link between the Hindu escetics and the Wicca. Sunniva, quiet and ethereal, a bit like Gwen but without her strength. And the new ones whose personalities were unknown but who radiated fear and doubt. They all had be be forged into a powerful unity and he was the only one who might be able to do it.

"Here we are *witches*," he began, letting conviction flow into his words. "Not cardboard characters to hang on a window. Not flower-children whose faces follow the sun. The Samhain rite we perform was drawn on the walls of ice-age caves in Southern France. The altar at our Mother Circle of Caer Maen is almost as old."

Arthur summoned the majesty of his age and experience to inspire the motley circle. Glasfryn shed his laconic facade and sat forward in his chair. The older members eased into a closer rapport with each other and Sara edged further away. Arthur hesitated; these youngsters were uninitiated: unsworn to the mysteries and unaccustomed to oaths. All his instincts told him to bar them from the ritual, yet his instincts had let the High Coven fragment and die. These newcomers might be the very ones the Gods had chosen to receive the talisman.

"This is an altar of the High Covens," he continued. "The power of life and death harkens to our call. The forces of the Otherworld mass against our strength. Nightmares. Nightmares! Branwen, innocent that you and your friends are, last year was nothing; They ignored us." Rowen shuddered as Arthur spoke, a gesture not lost on the rest. "From Samhain to Beltane—the Underside of the year—not merely winter, or rather say that winter is a symptom of the Underside when both life and death walk in fear.

"We do not know what power ravages on the far side of the Rift we will open tonight. We do not know whose names shall be called for death and rebirth, but it is our sacred responsibility to see that those names are called and safe-passage made for them."

"The Dance of Life and Death. Shiva Nataraja—the Lord of the Dance. In the wake of destruction and death comes life. It is the WAY—there is no other," Yama recited softly, clasping Devi's hand in his own.

"I do not speak of gods nor of ordinary life and death. With your notions of karma, Yama, have you never considered that there are spirits who cannot be redeemed?" Arthur's voice had softened without losing its intensity.

"There is a place for everything on the Karmic Wheel."

"Then, for some, that place is neither Here nor There but in the inversion that is totally Other; the place of which Hell is only a shadow. An eternity where there are no Gods and there is neither life nor death. We have no name for it; it is simply Other. But we know, we have known since the beginning that the Other envied our life and our death. We hold it back in all our rituals, but in doing so we hold life apart from death as well—and the Other knows this. It waits at the border, knowing there must be communion between life and death—there must be Samhain—a time when the realms of life and death exchange souls and those few which must be spat out of the Great Chain of Being are forever exiled to the Otherworld. We of the High Covens stand at the Rift, sealing out those who have already been exiled. We must never fail!"

"Nothing is that evil," Sunniva said, though she had attended the previous Samhain rite and should have known better.

"Oh, yes it is," Rowen countered, her soft voice turned shrill.

The uninitiated witch, Sara, trembled and edged still further from them. If she were the one to whom the burden would fall her transition would be miraculous. The High Covens never prosletyzed; they accepted no-one who did not first choose them. Could he, in any justice, let this frightened girl join them in the Samhain circle? Did he have the right to alter her life for all eternity by exposing her to the Otherworld? Did he have the right to risk everything by ignoring her weaknesses?

Sara might have guessed Arthur's doubts. She fished a handkerchief out of the borrowed gown and dabbed at her eyes. The rest of the coven had already cast judgment by ignoring her—but they were only following Rowen.

"We have serious work to do tonight," Arthur began again. "I had believed it was most important to have our full strength in the circle this evening—that itself is impossible without Stella and Uidred. Since we cannot have the strength of numbers we should concentrate on the strength of spirit. Take a few moments, each of you, consider what has been said; meditate on your purposes and if you find yourself wanting, then leave us without guilt."

Summoning the power of all the esoteric disciplines he knew, Arthur purged the tension from his mind and body. He found his center and rebuilt his peace of mind around it. When serenity had been established he focused his eyes on the group again and saw that both Fleet and Sara had retreated. He exhaled slowly and felt the renewed strength and purpose of his coven.

"We shall begin again in a more orderly fashion. Rowen . . ." Arthur opened his hand to the High Priestess and gestured to the unlit candles. She found a long taper and lit them.

The electric lamps were turned off. The circle formed around the altar. Rowen breathed life on the incense. Arthur attempted to forget the world outside the candlelight but the sound of breaking glass in the bedroom caught his attention.

His sigh was magnified by the effort of rising to his feet. Rowen rose to one knee, guessing his destination, but he waved her aside. He closed the French doors behind him and entered the bedroom.

The young pair was crouched on the floor picking up fragments of a glass vase Gwen's mother had given her at their wedding.

"I'm so sorry," Sara said, choking back sobs and rushed toward him. "I know I shouldn't have touched it . . . It slipped while I was putting it back on the dresser. I'll get you another one, I promise I will."

Arthur removed her hand from his own. Like so many other things, the vase could never be replaced. He shook his head and looked at Sara. "No, no that won't be necessary. It was only glass and not very valuable. Don't worry about it."

"I'm so sorry," she repeated and Arthur wondered how old she was.

"Oh, Damn!"

The young man cursed and jumped up, sucking his finger. "I cut myself. Do you have a band-aid?" He shook his hand and a spot of blood appeared on the bedspread. "Oh, Damn again!" He swiped at the blood-bead, succeeding in smearing the redness further.

Both of the children, Arthur could help but think of them as children, stared at him in frantic embarrassment.

"Ice water," Sara said earnestly. "If you've got ice water then I can get the stain up. If you let it dry it'll never come out."

Arthur shook his head. They were sincere enough but he was running out of time and patience. "No, don't worry about that either—just get your things and go."

"Are you sure we can't fix it? We've made such a mess." Sara tried to take his hand again, but he eluded her.

"No, just get your coats and be on your way—please."

Arthur followed them down the hallway and held the door while they hurried down the stairs. It was not until he heard the unmistakable click of a peephole cover snapping shut that he remembered he was in his priestly robes and that the scene would undoubtedly get reported at the stroke of nine the next morning. The anger he had not vented at the young people or at his coven rushed to control him.

"Damn you all!" he exclaimed before he could stiffle the words.

Releasing the door he let it bounce shut and spun on his heels. The sudden movement and seething anger sent grey dizziness washing over him. Gasping he leaned against the wall, clutching the front of his robe over his heart. A throbbing pulse of agony shot through his neck and shoulders. His knees buckled and he was sliding down the wall when the pain was suddenly over and only a trickle of sweat remained on his brow to mark the spasm.

He paused in the kitchen to dry his face before rejoining the coven in the livingroom.

Chapter Three

The air in the livingroom was heavy with the scents of Samhain: myrrh, henbane and black poppy. Rowen had recovered the balance and majesty of her role and led the circle in a traditional prayer as Arthur opened the door. She had chosen a commonly known invocation, one that was chanted in many of the newer pagan circles, not merely in the ancient High Covens: a tactful choice on her part. He turned the knob so that the door shut tightly but did not disturb his now-united group.

"Are we ready, Anerien?" Rowen asked, rising to her feet.

"Yes, I think the time is right now."

He took his place at the southern face of the altar, the others rose silently to their feet. Arthur, Glasfryn and Branwen drew black-handled knives etched with runes from sheathes concealed within their robes. The rest selected similar but plain-bladed weapons from those already set on the altar, except for Rowen who, in the shadowy darkness, produced a silver-gilt sword some two and a half feet in length.

She kissed the blackened runes along its blade then stepped between Arthur and the serene glass goddess. After a moment of thought known only to herself and the Gods, Rowen moved to the candle set behind Arthur and beyond the circle.

"To the Guardian of the South—all praise and thanksgiving! Draw near to us and guard our ritual from evil or malice. Sanctify that which we do in Your name and in the names of the Lady and the Horned God!" As she concluded, Rowen flourished the sword in a star-shaped salute that flashed the candle's light back to the others who repeated her movements.

As High Priestess she stood before each of the cardinal points in turn, invoking the guardian benevolence of the attending spirits. She lingered an extra moment in the East, as was her custom, requesting special consideration from that benign and gentle power. With the directional Guardians invoked she returned the sword to the altar and took up the censer. Starting with the North and moving clockwise, as the members of the circle rotated to face her, Rowen marked out a circle just behind them and within the limits marked by the cardinal candles.

"Be thou consecrated a place of Power; a boundary between the realm of men and all other realms, a boundary which guides and preserves Your servants as we do the Gods' work this night of Samhain. With myrrh, henbane and black poppy I consecrate this circle."

As the others repeated her words over the censer, Rowen placed it on the altar. She took up a shallow bowl and cast grains of salt onto the path she had marked with the incense. She summoned the leeching powers of the salt and invoked them in the protection of the celebrants. They repeated her words. Rowen made a third, and final, circuit of the room with water she had first touched with the tip of the silver-gilt sword.

The circle was sealed, they had only to fill it with the coven's power. This Rowen would not do out of loyalty to Gwen's memory. She stood motionless, her arms lost in the flowing drapery of her heavy gown. Finally, after a moment that seemed too long, Arthur extended his hands. Their touch brought a shower of visible sparks. They withdrew then. touched again, this time peacefully. With dancer-like grace they exchanged places so now Arthur stood facing the Goddess and Rowen was only another member of the circle.

A reminding trickle of cold sweat sped down his back as he prepared to raise the untested power of this High Coven circle. He heard his name whispered around the boundary Rowen had marked out, but glancing around he saw than no-one had called him. A second bead of sweat followed the first, then he felt the warm presence of the Goddess, unbidden, within the circle.

"Night-prime of winter. Birth of Death! These and more

are with us as Samhain lies heavy in the air. Ancient ones, crones and druids who have attended us in the past, draw nigh again as we enact our sacred rite."

Arthur's fingers jerked of their own accord as he extended his arms upward. For a terrible moment he feared the return of the spasm he had felt in the hallway. He forced his mind back to the ritual, succeeded in his quest and began to weave the protective power of the Samhain spells: first acts in preparation for the annual incursion into the Otherworld. He had meant to make his invocation peaceful, but the leavening of fear had put a harshness and doom-saying into his voice. The air around them grew cold and restive. The candles flickered erratically. The windows rattled in their warped, old frames. In the hallway outside the apartment a gust of wind whipped up the stairwell, momentarily drowning out the clanking pipes with its mournful *skree*.

They were witches, at least the older of them were, and believers in magick. They were also children of the twentieth century where magick lived a weakened life along the border of coincidence. The storm, outside the apartment, was the coincident cause of the flickering, rattling and skree-ing, just as the crows in the upstate grove had done nothing outside the bounds of coincidence: uncanny coincidence, like rolling snake-eyes ten times in a row. Perhaps the whispering of his name was coincidence, too.

The creamy pillar-candle set as the Guardian of the West sputtered and went out in a plume of waxy smoke. Coincidence or not, all eyes focused on the new darkness.

"The Guardian of the West abides in darkness even as the sun abides after it has set," Arthur intoned, though he had felt a twinge of primal fear when the candle guttered.

The guardian candles, purchased in bulk from an ecclesiastical supply house, were guaranteed against the errant breezes of the most drafty sanctuary. Arthur held silence for a moment, poised for some new outrage of coincidence, but there was none and he continued with the ritual, describing the purpose of their gathering as if time itself might have forgotten the generations of the High Covens.

They were people of mystery and faith and though the structure of their sabbats was hoary with tradition, they were not bound to a fixed litany of meaningless phrases. Arthur found new words of explanation flowing from his heart rather than from any of the thoughts he had carefully nurtured over these last months or years.

There was a place in the ritual where the circle would commend its own departed to the Gods and offer prayers of well-being for their souls now resting in the Summerland. Since Gwen's death Arthur had called upon each celebrant to make their peace in silence; he could never share his grief with them. But untoward urgency kept him speaking after he would have fallen silent. He recounted those who had departed from the High Coven of Gretna in his youth, then proceeded resolutely through his memories without faltering, even when Rowen could be heard sobbing softly behind him. Tears ran down his face when he spoke of Gwen and the pent-up grief of five years' enduring made its escape. When there were no more to commend he whispered through a sob-tightened throat that they might all take a moment in silence to greet those reviving souls who would enter this world in the coming year and to bid farewell to those whose names were now being called and who would depart before the next Samhain.

The candle-flames were the color of her hair the morning they married, respectably enough, in the old Norman church near Caer Maen (whose altar had a lengthy, and largely unofficial, association with the High Coven.) She had worn the same ivory satin gown for her funeral, though she had complained in the hospital that the dress would fit only because they'd never had children. There had been flames, too, at the end because New York would not allow him to inter a body in the grove while they would allow ashes. He could smile now when he thought of that macabre comedy-of-errors. The crystal gaiety of her laughter came to him and at the core of his being he was no longer without her.

His contentment abolished the somber moment of meditation and restored a mood of confidence and life to the coven.

With Gwen's spirit within him, Arthur called on the circle to commence its proper, magickal work.

"On this most sacred and terrible night of Samhain
When the spheres are stained and bursting
And the fires of life and death burn brightest,
"We come together in our ancient, august ritual
With shouts and songs to fling apart
The drawn curtains of our lives and all else,
"To bid fond, sad parting to those who must now depart
And greet with joyous thoughts and song
Each spirit whose journey is now begun,
"With fear and trembling, yet stalwart in our duties—
EVOI! EVOI! EKO! EVOK!

Arthur's sudden shouts startled the circle which had already slipped into the rhythm of his chant. Rowen and the rest who had experienced the ritual before echoed his words as a congregation responds to a pious, reverent drone. The remainder, who were not yet certain of the rite, whispered the response a half-breath later. And all listened more closely as Arthur continued with the chant that, though the product of generations of revision and interpretation, recalled the misty dawning of man with images of caves and naked dancers.

The pace increased and with it the volume of the chorus until the shouts were neither self-conscious nor hesitant and the neighbors in all directions were certain to hear the seemingly meaningless syllables. Arthur began clapping, the coven followed until the circle swayed back and forth oblivious to time or coincidence. Arthur spread his hands over his head; they scrambled to their feet to imitate him and those who could joined him in a gutteral, yet lyric, language that might once have been Basque or might always have been meaningless.

Yet Arthur had grown up in Gretna believing that these sounds, and these alone, could not be changed as the Coven moved forward in the stream of the centuries. And despite their meaninglessness, they were exactly the same as the ones

Gwen had copied from the Caer Maen Grimoires—the only prayer of which that could be said.

"HUREH-HAREH-HA!"

The final shout and the room was silent except for the storm's battering. By all the power and tradition vested in a High Coven they had opened the awesome Rift between all imaginable opposites. Now, while they sat counting a thousand heartbeats the intangible movement of souls was taking place. In a voice little louder than a whisper, Arthur bid his fellows to cast their spirits into the unseen swirl for enlightenment while he picked up the oak-sprig and held it over the altar.

His thoughts flowed fully into the act he was about to perform so that though a commotion outside the apartment was perceived, it was not consciously noted. He expected a momentary, yet total, reliving of his half-century of priesthood and was caught in the onslaught of memory. The disturbance, the movements of the circle as it responded to the loud noises and banging were reduced to utter insignificance beside the fullness of his spiritual stimulation until, with a crash that rattled the glass-panelled doors of the livingroom, the front door of the apartment was flung open and heavy footsteps thundered down toward their sacred gathering.

"Keep together, they're down there to the left. Burns, you and Harry go through first. Fan out and cover them."

"Right."

"Jesus, what's that smell?"

The French-doors sprang apart, ripping the flimsy skeleton lock away from the old wood and popping a pane of glass free from its cracked caulking. The glass shattered loudly. Arthur, still gripping the talisman, stared at the intruders—a deputation from the New York Police Department.

"Impertinent insolents! Be gone from here! You don't know what you're interrupting. Be gone!" He waved his hands in a manner suggesting a fantasy magician shooing away some annoying demon of his wayward conjuring.

The policeman furthest into the room drew his pistol and

dropped to one knee, holding the weapon with both hands, ready to fire at any of the Wiccans. His partner crouched to his left, his gun leveled at Arthur's head. But it was a younger man, further back in the pack who spoke up.

"Nobody move. We have a warrant to search you and these premises for illegal substances."

He waved a piece of paper at them, then appraised them of their rights, as required by law. The police stepped through the door, spreading themselves along the walls. They eyed the glittering black knives and the obviously non-Christian altar, and the people in the richly, arcanely embroidered robes. Illegal substance searches were dangerous but routine; stumbling into a den of witches on Hallowe'en left the men in the grip of fear. One of them found the lightswitch, hit it, and brought the coldly reassuring light of electric reality to what had been darkly mysterious. The cops relaxed.

"Now step back, slowly. Keep your hands out in front of you where we can see them."

"You cannot do this!" The towering rage in Arthur's voice had been replaced by his own fear and disbelief. He spoke to the Rift, to the Otherworld and to his own Gods, but not the police who were ordering Yama to lean against the wall.

Rowen's face had gone ashen. She swayed to one side, a leg buckling beneath her. Angry and panic-stricken voices filled the room. A policeman rushed forward, finally understanding what was happening to her. When the blue uniform broke the perimeter of the circle the remnants of Arthur's self-control vanished. He swung wildly with a knobby, untrained fist—missing the officer by a foot.

A stab of white-hot pain sprang through his arm, paralyzing him with shock. A numbed part of him said he'd been shot, but a calmer part already knew it was his heart and that he was dying. His fingers went into wild spasms. He felt his heart shudder, stop and begin a relentless pounding. It seemed as he hung there, poised but unbalanced, his weight forward on his feet; that the world had stopped and would not restart until he had completed his dying.

Arthur fell forward, narrowly missing the altar. The oak-sprig slipped out of his fingers.

"Mother-of-god, the old geezer's down."

"Anerien!"

The police pressed forward to separate the coveners from their fallen priest while one of their own knelt by Arthur, rolling him onto his back.

"What's going on down there? What's all the confusion?"

"Man down! *Man down!*"

"Someone's been shot!"

"Everybody! All of you! Get out of here—go back to your own apartments!"

"He ain't gone yet. Get on the land-line—call 911. Do *something*!"

The one who had held the gun on Arthur thrust the weapon into its holster and came up with a hand-held radio, smoothly—as if he were unimpressed by seeing his suspects collapse. He called his dispatcher and another cop grabbed the phone from the desk.

Arthur stared up at them. He was weightless yet he could not move. His mind was still clear. He feared being stepped on as huge feet crossed over him and someone beat violently upon his chest. For a moment his fear was all that remained in the world, then he remembered the interrupted ritual and the talisman. Summoning super-human concentration he looked for the sprig, focusing on it just as the last fleck of gold was absorbed into the abyss of the Otherworld. He wanted to scream, but there was only white pain searing through his body.

"He's going again!"

"Jesus! Sweet Mary—where're the medics?"

"Everybody back—*Everybody get back*! Nothing's wrong—it's all routine. EVERYBODY GET OUTTA HERE!"

"Mister Andrews? Mr. Andrews?"

A gust of raw air brought a breath of life back to the stricken man. He was strapped tightly into a stretcher and held by three people he did not recognize.

"Mister Andrews?"

Sam. Arthur recognized the aged doorman's face hovering above him. He could see fear in Sam's eyes, but he could not answer him. His spirit was drifting free of his body. He felt the cold winds of the Otherworld more keenly than he felt the few raindrops that splattered through the sheet they folded over his face as he was gently bounced into the ambulance.

A red-haired nurse folded back the sheet as the ambulance roared from the curb. Her eyes were a clear green and her skin was the color of clouds in a sunrise.

"Gwen? Gwen? Not yet Gwen. It's not closed! It's got the talisman! I can't go with you until the ritual's over."

"Now, Mr. Andrews, don't try to speak."

She jabbed a needle into his arm, an action he could see but not feel. His world faded until there was no color beside those green eyes. He heard his name, Anerien, shouted in his head.

"Gwen! Gwen! Stop them! It's not time—it's not time—!"

Chapter Four

The taxicab sent up a plume of curbside water as it raced toward the changing light at the corner. Lise stared down at her splattered raincoat and wished she hadn't given him a tip—or that she'd given him a larger one. In seconds, though, the new water-marks had blended in with the old. It had rained every day since Hallowe'en: eleven days in all. A radio DJ had announced that he was building an ark in Central Park; the way Lise's apartment hunt was going, if the ark would accept singles she'd move in.

Riverside Drive had sounded promising but the building itself, well-maintained and dignified, looked a bit rich for her blood. It was also a "deal"; the not-so-close friend of a not-so-close friend had offered Lise the sort of apartment that never made its way into the ads.

An elderly black man emerged from the lobby and held the brass-fitted door open for her. The lobby had the aura of luxury become genteel poverty and it was easy to imagine the days when a working girl need not bother looking at a vacant apartment.

"I'm here to see Mr. Fine," she said to the doorman, emphasizing her contact's name. "I'm supposed to meet him to see the vacant apartment."

"We don't have any vacancies," he replied impassively.

"I was told an apartment had just become available and that Mr. Fine would show it to me before he listed it." Lise spoke with a learned confidence that masked any number of insecurities.

Monday morning the idea of getting an apartment through contacts had sounded exciting and sophisticated. In real life it only reminded her that she was still just two years out of the Midwest and hadn't learned all the rules yet. She knew she was being tested but until the doorman smiled she couldn't guess if she had passed.

"He'll met you upstairs at apartment 647. It's a beautiful place. You must be the Miss Brown they said was comin' to look at it—I'd been expecting someone a bit older." He paused. "Very sudden—just like that. Mr. Andrews was down here talking with me not three hours before they carried him out on a stretcher. He was a good man."

There was a defensiveness in his tone that roused Lise's sense of caution. She had known from the start that the previous tenant had been an elderly man who had been fatally stricken by a heart attack on Hallowe'en. There was something more to it; blind instinct suggested the occult, though it was hard to believe that a building like this could be tainted by ghosts.

She considered questioning the doorman further, thought better of it and meekly followed his directions to what appeared to be the oldest, tiniest excuse for an elevator in the City. The morning sounds the cables made belonged in a grade-B movie and incubated phobias Lise had never suspected she had.

Fine was already on the landing outside the apartment. He was a round person: round face, round glasses, round body. She had been told he was the owner of the building. If that were true, then being a landowner had not given him much of an air of aristocracy. His cigar was knotted and bent at half-a-dozen angles; an inch of ash fell from its tip as she approached.

"The place is a mess," Fine explained, fumbling with the locks. "The old man lived by himself. We had no complaints until about a year ago. The new couple across the hall started getting upset. Parties! *Orgies!* Arthur Andrews was eighty if he was a day. If he could enjoy an orgy—well, good for him. I should be so lucky. Anyways, they call the police Hallowe'en. 'Big party.' 'Lotsa noise.' '*Knives!*' the old man ups and has a heart attack from the shock. Dies on the way to the hospital." He pushed the door open and flicked on the light.

The pullman-style hallway of the apartment was a dreary blend of dull paint and faded carpeting. The ceiling fixture cast unforgiving shadows and the bald light from the unseen rooms at the end of the hall only added to the gloom. The Andrews' place had none of the glamor she had been imagining. Only an unmailed letter, sitting on a hall table proclaimed that this had once been a home.

When they were inside and the door closed, the air smelled of candlewax, smoke and incense. Fine conceded that there must have been something to the neighbor's complaints but Lise, standing in the kitchen where a clean bone-china teacup sat alone in the sink, did not think the old man who had lived here was the type to throw wild parties.

The livingroom was another story. There was something more than normal disorder in this room that should have been a study in Edwardian interior decoration. The heavy damask draperies had been torn away from the windows. Plump velour cushions were strewn haphazardly on the paisley carpet. If Andrews had had his heart attack in this room, Lise thought, he had fought death every inch of the way.

A treestump sat in the center of the chaos; an odd piece that did not seem to fit the decor and yet was the most distinctive thing in the room. Guttered candles and fragrant ash gave the stump a mystery that Lise could not immediately unravel. But when Fine shed another half-inch of ash beside the burnt incense cones, her mind shouted "sacriledge."

"Can't make much sense of it myself," Fine said, drawing deeply on the cigar. "I'll be honest with you: the police think it's witchcraft. Andrews was a partner in some Wall Street law firm—hardly the place for black magick types, but it takes all kinds, I guess. Who knows, maybe the police came back and did it themselves to coverup."

He made a feeble attempt to straighten the drapes and only succeeded in pulling them off the rod altogether. Lise tried to imagine the room with everything in its proper place. She gathered up the letter paper scattered across the table and jollied it back into line. Fine was quiet now, stubbing out the cigar in what he took to be an ashtray on the stump. The rain had let up slightly; a lighter shade of yellow-grey was visible across the river.

"It must be lovely here when the sun sets," Lise whispered.

"Yeah, I get ten percent more for the view."

Lise's hand went to her purse where a thousand dollars hid in the lining. The friend-of-a-friend had said to bring cash.

"Really, Mr. Fine, this is a lovely apartment—despite the mess. And, like you say, the view is worth ten percent. But I'm afraid we've been misinformed about each other. I don't think I could afford this place."

"Have we talked money?" Fine retorted. "Have I said anything about money? How should you know you can't afford it if I haven't told you how much."

"Well, no—but, really—"

"Four-fifty."

It was not a figure to be taken seriously.

"Mr. Fine, you *are* a business man and I didn't blow in from Michigan last Friday. You could get twice that for this place, easily. My boss would pay you twice that—"

Fine thumped a cushion back into place on the sofa. "So, he's not here and you are."

While part of Lise's thought exalted and argued for agreement before Fine came to his senses, the suspicious, dominant part demanded more information. "What's wrong with this place, Mr. Fine? Where's the line of people waiting to get in here? How come you're making this offer to me?"

"Vibes," Fine mumbled.

"What?"

"Vibes—good vibes, bad vibes. Sure there was a waiting list—Andrews couldn't go on forever. Ratners across the hall wanted this place since a year ago. All the time they're trying to evict the old man—orgies! An eighty-year-old man with orgies! *Mazel Tov!*

"Hallowe'en they called the police—big megillah. November first Ratners want to see the place, but the police got a lock on the door. Next day, what was it—Tuesday? Ratner calls up and doesn't want to see the place. It's got bad vibes; makes funny noises at night. His wife thinks its haunted. Everybody on the waiting list takes one look at it and says the same thing. You ain't said it yet, so I figure you don't have 'em.''

Fine didn't say anything more; he was staring at New Jersey. Lise walked into the bedroom, which had escaped the disorder, and thought about his speech. Once the subject had been mentioned she could feel what everyone was calling vibes, but they didn't really bother her. Oh, there was something a little off, but certainly no more discordant than the average Stravinsky symphony. She liked Stravinsky.

She opened the doors of a large walnut wardrobe that supplemented the room's tiny closet. A woman's clothes hung there; the old man had been married and his wife had pre-deceased him. Lise lifted out a royal blue gown and held it between herself and the mirror. The bead-work alone was worth more than she earned in a week.

—She was my size—Lise lifted another more somber but equally elegant dress out for examination.

Fine was moving about again; she hastily thrust the dresses back before he joined her.

''Yeah, clothes—that's the worst part. First time I had someone die, my wife came in to clean up. Never again, she says—it's like undressing a corpse—an' she would know; she was a nurse.''

The image clung like an oily film; Lise had seen, touched and now felt unclean. Here in the bedroom the smell of wax and incense was replaced by the undefinable scent of people she could not ever know. Her first impulse was to run from the room and the apartment, adding her name to those who felt the bad vibes, but Fine blocked the doorway.

''They were good tenants, here before I bought the building in fifty-five. Limeys; never lost their accents.''

''Limeys—English,'' Lise corrected. People even more out of place in this city than she was. Maybe that was why the bad feeling had subsided so quickly. This apartment felt foreign and most of the time she felt a little foreign here, too. But surely in a city of this size there would be someone willing to pay the going rate for this apartment without concern for legends and vague feelings? Still, as Fine said:

she had the offer now, and she didn't believe in ghosts. Why not seize an opportunity?

"What sort of lease is it?"

"Two years, with an option."

Two years at four-fifty a month: her salary could stretch that far; she was due for a raise anyway. Even if they co-oped the building tomorrow it was a good deal. Who could say what she'd be ready for in two years. She needed the time and space now and Fine was offering it cheaply.

"I'll take it."

There followed the usual *baksheesh*: though the apartment was furnished the stove belonged to the management; fifty dollars to keep it instead of getting a less desirable one up from the basement. The extra locks on the door: another twenty. An hour after she had entered the apartment Lise left without her ten one-hundred dollar bills but with three new keys and the letter from the hall table which she dropped in the nearest mailbox.

Chapter Five

"I'm home!"

Lise kicked off her wet shoes as she closed the door behind her. The apartment was redolent with the aromas of tomato, onion, garlic and sweet sausage. Maria was simmering their dinner while she chatted on the phone. For the first time in hours the taint of incense and candlewax faded and Lise's appetite returned.

"You're late—are the trains fouled up?" Maria asked as she hung up the phone. She offered Lise a taste of the bubbling sauce.

"Mmm, fantastic, as always. No, I walked instead."

"In this weather? You must have had a really bad day."

Maria had already changed down into jeans. Her job was in easy walking distance of the East Twenties apartment they shared. Flushed with the joy of her recent marriage, Maria took advantage of the extra time to start dinner and do all the other chores which were theoretically shared.

"Remember that apartment I was telling you about?" Lise began, unable to burst out with the news that haunted rather than cheered her now that she was away from the Riverside Drive apartment. "You know the one that Mina said had come open in her brother-in-law's building?"

"The one up on Riverside Drive where her son-the-dentist is?"

"Yeah, that's the one. When's dinner?" Lise interrupted herself to open the refrigerator.

"Not until seven. Bob's working late. Did you go up there and see it?"

"More than that—I signed the lease," Lise admitted with her head still inside the refrigerator.

"You got a place!"

The wooden spoon splattered red dots all over the stove as Maria abandoned her cooking. Maria was expansive with her emotions, ready to cry or laugh and make someone a member of her family with a kiss. Lise, by contrast, needed a thick layer of space around herself—even with those she loved. Maria had to drape herself around the refrigerator door.

Lise selected a celery stalk and shut the door.

"For someone who's finally found a decent place after three months of non-stop looking, you don't seem very happy. Whatsa matter? It's not decent?"

"No, it's decent. There's a doorman and an elevator. It's a good place, I guess."

"You blew your budget?"

"No, it was less than I'd expected."

"Then what's the hitch—there's gotta be a hitch. No-one's pushing you out," Maria added, though it was no secret that the two months since her marriage had been a strain on them all. The one bedroom apartment had not been meant for three people, especially when two of those people didn't get along very well. "If it's not the right place; don't go. Isn't there some kind of law that you've got forty-eight hours to un-sign any contract?"

"No, it's the right apartment. After seeing twenty-seven that weren't I ought to know the right one. I guess I can't believe I did it. I thought I'd be all excited and relieved, but it hasn't worked that way. I've been nauseous all afternoon. I'm drained."

"You better get a glass of wine and take a bath."

Smiling weakly but sincerely Lise accepted a plastic glass of wine from the half-empty jug that sat over the sink. Bathtub retreats were a combination of tradition: Lise had always used extravagantly scented bath oil for sudden crises and Maria was inclined to measure out three fingers of chianti when the going got rough.

"I'll call Bob back and have him pick up a bottle of wine with a cork in it for dinner so we can celebrate," Maria called after Lise.

Lise nodded. They might not be forcing her out, she thought as she moved the umbrella, raincoats and assorted laundry from the bathtub, but the conditions here were taking their toll. Two bottles of bath oil had gone down the drain since Labor Day. Even Bob acknowledged that the bathroom was the only private room anyone had. Her new apartment, with its strange odors and tainted closets, was more inviting when considered in contrast to where she was now.

The steamy fragrant water and the wine restored her spirits while reminding her that she had not even checked the bathroom of her new home. It had to be there; even fifty years ago apartments had some sort of indoor plumbing. She wondered how many other things she had overlooked, but the wine-induced euphoria kept her from worrying.

She was still wrapped in a giant-size towel, mentally moving her possessions to their new home, when a masculine voice reminded her of the very finite limits of privacy in her current home.

"Bad day at the office?" Bob inquired as the fogbank rolled out of the bathroom. "Mari didn't tell me what we're celebrating but I'd gotten the idea it was good news."

"It is—I'm moving out." Lise juggled her clothes and clutched the towel.

"A new place! You're moving? Congratulations!"

He would have hugged her, damp towel and all, but Lise escaped into the bedroom, not caring if he were puzzled, confused or hurt by her move.

Awkwardness had been the fourth resident of the apartment since Bob had arrived, though it had lingered in the background since she'd moved to New York after graduating from college. Bob had been her only boyfriend for the last two years of college; they'd shared an off-campus apartment most of that time. When he said he was heading back to New York after graduation, Lise had naturally tagged along. She got a job, took classes at NYU and found that she and Bob didn't really have much in common once they were away from the ivory towers of college. She moved out of Bob's studio apartment and into this one with Maria, who was in one of her NYU classes. Then Bob had met Maria and found in her all those things that Lise wasn't about to offer him.

Thinking back Lise knew she should have stood on her own feet and walked out then, but she hadn't and it had taken two years, until Bob and Maria were getting married, for her to realize that she couldn't drift aimlessly between two people who were willing to make plans and commitments. Now that she finally had her own apartment waiting for her she couldn't comprehend how she had endured for two years, let alone the last two months. She resented the way his socks found a home in her bureau. She resented sleeping on the sofa and feeling like a guest in a place where she still paid rent. And she was on the verge of admitting her resentment that the fates had let Bob and Maria fall in love.

"Hey listen," she interrupted the newlyweds in the kitchen when she had gotten dressed. "I know I'm acting strange about this apartment thing. It's just, well, my new place—on the one hand it's every dream come true: a river-view, big rooms, even furniture and on the other hand something tells me that dreams don't usually come true. I keep on thinking about the past—you two and everything. Then I think about my new apartment again, and it gets spooky."

"Spooky? What gets spooky?" Maria asked.

"I got a funny feeling when I was there. I thought it was because the owner was so eager for me to rent the place, but now I'm not so sure—things will be so different up there."

"Maybe you've got weird neighbors." Bob took his turn coaxing Lise's misgivings from her—an action that only increased her anxiety by resurrecting her suspicion that she was the one who had cooled toward Bob; that she had driven him to Maria.

"I don't know," she said sharply. "I only saw one other family—a couple in the elevator when I left. They were all mink and Bergdorf Goodman."

"Sounds like a classy building," Maria commented.

"Very, like being in another world—not that my apartment doesn't need a little work—"

"Should be a safe building, then. People like that don't get robbed. Maybe you're just uncomfortable around all that money—after all, it's not Michigan," Bob commented while carrying spaghetti to the table.

Lise was not going to be baited into another discussion of her origins; in fact, she wasn't going to be baited into a discussion of anything and spent the meal listening to them talk and plan. Only when the last sauce had been devoured and the wine bottle emptied did she speak again of her anxieties.

"It's full of death," she announced.

"What's full of death?" Maria asked.

"My apartment. No, death's the wrong word—it's full of life."

"I'd think it would be rather difficult to confuse the two," Bob said, draining his wine glass and leaning back in his chair.

"I don't know which bothers me more: that the old man who lived there died last week or that all the closets and drawers are filled with his wife's clothes and I don't know when she died."

"I'd say your problem is with death, then," Bob concluded.

"No, it's life, Bob. I was sixteen when my Aunt Theresa died and we had to clean her apartment. It was like trespassing. We had to go through everything: all her clothes, the stuff from Italy she'd never shown anybody. The whole time I kept expecting to hear her come through the door screaming that we had some nerve to be going through her things. They were hers, after all—even if she wasn't there anymore. I don't know how the people who moved in felt."

"At least you knew whose belongings you were sorting through. I don't even know these people and I've got to get rid of all their earthly possessions." Lise stared at her wineglass as she spoke.

"So, hire someone to do it. Tell them what to leave behind and forget about the rest," Bob said in a tone that meant he considered the matter settled.

"I couldn't do that. I couldn't possibly turn them over to strangers. Who'd protect them? I'm all they've got now," Lise replied without irony.

"Strangers! You just said you didn't know their names." Bob sat upright in his chair, his face drawn into a grimace of exasperation.

"I don't know—I couldn't. There was a letter sitting on a table by the door. I picked it up on my way out and mailed it.

It was going to England. Now I feel like I should have copied the address so I could write and tell those people what had happened and who I was."

"That's ridiculous, Lise, and you know it. How many people die in this city in one day? What about the lady downstairs? They had a hundred applicants for her apartment before she was cold. No one felt squeamish. You remember that, don't you Mari?"

"Okay, okay—that's another thing that makes me nervous about this place. Nobody wanted the place; Fine didn't charge me a fraction of what it's worth. He was apologetic when I said I couldn't afford the place. If I'd wanted to I could have talked him down a hundred dollars—maybe more. He wanted to get someone into that apartment quickly and quietly." Lise said before Maria could answer Bob and catching herself just before she mentioned the rumors of witchcraft.

"That is odd. Maybe there's something very wrong and he knew but didn't want to fix it before he had tenants," Maria suggested.

"I thought that too, but it's wrong. God knows it sounds ridiculous but he was afraid I wouldn't rent the place. I felt it. He'd never laid eyes on me, but apartment 647 was supposed to be mine and he was just afraid that I wouldn't take it from him. Worse: I knew it was my apartment too; it fit me like a glove, like I'd lived there before. Do you realize I walked out of there not knowing where the john was?"

"That's it, Lise! It's all clear now—everyone suspects the rich are different; there's no plumbing. Everytime nature calls you'll have to go downstairs to the curb." Bob laughed and ignored the scowls of both women.

Silently Lise scraped and piled the dishes. By the customary division of chores she'd be alone to do the dishes—but Maria followed her into the kitchen.

"It probably really is just the clothes and stuff making the place seem uncomfortable," she said. "Once it's cleaned out you won't feel like you're trespassing. I'll help; so will Bob. Some of the things we found at Aunt Theresa's were a lot more valuable than any of us, including Aunt Theresa, thought they were. We had a little treasure hunt."

"Umm."

"There's something else, isn't there? Lise, you almost say what's really eating at you and then you swallow it back. Cleaning out the apartment isn't the problem. Did you see something that made you think you don't want to know these people? Something off-the-wall or kinky?"

"Not kinky," Lise admitted slowly, "maybe off-the-wall. Fine said the old man died of a heart attack when the police raided the place . . ."

"Old man—police raid?"

"But the place was raided. The livingroom looked like it had been ransacked: draperies dangling, cushions off the chairs, papers all over the carpet and a tree stump, of all things, sitting in the middle of the room with burned-out candles and incense on top of it."

"Meaning that since it was Hallowe'en, they might have been doing something occult-ish in there?"

"The raid was on Hallowe'en—Fine told me that much. He also said that the neighbors had been complaining about witchcraft. There had been a waiting list—but when it got down to it—no one was comfortable in the room, except me, I thought it was sort of peaceful.

"Well, like you said," Maria stated as she left the kitchen, "the place is filled with dead people's things and their superstitions as well. Look, I'll take Friday off and we'll both go up there and start tossing. We'll scrub it down with disinfectant if we have to."

Lise nodded. The kitchen reverberated with the sound of a toilet flushing upstairs and she pulled her hands back from the faucet as a rush of scalding water poured out. The plumbing probably wouldn't be much better in her new place, but undoubtedly there'd be fewer dishes to wash.

The sounds of a tickle-fight emerged from the livingroom. Lise thrust her hands back into the dishwater, attacking the baked-on tomato. If they worked hard over the weekend; if she was willing to accept most of the old man's possessions as they were, she could be moved in by Sunday night and her precious friendship with Bob and Maria might yet survive.

Chapter Six

"You'll never get it open that way," Maria chided, bringing a tray of iced tea and cookies into the livingroom of Lise's new apartment.

Lise was crouched on the floor, a bent nailfile in her hands and an assortment of other long, thin items on the carpet beside her. She shoved the file into the keyhole of a dark wood cabinet, twisted it and sat back in dismay as the lock-housing snapped the file in two.

"There must be keys for this somewhere," she muttered, picking up the tea from the tray which sat on the freshly polished tree stump.

"If it bothers you so much, throw the whole thing out."

"Whatever's in there has to do with the stuff we found on the tree stump and why this room was such a mess."

"You sound just like Nancy Drew," Maria complained. "Drink your tea. Bob should be here in a little while. Where do you want to go for dinner?"

Lise ignored the question, preferring to stare out the window. The city had broken out of the dreary days and was bathed in pale, brisk light. With the sun and a good breeze whistling through the window screens, she had purged her home of its oppressiveness. Odors, disorder and mystery had been all but banished.

"Tomorrow when we borrow your folk's car we'll move out all the old man's stuff—and some of his wife's things too. I'll do some food shopping and then Sunday I'll be moved in. Maybe I'll have to leave a few things behind, but I'll still be moved in."

"Shouldn't be any problems. You'll be set up Sunday night. That *is* one incredible view," Maria added, joining Lise by the windows.

The sun had slipped into redness, filling the apartment

with warm, friendly light—though the breeze reminded them that it was November now and the air would not hold the heat for long. They closed the windows and the atmosphere of the rooms reasserted itself. An endless succession of teaballs, rose-petal pomanders and woodsy-scented soaps had dwelt in the apartment. The heavy, waxen aromas of incense lingered as well; whatever had happened in the livingroom, it had happened more than once.

The gloom was balanced now by those pleasant, human traces of the old couple. On the whole the apartment seemed to welcome its new resident rather than repel her.

Lise went into the bedroom to shut the windows there. She opened the wardrobe, inhaled deeply of its rose-laden aroma and noticed, for the first time, that the petals in the glass pomanders still held their colors. They could have been picked no earlier than this past summer. Lise tried to imagine the old man replenishing the pomanders in his dead wife's closet.

"This place is full of surprises," she explained, bringing the pomander back to the livingroom.

"Maybe no more than any other place is—any place that's lived in. The food in the refrigerator is good; we've gotten rid of the mustiness—so it's like any other apartment, except that now it's yours."

Lise nodded and exchanged the pomander for a crumbly cookie. "But, even *her* things are fresh and cared for. And Sam, downstairs, said Mrs. Andrews died five years ago."

"Maybe he was a meticulous, lonely old man—or maybe he had a housekeeper who, seeing that he wouldn't get rid of her things, did the best she could to keep them from overpowering everything. Apartments should have attics. Everything's on top of you in an apartment—there's no place for the past."

"He didn't have a housekeeper," Lise answered quickly.

"Nancy Drew strikes again?"

"We'd have seen her."

"She came on Fridays?"

"No," Lise explained without acknowledging the jibes, "but she would have come sometime between when he died and now—slipped a note under the door or left one in the mailbox—something."

"Maybe the doorman just spotted her coming in and said 'Hey there, the old man's dead. No need to clean this week.' Doormen can do that sort of thing, you know. It's his job to know what's happening. He might have been the one to stop the mail deliveries, too."

Lise retreated from the discussion. Old man Andrews, as she thought of him, was a neat, orderly person, but he didn't collect rose petals and he hadn't paid a housekeeper to collect them, either. Someone else had kept a watchful eye over these rooms; that same someone could just as easily redirect the mail. A someone who might resent her intrusions into this comfortable residence? With that thought Lise smelled the traces of bitter incense amid the roses.

She froze a minute, probing the room with her thoughts. Or was the very lack of tangible menace all the reassurance she should need to know she had broken no hidden taboos and was accepted here. And why did she care so much, anyway? Lise struggled to get the better of her wayward thoughts.

"Did you hear something?" Maria inquired, noting her friend's cocked head and intense expression. "Bob did say he'd try to get away early."

"There's someone coming upstairs," she answered, though the faintly twanging cables were scarcely the cause of her reverie.

"That must be him. It's like you've lived here for years already," Maria called as she headed for the door, opening it before Bob could ring the bell.

Even back on Twentieth Street, which was a more active building, Lise had kept track of the elevator: known when it would stop on the twelfth floor and often who it was disgorging. It was as if she was always half-waiting for someone to arrive. Her mother had always said: 'Lise, you never stop waiting for something: Christmas, birthdays, when school gets out, when it starts again. You'll waste your life waiting.'

Bob broke Lise's thoughts with a critical appraisal of her new home.

"Late Victorian by way of the Midwest. How on earth did you find a place like this in Manhattan?" he asked, turning his back to her and removing a dusty book from the shelves.

Lise bristled, though he was just being Bob and had no intention of annoying her; he almost never did. Her angers and rages rose precipitously whenever he was friendly and bantering; whenever it seemed he had forgotten that they had once been special to each other, until she had drifted away.

"Instinct," she said, a trifle too slowly. "I was drawn by mysterious forces to the one place in Manhattan where I would truly feel at home."

"Almost at home—it's not snowing," Maria corrected. She had never been to Michigan, but she'd learned the punchlines to all the jokes and used them expertly to defuse the tension between Bob and Lise.

"True, true. The snow drifts will never rise above your windows. Now, then—there's a little restaurant about ten blocks from here which makes the best Moo Shoo Pork in the City."

"Sounds good, Bob," Lise said. When the mercurial moods ended she could see Bob for himself and would try, for a few minutes, to return his friendship. "Maria can show you around the place while I wash the dishes."

"Afraid the ghosts won't approve if you leave dirty dishes in the sink?"

Lise ignored him and carried the tray into the kitchen. There was a logic to the kitchen; dishpan soap and towels were all where she thought they should be. Only the serving plate proved to belong in a cabinet other than the one she first selected.

Feeling very much in command of the situation, she opened one of the drawers, expecting to find a ring of keys lying within it; such a ring of keys was in a similar drawer back home. But the drawer was filled with rolls of waxed-paper and an open box of sugar cookies. A red-brown cock-roach skittered under the paper. Lise smashed at the fleeing creature but the roach escaped and she stood, staring into the drawer, knowing she was a single movement away from tears and hysteria.

"Bob tried on that cashmere robe. It fit him per—" Maria stopped short, alerted to the precariousness of Lise's emotions as their eyes met. "What's wrong?"

"Roaches—a big one," Lise said with difficulty.

"Oh, come on—don't worry about it," Maria shrugged, "In a building as old as this one there're bound to be roaches. Don't worry until you see little ones—the big ones are just passing through."

It wasn't the roach, of course. Lise was used to the island's endemic wildlife by now. The bug was the intruder and the bug had gotten here first. It was back there, under the paper, hiding from her along with the discordant smells, the feeling of death and something Lise could not put a name to.

She caught a vagrant tear on the sleeve of her blouse and stiffened her back as Bob brought their coats into the kitchen. Maria didn't say anything and in a few moments, after they'd left the building, the spasm of panic faded away.

They spent Saturday sorting through Lise's new possessions and wishing they were in the nearby park enjoying the good weather. Bob was more enthusiastic than the women; the old man's wardrobe fit him perfectly and would not be banished to a thrift shop.

"Maybe Mari and I should move up here instead of you—" he said studying the silhouette of the second blazer he'd tried on.

Lise choked back sudden, vehement objections. "It's hardly the place to start a family," she said, hoping Maria would voice agreement quickly.

"And then we'd have to move furniture instead of men's clothes. And women's clothes! Whoever the old man married, she couldn't have stood over five-four and probably never weighed more than one-twenty in her life." Maria laughed and held up a beaded dress. "We earth-mother types were never meant to be thin."

Though Lise would have preferred a more neutral response, she let the subject slide away into a discussion of dinners over the next few weeks; dinners, she reminded herself, she would no longer automatically be sharing. In silent counterpoint to their exchange of schedules she imagined fixing meals in the bright kitchen, reading in the livingroom and soaking in the tub for hours at a time.

Chapter Seven

Sunday's plans fell victim to a hard-fought NFL game and an unexpected visit from one of Maria's cousins. Lise swallowed her hope for help, packed a suitcase with the lightest of her remaining possessions and departed with a promise to return later in the week for the rest. She hadn't been this alone in the City on her first day in from Michigan.

Sam wasn't on duty and his replacement, a surly man with an incomprehensible accent, had not been warned about a new tenant. An embarrassing call to Fine at his home in New Jersey was necessary before she could get to the elevator with her suitcase. A man and woman were waiting there, rapt in a debate over an as-yet unpurchased car. The man pressed the button for the sixth floor.

"I guess I'm your new neighbor," Lise offered into the silence of the crowded elevator car.

"I told you Fine'd rented the Andrews place," the woman said significantly.

"Now, Rachel," her partner chided, but he made his own lingering study of the suitcase that had not been new when her parents had taken it on their honeymoon. "You'll be living there by yourself?" he asked after a moment.

Lise met his stare. "For the time being."

"I haven't seen anyone moving the furniture out," Rachel said.

—And she would have—Lise thought to herself. But these were her neighbors; the people she would trust to watch her home when she couldn't and to answer her cries for help if she were in danger. It was not worthwhile to antagonize them so quickly.

"I don't have much furniture of my own," she replied with determined friendliness. "So, when Mr. Fine offered to leave the cleaning-out to me I decided to keep just about everything. The stuff may be old-fashioned, but it's better than orange-crates."

The elevator whined to an uncertain halt. Lise stepped out first, propping the heavy, non-automatic outer door open with her suitcase.

"I'm Mark Ratner," the man said extending his hand, not noticing her struggle with the door. "This is my wife, Rachel. We're across the hall from you."

Lise dropped her purse and shook his hand. "I'm Annalise Brown; most people call me Lise."

"Well, Lise, we hope you like it here," Mark offered hastily as his wife shoved past them both.

Lise waited until they had withdrawn into their apartment before walking the length of the landing herself. The apartment welcomed her with streams of sunlight coming through the bedroom and livingroom windows.

She left the unpacking and bedmaking until later, made a cup of tea and settled into the livingroom to watch the sun sink into the Palisades. No phone, no football, no Ratners—only the pleasant sound of her favorite radio station playing in the background. The velvet patchwork pillows with their handmade doilies smelled of incense and roses. She fluffed one up behind her head and pulled an old novel from the bookshelves. She began it eagerly but was fast asleep by the end of chapter two.

It was late when Lise awoke again. The stereo was broadcasting static. Her watch had stopped but it was at least ten-thirty.

—Fantastic—she thought, retrieving the novel from the floor. —I'll never get back to sleep now. Tomorrow's Monday; I'll go through the whole week like a zombie.—

She glared at the corners of the room as if they had been responsible for her unplanned nap. It was too late to venture out into an unfamiliar neighborhood in search of an open deli; she'd have to go hungry as well. The bed was still unmade and she remembered her alarm clock was still by the DelVecchio's sofa. She was fighting with the fitted sheet when the stereo once again slid into static and doubled its volume.

"What in blazes?"

The channel knob had spun to the high end of the dial. She readjusted the selector only to have it move again the moment her fingers released it. Sighing she turned it off and headed back to the bedroom.

It was, on the whole, a noisy building. She reached this conclusion as she sat reading in the freshly made bed hoping for drowsiness to overtake her again. The radiators were especially inclined to emit nerve-shattering clangs. Was it air bubbles in the pipes or water pockets in the coils that provoked the steam's irate performance? She didn't know the cause or the cure, nor how she had slept through them earlier.

By two the dated novel was getting interesting. Scores of insomnia tracts notwithstanding, Lise turned off the light and lay back on the pillows to force herself to sleep.

The streetlamps caught the patterns of the tree branches in the park and cast scraggly, narrow shadows across the ceiling: skeletal hands wringing uncounted fingers. Lise listened for the wind, and heard it in the grating of the bone-branches. She rolled over on her side only to see the shadows, handlike and menacing, more clearly with her mind's eye.

It was four and if she fell asleep now she'd never wake up in time for work.

But she did fall asleep and into a nightmare where the branches writhed at the edge of a fire-lit circle. Within the dream she did not know if the threat came from the bone-branches or the circle itself. Waking brought no greater relief than the knowledge that it was six-forty-five of a Monday morning and the sky was a distant, noncommital grey.

Andrews had apparently scorned coffee, forcing Lise to improvise her morning jolt to wakefulness. By overstuffing the teaball and by letting it steep the whole time she dressed, she concocted a bitter, smokey brew with an aftertaste that didn't quit until long after she'd gotten on the subway.

"So, did you see my son's office?" Mina injected into Lise's morning before she could retreat behind the *Times* for a respectable cup of coffee.

"No, it must not be near the elevator."

"Of course not, it's in the corner, with a door on the street.

He keeps *that* one locked—with a steel bar. That neighborhood's not what it used to be."

—So, now she tells me?—Lise smoothed the *Times* flat on her desk. "Well, I'll stop in and say 'hello' sometime. Maybe I'll even make an apointment to get my teeth cleaned. What night does he have hours?"

"Evenings? Up there?"

Mina went on to explain why her son kept banker's hours. Lise listened carefully; she had moved into a building a few blocks from "all those crazy island people" with their "chopped up chickens and goats." This information did not make her morning go faster.

"I've got it figured out," Lise explained to Maria over a quick lunch at one of the innumerable greasy-spoons scattered between her office and Maria's boutique.

"Figured what out?"

"How I got the apartment so cheap. I'm two blocks south of the voodoo center of New York. People are probably bailing out right and left. The old man probably got a wax doll in his mail."

"How much worse could that be than living three blocks from the emergency ward at Bellevue?"

Lise nodded. They had survived two years on the ambulance run. "You're probably right. It bothers me though that I didn't realize where I was moving earlier. I never even asked Fine what the neighborhood was like. I've been very careless."

"So, what did you do? Stay up all night worrying about it? You don't look so great."

Lise shrugged and recounted her first night in the apartment, finding humor in the nightmares now that it was daylight. They ended the meal with Lise's promise to return to Twentieth Street for her clock-radio after work.

It was past seven and dark by the time she schlepped groceries, radio, newspaper, pizza slices and purse into the apartment. Her quest for better nutrition was already compromised as she sprinkled garlic powder and hot pepper on the pizza. She ate both slices before wandering down the hall to check out the rest of her domain.

A pillow lay in the middle of the livingroom carpet; a candle had fallen from the bookshelves and broken in two. She bent over to get the pillow and got a static spark that made her pull back in pain. An angry blister rose on her finger, she put the finger in her mouth and glared back at the pillow. When she grabbed it a second time she thumped it soundly against her thigh and set it amid the rest with a little punch. She had no problems with the candle.

Lise spent the evening in the wing chair with the radio producing just enough background noise to blot out the noises of the building and street. Her tea-making had improved to the point where she enjoyed the cooling cup on the shelf beside her. Sitting alone, half-reading, half-dozing was an unfamiliar pleasantness. The knowledge that both time and space here belonged to her more than outweighed any voodoo that might be going on on the next block.

The jagged tracery on the ceiling over her bed did not seem as menacing when her thoughts were pleasant rather than filled with the dread of oversleeping. And her dreams, if she had any, did not mar her rest.

She awoke suddenly, already sitting bolt-upright. The radio showed two-thirty and the livingroom stereo was blaring static throughout the apartment. Lise clutched the blanket in a death-grip, caught by a fear that was beyond words, beyond movement. She listened for the sounds of an intruder's footsteps, all the while knowing the static sound would block it. The apartment was unnaturally dark: the shadows above her bed were reduced to a uniform blackness. Her eyes could not adjust to the dark. She flailed about with her free hand, groping for a lightswitch whose location she could not remember.

A crash in the livingroom forced a whimper from her as she finally closed on the brass-bead chain of the bedlamp. She yanked the chain and brought light to her room. And danger. On the edge of hysteria, she watched the dark doorway to the hall. When nothing crossed from darkness to light she began to breathe easier, though the fear had not abated. Strange sounds, louder than the background static, belched out of the livingroom, demanding her terrified investigation.

Moving with conscious deliberation and hands that shook from cold and nerves, Lise inched silently out of her bed. Her eye caught sight of a heavy silver mirror on the dressing table. She paused to pick it up. The wall-mirror revealed a sleep-bedraggled wraith in an unfamiliar room. A scream was rising from her innards before she recognized herself and smiled at the reflection.

She forced her mind to a fevered pitch with remembering the placement of each lightswitch, and which one could be reached with the least exposure to the ungodly racket coming from the livingroom. The overhead fixture in the bedroom pushed a dusting of light into the hall. The switch just outside her bedroom door, one she had never used before, turned on the light over the front door. She edged down the hallway, watching the dark doorway to the livingroom, and felt the locks with her cold fingertips. None had been tampered with, which meant—no, she wouldn't let herself think about what it meant. She fumbled with each lock until it was open and she would be able to leave the apartment by simply turning the knob—if she had to.

The kitchen was unaffected. Fluorescent light bounced off the enamelled walls, illuminating every corner and assuring Lise that this room was safe. The delicate violets balanced on the window ledges hadn't been disturbed. It was time for the livingroom.

There were no switches by the French doors; the nearest lamp was some four steps into the blackness. Her mouth was pasty and her knees rubbery as she made the first step into the noisy darkness. The second; the third—and she couldn't force her feet further. She reached gingerly toward the floor-lamp, felt nothing and pulled her hand back. The weakness in her knees shot up past her stomach; she might faint—but even in the throes of terror, Lise Brown did not faint. She got a grip on her nerves again, banished the skeletal imaginings of her terror from her thoughts and reached again, more carefully, more consciously. The ridged button was between her finger-tips. Holding her breath, she turned the lamp on.

The static belonged to the stereo, whose tuning knobs

careened from one limit to the other, but the violent, belching sound came from no object her eyes could see though the source should have been clearly visible in the center of the room. She stared at what she could not see and backed toward the stereo. A single tug on the cord was not enough to unplug it; she'd have to squat down and turn her back to the room to stop the static. Holding her breath again, she pulled the cord from the socket.

Deep pitched, gutteral sounds of something in horrendous pain filled the livingroom the instant the cord was disconnected. Lise spun about too quickly and went to one knee under the writing table, hitting her head as she went, but still certain she had seen the withered brown leaves fall from nowhere to the carpet. The room was quiet.

Still clutching her silver mirror, Lise crawled toward the leaves. She poked at them once with the mirror, waited in silence, then picked them up in her free hand. She was standing up, examining the leaves, deciding they were oak and just beginning to wonder how, exactly, they'd come to be on the carpet when she caught a flash of movement behind her and whirled to face an onslaught of pillows from the sofa.

They pelted her in the face, dropped to the floor and sprang up again with renewed intensity. Lise batted at them with the heavy mirror, knocking one or two away for a moment but no longer. They didn't really hurt, not even enough to knock her over, but she couldn't make them stop and in seconds that had driven her to a crazed helplessness. She folded her hands, still holding the leaves and the mirror, over her face. The pillows knocked the mirror from one hand; she screamed. They sprang at her in unison, sending fragments of dry, sharp-edged oak leaves into her mouth.

When the reflexive choking and coughing had past, Lise opened her eyes and saw the half-dozen pillows lying on the floor around her feet. She ignored the velvet-and-lace patchwork, sinking to the floor just beyond them, rocking back and forth in rhythm with her misery instead.

Someone was knocking at the door, but she didn't answer. After a few moments the calling stopped. Lise regenerated strength from the sound of her own crying; the trembling and rocking slowed and, finally, so did the tears. She dressed again in the clothes she had left on the bathroom floor and scuttled down to the lobby.

"Why, Miss Brown, what are you doing up at this hour?" Sam hailed her as she slouched toward the doors.

Lise froze. She knew she looked like a madwoman and suspected that she was one.

"Now, Miss Brown—you shouldn't go outside by yourself at this hour."

Lise stepped back as Sam stepped forward. "I'm going home," she said, turning the words into a warning. "I'm not going back up there."

Sam nodded. "I understand," he said softly, "but don't go out by yourself. Let me get you a cab. You sit right there—I'll call you one."

She edged onto the chair in his cubby-hole office where the TV was set on the all-night movies. The movie didn't tempt her and she watched his every move with feral suspicion.

"They'll be here in a bit. You look like you could use a cup of hot chocolate."

Lise nodded. He filled the mug part way so her shaking hands would not embarrass her.

"You sure you want to go outside. Maybe your people are sleeping. You'll scare 'em pretty good if you go bargin' in at this hour." Lise stared at him. "You could just sit here until dawn. Everything looks different when the sun's up."

She thought about Bob and Maria sleeping together. It didn't take much imagination to guess their reactions if she unlocked their door. They'd take her in, but things wouldn't be the same. She drank Sam's hot chocolate. He cancelled her cab and went back to his paperback while she searched for the plot of an Errol Flynn swashbuckler.

Chapter Eight

The City stretched itself awake from a restless night long before the sun rose. Traffic on the streets and highways thickened. The mysterious slunk back to the alleys and basements displaced by the predictability of alarm clocks, steaming coffee and the morning news. Lise stretched herself and eased the knots out of her back. Sam dozed behind his novel and the TV assaulted the day with an ecumenical prayer. It was six AM.

"I'll be going now," Lise announced softly.

"Hmm? Oh, yes. Now, you be careful," Sam warned, not seeming to notice that she headed for the elevator rather than to the street.

Like the streets outside, the apartment was fast losing its mystery. Neighbors she hadn't met were heading for the curbs with their equally sleepy dogs as Lise got off the elevator. All the lights were still on in her apartment, mute witnesses to the terror that had sent her panicking to the lobby. The pillows and the mirror were where she had left them on the rug.

She hesitated before setting foot in that room again. Dawn and the all-night movies had built a barrier between the nightmare and reality. In fact, when she had left Sam's cubicle she had believed it had been a nightmare. Staring at the floor she could remember being terrified, but the terror itself was mercifully absent from her memory. There remained only the twinge of knowing what had happened, nothing more.

"—causing delays on the A-train. A stalled car is blocking—"

Lise jumped, bringing her hands over her eyes and for a heartbeat the true terror returned unadulterated. But this time there was a real explanation—the damned clock-radio—to stop the panic.

She thumped the pillows back into place on the sofa then sat leaning against them. Two nights without rest, a nightmare that was not a dream and an announcement that the subway was already fouled up. It seemed time to take an unauthorized sick-day from the office. The phone wasn't working yet and to call her office from the delicatessen was almost as much effort as going to work, but the day off was worth it. By half-past ten she was back in her nightgown and surrounded by blankets that smelled of roses.

The intercom buzzer, remorseless disrupter of naps, brought Lise to yet another disoriented; panic-filled waking.

"Sam," she queried of the speaker when she had finally made her way to the front door.

"He's not here," an unfamiliar voice answered. "You want him, you got to wait until six."

"No, didn't you just ring this apartment?" she asked, thinking that she might have dreamed *that*, too.

"Yeah, you got visitors. I send them up, already."

She stepped back from the speaker, no longer sharing Maria's faith in doormen. But, though she was convinced she could have no legitimate visitors, she raced back down the corridor to her bedroom to look for a bathrobe; her own was something else she'd left behind.

The doorbell had rung when her fingers closed on a soft, dove-grey fabric. Fumbling with its buttons as she returned to the door, Lise had to conclude that what she was now wearing had never been intended to cover a flannel nightgown. She spun the peephole cover up and peered out at a serious-seeming couple.

They could only be friends of the old man, and she was dressed in his late wife's evening gown. Running one hand through her hair she opened the door a crack. From the sudden grimness of their expressions she knew they saw the gown as soon as they saw her face and that they approved of neither.

"I'm terribly sorry," she began.

"Do you live here now?" the woman demanded, unaffected by Lise's humility. She was petite, with severe features and a first-grade teacher's no-nonsense voice.

"Yes, I do. I moved in last weekend," Lise answered promptly.

"May we come in and speak with you privately?" the man asked.

They were older than her parents, well dressed: scarcely what one would expect in the way of thieves, but Lise held the door firmly and would not let them in.

"I haven't been feeling well. I was in bed . . ."

"Miss Brown, if you'll just let us in we can explain all this to you. Arthur was a *special* friend of ours. We don't care if you have someone with you."

Lise didn't believe them, especially the woman—who did care. She couldn't see them as bereaved friends; they were intruders who could cast judgment on her worthiness to live in this place. Their purposeful stares were more than she cared to confront in her current condition. "Please, maybe some other day—really, I'm simply not feeling well."

"We understand. We can help you," the man said with too much intensity.

"No, I'm sorry your friend died, but I live here now. It's all legal; this is my home."

With a last apology she shut the door, threw the bolt and then, fearful that they might have keys to the as-yet unchanged locks, dragged a chair from the kitchen and wedged it, detective-fashion, under the knob. As she surveyed her handiwork, a business card slipped under the door.

"J. Robert Hynes," it read in the fine engraved letters above a large bank's gold-embossed logo. She reversed the card. A distinctive, bold hand scrawled across the back: "Please call us. There is much you *must* know—Marjory," along with a phone number.

The card and her hand shook as she stared at it. It belonged in the garbage, but disposing of engraved business cards was not like tossing out Kleenex or old newspapers. Business cards, like telephones, had imperatives. She left the card, face down, on the hall table.

But the place was quieter after the couple's visit. The locks were changed late that same afternoon. The phone company called the following evening, reanimating her phone. By Friday morning she had survived three full nights in the apartment and had put the horrors of her first two nights there into a seldom disturbed attic of her mind. When Maria said Bob was sitting in at a late night poker game, Lise had no hesitations about inviting her friend up for the evening.

"There, that should be just about it." Maria grunted as she swung a heavy suitcase onto Lise's bed. "I checked through every closet, all the boxes in the bedroom and the stuff behind the couch."

"I really didn't think I owned this much," Lise admitted, dragging a second suitcase into the room. "I've completely taken over here. If I buy anything more I've got to start throwing things out. I don't even know where I'll put this stuff." She turned her back on the suitcases and led the way to the livingroom.

"It's starting to look like you," Maria commented as she sank onto the sofa.

"It is?"

"Yeah. A week's worth of *New York Times* on the table; an open book in every room and an empty soda bottle scattered hither and yon."

Lise quickly picked up the empty bottle from the writing table, as if she were embarrassed at being caught in the act of comfort. Yet her personality was surfacing in the room. Her favorite posters hung on the walls; a huge jar of coffee sat beside the stove in the kitchen.

In homage to natural foods and the cult of perpetual dieting, they ate salad greens and yogurt for dinner and looked for distraction from swiftly returning hunger. A stiff breeze was rolling up from the river, rattling the closed windows and shaking the hanging plants in front of them, but the stereo buffered out the noise of the weather.

"Did you ever get that opened?" Maria pointed to the low cabinet beside the sofa.

"Haven't tried again all week."

Maria sat down in front of it, jiggling the door they both knew was locked. "Kids are supposed to be able to open locks like this in no time at all. Kinda makes you wonder what they know that we don't."

"Kids can open things like that because they don't know it's mahogany; and even if they did they wouldn't care. We get in trouble because we want to know what's inside the box without breaking it."

Maria nodded but continued to probe at the keyhole. "You've tried a credit card?"

"No good. The door opens out."

But they'd found a diversion. When they'd tried pins, needles and other gentle lock-picking devices, they searched the apartment for the key. Lise removed each book from the shelves looking for hidden compartments while Maria roamed the other rooms.

"I've found it!" Maria exaulted. "Or, at least I've found an old key."

Under the stamps, string, rubber bands and thumbtacks in the single drawer of the hall table, Maria had found a rusty keyring and three old keys.

"Who's Marjory," she asked, inspecting the business card Lise had left there.

"Some friend of the old man's, I think," Lise answered quickly.

"Did you call and find out what it was that you *must* know?"

"No, not yet."

"I wonder what it is. Maybe she was supposed to get the furniture."

It was a possibility Lise had not considered, and one which she rejected at once. Furniture had not been in the couple's eyes as they stood in the hallway.

One of the old keys fit the lock and gentle coaxing eased the door open.

"My god, that's beautiful!" Maria exclaimed.

"Goddess."

Lise unhooked the chamoise-covered restraints and lifted

the glass statue of the High Coven's goddess from its niche.

"I've never seen anything like that outside a museum," Maria admitted.

Lise nodded and set the statue on the nearby tree stump. A goddess, definitely, with a serene unreadable expression; a goddess reaching out for something with slender glass arms.

"Odd that they'd keep it hidden away like that—unless it's so valuable it can't be displayed. It is glass, isn't it?" Maria asked without touching.

"Maybe it was an heirloom and they didn't need to see it all the time."

"There're lots more things in there."

Reluctantly Lise directed her attention back to the cabinet from which Maria was removing a disturbing array of objects in brass and silver—including a velvet-covered box with thirteen nasty-looking steak knives nestled in green plush. Suspicions formed in Lise's mind; voiceless suspicions that linked these discoveries to the brass plates left on the tree stump when she'd signed the lease. But the insight that tied everything into a neat package eluded her and the confusion worsened.

"It smells like a church in that box—almost." Maria said.

"Consider the Inquisition."

Maria looked up. "No, people who wore cashmere dressing gowns are not the right type for the Inquisition."

Lise was not so certain, but she would have to explain what had happened earlier in the week if she wanted to convince Maria. Everything, including the statue, probably belonged in the incinerator, but Lise, the product of centuries of Calvinism, was more reluctant to admit the reality of superstition than to destroy its source.

"I'm not putting the statue back in the box," she announced. "It's a work of art. It shouldn't be hidden away."

"And the other stuff?" Maria asked.

"That can go back—until I can get it to a thrift shop or the Salvation Army."

They packed everything but the statue back in the cabinet and re-locked it. They had gotten through two hours of post-dinner stomach grinding and agreed to reward themselves by heading out for dessert. By the time they'd lingered over a second cup of espresso, it was too late for Maria to take the subway home, and the neighborhood was cab-less. Even Lise began to get edgy as they waited for a cab. Finally, to Maria's obvious relief, she invited her to spend the night.

"Thanks. Next time I think I'll just plan on staying. Your neighborhood is not good at night," Maria said as they stepped out of the elevator.

"Should have thought of it sooner myself."

Loud radio static greeted them as Lise opened the door. This time all the lights in the apartment were turned on; they flickered once while the women stood in the doorway then dimmed out. Maria dug her fingers into Lise's elbow. Lise groped for the lightswitch, but flicking it on had no effect. A moan, not unlike that of the elevator cables, but deeper and more resonant erupted from the livingroom. Glass shattered somewhere in the darkness.

"Burglars?" Maria whispered.

"No."

Lise was numb from the waist down and as frightened as she'd been the last time, but she was angry as well and used the anger to force herself down the hallway to the livingroom.

"Don't, Lise," Maria pleaded from the doorway.

The French doors, which had been open, were shut tightly; she gripped the knob and twisted it sharply, pushing the door open against its will. Behind her the lights came up, but the livingroom was still in mystery. A dull orange glow filled the lamps in front of her, making them malevolently visible without bringing any useful light to the room. A shimmering blue-white aura rippled over the glass statue; as she watched it burst into a brilliant red that was far deeper and bloodier than any natural light should be. There was a rustle in the darkness—a sound Lise knew to be the pillows rising.

"Get out of here!" she shouted. Maria, who had crept a few feet down the hall, raced back to the door; but Lise walked into the dark room. "Get out of here!" she bellowed as the pillows struck her. "Get out of my home. Go back where you came from!'' She caught one of the pillows by its tassel and heaved it at the sofa. The red light flickered and approached her. She extended her arms out sideways. ''Get out of here! You hear me? I said: *Get out*!''

The moaning sounds pressed against her ears; the pillows shone with red light as they pelted her, but Lise was beyond fear now and bellowed her commands a second time.

Reluctantly the menace retreated, lingering at the limit of vision to take a last appraisal of the fury that was exiling it. The blue-white aura around the statue reappeared; then it, too, was inhaled. The lights returned to normal brightness and, save for the pillows on the floor, the room showed no changes.

In the calm Lise could reflect on the risks of brazen courage. A trickle of moisture curved down her thigh, another down her back. A cold breeze from nowhere gave her the shivers and roller-coaster nausea.

''Lise?''

Maria's voice, floating down the hallway.

''Lise, I want to go home.''

With her fury exhausted, it was all Lise could do to take a step backward out of the room. She would not be driven out of her home by anything, anyone, but it might be a good time for a strategic withdrawal. She'd come back—she promised herself that as she took another backward step—but, maybe not tomorrow. This was her home, though; she'd signed the papers, made the plans, made the commitments to living here. Nothing was going to drive her off.

''Wait up, Maria—I'm coming with you—for now.''

Chapter Nine

The tides changed, bringing a different tang to the breezes that swept off the coast. Edith Brompton, lifelong resident of the wild Cornish headlands, knew it was time to head back to the farmhouse. Slipping Arthur's letter into the deep pocket of her sweater she clambered over ancient carved rocks that were the oldest extant part of Caer Maen.

As a child she had imagined the ghosts of druids and bards easing through the interwoven pines that sheltered this ramshackle collection of stones from prying eyes. As a university student she had wanted to bring her tutors to visit these ruins; that had been the one time her mother had exercised the High Priestess's total authority over her witches and forbidden such notions from consideration. Now, thirty years later, Edith was High Priestess; she protected the treasures of Caer Maen, using them in the time-honored ways and riding the waves of a new generation's curiosity.

Some two hundred yards from the grove she unlaced the cord holding a barbed-wire fence shut, rousing the vague interest of the arthritic horses the coven pastured near its grove. Enthusiastic tourists and hikers along the seacoast avoided the fenced-in animals more than they would have avoided a No Trespassing sign.

She followed the dirt path through undisturbed countryside. The Bromptons owned a sizable portion of these moors near the sleepy town of Saint Ives, or rather the High Coven of Caer Maen did. Since the sixteenth century a Brompton daughter had lived in the stone farmhouse, presiding over its heritage; her husband always took her name and nominal charge of the farm. Before that, there had been another farmhouse; its stones lay in the foundations of the current house. But there had been a coven of some sort here before the Conquest, before the Romans too. The meander-

stones in the grove had been carved by the Bronze age tribes who first settled the peninsula some four thousand years ago.

When the farmhouse and the road came into view the grove and its stones were long hidden from sight. A tiny blue car tooted its greetings; Edith waved to her husband as the car headed up the gravel drive to their home. Though it was Friday, and he often returned early on Friday, Edith thanked the Gods that he would be there waiting for her.

"Well, Arthur's been saying he'd do this for years, since Gwen's death. Riverside was never any joy to them—a flat's not a proper place for our sort of work," Bert said, folding the letter back into its envelope and taking the glass of sherry his wife offered him. "I know you hoped he'd come around, but that was never very likely."

"No—I suppose not. But, Bert, it's not what's *in* the letter so much as the letter itself. That letter was mailed on the tenth!"

"Two weeks for an air letter. Their mail's as bad as ours."

"But the tenth, Bert. That's ten days after Samhain."

Bert set down his glass and studied the envelope; his casualness evaporated. "Tisn't likely he'd send this ten days after the fact. Might've added another to it, or not sent it at all. Not like Arthur. But what're we to do about it? Maybe we'd've done best to get the telephone in."

"He'd no more call us with that sort of thought than we'd call him," Edith chided.

"But, Edith, I would call him. I'll have a run down to the office when we're finished and put a call through—what's the time over there, anyway?"

Edith stared out the window and counted on her fingers. "Seven hours, I think. Should be just after noon for him."

In twenty-five years of marriage Edith had learned to respect Bert's calm facade, to know that he was already aware of the implications of the post-mark. They ate in compatable silence.

The Samhain rite at Caer Maen had also been a grueling night. Not since their early years had the High Priest and

Priestess encountered such difficulty in assuring themselves that the rite had ended with a successful re-closing of the Rift. Inexplicable, petty disasters had marred the evening: two goblets broke for no apparent reason and hot wax had set the altar coverings to smouldering. The inexplicable was expected on Samhain and no one had thought the worse of it until, when the witches clasped hands for the closing prayer, Elizabeth, their only child, had collapsed in a faint murmuring the names Anerien and Morwedd.

Elizabeth had gone back up to London on the second, but had twice called her father to report recurring headaches and chills. As Edith daubed up the last of the steak-and-kidney pie with a piece of bread, she guessed it was no coincidence that Elizabeth, who with her green eyes and red hair was the image of the young Gwen Andrews, would have been the first to feel a crisis at Riverside.

The ride from the moorland plateau of the farmhouse down to the harbor town of Saint Ives was, as always, a distraction from even the most wearing anxieties. The bumpy old roads with their blind, hairpin curves demanded total concentration lest the car turn top-over-teakettle into someone's garden or kitchen. Edith would sooner have driven to London in the fog than ventured down the unlit hills after dark, but she was not driving—merely holding her breath.

Bert shared his offices with two junior partners, both long since departed for their homes. While Edith made notes on a scrap of paper he set about placing the overseas call.

"She says it's a holiday weekend over there and the calls're backed up for hours," he informed Edith as the wait lengthened.

"We're going to get through," she replied tersely.

Bert drew intricate lacings of elephant tusks and roses on the blotter and waited for the connection to be completed. He ignored his wife's pacing and the sound of a distant fog horn.

"Brompton here—What?—No other line, you're sure of that? Well, no—how could I possibly place a call when I haven't got a number?"

Edith heard the uncharacteristic fluster in Bert's voice; the unmistakable sign that something was wrong—and wrong in a way they hadn't anticipated. She left off pacing and stood close by the phone.

"His line's off," Bert explained. "The number's cancelled and not replaced. We can't get through to him."

Edith stared at the harbor. She had considered that some accident had befallen her brother-in-law; that he might be ill or in hospital, but she hadn't considered that he might simply have vanished from their fragile communications network.

"Well, I'll write at once," she announced before she had resolved all the questions loose in her mind.

"Write where, and to whom?" Bert asked gently.

"Let's go home then. I don't know how you can think at all in a place like this—" she gestured to the clutter that had defeated three char-women in as many years.

She did most of her thinking alone in the earth-floored cellar beneath the farmhouse where the coven's history was stored on dry, wooden racks like fine wine. She read over all her American correspondence, searching for an address—a name she might contact—but Riverside had never really taken its place with the other High Covens. Perhaps that was because it was so new, or perhaps because it was American it had never evolved the communications network that marked Caer Maen and the other English High Coven. By virtue of generations of marriages and other alliances, Edith could have secured the Craft-name, family name and address of almost any respectable occultist in Europe—and a few whose reputations were less than savory—but she had few contacts in America.

Returning the little pile of letters to its box, she turned next to a handsomely bound book. She brought the heavy volume to a rocking chair located beside the warm chimney. Her mother's neat handwriting recorded the unprecidented events that had led to the founding ot ehe Riverside High Coven. Caer Maen had waited almost a year after first suspecting something was wrong, communicating with the other known

High Covens and hoping that some native tradition would assemble at the Rift and take up the burden of guarding it.

In the end Ravenna, with the blessings of her sister Priestesses, had sent her daughter and Arthur to tame the Rift. But Lady Ravenna knew nothing about the people Gwen and Arthur had found to fill their circle.

The volume now closed, Edith let her thoughts wander. The grey cat who ruled both house and farmyard bounded into her lap while a gawky pair of adolescent kittens waited in the shadows.

The warrens of Caer Maen, as the earthwork maze beneath the farmhouse was known, were larger than the house above them. In more ominious times a tunnel had led from the potato-cellar all the way out to the grove though that had collapsed shortly after Waterloo and there'd been no need to re-dig it. The information they'd need to excavate another tunnel, if need arose, and how to build houses with secret passages was carefully preserved in the corner of one of the many shelves.

It was said, even in the lesser circles, that the Wiccans who survived the Burning Times shunned written records and performed few rituals that were more than a hundred years old. The High Covens had always followed their own path—and their survival seemed to justify them. The vast records were the last mystery revealed to a High Coven witch and in more harrowing times only the High Priestess had known of them. The High Priestess, who often concealed her literacy, kept the geneologies and ritual intact and could vouch for the greater antiquity of many of the modern rituals.

Edith had access to every solution ever contemplated for every crisis the High Coven of Caer Maen had faced in a thousand years—but Caer Maen had founded only one subsidiary High Coven and had never before grappled with the possibility that High Coven Guardians had failed in their sacred tasks. She pondered such disturbing thoughts in the darkness with all three cats curled in her lap.

A letter to Arthur—or to Arthur's address—the whole problem might be no more than a nasty mix-up. She'd send a second letter up to Gretna where Arthur had grown up; he was their child and it was only courtesy to let them know. Lady Vivian would apply her own not inconsiderable connections and insights to the problem. But her best hope, Edith concluded, lay a day's journey away in a velvet-curtained London basement and in the erratic talents of a psychic known simply as Hector.

"Have you found an answer?" Bert asked as she ascended the stairs.

"No, but I shall go up to London Monday and have a sit-down with Hector."

"Is this a good time of the year for him?" Bert asked sincerely.

"Should be, it's the Underside. If we're right and Arthur has died his spirit should be easy—"

"But, if he died in Circle—a possibility we mustn't overlook in view of Elizabeth's reactions—it would be a bit of a risk to send a psychic out looking for him, wouldn't it?"

Edith regarded him grimly. "If he died in Circle there won't be a legitimate operative from here to next Thursday who won't know about it sooner or later—and probably under considerably more unpleasant circumstances."

"Well, it is a small possibility, after all. I should think we'd have had more trouble ourselves. Wasn't that the case when your mother decided that there was a Riverside Rift?"

"It's hard to say. Mother's notes tend to get poetic. What is a 'cold, timeless babble blowing from the Otherplace'? Is that the same sort of thing that made Liz faint?"

"We could check that, you know."

"There're only the two of us—It's too late to roust the rest and if there is a problem we'd not want to face it alone."

"Well, then—tomorrow. They'll mostly all be home with the weather like this and as we're not about to open the Rift you needn't get the First String down here. I'm sure a day or so in the country would do 'Lizabeth a world of good and you could drive back up to London with her."

"After what Liz's been through it wouldn't be fair to ask her to sit in on this," Edith countered, but she was already composing the rest of the circle in her mind.

"After what she's been through; after what she may very well go through it wouldn't be fair to exclude her, my dear. She'll need the circle more than the rest of us."

"I'll call her in the morning then."

"Damnable nuisance it's becoming—all this heading into town for phone calls. Perhaps we ought to get a phone."

"Not until they'll bury the wires. I'm not having an electric spider web wandering onto our land," Edith announced. "I'll pedal down to Saint Ives in the morning. It's too late to call anyone now."

Headaches, nightmares and University exams notwithstanding, Elizabeth came out to Saint Ives the next day along with all the other members of the coven who had partaken in the Samhain rite. They arrived in the late afternoon; a discreet display of middle-class, well-maintained cars.

Unlike the Riverside coven, the manner of these people did little to suggest the occult or arcane. They chatted about jobs and family through the cold buffet Edith provided them. Only when the last teacup was dry did the purpose of the gathering come under discussion; they decided they need not make the trek to the grove in the November damp but would have their circle within the warrens.

Robes and jewelry were extracted from valises that seemed too small to have contained them. Edith swept her short, snowy hair under a silver-blue silk veil that complimented her otherwise unadorned midnight-blue gown. All essence of country-housewife disappeared as she smoothed the veil back over her shoulders and led the way downstairs. Bert, in similarly austere garb, was waiting for her.

"I've given this some thought," she explained from outside the ring Bert had marked in the earth floor, "and, as we've never done anything like this before but foreseeably we'll have to do it again—I think we'll want to follow a fairly simple, easily reconstructed form."

She removed the High Priestess' crown from a bag and placed it over her veil, centering the upturned crescent of Hathor on her forehead. She spoke as Lady Camulac, High

Priestess of Caer Maen, and no-one would gainsay her without good reason.

"You will construct the full Samhain circle, though, won't you?" Elizabeth asked.

Lady Camulac nodded and the witches chose their places at the perimeter. The altar candles and statuary sat upon a hand-chiseled stone that had been hauled from the grove years before the farmhouse had been built. Lady Camulac got her sword and moved closer to the altar.

Yes, she would have to draw the Samhain circle with its mournful incense and baleful charging; not a pleasant thing to forge out of oneself. A lighter circle could be drawn, but if it failed the disaster would be her fault. At least she had no need for blood, not even in symbolic amounts.

She completed the circuits and the candle-lighting and returned to the altar to meditate while the unity of the circle grew more solid in her mind. The coven had a sense of purpose that should daunt the hungers of the Otherworld—though who was to say what logic or rationale operated there?

When she raised her head she was escorted back to the outer ring and Bert undertook to pass the goblets and wine around. Everyone found a more-or-less comfortable position and sipped at the ritual offering whose transitive powers had been known long before the days of the new church in Rome.

"Cast your thoughts beyond yourselves," Lady Camulac instructed when she had all but emptied her glass. "Set your senses drifting. We're looking for disruptions in the Great Curtain; disruptions that might mean a Rift was left unclosed at Samhain. I've no idea what form the signal might take—but—there will be no mistaking it."

This was a working circle without ritual or poetry, convened for a single purpose: an ad hoc session of the High Coven. Though she had not specified it, many of the witches reached for the hands of their partners and spontaneously a circle of flesh was formed above the one Lady Camulac had marked on the floor.

They all had experiences to use as a guide in exploring the fringes of the Otherworld. Elizabeth whose experience was still on-going met the Otherworld first. As she had done on

Samhain the young, red-haired woman began shivering; only the hands holding her on either side kept her from collapsing completely when the shivering became a fainting spell.

"Lady Camulac?" a neighbor whispered to gain the High Priestess' attention.

Aroused, Lady Camulac brought her neighbors' hands together behind her back and broke out of the circle. There were no ritualized reasons for the circle of flesh, nor any reason to feel there would be greater danger if that circle were broken—but primal prudence said she should not leave an opening at her back.

"She's like ice," the High Priestess muttered as she touched her daughter's face. "Sarah! Break the circle!"

It was well, then, that they were all consecrated priests and preistesses and that any of them could undo what Lady Camulac had woven around them. A tall, slender woman picked up the silver sword and after a brief moment of thought passed its tip through fire, salt and water. Another witch poured a second goblet of wine for their stricken companion. By the time Sarah had dissipated the power and energy of the gathering, color had begun to return to Elizabeth's cheeks and her trembling had ceased. Her father carried her upstairs to the warm livingroom where he laid her on a carpet before the fire.

"It was like before, like the dreams—icy cold. I fought it, but this time I couldn't get away."

Edith sat beside her daughter, smoothing the hair back from her face.

"Uncle Arthur had called me, Mother, but he led me to the Otherworld."

Edith looked away from Elizabeth's distraught face. Only Hector could say for sure but the situation could not seem worse; Arthur's spirit had been subverted, somehow, and had nearly led his niece to her doom.

"They're waiting," she whispered to no-one. "I've been a fool to think they weren't. I shouldn't have needed a circle to tell me what I already know: They're waiting and They've already got Riverside."

Chapter Ten

Edith glanced quickly toward the passenger seat. Elizabeth still stared silently out the window, entranced by an unremarkable Devonshire landscape. There was little traffic on this portion of the road up to London; Edith could give most of her attention to the events of the weekend and her daughter's continued distraction. Elizabeth's lustrous hair and smooth complexion could shrug off the effects of a few sleepless nights but a mother's practiced eye saw the beginnings of sad, dark hollows under her eyes.

"We can stop for tea somewhere along here, if you'd like," she suggested. "Maybe some berries and cream—we won't get as fresh up in London, you know."

Elizabeth nodded and spoke for the first time since leaving Caer Maen a good many hours before. "Someplace small and quiet. No crowds."

Drawing upon a half-century of backroad wandering, Edith left the highway and threaded her way through the countryside to a gabled inn that swayed precariously over its gardens. A signboard proclaimed that the Black Duck had been open for business since 1548.

"Riding the M-roads is a bit like going to sea—puts a lot of space between you and your problems rather quickly," Edith began once a pot of tea was on the table and their orders had been sent to the kitchen.

Elizabeth looked past her mother. "I guess you're right, Mum. It feels behind me now."

"Far enough behind that you can talk about it?" Edith pressed gently.

The young woman sighed. "Talk about what? Now I've felt the Otherworld. It wasn't particularly unlike what I've heard tell of, only this time, because it was *me*—" She stared at the tablecloth. "Oh, Mum, you must know what I feel like without my telling you."

"Oddly enough, Liz, I don't. The Otherworld has never come after me that way." Edith stated with a frankness that firmly caught her daughter's attention. "No, nothing individual at all. As far as the Other's concerned I guess I'm fairly uninteresting—"

"And I suppose I've done something to catch notice?" Elizabeth grumbled. "I haven't the faintest idea what I did, or I'd un-do it."

"Did isn't quite the right word, Liz. You remind everyone and everyTHING of your Aunt Gwen."

Elizabeth poked through the rich, clotted cream and stabbed one of the half-hidden berries. "I wasn't reminding anyone or any*thing* of Aunt Gwen at Samhain. I felt something reaching at me and I called for her." She paused to stab a second berry. "I've felt I should have called for you or Dad, but I didn't—maybe because you were already there. I don't know." She stared out the window again, speaking so softly her mother had to lean across the table to hear her. "I was frightened; afraid They were going to make me die and I turned to a woman I saw maybe a half-dozen times in my life and who has been dead five years. My parents, the people I've known all my life were right there in the circle with me and I called for Aunt Gwen. I don't understand."

"Have you considered that your aunt might have been reaching for you?"

"No."

"Maybe your Aunt needed your strength because something had gone wrong at Riverside."

"No, it wasn't like that—though I take it that something went *very* wrong at Riverside and you think that Aunt Gwen could have reached across from the Summerland to me?"

Edith wouldn't answer. She had said enough about her own theories; anything more was best left unsaid until after they saw Hector. She had decided, though, without thinking or asking that Elizabeth would be with her when she talked to the psychic.

She knew both as mother and High Priestess that Elizabeth yearned for Riverside rather than provincial Caer Maen.

When Arthur's bitterness had become entrenched, Liz had asked to emigrate. And now? No, they had lost enough. What her own mother had done in innocence had brought them all to the edge of an abyss. Caer Maen would have to repair whatever damage they might inadvertently caused since 1928, but Riverside would have to form its own coven.

The London streets were as quiet as they would get with a few post-midnight travellers moving purposefully along the rain-dampened streets.

"I'm bringing you to Hector's with me," Edith commented as they passed yet another of the streets that would have taken them to the flat Elizabeth shared with two other women.

"I'd guessed as much. It's nearly one, though—a bit late for visiting, isn't it?"

Edith tucked the car into the shadows between two buildings.

"Early for Hector, I'm afraid. I'm not entirely certain he'll see us before two."

"Eccentric old man?" Elizabeth joked as she followed cautiously down the pitch-dark pathway after her mother.

"Not old, late twenties or early thirties, I should guess—unless that's still old to you. He finds it easier to be awake when everyone else is asleep."

They waited by an unmarked backdoor until a light came on. A pale man with an unruly mane of black hair and wild, but gentle eyes, opened the door slowly. He seemed reluctant to admit them to his home. Elizabeth retreated to the shadows, but Edith greeted the psychic by name.

"Yes, Mrs. Brompton, come in. Your husband called earlier and said you'd be getting here past midnight. Forgive me—he did say it was urgent but—"

He made a small helpless gesture with his hands and led them into what had once been the servants' hall of an extensive urban household but which was now given over to comfortable chairs and tables piled high with books. Edith had been upstairs many times: an old family of impeccable heritage and a tendency towards fragile, psychic children; Hector was the most gifted the family had ever seen. He could have made a more than comfortable living making predictions for the picture-press, but he'd chosen a secluded life sharing his talents quietly with a select group of occultists and detectives.

The trio exchanged introductions, pleasantries and a glass of port before Hector led them to a small room which was empty except for three uncomfortable-looking straight-back chairs.

"Your husband said you'd be coming alone—but I had foreseen a third at our gathering. I usually like music in the background—as an anchor. Will you be comfortable with Bach?" he asked and when Edith nodded he left them alone in the room.

"*This* is the best psychic in the UK?" Elizabeth asked.

"By far and away. You surprise me. I shouldn't think you'd need fripperies to convince you he had talent."

"I guess I can still be surprised by who is and who isn't."

Hector returned to the room as the music began. In silence he assigned each woman to a chair before settling himself between them. The light of the room, such as it was, crept in through the cracks around the door and touched their faces with deep shadows. Hector pressed himself against the back of his chair, gripping the ball-and-talon armrests resolutely and waiting in increasing apprehension.

Edith held her breath and waited with him. For all that she was Priestess of a High Coven her talents were only those of a woman with intelligence and determination; Gwen had been the sister with magick. Years of work within the Circle and elsewhere had convinced her of the tangible power of magick, but as she had indicated to her daughter, she had never had one of those self-defining experiences that sets a modern person utterly apart from his contemporaries.

Heavy shadows moved across Hector's face. His brows knotted as he applied a talent that might rightly be said not to exist. Elizabeth raked her hair with faintly trembling fingers. Edith remembered that at her daughter's age she was already the High Priestess of Caer Maen and had never been allowed the luxury of visible discomfort. The psychic covered his face with his hands; his fingers kneaded concentration-cramped muscles. He looked over to Edith.

"I cannot find the one you ask for. If he walks among the living, his mind is vacant. If he is dead—" The young man shrugged noncommittally.

"The letter, Mother, you've got the letter with you. Perhaps he can find Uncle Arthur with that."

The weariness sloughed off Hector's face as he drew himself erect in the chair. "I don't require touchstones—superstitious jumble, all of it! A name and a purpose—that's all I require."

Edith saw the angry blush rise to her daughter's cheeks and hoped that Hector hadn't seen it. The young man's reputation warrented his pride, but he had always sought after the minds of ordinary men and women for ordinary purposes; her brother-in-law had been no ordinary man. If Hector were like all those other talented individuals existing outside High Coven circles he would exercise his gifts until his death and never suspect that the Otherworld, or the High Covens, existed.

"I do have a letter—the very one which led me to contact you. It may indeed be that something has happened to his mind. In lieu of his name, perhaps the texture of his writing would lead you to him?"

Hector's pride flashed. "I do not seek after the deranged."

"And I would not ask you to. I'll get the letter."

Hector's arrogance came from the summoning of mental traces and extracting small bits of knowledge from them; Edith's authority had been hard-won while guiding a half-hundred sincere and free-thinking Wiccans. The ephemera of genius crumpled before carefully exerted experience. Hector nodded and Edith left the room to get the letter.

The writing was typical of Arthur: unevenly-sized but well-formed letters; a few marks that might have been skips of an absently guided pen; a firm, instinctive signature. But would this be enough to find him if he were lost between here and the Summerland? Edith pursed her lips and returned to the room where Hector waited.

"He wrote it November Eve," she explained handing it to him.

"Who beside yourself has handled this?"

"Half the postal workers between Cornwall and America, I should think."

Hector smiled tolerantly. "Static," he mumbled, "the world is filled with people who touch and think without ever having touched or thought at all. So, it's just yourself and Arthur Andrews, then?"

"And my husband, Bert."

Hector held the letter in his hands and resumed his stiff position on the chair save that now his eyes were open and fixed on the piece of paper. Edith went back to her chair and avoided Elizabeth's questioning glances. She lost track of time while the psychic worked. Her memory took her back to the days when Arthur Andrews was the gallant war hero come down from Scotland to take her older sister off to America. She had wished for a man as dashing and romantic—and gotten him only to see Tom swallowed by the English Channel in the dark days of 1940 and another war. The Gods gave the High Coven witches full and rich lives, but They didn't spare Their servants the tempering flames of sorrow. Edith had never sought Tom the way they now sought Arthur—and never would.

A thin sheen of sweat covered Hector's forehead. The letter vibrated in his clenched hands. He closed his eyes but the trembling continued. Edith sat forward in her chair, looking between the fluttering paper and his face, certain he'd been caught in an Otherworld web.

In a circle, as the High Covens raised them, a few words and some salted wine usually ended any danger from the Otherworld. But Hector had no such precautionary defenses. Neither the living nor the dead had ever been a threat to him and Edith had allowed her hopes to supersede her normal cautions.

Elizabeth darted forward and pulled the letter from his

hands, calling his name and bringing him back from wherever it was that he had been drawn. His panic had been felt among his blood kin as noises could now be heard on the upper floors and in a nearby room a child was screaming.

Hector glared at Edith. "What manner of man was he? You do well to fear for him," he whispered, taking the letter from Elizabeth and returning it to Edith.

"He is dead, then?" Edith asked—she had no intention of revealing what manner of man they sought.

Hector nodded and led them back into the kitchen where his wife was heating a pan of milk for the whimpering child.

"Would you like more port?" he asked, refilling all three glasses.

"He's safely dead?" Edith asked sincerely.

Hector regarded her carefully. Though Edith possessed a great store of talismanic jewelry, it was not her custom to wear any of it outside a circle. A band of gold and silver adorned one finger to proclaim that she was married, but there was nothing to say she was High Priestess.

"Safely dead—an interesting phrase: as if there were varieties of death and not all of them equal." Hector shook his head. "Well then—what can I tell you about your late brother-in-law, Arthur Andrews? He's dead—very disoriented but, one would suspect, safely dead. His spirit isn't wandering the Earth, not that spirits do, but it is troubled. He is desperately searching for something and won't respond to my calls.

"It's strange: for all the tales of questing ghosts, your brother-in-law is the first I've encountered. They most often accept their deaths more calmly than the living do—but your Arthur quests and is, I suspect, quested after."

"What does he seek?" Edith asked, since she knew what sought him.

"Oh, he's not looking for you—he's not looking for anything out here. Do you believe in reincarnation? I do, of course. Your brother-in-law would appear to have strayed from his path." Hector laughed and something of the empty, panicked look returned to his eyes. "But, for now there's no communicating with him. He both seeks and hides as no man has done before."

Edith thanked him for the grim information and shared in trivial conversation that was forgotten as soon as it was uttered. It was late. Elizabeth was impatiently signalling that she wanted to leave; would have preferred to have left some time before, but the High Priestess wasn't ready.

The worst had indeed happened. Cold certainty said Arthur had died with the Curtain of Being parted open and the Otherworld sniffing out the fringes of its exile, ready to snare a High Coven soul or subvert its journey to the Summerland. She told Elizabeth so when they were back in the tiny car and headed away from the mews.

"But how can you be so certain?" Elizabeth asked.

"I knew. I should have known the moment we had trouble—the moment you called them both on Samhain. I had a notion, but I let it slip." Edith's voice was bitter.

Elizabeth's sigh echoed through the car. "Mother, New York is seven hours different from Cornwall. Uncle Arthur was probably eating dinner when I fainted. There's no reasonable way he could have been in Circle when we were. It's pure co-incidence. Stop blaming yourself."

"Twentieth century poppycock," her mother retorted. "We've been doing Samhain rituals since the world was flat. We believe the Rifts open and close at the same time and no calculating scientist at Greenwich can contradict us. We believe it; it's one of the few things we *all* believe and it's one of the few things that binds *Them*."

"You're serious, aren't you, Mother?"

"Of course I am. I don't need an Oxford text to tell me about the Otherworld."

An object that might have been a cat or a lump of newspaper shot across the street. Edith swerved sharply to avoid it, jerking Elizabeth against the door and sending her own stomach to her throat. She rarely drove in London this late at night, this tired, this anxious or after two glasses of port.

"You'll go to New York, then?" Elizabeth asked into the tense silence. "Or will you send me like Grandmum sent Aunt Gwen?"

Edith gripped the wheel until her short fingernails dug into the palms of her hands. "I'll go myself, when the time comes. What's happened there has happened. We can't close that Rift again until next Samhain: many places but one time, you know that. For now we'll warn the other High Covens and prepare ourselves. We'll need more than that, but it's all we've got for now.

"And, Liz—you'll not go to Riverside with my blessings. I'd like to see you take my place when the time comes, but that will be your choice. I won't see any more of Caer Maen lost to Riverside and the Otherworld—that's my choice."

Chapter Eleven

Lise picked up the pillows from the floor and arranged them behind her on the sofa. A homemade chocolate pastry sat between the crystal statue and a steaming cup of coffee on the tree stump. She picked up a section of the Sunday *Times* and glanced at the pastry. It was still too early——maybe she'd be hungry by lunchtime.

If there was one thing at which Maria's family excelled, it was food. A dinner at the cramped Brooklyn house with its pictures of the Kennedys, the Cardinals and all the relatives both here and in Italy was a meal to remember. It was also a meal to train for. Lise had fasted for eighteen hours and almost a day later had yet to eat her dessert.

Mama Agnelli understood that her brood was now American as well as Italian. She roasted a turkey and served it with the patriotic accompaniments of stuffing, yams and a small mountain of mashed potatoes. She also prepared lasagne, occi bucci, calamari and a somewhat larger mountain of pasta with the traditional Agnelli sauce. Lise had eaten a bit of everything except the calamari—squid by any other name was still squid and no amount of teasing would get any on her fork.

Lise's thoughts drifted away from the meal and back to the paper. She read the magazine section with more thoroughness than the articles truly deserved. The apartment had calmed down since that night when she and Maria had run away—and Lise had waited four days before returning. Oh, the pillows were still more often on the floor than on the sofa; the stereo was best left unplugged, but nothing had dared attack her directly again.

She took a bite from the pastry, found a pencil and began the crossword puzzle. The single life wasn't turning out too badly, though she had a lot more time on her hands than she was used to. Besides, there was Alan. She set aside the puzzle and looked at the phone.

Alan had just transferred to her office section—a management trainee out of Harvard doing his tour of the company before getting his own command. He was blond, thirty, divorced and marked as fair game by every woman within three floors of his neatly organized desk.

Lise had worked with him on a couple of projects since his arrival. They'd eaten lunch together a few times—at first out of convenience and then, she thought, because they got along fairly well. Though he could have gotten her phone number from any of a dozen not-terribly-confidential files in the office, he'd asked her for it and asked, at the same time, if she was doing anything Sunday. He hadn't made definite plans, but instead of wearing her usual threadbare jeans and frayed shirt, she was doing the crossword puzzle in Ms. Vanderbilt's velveteens and a handknit sweater whose moss-rose tone, she'd been told, was ideal for her fair skin and light brown hair.

It was two o'clock and the likelihood of his calling diminished with each passing moment. Lise slipped into sour-grapes moralizing on the dangers of dealing with recently divorced men who looked anything at all like Robert Redford.

By dinner time she had finished the pastry and the crossword puzzle—and her infatuation with Alan. The evening stretched endlessly before her. She picked up her knitting, made two mistakes in the first row then set the project aside again. The novel that had seemed interesting on Friday no longer held her interest and she had already washed her hair once today.

An airmail letter from Britain sat, unopened, on the writing table where she had placed it Saturday before heading out to Brooklyn. It had been addressed to "current resident" and had not been forwarded to whomever was collecting Arthur's mail. Lise recognized the return address from the letter she had mailed the day she signed the lease. Like the business card that still sat on the hall table, the letter radiated imperatives and a past she approached reluctantly if at all.

She found the paper knife and slit the sides of the letter. The writing inside was neat and crowded the edges of the paper. It was signed by an Edith Brompton and began with an apology for not being able to greet Lise by name. Mrs. Brompton did not mince her words in describing the apartment. She knew most of its furnishings in great detail, especially the glass statue and the other materials Maria and Lise had discovered in the locked cabinet.

Edith Brompton was the High Priestess of a coven in Cornwall and though she declined to say much about herself, she made it clear that there had been witchcraft in the apartment the night Arthur died. Witchcraft that, having been left incomplete by his death, was responsible for whatever untoward events had been occurring the apartment—and Edith was certain there would have been some. The new tenant might well believe the apartment was haunted.

"—which it most certainly is not," the letter informed in underlined letters. "I can assure you that ghosts have nothing to do with this. But, if my brother-in-law's death were as untimely as we fear it to have been, he has left undone things which, for the safety of us all, must be done. I have been unable to contact any of the original Riverside coven directly, but Arthur should have arranged for his apartment to be turned over to someone who would understand. The damage must be repaired—if you need help, our resources are at your service."

Lise folded the letter and set it under a paperweight on the table. Someone from the Riverside coven, whatever that was, had probably been collecting Arthur's mail and probably would have understood all that the letter implied. She could even guess that J. Robert Hynes and Marjory had been members of that coven and had wanted to discuss the same things the letter had stated so baldly. What Fine had called bad vibes were scarcely an adequate description for what the witches had left in her apartment. The worst of Lise's suspicions had been confirmed and, though she hadn't really wanted to know the truth, now she could be prepared. Riverside coven wasn't going to get back in here—as Shakespeare had said they were protesting too much; she didn't trust their intentions or their abilities. Better to let whatever unreal disturbance they had created subside on its own—as it was certain to do in this rational world.

She studied the glass statue. And it was a statue, very pretty, very valuable—but just a statue. She wasn't some fool who believed in hexes and voodoo dolls. She got the business card from the hall table and dialed the number; she'd tell Marjory that, too.

The number rang fifteen times before she hung up. By then the impulse to give the witches a piece of her righteous indignation seemed less wise, but she left the card under the dial and sought other ways of getting herself through the long, lonely Sunday evening.

When the phone rang a little after ten she answered it cautiously. At home there were only two types of after-nine phone-calls: emergencies and cranks. She waited for the caller to say the first word which, after a few seconds, he did.

"Is Lise Brown there?"

"Yes, this is Lise," she replied, not recognizing the voice and poised to slam the receiver into the cradle.

"Hi! It's Alan—remember me? For a minute there I thought I'd dialed the wrong number. I didn't wake you up, did I?"

"No," she said after a pause. "I was just sitting here working on a sweater for my brother. Christmas seems to be coming fast this year."

He was casual and friendly—blissfully unaware that she had spent the better part of the day waiting for this call.

"Would you be interested in an end-of-weekend drink?" he asked. "I figure I'm about five minutes away from your place. If it's too late—just say so. I've got to get up early tomorrow too."

She was still dressed for a visit to any trendy bar and he *had* called, however late. Caution and propriety had limited her social life in New York City—it was, perhaps, time to bend a little. She agreed to the drink and went down to the lobby to wait for him.

"You want me to get a cab for you?" Sam asked as she sat down in one of the lumpy, vinyl-taped chairs.

She smiled and shook her head. "No, not tonight—I've got a date."

Alan had fifteen minutes; traffic lights and parking problems allowed him that much grace—but by ten-forty-five she'd be back in her apartment rehearsing some scathing remarks to use at work. Not that she'd actually say them; it was all fantasy and it would never occur to her to rehearse what she would say when he showed up—which he did.

"You didn't think I'd show up," he said bluntly as they got into his double-parked car.

"Well," she admitted, "I guess I wasn't sure."

"Truth to tell: I was best man at a wedding up in Boston yesterday; I was in no shape to drive back here."

Lise told him about the meal Mama Agnelli had prepared and how she'd brought her dessert home with her. He described one of the many times he'd gotten lost in Brooklyn. Despite her reservations, Lise found herself forgetting the long wait for his telephone call. He told jokes and she laughed. More important—he laughed when she told a joke.

Then it was midnight and she felt the first touch of impending awkwardness as surely as Cinderella had felt the coach turn into a pumpkin.

"Yeah, I just looked too," he said. "Midnight, already. That's what happens when you don't get to wherever you're going until eleven. If I'm going to be in any shape for that bond portfolio meeting tomorrow I'd better take you home now."

Lise relaxed, finished her drink and enjoyed his company all the way back up Riverside Drive. He said goodnight with a purely friendly kiss. Sam said goodnight with a wave of his hand. It wasn't until after she'd crawled into bed and turned out the lights that she began to think about why he had really wanted to see her. She wondered, in turn, if she really liked him, either, or if she was only desperate for someone's company.

Asking herself what did matter to her, she found that the problems riding closest to the surface of her mind had to do with her apartment and the witchcraft that had been performed within it. Her mind, in a sleepy way, built bridges from one thought to another. The couple who had brought the business card; they were witches. He was an investment banker; Alan would in all probability become a similarly well-positioned executive. The Englishwoman was a witch who spoke of having a husband and family. Lise tried to imagine the everyday life of a witch. She rolled over in frustration.

The peace she had with her apartment—if it were to hold through the night and not slide into another sequence of nightmares—depended on achieving sleep in a relatively calm frame of mind. She was one who could generate anxiety and frustration quickly if her equilibrium was at all damaged—even by thinking thoughts that had no resolutions. She set the timer on her clock-radio, turned the volume up and listened to classical music. She tried to think of her knitting instead of Alan or witches.

Chapter Twelve

She slept soundly without dreams or interruptions and still managed to wake up feeling and looking exhausted. There should have been nightmares, though she was glad she couldn't remember them. Still, it would take two cups of coffee to get going and she could forget about getting to the office early. Dark, swollen half-circles glared out at her from the bathroom mirror; she looked more like a raccoon than a career-woman. She intended to look good today, if it took every bottle on her cosmetics shelf to do it.

Almost everyone else had arrived by the time she reached the office. She left the *Times* unread on her desk and joined her peers at the coffee machine where Alan was most apt to begin his day. She got a few compliments for the pale lavender dress she wore, though she had worn it before without anyone noticing. But she did not meet Alan; he headed straight for his office and then on to his meeting without noticing her.

Lise shoved a school-girl hurt into a far corner of her mind and turned her attention to the in-basket. After several more futile attempts she got through to J. Robert Hynes, having decided that it would be best to deal with the witches on a business-like level. A crisply efficient secretary informed her that Mr. Hynes was not expected back at his office until the fifteenth of January; his portfolios were being handled by Susanne Hirshhorn who would be glad to answer any questions—if Lise would leave her name and a return number.

"Well, no—I really wanted to speak with Mr. Hynes himself." Lise mumbled.

"I assure you that Ms. Hirshhorn can answer all your questions most satisfactorily," the secretary said with such determination that Lise believed she was speaking with Ms. Hirshhorn.

"No, really—it's a personal matter. A mutual friend—"

"Oh." The phone cooled in her hand. "Shall I take a message? He'll be out of the country, you know."

She didn't know, and she didn't leave a message. She also found herself feeling vulnerable. She had gathered the month's worth of frustration and fright and intended to dump it on the couple along with Edith Brompton's letter and the paraphernalia from the cabinet. She had convinced herself that would end her problems with the apartment. Now, she found she had stirred her emotions and her hopes to no useful end.

"You're looking glum."

At the sound of Alan's voice she flung her pen halfway across the desk. She shrugged and tried to retrieve her pen without drawing more attention to it.

"Out late last night?" he asked with a wink; she replied with a smile. "Got a minute? I'd like to talk to you in my office."

His cubicle was clearly visible to the rest of the room: hardly the place for a private conversation. Lise was already pondering the disadvantages of office romance when she sat down beside his desk.

"—it's a rush year-end job and I told Krozier I'd need an assistant. He agreed, so I asked for you. You've got the best record of anyone in the bullpen for accuracy and speed—besides, I'm pretty sure we'll work well together." He winked again.

When they'd gone out the night before she'd day-dreamed of a longterm relationship. The five-year difference in their ages and the thousands of dollars difference in their salaries had seemed an advantage, then. When she looked at him now, on the executive escalator, the light of ambition in his eyes while she was still a troop-in-waiting, the differences seemed unbridgeable. She grew steadily more distressed while he waxed enthusiastic.

Her feet came alive with the prickling of imaginary needles and she realized she had sat for almost three hours without moving. When she stood up to leave there was a moment of dizziness—as if all the blood in her body lay in her feet.

"You doing anything Friday night?" he asked as she got her balance.

"No," she answered, drawing out the word and thinking more about getting home in one piece than the end of the week.

"Fine—dinner? After work—or would later be better for you?"

"After work's fine—I guess."

It didn't sound like her own voice; it wasn't what she'd planned to say. Her own voice would have said she didn't date the person responsible for her next promotion. At the very least her own voice would have said that she was busy. But then again, her own voice belonged to a person who didn't take risks and lived a quiet boring life—and maybe she wasn't that person anymore.

—Not everyone can live in a haunted apartment—she thought to herself during the daily replacement of the pillows. —I could start charging admission. For a small fortune you, too, can see the Phenomena of Riverside Drive. See the Amazing Flying Pillows do their thing right before your very amazed blue eyes. How is it done, you ask. How is it done?—

The exhilaration faded as reality oozed in. She didn't know how it was done; she didn't really believe it was possible that it happened at all. Maria would visit only when she could leave before dark; she always wore a silver cross, though Lise pretended not to notice.

"I'm stronger than you are," she warned the empty room, "and at least twice as stubborn." The ebullience was gone, only the anxiety remained.

She had expected the room to vibrate to her challenge, but it remained inert. The sense of confidence came back, a little, and remained with her throughout the evening. She was in her nightgown when the phone rang.

"Hello?"

"When you hear the tone the time will be eleven forty-two PM and twenty seconds–When you hear the tone the time will be eleven forty-two PM and forty seconds–"

She held the receiver away from her ear a moment longer before letting it drop back into the cradle. A cold draft moved across her back. The room was still, but not empty and she tensed with incipient panic, waiting for the pillows to rise or the lights to dim. When the clock had clicked through five, unending minutes she told herself it was a trick of the breezes and the windows; the livingroom had only seemed to harbor a malignant presence. And getting a phone call from the time-recording was a joke; a hey-you'll-never-guess-what-happened-to-me to be shared over coffee at the office.

She gave the nearest pillow a satisfyingly solid punch, though it hadn't moved an inch. She was even calm enough to be angry and to eat an orange before going to bed. The lights in every room, however, burned throughout the night and a heavy-duty flashlight, a present from Maria, shared her bed.

"It's getting to me," Lise confided to Maria when they met for lunch Wednesday. "I'm starting to *believe* that those Phenomena are real. The other night I practically scared myself to death because I'd gotten a phone call from the time-recording lady."

Maria's eyes widened, but she said nothing.

"Well, I can't very well believe it's real, now—can I?" Lise demanded. "I wasn't raised to believe in spirits and ghosts!"

Maria stared into her coffee. "I'd believe it," she muttered without looking up.

"Maria—fun's fun, and all that—but there's got to be a simple, rational, scientific explanation for all of this. A simple, unmysterious answer—except that I don't know what it might be."

"If all I knew was what you'd told me; if I'd never seen any of it myself—well, I'd say you're right. But, I saw those things myself."

"So, there's such a thing as mass hysteria—two people, whole crowds of people can think they've seen the same not-real thing—if they're receptive to that idea in the first place—and we were after opening that cabinet and all—"

"Sure, Lise, I've seen lightbulbs glow like that—just before a blackout. Maybe you could even convince me that there was some chemical in the air that made the statue glow. There probably is a good reason for everything that has happened—even miracles can have an explanation of *what* happened. But the only explanation for *why* it happened is in the letter you got from the English lady."

Lise stared out the window; the sidewalks had their normal quota of lunchtime strollers. Trucks and taxis rumbled uptown. There was a real world out there and she had expected Maria to insist that it had the upper hand—or else she never would have shared the letter with her.

"Okay," she grumbled, "the craziness wins: I live in a haunted apartment. Witches here and in England would be thrilled to live there. I've lost five pounds since I moved in—so it hasn't been a complete waste. Of course, if I keep that up I'll disappear before the lease is up—"

"You could go to church," Maria suggested timidly.

Lise rolled her eyes upward. "Presbyterians don't do exorcisms."

"It might help. It helped me—after what happened that night."

Maria's voice was little more than a whisper and Lise was dumbfounded by the thought. She had abandoned the family religion before she got to college. Throughout all the sleepless nights and moments of terror her thoughts had never turned to foxhole religion.

"I guess there's no harm in admitting I'm afraid of the Phenomena," she said slowly. "Sometimes I'm afraid I'll get sick before I can get the door unlocked when I come home. But, still, I don't have any religion left in me. I'd go to a psychiatrist before I'd go to church."

"Well, you could do that, too."

"The apartment's crazy—not me. It needs the help."

"Well, do something. Go talk to the witches," Maria's voice had taken on an edge of irritation.

"In the yellow pages?"

"No, there're ways of contacting them; places you can leave your name and they'll get in touch with you. There're a lot of witches in the City. Some of them would try to help."

"You've obviously given this a lot of thought," Lise acknowledged, sitting back in her chair. "So, tell me: how do you get in touch with the witches? Shall I whisper a secret word three times under the clock in Grand Central Station." She made no attempt to purge the sarcasm and bitterness from her voice.

"You act like it's a joke—but you're scared; you look like a wreck," Maria complained. "Father Galen told me about the witches; he's met some of them. There's some sort of witches' rights organization here and they send delegates to all the ecumenical meetings."

" 'Eye of newt, toe of frog,' cauldron-carrying witches?" Lise joked. "I'm not certain they'd really be much help."

"There's a store up on the West Sixties. It's owned by witches."

"In the Sixties?"

"Culpeper's."

Lise affected to ignore the information but it stayed with her—especially as she couldn't get in touch with the couple who'd left the card. She was getting by in the apartment by turning her fright into anger at the witches for doing this to her—but for the anger not to become malignant itself, she had to know that there really was someone she could scream at—even if she never opened her mouth. As long as Alan and her work distracted her; as long as the livingroom stayed quiescent she could survive nicely just knowing there was a witchcraft store called Culpeper's and not knowing anything more.

Chapter Thirteen

Alan did keep her thoughts occupied both in and out of the office. He proved to be a taskmaster, inspired by computer-generated progress charts and a technicolor graph of daily milestones of the three-month journey to his next round of corporate congratulations. But he wound up their first Friday afternoon conference a half-hour before quitting time and disappeared until well after the office emptied out. Lise used the company washroom to affect her transformation from bull-pen worker to such stylish sophistication as her personality and budget allowed.

Alan had mastered the City. Taxis screeched to a halt when he raised his hand; maitre'd's remembered his reservations without looking in their leather-bound books; his tables were in quiet corners, surrounded by attentive staff.

He suggested visiting a disco recently praised in the pages of *New York Magazine*. She declined, suggesting instead a movie lately imported from France. He agreed and they sat chastely attentive through a pagent of sub-titled passion. They went to a dark, little bar, drank cognac and discussed the movie in properly intellectual platitudes.

If she had a choice, and she probably would, she would rather bring him back to her place with its romantic wooden furniture, thick carpets and faintly scented air. He hadn't said much about where he lived, except that his wife had taken all the furniture after the separation and divorce. She could imagine them in her wood-frame bed but couldn't imagine herself wrestling with the sofa-bed she suspected he slept on.

"You'll stop for coffee, if nothing else, won't you?" she asked as he held her coat for her. "I'd like to show off my apartment—I don't get many chances. It's not quite like your average apartment,'' and for once she was thinking of the charm of the livingroom when it was flooded by moonlight and not about the pillows.

He nodded and smiled without saying a word. They rode up the elevator where the twanging cables brought a shadow of discomfort to Alan's face and Lise realized she no longer consciously heard the sound.

''This elevator's on it's last legs,'' he said as it snapped to a halt then settled four or five inches back to the floor level.

''Everyone assures me it's perfectly safe. Well, actually, they assure me it's always sounded like this and hasn't killed anyone yet.''

''The Phantom of Riverside Drive,'' he said as they stepped onto the landing; Lise smiled and said nothing. The Phantoms of Riverside Drive did not dwell in the elevator shaft.

''Your place smells of incense,'' Alan remarked before they were more than a few feet beyond her door. Lise inhaled deeply, once again surprised at how accustomed she had become to the scent.

''Part of the charm of the place—'' she muttered and wondered if she'd had such a good idea. But the pillows were neatly piled on the sofa, the books were properly aligned on the shelves and though the glass statue caught his eye at once, it was radiating only its usual lovliness.

''*That* must be worth a fortune,'' he exclaimed. ''What're you doing driving a calculator if you can afford things like that?''

''The landlord let me rent the place furnished. I found her in one of the cabinets.''

''You found that?'' Alan's fingers made gentle contact with the statue then withdrew. Lise watched as his gaze darted from object to object. ''What wasn't here when you moved in—if you don't mind my asking?''

''Oh, my clothes—things like that. Most of the plants—though I inherited some African Violets that don't seem to have died on me yet. And some fancy evening gowns I'll never wear.''

She headed to the kitchen to put the water on for coffee.

"You know, you're damned lucky," he said after a minute or so.

Lise jumped and lost count of the spoonfuls she'd ladled into the pot. He lounged easily against the doorjamb, unaware of the terror she had felt—seeing him there for an instant before she recognized him. "Lucky," she muttered, trying to remember if there were three or four scoops in the pot.

"Yeah, you have a furnished apartment that actually lives up to its billing. You're working on a project that's going to Board-level with your initials on it. You've got me."

Lise watched him from the corner of her eye, no longer caring how much coffee she dropped in the pot. His posture was assured, almost cocky—but his posture was offset by something in his voice. This handsome man with the Harvard MBA and a guaranteed spot in the executive corps had been left behind by an even more attractive, ambitious wife (if any of the rumors were true). He might just be more of an emotional castaway than she was—Phenomena notwithstanding.

"Still want coffee?" she asked.

"I've got a choice?"

"Yeah, coffee if you're going home from here; wine if you're not."

"Wine, then."

Lise quivered. It had happened so quickly, before she'd had a chance to think and get tongue-tied. She'd asked him to stay, and he was staying. If he hadn't been there she would have bounced around the kitchen for joy. Of course, if he hadn't been there, there would have been no cause for joy.

They shared a non-vintage California wine from a bottle that had a pop-top instead of a cork—not that they needed to worry about leftovers, anyway. Lise slouched back against the pillows on the sofa—in case they developed wanderlust—and listened to his ramblings.

He hadn't recovered from his divorce, despite his protests to the contrary, or he would have been able to mention *her* name at least once. He hadn't gotten his confidence back, either; hadn't even gotten around to admitting how badly he'd been shaken up by everything.

It was past two; the time when the wine, the hour and the normal end-of-week slump caught up with them. It was slightly past the time when Alan's desires and determination could overcome the wine. They got into bed with the loving disinterest of couples who have spent years of nights together. He was asleep before he had finished his litany of apologies and Lise, hiding her disappointment, contented herself with touching his shoulder.

She closed her eyes, expecting not to open them again until sunlight flooded the room but found, instead that the sound of someone else's breathing was not the soporific she'd hoped it would be. She was acutely uncomfortable; aware of each move he made, of irregularities in his breathing and, most of all, of how hard he made it to hear all the other noises in the building.

He grunted as she inched away from him. An arm flailed, searching for her, but she avoided it and he was quiet. She resented that a stranger could sleep so soundly in her bed; in her home where nothing was truly inanimate and she had to stay awake to keep track of things. Of course, she reminded herself, she'd kept all that from him—so he could hardly be blamed—though she did blame him; he should have been able to guess the truth. Maybe it was an honor, of some liberated sort, that he'd become drowsy on *her* wine, confided a portion of his woes and slept the sleep of the innocent beside her.

Giving the pillow a quarter turn so that she could curl around it, Lise settled down to match pace with his breathing: a trick she'd learned while living with Bob. He'd been the first: there were only four—if she counted Alan; if she could count Alan. It was called "sleeping together" but sleeping wasn't how the score was kept. If it were just sleeping then she'd have to count her cousin with whom she'd shared a double-sleeping-bag when she was eight and determined to see the Leonid meteor shower. No, at least for now, there were only three. She sighed, consciously and melodramatically. There was always the morning.

They awoke together: Alan with a mattress-jarring leap, Lise with the knowledge that, once again, something was wrong in the livingroom. She had forgotten to unplug the stereo, from the sound of things.

The sounds from the other room still frightened her whenever they occurred, but it was a familiar fright—like the sounds of a war that has dragged on for years. The light from the livingroom steadied and if she concentrated she could probably go back to sleep. After all, she'd long since decided that when the lights were bright and steady the Phenomena had subsided. The pillows were already on the floor; it would all still be there in a few hours, along with sunlight.

Alan slipped out from under the blankets. She rolled over, raising her head. He waved at her to be still and pointed toward the livingroom; he clearly expected she would heed his warnings. There was fear in his face, but he was going to investigate. Lise drew herself into a sitting position; he glared at her and took a few more steps toward the light and noise.

—So, it will only frighten him a bit more—she thought. —He can't have guessed what's really happened—But, she got out of bed to follow him anyway. He did not seem to notice she stood beside him at the French doors; he was transfixed by the dazzling green cloud that hung over the carpet.

"Will-o-the-wisp," Lise whispered as she watched the dancing spiral.

"What?"

"Swamp gas—natural phosphorescence—agitated methane. I suppose I should have expected something like this, eventually." She stepped forward, shrugging off his restraining grip, determined not to share the terror. If she'd been alone she would have been in the lobby by now—and she knew it. But, as with Maria, the presence of another person, an innocent person, charged her with unexpected courage. She confronted the cloud. "Get out of here!" she bellowed at it.

It elongated and bent toward her. Alan picked up a book that had fallen on the floor nearby. He heaved it at the Phenomenon, not realizing that it would most likely strike the glass statue dimly visible through the green mist. Lise lunged after the book, passing through the mist herself as she did.

Aching, numbing cold so intense it could have been searing fire clung where the insubstantial fog had touched her. An oily film oozed over her skin; she thrashed on the carpet like a beached fish trying to rub the invisible stuff off. She opened her eyes and saw her arms and legs glowing with the green of the dancing spiral. Clawing at the clinging nothingness, Lise drew blood between gasps of pain. The cold mist whirled farther up her arms and legs, seeping over her body until it became a second skin locked over her chest. She could feel nothing, move nothing, and as she struggled to loose one last scream a green tendril snaked across her vision and, at last, she fainted.

Alan was beside her when she came to. A puzzled man, holding his wrinkled shirt which he had used to dry away the perspiration on her skin. Lise wiped away her tears.

"It's gone," she announced, gathering her shattered dignity like an invisible cloak around her.

"But, what was it?" he asked, stroking her dishevelled hair and holding her closer.

She didn't have the answers for herself, much less for him and kept quiet while her body caught the warmth from his. He stroked more than her hair and she pressed closely against him as they returned to the bedroom.

She could count four now, without doubt or adjustment.

Lise awoke more calmly in the morning, still entwined in his arms. She left him lying dreamily in the pillows and blankets and set about her morning activities—uncomfortably aware that there was a man in the adjoining room; a man with whom she had made love and who had seen the Phenomena in action.

When she remembered the mist the bathroom swung crazily and she had to hold the sink for balance. Long scratches on her arms and legs insisted that the experience had been real. No longer thinking of Alan, she turned the shower on full blast and scrubbed herself down with a rough natural sponge until her skin hurt all over. Alan was sitting on the edge of the bed when she emerged, bright pink, into her bedroom.

"Your turn," she announced, stepping out of range. He wanted to touch her, hold her—and she could not bear the thought of anything near her skin.

Frowning, Alan shut the door of the bathroom behind him. Lise dressed quickly and went boldly into the livingroom. The nightmare recurred in its cold, daylight form. A broken book lay beside the statue; Alan's shirt was on the floor where they had left it. The yellow fabric appeared unaffected by its ordeal, but Lise felt a wave of nausea when she touched it. Though the pillows had always been innocent when they weren't infested by Phenomena, the shirt had not been so fortunate.

With a pair of scissors, fighting riots in her stomach Lise reduced the shirt to a jumble of shapeless scraps fit for the incinerator.

"That's my shirt," Alan interrupted from the doorway, his face filled with the exasperation that could not be contained in his voice.

His hair was still damp from the shower; the skin of his chest and shoulders was pink where the hot water surges had surprised him. Lise smiled and without answering, snipped another scrap in half. "Take one from the closet," she told him.

—He thinks I've gone crazy—she thought, continuing to reduce the scraps to shreds. —Unfortunately, I suspect he's right, I'm not really sure myself anymore. —"We can go down to Bloomingdale's later," she added in a effort to sound sane. "I'll get you another one."

"Fine," though from his expression nothing was fine. "Wonderful! And what do I wear in the meantime? You're hardly my size."

"And neither are the shirts in the closet. You'll find

something—trust me." She wasn't sounding sane, not even to herself and set down the scissors to get him a new shirt from Arthur's clothes that Bob had never picked up. "They're a bit conservative, but more than adaquate. Here, what about this?" She handed him a light blue sweater.

"Lise," he muttered, pulling the sweater over his head. "What in Hell's going on here? That thing in the livingroom, slicing up my shirt, a closet full of men's clothes?" His words came slowly; he teetered between indignation and fear. Lise could appreciate his position.

"This place, here—where I live; it's not *normal*. I mean, I'm *normal*, or I was, or I am when I'm not here. But when I'm here, different rules apply. Your shirt is *evil* now. I know that's ridiculous—but, I also know it's *evil*; you couldn't wear it again. I live here; I know what happens here. I don't like it, but I have to face facts. The things in the livingroom, the Phenomena, I call them—they all come with this apartment you think I'm so lucky to have. I shouldn't let innocents come up here—but, sometimes I slip; I get lonely."

"So, leave this place. Get out of here." Alan smoothed the sweater over his belt.

"I've given myself the same advice innumerable times. Almost every morning I think I should look for someplace new. But, I don't, and I won't. It's crazy—I mean this *is* crazy—but I've chosen this place as my home and I'm going to make a success of it. I haven't been here two months; I'm just not going to run away. You can leave if you want, but keep the sweater, it's only fair."

She stared at him, letting her face go blank. It was crazy and she did sound crazier than the apartment. She expected him to walk out and was astounded when he hugged her tightly instead.

"You need help," he whispered.

She wrested away from him. "I'm not some hallucinating hysteric. None of this should be real—but it happens and I can't stop it from happening, yet. I *would* need help if I pretended that nothing happened here last night. But, I'm not crazy and there are Phenomena in my livingroom. Your shirt was evil, but I don't need a shrink."

"I didn't say you did. You need something more along the lines of an exorcist."

"Rot."

"This place is haunted, Lise. I trust my own eyes."

"But I don't believe in ghosts. I have to believe in the livingroom but not in ghosts, demons or exorcists!" She began making the bed with a vengeance. "It's mine and I'll cope with it as I see fit, all by myself—thank you."

"Lise, I'm only trying to help. I'll believe everything that you say except that you can cope with this by yourself. I saw you last night. Whatever made my shirt evil was all over you first. Think what could have happened to you last night!"

Lise froze, the blanket clutched against her breasts. She didn't want to think about that. Waves of nausea and weakness broke over her.

"Let me help you—at least let me care about you. I need to care about someone. There's a place in the West Sixties. I went to Columbia with a couple of guys who worked there. If there's an explanation for what's going on here, they'll be able to get it for us."

Lise said nothing. She wouldn't let him help her any more than she'd allowed Maria or the witches that priveledge. Still, he was the second person to tell her about Culpeper's in one week. Perhaps she would have to pay the place a visit someday.

Chapter Fourteen

The Ides of December were dark and drizzily; weather that passes for early winter in New York City. Raw and unpredictable breezes blew from every direction, but always in Lise's face and never at her back. She pulled her scarf tighter and wondered again how come forty degrees in New York felt colder than twenty below in Michigan.

A hand-painted sign announced the location of Culpeper's Herbal on the second floor of a dingy loft building. The ground-floor windows had been boarded up and plaster with several years' worth of handbills from nearby Lincoln Center. The sidewalk doors to the basement were rusted through and liquor bottles, still wrapped in brown paper, were lined up beside the main door. Though it was two o'clock in the afternoon (Lise had taken the afternoon off) the street was deserted and she hesitated before opening the sheet-metal door to the lofts above.

The stairwell rose in a single, unbroken slope to a skylight above the fifth floor. Bald, grey light filtering through that dirty glass provided enough light to count the peeling coats of paint as she climbed the stairs. Subtle incense beckoned at the first landing where a more elaborate sign informed her that she had reached Culpeper's Herbal at last. The sign said to ring the bell and wait, she did and was let into the store.

"May I help you?" a soft-spoken man asked. He stood behind a glass display counter that stretched the width of the loft at the front of the building.

"No, I'm just looking, thank you."

"If you need anything—" He nodded and went back to reading.

Momentarily Lise wished Maria or Alan had come along with her; certainly they'd both offered often enough. She wasn't comfortable in this place that was both like and unlike her home and she certainly didn't want to discuss the Phenomena with people who might revere them.

Living up to its name, Culpeper's was filled with a seemingly endless array of dried herbs and herbal oils, candles and incense; each was prominently labelled with its traditional, Wiccan, astrological or voodoo attributes. Piles of arcane books tumbled over trestle tables at the center of the room. Lise scanned the books, hoping one might miraculously bear the title: Livingroom Phenomena, Causes, but more importantly, Cures. Aside from a tattered, used copy of *Rosemary's Baby* though, there was nothing relevant in any of the piles.

A line of black draperies separated the front part of the loft from the back. Announcements had been pinned to the velvet announcing Yule celebrations to take place the following week and several courses in occult practices being taught by people with names like Starfollower and Master Beltane. One of the announcements was decorated with a female figure not unlike the glass statue but the lecture advertised was for numerology and did not sound promising.

"Are you sure there's nothing I can help you with?" the man asked a second time.

Lise thought of the letter in her pocket and patted her side to be sure it was still there. At the same time she insisted she was just looking. Her attention caught on the display case. She glanced over the X-rated Tarot decks and mother-of-pearl ouija boards, lingered moments longer at the matched knives that were identical to the ones in the locked cabinet and was completely transfixed by a bleached skull with a brass spike protruding from its cranial dome.

"It's not real," the man said gently. "Everybody stares at it that way. It's one of those new plastics the museums use instead of bone and ivory. Lifelike enough, isn't it? Even down to different colors for the teeth."

"Too lifelike," Lise admitted. "What in god's name would someone do with it?"

"Put it on an altar with a candle. It takes all kinds," he added with a deprecating shrug.

He was not a young man; there was more than a smattering of grey in his reddish-brown hair. She doubted that Alan had gone to school with him. His glasses were thick, rimmed with gold-wire and made his pale blue eyes look too large for his face. He wore his clothes as if he'd borrowed them from a scarecrow. Aside from the uniquely urban pallor of his skin he looked as if he should have been in Maine or Vermont—or even Michigan. She decided she liked him, despite the skull and the red candle he had pushed onto the spike.

"It's not my style," she said in what was supposed to be a jesting manner.

"Wouldn't have thought so. But, what are you here for. You don't have the classic patterns of a browser."

"Browsing, really. I heard about this place. A friend of mine said he went to school with some of the people who worked here."

"Who?"

"The friend?—Alan Porter."

"No, the people who worked here."

"Friends of his from Columbia—I don't know their names."

"They've been gone a few years now," the man wrinkled his brow as if the memories smelled bad. "My lady-wife and I have been running C-P's for a while now."

It was too good to be true—the people Alan knew no longer were in favor here. She could be completely honest about her visit, add another gripe to her list and still not have to tell them about the Phenomena. All she had to do was walk out, but she couldn't do it.

"Sometimes people come up here just out of curiosity—usually around Samhain—Hallowe'en. Sometimes they're looking for something they don't have a name for. Which kind are you?" he asked.

"Just a browser, like I said," she mumbled. "Curiosity, I guess."

"And what else?"

"Nothing else."

He put the skull back in the case and locked it. "I'm Jason

Star, co-owner of Culpeper's Herbal and one-time practicioner of the mysteries of psychiatry. If you've come here for help or advice, you've got to give me a bit more; I'm not a mindreader."

"I've got Phenomena in my livingroom."

Jason accepted her remark with equanimity. He quizzed her lightly about these Phenomena without revealing a glimmer of his own opinions until she had run out of things to say.

"Now, what do you want to do about these Phenomena," he asked in properly psychiatric tones.

"Make them go away."

"You can't make them go away. Magick doesn't work that way; it's not stronger than you are. You have to believe they will go away first—then you can turn to magick for help."

"I don't think you understand. I don't intend to believe in magick. I believe in the Phenomena because I have no choice. I want to get rid of the Phenomena, not pick up a lot of excess supersticions along the way."

He smiled tolerantly. "It's a slow day. Why don't we go in the back. Sally can heat up some water for coffee and we can talk for a while. You see—if you believe in the Phenomena you already believe in magick; you just don't believe anything good can come of it."

Glad that no-one she knew was there to witness her capitulation, Lise followed Jason behind the velvet curtains where, amid stacks of invoices, plastic vials and mounds of holly, Sally was working.

Now, Sally looked like a witch—not the Wicked-Witch-of-the-West witch with a warty nose and bony knuckles but the ethereal good-witch. Her waist-length hair was scarcely confined by a copper band she wore across her rather high and broad forehead. She had the same awesome serenity that marked the glass statue and Lise felt immediately uncomfortable.

"Do you have reason to think that any sort of Craft was practiced in your home before you moved there?" Sally asked.

Lise nodded as she sat down. "Yes, the landlord said the

place had been raided on Hallowe'en—the neighbors thought there was a orgy or something going on. I wasn't there, of course. There was a lot of old incense around. And later on I found some knives like the ones you have out front—other stuff, too.'' She wasn't ready to talk about the letter.

Jason and Sally watched each other a moment and Lise thought that they might, after all, comprehend her problems with witches.

''Perhaps your apartment needs a sort of purification. Maybe you could contact the people who lived there before—or, if you're too nervous to do that, we could do it for you.''

''The old man who lived there died in the raid.''

''Oh,'' Sally went on without a pause. ''The aura of ill-practiced magick can torment someone who had nothing to do with the original spell.'' The witch-woman closed her eyes. ''You might try scattering garlic cloves throughout your home then burning them at the full moon. Stay upwind, though, you wouldn't want to breathe the smoke.''

Lise shook her head. ''Garlic belongs on pizza. I just want to get rid of the Phenomena. I don't want to get involved in some silly charade by the light of the moon. Witchcraft created this mess; I don't see where more of it will help.''

If either Jason or Sally were offended they managed to conceal their emotions.

''If just *want* were sufficient, Lise, you wouldn't be here in the first place,'' Jason pointed out. ''And, it's unfortunately true that there are many varieties of witchcraft, not all of which are wholesome.''

Lise was outnumbered, outmaneuvered and getting too tired to fight. She told them about Hynes and Marjory and produced the letter from Edith Brompton for their examination. ''That's the kind of witchcraft they practiced in my apartment,'' she told them with distaste.

''It could be,'' Sally said softly, folding the fragile paper and returning it to Lise. ''I'd heard once that there was a coven in that area: an old one. I wouldn't have heard of them at all but the past few years they've been short a full circle and looking for new members."

"They must've been diabolic."

"Devil worshippers?" Jason replied to Lise. "No, I doubt it. If they were a daughter-coven of this Cornish coven they probably had their origins in the Celtic traditions. Some of the old covens are almost invisible to this day; they don't see any need to enter the pagan renaissance. After the Inquisition I doubt that anything will convince them it's safe to go back in the water."

"It sounds like they practiced an awfully intense Samhain, though," Sally added.

"So, what can I do to make the Phenomena stop?" Lise interrupted, lest they get carried away in discussions of that which did not interest her.

"You've written to this Mrs. Brompton?" Sally asked.

"No, I didn't know what to say to her. I don't want her help; I don't want to have anything to do with someone as—as *intimate* with the Phenomena as she seems to be."

"Well, it would take until January before we'd get an answer back from England, and Lise wants help now," Jason added for her.

"Then, we'll have to do what we can from here," Sally agreed.

"Such as?"

"Well, a variety of things. We'll work our way along until we find something that's effective for both you and the Phenomena of your apartment."

Jason left to answer the doorbell; Lise sat with Sally and listened increduously as the occult campaign was detailed. They would try garlic—or rather Lise would, as a favor to them—because the plant was a traditional purifier. She would purchase a few candles and incense which Sally would compound expressly for the protection of property and the purification of ritual vessels. When Lise reluctantly admitted that the glass statue was still in her possession, Sally produced a loose-leaf binder from which Lise handcopied several pages of poetry and the ritual instruction that were scattered in the margins. Lise bristled and Sally calmly announced that she would come to the apartment and perform the rededication ritual herself on the following Monday; she'd even bring a friend to help her—since it was plain that Lise wouldn't.

It was obvious to Lise that Sally *believed*. What Jason said made sense; it would take a religious fervor to defeat the Phenomena. She felt smug when she finally left the shop with purchases she had no intention of using and instructions she would not follow. Come Monday Sally and her witch-y friend would do the dirty work and she would reap the benefits. It seemed delightfully simple.

Chapter Fifteen

Lise opened the door to her apartment that next Monday evening with mild trepidation. Whatever else they were, they were still witches and they made her nervous. There was no predicting what the Phenomena would do and nothing but their word to guarantee that the witches would work against the Phenomena and not for it.

Jessica, Sally's friend, could have been any age between twenty and fifty. Her face was girlish but her eyes had a penetrating wisdom Lise associated with someone of considerable experience; specifically someone who had endured horror and trauma. Jessica was tiny and brittle rather than fragile—as if the sinews which held her in perfect balance might shatter if the right note were sounded. Her black hair was arranged in a simple, shoulder-length sweep; her clothes were neat and unpretentious and though the effect was totally unwitch-y neither could it be called casual. Lise was careful not to touch her guest's hand while taking her coat.

"Can I get either of you anything to drink," she asked as the threesome moved into the livingroom she had hurriedly cleaned after finishing packing for her Christmas vacation which was to begin the next morning.

"Whatever's handy," Sally answered with a smile.

"Warm water—and a spoon, please."

Jessica's voice was a husky rasp out of all proportion with her size yet not inconsistent with those too dark, too intense eyes. Lise scurried to the kitchen to comply with their requests. When she returned with rootbeer and water neither woman appeared to have moved at all. Jessica removed an unlabelled vial from her purse and sprinkled an ashy powder across the warm water.

"Jessica's going to 'feel' the past of the room—to help us learn what happened here. That way we can be more certain of rooting out your Phenomena," Sally explained to a very skeptical Lise.

"Is there anything I can do to help? Music? Should I turn out the lights?"

"No!" Jessica injected. Her eyes came into bright focus and her shoulders tightened with nearly audible tension. "No, everything is fine just the way it is."

Lise sipped her root beer and felt all the uneasiness she had repressed since her visit to Culpeper's. Even Maria had questioned her judgment in blithely assuming she could set one set of witches successfully against another and suggested Lise spend the weekend boning up on the occult in general and the witches in specific. And, for once, Lise would have taken someone's advice—but she'd been at the office most of the weekend doing the work she wouldn't do in the next week and when she wasn't at work she was with Alan.

"I'm ready now," Jessica announced as she set the grit-stained glass at her feet.

The tiny woman moved about the room as if she were blind; her eyes actually wandered aimlessly as her fingers dusted nervously over every accessible surface. Lise clutched the arm of her chair when Jessica handled a book that had once fallen off the shelves in a Phenomena outburst, but she put it back with the rest without comment.

Jessica passed over those objects Lise had bought or brought with her as if they weren't really there; she paused over those objects Lise knew to be connected with the room's occult past and she examined closely but unemotionally those normally neutral things that had been touched by the Phenomena.

For fifteen silent minutes, each marked by a click from the digital clock, Jessica searched the room. She was still many minutes from the statue and the pillows, all of which Lise expected would produce some sort of profound reaction from the woman. She fidgeted with impatience until Sally caught her eye and led her into the hallway, closing the French doors behind them.

"If you distract her she'll only have to start over again—

and it won't go any faster the second time. She won't be sure if what she senses is real or just an echo of her suspicions."

"As sure of what? What's she feeling?" Lise demanded. "The stuff she should be interested in is on the sofa—and she'll get to that last. She ought to have a lot of suspicions by then. I'm really surprised she didn't start with the glass statue."

"Do you think that was their image of the Lady?"

Lise nodded; she'd read enough to know that the witches called their goddess the Lady.

"I thought so as soon as I saw it. That coven didn't outfit itself from Culpeper's. We never have items like that—who could afford it? I wonder, though, what they used to represent the Horned One?"

"Horned One?" Lise controlled her apprehension; that sounded like a devil and Black Mass notions which Sally had said she didn't have to worry about. But then, that was before Sally got here. Lise wasn't trusting the witches any more than before.

"No, not the devil," Sally chided gently. "The male principle—the Fertilizer—the One-who-balances. If the Lady is birth and living then the Horned One is death and dying—except it's not that simple. Sometimes the Lady is death and dying. Do you know about Yin and Yang?"

Lise shrugged with disinterest.

"Well," Sally sighed, "they must have used something. Mono-polar covens don't usually have men in them."

Lise shrugged again. "Maybe Jessica'll find out. God knows she's looking hard enough."

"Making you nervous?"

"Nervous? No—I just wish she'd get finished. In the end I expect I'll believe she's very sincere—but a fraud none-the-less, sorry."

"Then what will you have? Nightmares, telekinetic phenomena, hallucinations? What will you have next? You believe all that happens here is real in some sense; you already know more about this place than Jessica can possibly discover. Something here's locked in on you, lady."

The words to counter Sally's assertions did not come quickly. Lise was filled with an anger that was directed more at the truth than at the witches. "I live here," she said finally. "These things happen around me but they aren't for me. I turned to you and your witchcraft because these things belong to your world—not mine—and the sooner you take them back, the sooner I'll get back to normal."

Sally stiffened. "Even if you believe these things happen by accident, and you haven't said that you do, you can't deny that they've happened to you and not someone else. You aren't going to be able to forget what's happened here; you won't deny it without going mad. Your feelings no longer really matter, Lise. You've been touched by the Gods now. Even if you moved out of here tomorrow a part of you would remain—with the Phenomena."

Lise knew Sally was right and that she'd put words to the real reason she hadn't moved out of the apartment. She summoned up her most scornful and deprecating stare, but Sally didn't wither away. Lise had to admit that at least one witch had a closer grasp of the truth than she did.

"I've finished now," Jessica announced, opening the doors and breaking the deadlock in the hallway.

The haunted look had faded from Jessica's eyes.

"So, what's the verdict," Lise asked as they re-entered the livingroom. She tried to sound friendly now.

"Nothing conclusive. People worked magick in this room—there're traces of it everywhere. It was powerful and intense magick, but nothing that should account for your nightmares, Lise—or the things Sally described to me. I'm sorry I couldn't find anything more useful."

Now that Jessica had finished the search and lost most of her strangeness Lise found it increasingly easy to talk to her—though, perhaps, that was only because she was embarrassed to talk to Sally.

"No black magick, then?" Sally asked.

"Not that I can feel. Whatever went on here wasn't directed at people at all." Jessica shook her head. "I'd say they only performed the seasonal rituals; they used very, very strong earth-magick."

"Here on the sixth floor of an apartment building?" Lise asked.

"I don't claim to understand what I feel, Lise, but there's no manipulative magick in this room and there never has been—just a powerful sense of the Celtic, lunar quarters."

Lise had heard about the solar quarters: equinoxes and solstices, but lunar quarters were something new. She'd have to ask a question, and they'd explain everything in great detail. But, that would be showing an interest in magick, and she didn't want to seem to have weakened that much.

"What about the objects themselves, Jessica? Or, any of the people in the coven. Has someone laid a curse on them, or on Lise for moving in here?" Sally continued.

"Well, there is death in here, but if the old man died here I would think that would explain everything—it's so recent."

"What about the statue," Lise asked, thinking it neutral enough.

"That statue's been here since it was cast; it's had no owners except the coven. The writing table's the oldest object in the room."

"So, we have a room, maybe the whole apartment, that's been used for years as a covenstead by a powerful coven that apparently gathered here to do nothing but celebrate Celtic quarter-days?" Sally summarized with a question.

Jessica bit her lip. "It's not like they just got together and chanted, Sally. The seasons begin and end in this room. Samhain was *here*; it's more real than the furniture."

This apparently was not at all easy for Sally to understand and the two of them argued in language that grew progressively less intelligible. The world of the modern day witch, Lise was discovering, was as filled with jargon as any other profession.

"—what's happening to Lise is the result of a Samhain circle interrupted by the death of one of the priests—probably the coven's High Priest and the man who lived here?" Jessica asked.

"It's the one explanation that covers everything," Sally insisted.

"Except that there's no personality here—just Samhain. It

can't have much to do with one man's death; I'd know in a moment if it did. Besides, the man who lived here was a *good* man, in a ritual sense, anyway."

"Then it's got to be something flowing in from outside."

"Sometimes I do feel a draft," Lise injected, and got their attentions at once. "Almost a wind." She thought of the night Maria had been here, and the night when Alan and she had seen the will-o-the-wisp dancing. "Sometimes the wind starts from nowhere special but always it blows away from me, taking me with it—"

"To where?" Jessica asked.

"I don't know. Once I saw something here in the middle of the room. It touched me and I felt like I was in an endless tunnel. It was cold—like another world." Lise shuddered involuntarily.

"Do you remember where you were standing?" Jessica stood up herself.

"Oh, right about there," Lise pointed at one of the medallions in the carpet. "I haven't felt it since, and you walked across that spot a dozen times."

But Jessica was determined to test the place. She closed her eyes and pressed her fingertips against her temples, straining to find whatever lurked in the unseen dimensions of the apartment. She moved in tiny, shuffling circles, adding a few inches to her search with each small step. Lise closed her eyes and dared to remember the evil, green mist.

Jessica shrieked. When Lise opened her eyes the will-o-the-wisp was there before her for an instant. Jessica collapsed on the carpet where the mist had disappeared.

"She's freezing!" Sally exclaimed. "Get a blanket or something."

"Get her off the rug!" Lise countermanded.

"It's so cold," Jessica moaned. "Eating at me—Eating at me!" She flailed wildy but with considerable strength, twisting until she was free of both Sally and Lise. *"It's got me!"* she screamed.

The neighbors were sure to hear and fill the landing with their curiosity. Lise could have gone to reassure them, if

Jessica had not suddenly stopped thrashing about. The dark-haired woman rolled into a fetal position with her fingers flared in an attempt to cover both her eyes and ears. Her cries had subsided into sobs and whimpers.

"I'm blind. I can't see; can't feel. I'm nothing—"

"We've got to get her out of here," Lise commanded; she did know more about the Phenomena than they did. "It *will* kill her."

She placed her hands under Jessica's shoulders and began dragging her across the carpet until Sally found a handhold and they were able to lift her.

"Anerien!" Jessica gasped as they left the livingroom.

But leaving the room did begin a reversal of Jessica's condition. Her color was coming back before they wrapped blankets around her and held her frigid hands in their own.

"Where am I?" she asked after several moments. "What's going on?"

"You found what you were looking for," Sally said.

"More likely, it found you," Lise corrected. Her own memories were clearer now, as if Jessica's terror had validated her own experiences.

"It was a hunger—pure, simple and brutal." Jessica's alertness and poise returned as rapidly as it had gone.

"You shouldn't talk about it. Get some rest," Sally cautioned.

"No, I've got to talk about it. I've got to get it out before it buries itself inside me and I can't ever face it or talk about it. It was Nothing—and it could have drained me until I was Nothing too: flesh and soul both. They weren't dead and they weren't alive, but they wanted me."

"They're evil," Lise added absently.

Jessica nodded. "They're beyond evil—they're beyond everything."

"Anerien—that's the old Celtic god of the underworld, isn't it?" Sally asked.

Jessica's eyes misted and she began to tremble toward a relapse. "No, Anerien is the one who was here. He's trapped there, by them. He was a good man, but they caught him as he died, I guess. They're using him—'' Jessica halted in mid-sentence, tears rolled from her face onto her sweater. ''He'll never get away from them.''

''Who won't?'' Sally asked.

''Anerien, the High Priest of the coven that met here. He's like them now: not dead, not alive. It doesn't matter that he was a good man.'' She rolled her head down into her lap.

''Jessica, you're here with us. You had a close call, but you're safe now,'' Sally insisted.

''Safe, I'm not safe any more,'' Jessica whispered. ''Every time I see something I see *it* too: cold, hungry, full of hate, wanting me—wanting to use me the way It uses Anerien.''

Jessica pulled away from them both and expended her tears until they were exhausted. Then, with delicate slowness, she sat up and faced them. A new dimension of empty horror lived in her eyes, but her cheeks were dry.

''I won't look again—never again. No matter what I do I'll know that other place exists and that Anerien is held there like a fly caught in amber—but I'll never look again. Never!'' She stood up and smoothed her clothing then turned to Lise with deliberate calm and said: ''Where did you put my coat?''

''Are you sure you know what you're doing, Jess? Shouldn't you rest a bit?'' Sally pleaded.

''I can't stay here.'' She grasped Sally's forearm. ''I'm sorry; I don't blame you, but I can't stay here and I can't come back—not even to New Moon. I've got to start over again—if I can—without a part of me. Maybe I'll be safe then. I have to—*It*'s waiting for me now.''

Lise went to the closet where she'd put their coats, unaware that Sally was following her.

''I think she'll feel better once she gets away; I've never seen anything like this happen to her before. I don't think I should let her go home alone, though—I hope you'll understand. I'm sorry we can't do the rituals we wanted to, but—well, maybe we should do some more thinking anyway. I do want to help you, but now I think I should get her back to Brooklyn.''

Lise nodded. Jessica was not a fraud; she would not recover quickly from her visions. When Lise had seen the other place Jessica spoke of she had not seen so clearly, but she had felt the hunger and the cold—and the hate. Now that Jessica had defined those things Lise could not, she herself would not rush boldly into green clouds; the danger was incalculable.

The hallway was smoky when Lise saw them to the elevator. She checked the incinerator closet for fire and found the odor was less pronounced the further she walked from her door. She stood still and let her nose guide her until she saw three large cones of incense resting on the ledge above her doorway. The burnt odor lingered long after the cones had been flushed down the toilet.

With her suitcase and two shopping bags loaded with brightly wrapped packages suspended from her arms, Lise carefully locked her apartment behind her. Her plane wasn't leaving until eleven AM, but she'd rather spend the night at a dull airport than stay home by herself.

Chapter Sixteen

Yuletide at Caer Maen: children racing to the kitchen for fresh cookies; teenagers huddled by the radio exchanging gossip and the latest dance steps; reunions in nearly every room. Edith, leaning against the kitchen doorway, couldn't even recall the names of all her houseguests yet she couldn't have been happier.

This was the way a Wiccan holiday should be celebrated. Twenty third-degree witches: each fully qualified to sit in a High Circle. There were two visitors from Gretna but the rest were all Caer Maen and its daughter-covens. In addition there were almost three dozen more Wiccans of lesser degree who would join them in the Yule Esbat late in the evening.

They filled the farmhouse. There were extra beds in the upstairs rooms, even caravans parked in the yard. The seventeenth-century open hearth and the Victorian iron-top stove strained to provide food for the small army of pagan families.

Mostly, though, the joy came from the children; that was the greatest gift of all. It was not so long ago—her own childhood—that a child wasn't exposed to the Wicca until he or she could be trusted never to reveal the mysteries. And at that, adolescents were not brought to the circle of their parents; a carryover from the Burning Times when the authorities could sweep through entire families if precautions weren't taken. Surely the gods could not be entirely displeased with the twentieth century.

Only a few of her guests knew about the problems in Riverside, but those few were Edith's touchstones in the circle should anything go awry later on. At first she had been against the Yule Esbat entirely, fearing the attraction such an accumulation of life and magick might have for the Otherworld. In the end, though, Bert and the prospect of a grand gathering had prevailed. This was Yule, after all: a solar festival from a completely different mythos. The Otherworld was only associated with the lunar quarter-days of which Samhain was the foremost.

"You're falling asleep on your feet, Mother. You should take advantage of the lull and get some sleep."

Edith rubbed her eyes as a fresh batch of cookies were removed from the oven. A swarm of children raced past, their shoes thundering on the wooden floor.

"Lull? Thanks for the thought, but I'm not tired—just gathering strength. Look at us all!"

Elizabeth had made a full recovery from the trials of the previous month. She had cut her hair in the latest fashion; her face was framed by windswept tendrils of copper-penny red. Though the effect was thoroughly modern it somehow accentuated her resemblance to her aunt.

"You don't like it. You really don't, do you?" Liz asked, pushing the wisps back from her forehead.

"What? Your hair? Goodness, child—I'd gotten mine cut by your age. My mind was just wandering; I'm getting old myself. You know, when your grandmother arranged Yule dinner we never had more than a dozen at the table."

"Even if the Wicca weren't different today, people just didn't get up and travel all the way out here for a weekend then, Mum. And, tell me, where was your mind wandering—really. Riverside?"

Edith smiled and remained silent. Her thoughts had been drifting inexorably Otherworld all day and she would not speak of it to anyone. When Liz could not be reassured by a mystic smile, Edith confessed to a headache and made her way, alone, down into the warrens.

The altar was already prepared; three concentric circles were marked in the hard earth around it. The warrens were chilly and damp, but nothing like the grove at the winter solstice. Edith's thoughts lightened by the altar. Even the warren records did not go back to the days before the Romans when many covens would come together for the Great Esbats, sharing the knowledge and news. Tonight's gathering was her own contribution to history: a return to a Caer Maen tradition lost for almost two thousand years.

The beginnings of a special invocation came to her, banishing any tiredness or Otherworld thoughts. She went to her rocking-chair to experience the prayers she would make after midnight.

"Lady Camulac, a word with you, please?"

An unrecognized voice grounded Edith's thoughts in irritation. There was more freedom now, but only her closest family and friends wandered unannounced in the warrens—she would not have failed to recognize one of their voices.

"Yes, of course," she said without a trace of her annoyance. "I'll join you upstairs."

"No, Lady Camulac—this is High Coven business."

Then her visitor had to be one of the Gretna witches and the business was Riverside.

"Very well then, let me find a candle and match. These floors can be treacherous if you're not used to them."

A small island of light grew around her. The guest was already garbed in her finest robes and struggling with a large, unwieldly box. Despite herself, Edith's curiosity was as aroused as a child's.

"I bear a gift for you from Lady Vivian, and all of us at Gretna—and an honor as well."

Now that Edith listened closely she could hear the trace of a burr in the otherwise Oxford-precise syllables. She guessed this was Greenspeed, Vivian's daughter-in-law and heiress-apparent in the Scottish circle.

"We accept both with open hearts," Edith responded automatically as the padlock was removed from the chest and four, partially burnt candles were removed.

"These were burnt first at Anerien's initiation and again at his elevations within the High Coven. Had he remained at Gretna they would have marked all the other occasions of his life. It is our way, but he did not choose to take them with him to Riverside. We lit them again when we learned of his death and would have kept them alight until they guttered but Lady Vivian spoke of his ties to Caer Maen and suggested we bring them to your Yule for their final burning. At Gretna we would set them beside the watchtowers.''

Edith had suspected much of the story from her first sight of the candles. The cream-colored wax was stained in places from age and damp—the Gretna warrens were, perhaps, less weather-worthy than her own. Runes had been carved the length of the candles, though some had melted away. Edith read, with surprise, that her brother-in-law had chosen the name of Greylag at his initiation and had only chosen Anerien after meeting Gwen and being absorbed into the more Brythonic traditions of Caer Maen. She took the candles, but felt awkward with them.

''It is an honor, indeed, to have these candles of our brother's life—but the altar is set already and the watchtowers erected—''

''They need not stand alone at the cardinal points. In less fortunate times we had many such sets of candles—and felt safer for their light.''

How much had Vivian told her witches? How much more had Vivian, or Greenspeed, guessed on her own. Edith had said nothing of her specific fears nor of Elizabeth's brushes with the Otherworld, but word of Hector's experience could have spread. Still, had Gretna been the one with Caer Maen's problem, and she the one on the outside—what would she have done to help?

She examined the uppermost candle closely. The smells of beeswax and heather came away with the warmth of her hand. These were High Coven candles sent by a friend who knew her Craft. Those who guarded the Rifts could not be rivals and could not risk offense. Caer Maen would set the candles beside their watchtowers. It was only in the lesser portions of her own mind that these candles spoke of the Riverside failures—to the rest they were Gretna, which stood by her duties and had never been found wanting.

''Our circle tonight shall be strengthened by these gifts. We are indeed honored to have the life-candles of Anerien; to share in your mysteries—'' Edith's voice broke as unexpected tears blurred her eyes; the first tears she had shed for Arthur. "With your permission, I'll set them in the circle myself, alone."

Greenspeed nodded and returned quietly up the stairs. Edith took the candles to the altar. Caer Maen, no—the High Priestess of Caer Maen, had been so concerned with danger and failure that no words of parting had been spoken for Arthur—and his own coven seemed unlikely to do so. She whispered a quick God's speed for the spirit of the one who had been Arthur Andrews, Anerien and Greylag; who had served well until his death.

She found swags of vibrant silk to wind around the brass-trimmed watchtowers and the candles. The Gretna gifts became flying buttresses for the structure Liz had already built. They strengthened the Guardians—or Edith believed they did. She left the warrens with a feeling of wisdom and contentment.

It was midnight when the candle-bearing procession wound its way down the stairs and to the altar cavern where sturdy oak pillars held up an earth-and-stone ceiling. They sang as they walked, mostly with church-trained voices and melodies borrowed from the Christmas repertoire—just as the Christians had once borrowed so much from the pagan solstices.

Bert escorted Edith. He was wearing green-black velvet and she shimmered in moire satin of midnight and silver. Yule had always been the festival of richness and splendor, when the wealth of the coven was displayed in acknowledgement of the Gods' bounty.

A trio of priestesses moved along the outer circle, marking the boundaries of the assembly's power, invoking the elemental forces of the cardinal points and lighting Anerien's candles—all while the High Priestess stood alone before the altar. The power of the Wiccans began to grow within her. With the circle sealed at the watchtowers the trio began a kiss of peace that braided through the concentric rings of celebrants, binding them into one unit of power, love and magic.

Lady Camulac, recently Edith Brompton, raised her arms

in a graceful crescent calling the Goddess into their circle. When the Lady was with them Bert would step forward and invoke the Consort-God in whose honor the winter solstice was celebrated.

A shower of sparks fell from Lady Camulac's arms as she began her prayer—or, was it only the candle reflection off the silver threads in her gown? It did not matter. She felt a shiver of transcendant power as their gathering made itself known in the realm of magick. The High Priestess felt the ether wrap around her and take the invocation directly from her mind, unmarred by the imperfection of words.

Her upreaching fingers strained to be free of palms, wrists and arms until they indeed were—or it seemed she no longer needed to hold them above her but wrapped her arms over her breasts and clutched the sterling crescent-and-triangle crest of Caer Maen that hung from her neck. Lady Camulac, Edith and the rest were left behind, below; the essence of the High Priestess of Caer Maen slipped loose from its worldly mooring. Her covens seemed frozen in time. Only the flames of the High Priest's life-candles flickered in this unmarked, windy plain. The High Priestess felt their summons and followed. She had broken through the Curtain and was adrift in the Otherworld, yet she found she was not afraid. The Otherworld itself was locked in a frozen dance with the power of her covens and the power of her covens was sufficient to permit her to follow the candle-flames in safety.

The Otherworld was an unsensory place apprehended in levels of consciousness where neither words nor images held sway. At the limits of all her perception a threshold of shimmering red manifested itself; the Riverside Rift, an open, bleeding sore on the fabric of the Curtain. She could perceive the properly closed and warded Rifts of the other High Covens; she could see the pinpoints that were Rifts tended by other rites of magick. One such jeweled mote erupted, spewing an ethereal jet into the Otherworld; at the same time another mote came to life and bound itself into the threads of the first. She saw the mysterious exchange of souls in the spiraling dance of life.

The magnetic power of concentration enveloped her,

drawing her across the frozen Otherworld, past incalculable points that were, or had been, Rifts in this world or some other. Like an arrow she moved toward one more throbbing gateway: the gaping Summerland Rift which corresponded to the Riverside Rift.

They called to her, those who had been Caer Maen, those few who had been Riverside and all who had known of either. The Summerland is a place of rejuvenation, of waiting and rebirth, of rest for those of the High Covens but it *is* magick—not a place for the working of magick. Not all the shadow generations of the High Covens had the power to seal the Rift which, the High Priestess realized suddenly, was held open by the enslaved spirit of Anerien.

The High Priestess fell back, through the thawing Otherworld, past the watchtower guardians, past Lady Camulac and deep into Edith Brompton. She might have sunk further, but the power of the circles caught her in the net of their voices, still singing, still waiting for the invocation of the Goddess. No time had passed for them.

"Lady of the Night Beyond—Hecuba, Hecate, White Goddess of Snow and Death—abide with us. Lend us strength to bear the sufferings of Your Consort. See Him through the Otherworld darkness. Bring Him home—"

The witches gasped at this unprecidented emphasis on the Otherworld in an open ritual; this was no Yule invocation of the Lady. Camulac's words caught the latent power of the circles and bent it away from Caer Maen and into the fathomless Otherworld. The sum of Edith, Camulac and all the archetype priestesses shaped the power of the coven—but it was not enough to reach the endangered Summerland or the tortured Anerien and in the end the power faded.

They called their priestess back from the altar to join them in the outer circles, awaiting an explanation for the electrifying, frozen moment when they had strained to follow her into the incomprehensible. But Lady Camulac would not speak. She knew what must be done next; she herself would go to Riverside where she would contemplate the unthinkable: the off-cycle closing of a Rift both here and in the Summerland.

Chapter Seventeen

Lise realized that she should have asked Maria or even Alan to pick her up at the airport after her holiday visit to Michigan; the return load of packages was no less bulky than the outgoing one, but now a fine, icy rain was falling. She paused a moment by the telephone booths in the terminal but did not alter her decision to go it alone.

She piled into a city bus that would take her to the nearest subway station. After setting her hands and feet carefully so that no package could be jostled free without her knowledge, she kidded herself into trying to relax and unwind after the disaster of her vacation home.

The family had been waiting for her. They hadn't said a word about her new address and phone number; she never paused to consider the suspiciousness of that silence. They had simply been waiting for Christmas. They knew every murder, rape and robbery that had been committed within thirty blocks of her apartment building. They had even found out about Arthur Andrews' death: the drug orgy version.

Their information was an inflammatory combination of truth and conjecture that Lise could not contort to her advantage. The complete truth would scarcely have reassured them. So she had defended herself piece-meal against their indictments, finally lapsing into a stoic silence. The truth, her own fears which she'd hoped to confide in them, stewed within her.

Only Rick, her brother, had seemed to support her. He reminded them all of what he, a local policeman in Michigan, knew about the surging rural crime wave. But then, as he drove her to the airport, he'd given her an illegal device that shot a pair of electrodes into any attacker and then administered an incapacitating jolt of electricity. Her hands shook as she'd tried to give the thing back to him—but he'd hear nothing of it and offered yet more bits of unwanted advice: her pants were too tight and her bra not tight enough; she was asking for IT.

Lise had fought back tears and anger for the entire flight and still fought them while she sat on the dark bus.

"Switches're frozen, Lady. It'll be another hour before a train gets through here again," the subway clerk told her when she slipped her money under the window.

"An hour?" she sighed. "Is there any other way I can get into Manhattan from here?"

"Call a cab or take the Q-33 bus out to the airport and get a charter bus there."

She sighed again and carted her luggage back up to street level where a lone taxicab glistened in the streetlights. The bus was well on its way to LaGuardia; she hailed the cab.

Sam was there at the awning to help her get into the lobby; the first friendly face she'd seen in days.

"Have a good vacation, Miss Brown?" he asked.

"I'm glad to be home," she answered with evasive truthfulness.

"Did you go skiing? I hear there's a lot of snow in Michigan already."

"Lots of snow, but no hills. I went ice skating, though."

She hadn't, but she hadn't wanted to rebuff him either. It wasn't fair that he should care whether she had a good time and her own family didn't. The moisture on her cheeks was not from the rain but, fortunately, Sam didn't seem to notice that.

He appraised her luggage, picked up the two heaviest pieces and led the way to the elevator. "Been rainin' like this almost since you left. Some mornings you could ice skate right outside our door."

Lise followed quietly behind him, grateful that he didn't stop talking long enough for her to answer—even if she'd been able to. She listened to Sam and the elevator and told herself that she was home—not merely back in the City, but *home*—she had no other any more. She was still sniffling when they stepped off the elevator at the sixth floor.

"At it again!" Sam grumbled as he hurried down the hall

ahead of her, leaving the suitcases propped against the elevator door.

There were more incense cones above her door, just like the ones she'd removed before she left. Sam was stomping on something, too—so there must have been even more on the mat. She dragged as much of her stuff with her as she could and joined him as he brushed the last of the cones off the upper doorsill.

"What's this place coming to?" He smashed the unburnt portions with his heel. "Fires, that's what we could have here—fires! And it's someone in the bulding 'cause I don't let anyone in who'd do this."

Lise remained prudently silent. She didn't want to open the door while Sam was still there.

"Vandals," Sam continued. "I told Mr. Fine himself last week. I don't know what's going on, Miss Brown. I don't know. All the stories about Mr. Andrews—you know they were lies—and now this."

"Maybe my neighbors are telling me I forgot to take my garbage out before I left?" She tried to joke with him.

Sam did not appreciate the humor but was, at last, headed back to the elevator. Lise unlocked the last bolt and let the door swing open. She shuttled everything in past the front door and locked it again before she braved the depths of the livingroom.

The rain beat against the windows at the front of the apartment; a steady drone that muffled all other sounds. The room was as she had left it. Nothing had fallen from the shelves. The pillows were an aesthetic clutter on the sofa, not the floor. The apartment must have known she would be coming home for good and had cleaned up its act for her.

Gathering her courage, Lise stepped firmly onto that spot where both she and Jessica had encountered something definitely not of this world. She stood, then sat and finally dug her fingernails into the dense pile of the carpet. Nothing. No trace of cold memory stirred in her mind and she could cry from relief.

"You let me know if that happens again," Sam told her when she came back for her mail a half-hour later. "You don't have to put up with that. I watch the doors here. Somebody starting fires like that; I', supposed to stop him—and if I'm not doin' my job—Don't wait for your neighbors—it just might be it's their idea."

Sam didn't usually talk with such intensity. Lise grabbed her double handful of envelopes and fled as quickly as politeness would allow. She was hearing words that sounded like he knew what was going on *inside* her apartment.

"It's just that he cares," she said aloud to herself in the elevator. "He cares about me, about the building—that's all. And it should make me relaxed—not uptight. He's my first line of defense, as Maria would say—and my only friend in this building. I shouldn't have to feel afraid of him like this—"

The incense aroma had begun to fade. She paused by the hall table to weed out that mail which wasn't even worth opening. The cold December rain became a friendly sound. It was all attitude; anything could sound friendly, be friendly. Almost anything. The soft thud of a pillow flopping off the sofa was an ominous sound that brought her to the French doors.

The whole pile of pillows was vibrating. As she watched another one broke free and joined the first on the carpet. Now that she had felt the truly great horrors the Phenomena could engender, the pillows were more pathetic than frightening. She distrusted them; disliked them; marched into the room, grabbed them by their tasseled corners and shook the strange electricity from them, but she wasn't afraid of them any more.

The phone rang; she wasn't tempted to pick it up. It stopped ringing and in a few moments started again. She divided her attention between the sofa and the writing table.

"Oh, it's just you," she said to Maria's cheery hello.

"Should I ask who you were expecting?" Maria was unrebuffed by the greeting. "I've been trying to get a hold of you; I thought the lines might be fouled up—did the phone just ring? I even called out to your folks to find out if you'd left on time. Something told me things didn't go well on the homefront."

"You've got it. They don't approve—" Lise sat down to unwind the tale. "They even found out about the old man's death and the police raid!"

"How'd they do that?"

"Who knows? No, come to think of it, Rick must have pulled some strings. I couldn't see telling them they were wrong—if you know what I mean—so things went down hill the whole time. But, I didn't think they'd be happy to know that rape had been replaced by the Phenomena."

There was an understanding silence across the lines. "Well, did you get caught up in your sleep, at least?"

Lise laughed and admitted she was more tired now than when she had left. She detailed the events of her last night in the City, so Maria would understand how *very* tired that must be. They postponed plans for a shopping trip and promised to get together later in the week. She had no sooner gotten the phone back on the table when it rang again; this time it was Alan.

Bored and feeling lonely because of the holidays, he'd actually spent the early evening at the airport but had been meeting the wrong airline's flights. Lise enjoyed being the focus of all his attention but wasn't quite prepared for an overnight visit. She invited him over for breakfast the next day.

After a long bath she got into bed hoping for a night of romantic, if not outright erotic, dreams but the will-o-the-wisp lingered in her thoughts instead of Alan. Even with the blankets held tightly over her suddenly cold shoulders, she could not recapture the bliss she'd felt while talking to him. The minutes slipped slowly through the clock. She stared into blackness and waited for exhaustion to catch up with her. It did, finally, and her sleep, though fitful, was without nightmares. She slept until the phone rang again and the sky outside had turned bright blue.

Alan was bringing an extra copy of the previous Sunday's *Times* so she could do the crossword puzzle. He also had a half-dozen fresh bagels so all she'd have to do was have the coffee ready in an hour and a half when he got there at ten-thirty.

A thin crust of ice clung to the branches of the trees in Riverside Park, but the sidewalks were clear and there'd be no iceskating on Riverside Drive today. Pigeons, squirrels, children and the other wildlife of Manhattan were enjoying a cold, Monday morning—a holiday for some since Christmas had fallen on the weekend. Lise sipped a cup of coffee and watched an oil-tanker decorated with a huge green wreath churn down the river. She followed the ship from window to window, from bedroom to livingroom until it was out of sight. She set the cup down on the windowsill and had meant to decide then what she'd wear, but the glistening carcass of an eviscerated bird, frozen onto her fire-escape, caught and held her attention.

It was a chicken, not a pigeon—a fresh chicken with its matted feathers intact and its head covered by a pink icicle that began at its slit neck. Lise swallowed hard and steadied herself against the wall. There were no chickens roaming Upper Manhattan, and no hawks to drag them this high up—not that a hawk had killed *that* chicken. She closed her eyes but was too inhibited to scream.

She watched the clock: nine thirty-eight; nine forty-five—waiting. She'd dressed—after a fashion; made the bed and the coffee. Now she only prayed that he'd be on time, or maybe early. Ten twenty-five, give or take a few seconds. She'd perked a second pot of coffee and was drawn back to the window to stare at the offense on the metal slats. She jumped against the window when the buzzer finally sounded.

"Gentleman to see you, Miss Brown," Sam's smile came through the tinny speakers undistorted.

"Send him up!"

Her hands shook when she tried to turn the locks. She inhaled, thinking to steady her nerves but took in a lungful of incense instead. It was the same arrangement as before: three cones on the doormat, three on the sill above. Tears only made the smell worse, so she sniffed them back and stood on her toes, reaching with a paper towel over her fingers, as the elevator rattled open.

"What's wrong?" he asked, closing his fingers over hers and holding her head against his shoulder.

"They hate me," she sobbed.

He pushed her gently through the doorway and shut the door before asking for further explanations. He poured the coffee for both of them while he listened to her incoherent discourse about incense, family and the frozen chicken on the fire-escape.

"They hate me. Everybody, everything's trying to make me crazy. I almost jumped out the window when the buzzer went off just now."

"But you didn't," Alan reminded her. "They haven't made you crazy yet." He left her staring at a bagel while he removed the last of the incense from her doorway. "Okay, now, where's this damned bird? You got something I can shovel it off with?"

She got a spatula and a paperbag before leading him to the window. "It's frozen on the metal; and the window's frozen too. It'll be there 'til Spring."

Using her hair-dryer to loosen the locks, Alan got the window open then prodded the mess with the spatula, assuring them both that it was, indeed quite solidly attached to the metal. He used the real-estate section of the *Times* to cover the bird then ripped it bodily from the metal. Lise dared to glance at him only once as he continued ripping feathers and worse from the fire escape.

"How can you stand it?" she asked. "I'm sick just looking at it—and I don't get sick looking at things."

"Let's not talk about that possibility, okay? We'll get it cleaned up, thrown out and we'll get out of here ourselves and then maybe we'll talk about it."

He shoved the last of the mess into the bag and slammed the window shut. His hands were shaking but whether from fear or cold was impossible to tell.

"Now, where's your garbage chute?"

"In the hall—"

"Fine—get your coat."

"—But the coffee, the bagels?"

"You don't *really* feel like eating, do you?"

Chapter Eighteen

It was late when Alan and Lise returned to her apartment after a day of wandering the streets. Sam nodded as they walked by his cubicle—a knowing nod though Lise had already decided she didn't really want a man underfoot as she tried to get ready for work in the morning. Especially not when the man she'd be tripping over was the man she'd be reporting to when she got to work.

"I don't really want to argue about it," Alan insisted as they rode the elevator, "and it's not as premeditated as it sounds, but I have a change of clothes in my car. Hell, it's not even romance. You look like you need a good night's sleep more than anything else. You haven't stopped yawning since dinner."

"I understand—but I really won't sleep as well if someone's here. I'm not used to it."

"I won't lay a hand on you—word of honor."

Lise laughed and got out her keys. "*That's* not the problem. Could you stop breathing for a night?"

"No-one's ever said I snore before."

But Lise's attention was already far from their conversation. The landing had an all too familiar aroma. The incense cones were in place once again. She cursed and stomped toward them.

"Look, just leave them alone," Alan advised. "Whoever's doing this is trying to rattle you. If you keep getting upset and cleaning everything up they'll just keep on putting more stuff here. Ignore them and they'll get bored."

Lise stepped uncertainly over the smouldering mounds. It was barely possible that he was right.

"So I guess it'll be coffee tonight, since I'm to go back home?"

Lise nodded. He prowled through the livingroom, checking everything out and Lise marvelled in her courage for sending him home. Regardless of the Phenomena—someone had been out on her fire escape the previous night and a single pane of glass was all that had kept him out of the livingroom. There were other dangers to living alone—as her parents so bluntly pointed out.

"All quiet on the western front?" she asked as she handed him the coffee.

He did not reply.

"Pretty, isn't it?" she said a little louder.

"Maybe—it's not the word I'd choose." He stepped back from the window, giving Lise a clear view of the dark design that had been scrawled on the glass.

"What the—" She ran a fingertip over the design, without feeling any paint. "It's on the outside—and—and this *isn't* the fire-escape? Alan—there's no way to get to the outside of this window like this."

Alan grunted in what could have been agreement and forced the window open. He scraped off a tiny portion of the design. They crowded together examining the brownish residue.

"I can't figure it. It must be rust of some sort—but how could it get there like that?" Lise shrugged and relocked the window. "God, it's on *all* of them," she complained after a quick study. "I guess the caulking's given out. The place'll be freezing on top of everything else now."

She had confirmed her worst suspicions about the bedroom and returned to the livingroom to find Alan busily tracing the design onto a sheet of paper. Before Lise could ask what he was doing, or why, the doorbell rang.

A cautious glance through the peephole revealed Mark Ratner's distorted face. She opened the door to find not only him and his wife standing in front of her, but a handful of neighbors whose names she had not learned as well.

Mark cleared his throat. "Miss Brown—ah, Lise—" He glanced at his wife and began again. "We've complained to Sam; we've complained to Fine and it hasn't done any good. This stuff—" he pointed at the extinguished but still aromatic incense, "not only stinks to high heaven—it's dangerous.

Frankly, we'd all hoped that with Andrews gone things would return to normal around here—instead it's only gotten worse. We've all heard the screams and crashes. Lise, this's got to stop; the building's got to have standards—you understand?''

Lise tensed her fingers on the doorknob, wanting to slam the door in their self-righteous, misinformed faces—yet knowing that she'd stammer some polite explanation, if she thought of one. ''I'm sorry, I truly am. I don't know who's putting this stuff outside my door. Sam said it's been going on for over a week, but I only got back last night.'' The gathering did not respond to her soft-spoken words. ''Well, it's not as if *I'm* putting the incense out here! I haven't been around!''

''I saw you in the hall cleaning it up—after those two women left. And the screams we heard that night. Well, maybe it is your friends, then; same difference. It was Andrews' friends too,'' a woman Lise did not recognize accused. ''This is no accident, young lady.''

''But Sam said he wasn't letting anyone into the building who'd be likely to do this sort of thing,'' Lise pleaded as Alan stepped up behind her.

''And that means,'' Alan elaborated, ''that it's most likely someone in this building—maybe somebody standing right here.''

''It's one of her friends,'' a voice snarled.

But Alan was obviously one of Lise's friends—and a more respectable specimen of the urban middle class could scarcely be found. Lise felt the tide swing toward her; felt gratitude for Alan's assistance and, almost at once, felt the uneasiness that came whenever she let someone else fight her battle for her.

''The problem does seem to be localized. I mean, it's only this apartment; no-one else attracts this sort of attention,'' Mark mused aloud.

''Maybe there's someone in the building with a thing about this apartment. Maybe 647 is their unlucky number. Who's to say? It's obvious that some of you can keep a better watch over this door than Lise can. Why don't you find out who *is* putting the incense here. Even if by some chance it is someone that Lise knows, it's still not one of her friends. She'd be grateful if you could tell her who it was."

—And that—Lise considered while everyone else looked away—is why Alan's going to run the company one of these days.

"No-one's seen anyone out here," Rachel Ratner conceded. "You turn your back and it's there. It had to be coming from the inside."

"But, no-one's been here for over a week," Lise reminded them.

"So—it can't have been Lise," Alan insisted. "Now, since your doorman is aware of the problem, why don't you all report any odd activity to him?" He put his hand on Lise's shoulder as he spoke and gently urged her back from the doorway. "That's certainly more productive than everyone standing here, isn't it?"

There was grumbling and muttering as the group broke up—but it broke up. Alan whispered to Lise, directing her to get a paper towel. She hurried to do his bidding—conscious that she'd let him take over but unable to think of a better tactic. The ashes were caught up in the towel before the last door had been locked.

"I should say thank-you," Lise admitted as they retreated behind her own locked door. "They took me by surprise. I didn't know what to say to them. Usually I can kill my own snakes."

" 'Kill your own snakes'? Another Michigan expression meaning that you don't appreciate my help?"

She reddened slightly. "The snakes're dead anyhow. I'm betting it's Rachel."

"Your mystery visitor isn't one of those clowns."

"No? What makes you so sure?"

"Well, whoever's putting the incense on your doorstep is the same person, or persons, who left that bird out on the fire escape and drew the pictures on your windows." He picked up a tracing he'd made and waved it at her. "There's a pattern to all this—and it doesn't have anything to do with anyone who actually lives in this building—except maybe Sam."

Lise bristled. "Sam is a perfectly kind old man. I can't imagine him out on the fire-escape in the middle of the night. Besides, he's got keys. If he wanted to get in he could; he wouldn't have to leave everything outside."

"Okay, we'll eliminate Sam—I would have anyway," Alan conceded. "Though it would be easier to get the drawings out there if the drawer were inside."

"They aren't drawings; no-one could have drawn anything on those windows. They're just some sort of stain."

"Yeah, a bloodstain."

Lise froze. He was smiling and he'd known the suggestion would upset her. It was one thing to play the protector-game with her neighbors, but it was something else to twist words like that. Her gratefulness had already been tainted by guilt, now there was anger and the new-born suspicion that all his help and concern was only a manipulation to get her dependent on him.

"Bloodstains!" she exploded. "What kind of game are you playing, chief? Do you want to turn me into a basket-case? Or, are you so determined to spend the night here that you don't care how you do it or what you do to me in the first place? You don't know that's blood; there's no way you could know—but you know you can frighten me by saying it's blood. Well, it won't work—you can frighten me but I can darn well kill my own snakes—and say 'good-night' and 'good-bye' too."

Alan let the papers drop to his side. "Lise, I'm only trying to help."

"You're trying to take over. You saw me get frightened and cry on your shoulder so you think I'm the frilly, dependent type just waiting for your Prince Charming. I'll take care of myself, thank you, and do it quite nicely."

He picked up his coat from the chair and draped it over one shoulder. "I guess I don't much care one way or the other what you think of me—or how ass-headed you are—but you *do* need help. I wanted to help—there weren't any price tags, it was just something I wanted to do. I'd already done some checking around. I thought that with the location of this building maybe you'd run into voodoo. Anyway I started checking it out. I don't have anything specific, but the incense and the bird are giveaways. These things on your windows—they're vévés and they're drawn with blood, among other things. I don't think I'm going to be at all reassured when I compare these tracing to my book—but you don't have to worry that I'll come running to you with the information."

"Voodoo," Lise repeated flatly.

It wasn't the magick, it was the image of wild-eyed witch doctors and half-naked savages creeping through swamps that got to her first. She tried to force it from her thoughts, but voodoo could itself only be replaced by her anger toward the person who had suggested it to her.

"That's your concern? Your help? I don't have enough to frighten me without voodoo? And you admit that you've been looking around for an explanation of *my* Phenomena; waiting, no doubt, for just the right moment to drop it on me. Well—okay, what am I supposed to do about it?" Lise's voice tightened and cracked, but she held her tears. "What am I supposed to do—wait for you to rescue me? Are you going to scrape the blood off my windows? Are you going to tuck me in and keep the boogey-man from my door? Or, am I supposed to get my toothbrush and move in with you?"

He opened his mouth, but Lise would have none of his explanations. "You're doing just what you set out to do—I'm scared of everything—I'm even scared of you now. I won't come running to you. I won't. I won't—"

It had all happened too fast; he was in the elevator before she really knew he was gone—and she was afraid of everything, too frightened to go into the bedroom where she couldn't see the fire-escape; too frightened to go to Sam—now that Alan had implicated him; too frightened even to call Maria and share the terror. A few tears seeped out, but the purging torrent remained locked inside, churning into a gut-numbing, hard, black knot that nothing—not even a sleepless night of twisting the new terror around her affection for Alan—could release.

At dawn she went into the bedroom; at eight-thirty she called the office and took a day-off: personal time, without pay. She drank a glass of orange juice and raced to the bathroom toilet—there was no room within her for anything but anger and terror. When, late in the afternoon, she finally did call Maria and relate the outrages she had suffered; her friend had the unmitigated audacity to laugh.

"Lise, you can't be serious. He *was* only trying to help."

"If he was trying to help, why did he wait until midnight—when he knew I wanted to be here by myself—to tell me; we'd had all day together."

"So, his timing's off—and maybe he is hot for your body, too—he still wanted to help, I'm sure of it. And, Lise, you could do with a set of strong arms around you now and again."

"What good would that do—no, don't bother answering," Lise snapped. "It's no different, not even with you."

"Lise, how can you say that?"

"You've all got your own ideas. Everybody wants to solve *my* problems *their* way. You've got a good marriage; he's got a divorce and you're both convinced all my problems come because I live alone—that's *not* the problem and it's not the solution. No-one is interested in helping me find a way out of my problems!"

"You don't want a solution and you don't want help. You want everyone to be just as miserable as you are. Your parents, your apartment, your boyfriend—everything's got to conform to *your* way," Maria snarled.

"No," Lise whispered back into the phone.

"Then, what *do* you want?"

"I don't know—I honestly don't know."

She set the phone on the table and walked away from it. The multitude of downward spirals that she felt around her and that she had, she realized, had always had around her in one form or another, had reached a final convergence. If the pillows had risen to assault her as she walked blindly past them, she wuld not have resisted their punishment; she might not even have noticed. But they were not lured by her depression. After a few moments, Maria stopped calling Lise's name; the phone buzzed a while then the room fell into lifeless silence.

Lise was never certain if she slept or remained awake that entire night until the alarm jolted her to the realization that it had become morning.

"I could lie here until I'm dead," she whispered after turning the radio back to silence. "No-one would know until the place started to smell—" A wry smile crossed her face, "—no, they'd think it was still the incense."

She nurtured the reactions her disappearance and death would have on all those who had abandoned without for one moment thinking that she might be abandoning them as well. Another twenty minutes of her life passed; habit informed her that though she might, in time, wither away, for the interim her kidneys expected their usual attentions and so did her stomach. Lise had little experience with the acute throes of depression; she didn't know enough to stay in bed and add physical discomfort to the others she was already wallowing in.

She went to the kitchen and got a glass of juice, then made a slice of toast and in due course brushed her teeth. She got dressed—and as nothing she owned was absolutely inappropriate at the office and as the sun was shining brightly she wandered down the stairs and to the subway where the sheer ordinariness of events kept her going until she was at her desk.

Thus began an era of somnambulance. Dishes grew fuzzy in the kitchen sink; the bed was never made. The designs on the window were water soluable and disappeared in the normal course of events not because she found a way to remove them. But, habit got her from one day to the next. She was rude to both Alan and Maria until the former communicated with her entirely by memo and the latter gave up entirely. Lise didn't care—it could hardly be said that she noticed.

At one point she dragged her pillows and blankets into the livingroom and tried sleeping on the sofa. The wool plush poked through the wrinkled bedding and gave her a rash that itched beyond her ability to ignore it. But it was the rash, and not the pillows or any other Phenomena that moved her back into the bedroom. The apartment like everything else was still oppressively quiet. Annalise Brown had discovered life on the razor edge of exhaustion.

She drank at least eight cups of coffee each day, starting in the morning with left-overs from the night before: oily, black and extra strong with a life of its own. The coffee had kept her from falling into a dazed sleep at her desk.

She had thought of getting help, but Culpeper's was closed until the end of the month for alterations. Ms. Hirshhorn at the bank said that J. Robert Hynes had returned from his vacation with an unspecified illness and was on disability. His home phone number was unlisted; Marjory was never at the number she had written down. Lise had no regular doctor and the thought of getting one meant breaking out of habit. As January wound into its raw, windy finale, Lise knew that sooner or later something would give out—most likely her health—but she did nothing to change her now-habitual downward course.

"Lise, would you step into my office?"

She hadn't heard Alan approach and should have jumped from surprise but she was too tired to do more than gulp the last of her current cup of coffee and follow him across the room. Her latest work-sheets were spread out on his desk. The deterioration in her handwriting was apparent even at a distance.

"Sit down, Lise," Alan said when she just stood there. "Lise, I just don't know what to say about this—" he rearranged the papers.

"I know it's messy," she began.

"It's not the messiness—though that doesn't help any." He shook his head and Lise felt a chill pass through her. "But, Lise—this is all wrong. The interest rate is wrong. The commissions are wrong. You used the wrong year's data and on top of everything your arithmetic is hopeless."

His voice was harsh. Lise arose from her habitual slouch

and inattention to realize that there was nothing she could say. She couldn't even say she'd correct the problems or that they wouldn't happen again; even she couldn't believe that. He knew the problem; he was the problem—she could remember that much. All this had started when *he* talked about voodoo.

"Lise, you can't go on like this!" Alan crumpled her work-sheets into the wastebasket. "I wasn't kidding when I brought you on board for this project; you were the best we had out there. Look kid, I can't cover for you. This job's important for me, too. If I have to drop you now frankly it will look bad for me too: a question of *my* judgment. And, anyway, I don't want to do that to you; I've got some idea of what you're up against."

—Let him think that, if he wants—she reasoned in bleak silence. The chasm that had come to separate her from everything had become too great to be bridged. Let him fire her—get it over with; then there'd be no reason for the habits of workday life. "You'll do what you have to do," she mumbled. "I'll understand."

"You'll understand? Well, then maybe you'll explain it to me 'cause I sure don't understand! You look like the living dead. You were tired at Christmas—how do you keep going now? Pills? I'm more amazed that you can keep up the pretense of working than that everything you do is wrong. Lise, exactly what *is* happening?" he demanded.

"I'd rather not talk about, it, if you don't mind. It's my personal life and if it's interfering with my work I'll take the responsibility for it. But, I don't have to talk about it."

"Yes, I do mind! This isn't your friend asking you—this is your boss—the guy who's going to sign your pink slip if you don't straighten out pretty quick. In your present condition I don't think you have enough energy to apply for unemployment much less get a new job." He paused, waiting for a response and when there was none he began on a new tactic. "Call it pure self-interest. I've never had to fire someone before. If I have to get a new assistant at this late date, I'm going to miss my deadline, too. Now, I know you can do this job, all I want to know is what is it going to take to get you in shape so you're reliable again?"

"I can't sleep right; I don't eat; I can't cope anymore, I just can't."

"If I could arrange to put you up in the hotel around the corner? You'd get meals, room service—all those things."

"Ye gods! You're *serious*!" she exclaimed, surprise momentarily surmounting apathy.

"I could probably do it: a few white lies in the right places. It'd be worth a try. I don't think you'd accept my other suggestions: move in with you for the duration or move you in with me."

"You're right—that wouldn't work at all." Lise tried to laugh but stopped short when her laughter became hysteric.

"Lise, you're shaking."

She clasped her hands together and forced the tremors out. "Withdrawal symptoms—I've been more than ten minutes between coffee cups."

He did not find her humor either funny or reassuring.

"I checked those drawings, by the way. I was wrong—they're for protection against evil not for attracting it."

"You mean no-one's hexed me?"

"Well, whoever put those drawings there didn't curse you, but you might have been cursed anyway or why would you need protective spirits?"

Lise let her attention wander. So the designs had been for protection. They'd been on the outside of the windows and, she guessed blindly, were really there to protect the world from her apartment. They'd bottled up whatever evil her livingroom contained or created. She alone moved freely through the door now, carrying the evil—

"Lise, you're not paying attention," Alan said loudly.

"I was thinking about what you'd said."

"Lise, when was your last decent meal?"

She shrugged. "Yesterday, last week—I really don't remember; they're all sort of blurred together. I'm exhausted until I get to bed, then I can't seem to stay asleep." She yawned. "I deserve whatever you're going to do about me," she said, mindful of his stare.

Alan laughed suddenly. "Should I take your word on that? I'm seriously thinking of sending you home right now and then coming up later with Chinese take-out—so you'll eat. Then I'm thinking of camping out in your livingroom so you'll sleep. Note: I said livingroom—this is purely professional desperation on my part. I need your flying fingers on the calculator to get these numbers together for me."

"Sometimes I can sleep in the afternoons—on weekends. It only makes the nights worse so I try not to nap—" She was too exhausted to argue any more with him or with herself.

"Then, go home! Get some sleep. If anyone asks, say you've got a fever or something. I'll clear things at this end. Anything special you want for dinner?"

"No."

Lulled into a drowsy serenity by the knowledge that everything had been finally taken out of her hands, Lise left the office building. She was daydreaming when she should have been getting off the subway and had to get off the train a good ten blocks further uptown. Rolling the collar of her coat up against the wind, she started the walk back downtown to home. It was a different sort of neighborhood, both foreign and ghetto. Even in her dulled state-of-mind Lise knew she was dangerously out of place. She picked up her pace and tucked her head down, determined not to be noticed until she was back in familiar territory. She caught sight of a storefront covered with the same sort of scrawls that had covered her windows. A sign over the door said: Mme. Odile's Botanica.

Without breaking stride Lise crossed the street as if the little shop had been her destination all along. It was risky, dangerous—and she could taste stupidity as she turned the rusted doorknob.

"Madame Odile?" she inquired of the dusty twilight.

A tall, slender negress rose and greeted her without warmth. "What do you want?"

Lise was immune to the woman's hostility. She looked

around the cluttered room. Bottles, jars and boxes were heaped on unpainted shelves. Furniture that could only have come from the curbside had been arranged to draw the eye to a table and a whitewashed wall covered with more of the red-brown symbols. The table was unmistakably an altar, but not a Chrisian one though a Cross stood prominently on it. Culpeper's Herbal was positively middle-class in comparison with Mme. Odile's.

"I'd like to know about the symbols painted on the outside of your shop," Lise asked after a long moment of silence.

"Grafitti, you say. Kids paint them in the summer." Madame Odile had a rich, accented voice that bespoke authority and, in this specific case, deceit.

"Don't they have some extra meaning? I'm certain I've seen them before," Lise disembled herself.

"Just grafitti. Now, you want something—really? You got too much curiosity for a white woman. You trying to make trouble?"

Odile had piercing eyes and a haughty manner. A droopy, handknit cardigan covered the bright cotton of her African-style dress. A bright turban added an extra six inches to her not inconsiderable height, but Lise was not tempted to gawk at the outlandishness of the costume.

"I'm here because of the grafitti: the vévés. Someone's drawn them on my windows. Someone's also left a dead chicken on my fire-escape and puts incense over my door. What can you tell me about things like that? How much does it cost?"

Odile darted around the front of the altar table, protecting it.

"Where you from?" Odile demanded.

"Why, Michigan."

"You come this far, from Michigan, to see me? Why?"

"No, I didn't come *here* from Michigan. I live on the Drive and I came in here because of the signs. Strange things have been happening to me and someone said it might be voodoo. That's what all this is, isn't it? Voodoo?"

Odile slumped against the table. Her hand tapped against

the wood in a sequence that was too complex to be accidental. "Yes, you go—and don't come back. The Baron—he'll watch you. You don't come back here. You don't bring your 'strange things' to Madame Odile."

"Who's this Baron? How do I get in touch with him? Will he really help me?"

Odile made a sign with her fingers, one which even Lise knew was against evil. "The Baron will find you himself." She reached into her sweater and came up with white confetti which she tossed into Lise's face.

The flakes ended Lise moments of courage and clarity as surely as a magician's wand dispells illusions. She saw the voodoo trappings a second time and backed out of the shop unable to control the trembling in her fingers or the weakness in her legs. Even the street looked different and she wasted precious moments reorienting herself.

Habit had kept her cautious; Alan had broken her habits and she lapsed into danger almost at once. By all the workings of her recent logic she should have seethed with anger toward him, but she only wanted to see him and tell him about the shop.

Sam wasn't around when she ghosted through the lobby and up to her apartment; the whole building seemed deserted at this hour. She felt unobserved and lighter than she had felt in weeks, though it might only be her reaction to the efforts of walking fast. The chaos her depression had wrought in the apartment was apparent for the first time and she made a feeble attempt to rectify the disorder. But Alan had told her to sleep and as soon as the bed was half-clear that was what she did.

Chapter Nineteen

Empty white cardboard containers from the Chinese food were scarcely noticable amid the disorder of the livingroom. Lise had rediscovered her appetite and gorged herself on spareribs. The nap and the food revived her, at least temporarily. For the moment she was content with her glass of root beer and the embellished story of her encounter with the voodoo woman.

"The signs on her shop were what attracted me. From a distance they looked just like the ones on the windows. It hit me funny. I mean, throughout all this I've never been tempted by those gypsy kids who give you little slips of colored paper that say to visit Madame Zloty who invariably has the second-floor on some seedy side-street and a neon-sign that says: Reader and Advisor, except advisor is always spelled with an 'e.' I thought I knew the difference between the occult and the fraudulent, but seven blocks north of here, in a neighborhood where no person of Anglo-Saxon heritage can feel truly safe, I marched right into Mme. Odile's." Lise told her carefully rehearsed story.

"Not that she was glad to see me. When I tried to talk about the windows she went wild. She said the Baron would take care of me and threw confetti at me—by then I'd sort of figured out I was in the wrong place and was leaving fast."

"Confetti?"

"Yeah, well—white, flaky stuff. I assume it was confetti. It brushed right off; I didn't bring any back with me. I think she was just trying to scare me—and she did a good job of it. Who, or what, is the Baron?" she asked as Alan fished the now-tattered paperback out of his briefcase.

"He's in here. I've already found connections between him and the general style of the vévé nearest the chicken. call him a lot of things: Cimitre, Cemetery, Samedi and sometimes Samhain. He's tied to their death cult; Saturday's connected with the dead. Anyway, the Baron's supposed to visit people when they die and share a meal with them; he likes fried chicken, not raw. You can identify the Baron by his clothes; he always wears black evening dress—whatever that is."

Samhain! Lise's thoughts whirled. Culpeper's had never mentioned this connection between voodoo and witchcraft. She fit the Baron's many names around the Phenomena. None of the names satisfied her completely, but they came close.

"Tell me more about this Baron Samhain," she urged when he looked from the book.

"There's not really all that much to tell," he complained, shutting the book. "This was the most complete I could find at Barnes & Noble, but it's short on particulars. It's got lists and drawings but no why's or wherefore's. I can't even tell if our man, or more exactly our *loa*, is a good-guy or a bad-guy."

Lise tried to listen attentively to what little information Alan could read but found herself on another tangent. No-one, it seemed, expected the Baron's final visit; she hadn't expected Marjory and Hynes' visit, either. It had been several days since she'd called Marjory's number.

"I thought you wanted to hear this," Alan complained when she went to the phone and began dialing. "Who're you calling, anyway?"

"Some people who knew the old man when he lived here. They came by in November when I'd only been here a few days. I wasn't ready to talk to them; I'm ready now. I've been ready for a while, actually, but I can't seem to get ahold of them. I call whenever the thought crosses my mind."

"Do you know who they are? If you've got a name maybe you could get an address and write—or visit," he suggested.

"I've thought of that," she explained, rummaging through her purse for the business card. "If I could get an address I'd have visited by now, but they seem to have fallen into the cracks."

She handed the card to him. He read the hand-written

message but was more impressed by the gold embossing on the front.

"I don't mean to sound prejudiced," he said handing the card back to her, but I doubt that this Mr. Hynes will know very much about the Baron."

"No, not about the Baron, but I expect he'll know quite a lot about Samhain. I've tried to reconstruct what I know and I'm convinced that he and Marjory were in the coven that was in this room the night the old man died.

"I've reached some other conclusions too. This is *his* office number and *her* home. There's no J. Robert Hynes in the phone book that match Marjory's number. There is a J. Robert Hynes somewhere in the city, but the number's unlisted and that means they won't give out the address either. I'm sure the phone company knows the address, they send bills don't they? But they won't tell their secrets."

"You really think they could help?" Alan asked.

It became Alan's turn to listen to a lengthy, distracted monolog as Lise unburdened herself of all she had learned at Culpeper's and of Jessica's pre-Christmas encounter with the Phenomena. She could forget Alan was in the room as she relived the evening Jessica and Sally had been there instead.

"Ready to sleep now?" Alan asked when she came up for air. "You've been letting that brew a long time."

Lise nodded and looked past him to the clock which showed she had talked for an hour. There were no words left to expend on the banal subject of who slept where. While she washed he took the extra pillow from her bed and settled down on the sofa. For an instant she thought to warn him of the pillows and the other Phenomena, but he'd picked the location and he knew the dangers. She turned out the lights and made her way to bed.

Alan was sitting at the kitchen table when she came out the next morning to put the water on. His beard had put forth a full day's stubble since midnight giving him an disreputable and disgusted air. She realized he hadn't slept well—if he'd slept at all.

"Coffee," she asked gently.

"Yeah, black and through an I-V." He stretched and rubbed his eyes which only made them redder. "Lise, how do you stand it?"

"I don't give myself a choice. I don't waste what little energy I've got asking myself if I can stand it. Did you have dreams? Sometimes they'd get to me. I didn't have any that I remember."

"What I had weren't dreams," he replied, dropping the temperature of the conversation into grimness. "There was a weight on my chest. I woke up when I couldn't breathe—and I couldn't get my breath when I was awake. I couldn't even sit up. It was all eyes and mouths, staring at me like I was something it hadn't caught in its web before."

Lise counted the spoonfuls into the pot, giving herself time to compose an answer. She had dreamt of fires and skeletons, been attacked by pillows but she'd never had a dream come to life. "Bad dreams always seem worse here," she equivocated.

"Yeah, I guess. Spiders all night. God, Lise, I hate spiders." He shuddered and brushed imaginary insects from his shoulders. "If I dreamt about one I dreamt about a thousand—and then it stopped being dreams. I'd go mad."

"Or you'd stop being afraid of spiders. You can't be that terrified for very long," she spoke from experience. "The edge dulls after a while. After the thousandth spider doesn't eat you, you stop caring."

Alan raised his undershirt to reveal a double octagon of red marks. "I don't think I'd last to the thousandth spider."

Lise couldn't swallow her coffee as she stared at the tiny punctures. "I don't think you should stay here again," she said slowly. "They've never hurt me—never broken skin." She added as much for herself as for him.

Morbid, but insatiable, curiosity got the better of her and while he negotiated the obstacle course in her bathroom she went to the livingroom. It was quiet enough, as it had been since the vévés appeared. She folded the blankets and went to fluff the pillows. Tiny, but complete, webs stretched from one to another. There was a larger web on the arm of the sofa and, on close examination, the remains of several more ground into the maroon plush. But the largest web, an engineering paradox, stretched from the carpet where Jessica had fallen and the will-o-the-wisp had danced, upward into a patch of nothingness.

Grabbing the ivory-handled paperknife, Lise attacked the impossible web, not realizing she had held her breath until all the grey filaments were wrapped around the blade and her lungs screamed for air. Still unwilling to touch the silk, she held the knife in the stove-burner where she was interrupted by Alan.

"You ready to go?" he asked, raising an eyebrow at her activity.

She set the knife and aside and left the apartment with him. Though one night of sleep had hardly brought about a full recovery, she got through the day on less coffee and without an after-lunch bout of nausea. Everyone noticed the improvement. With considerable persuasion but without mentioning spiders she was able to convince Alan that his visit had enabled her to turn the corner of her despair and he needn't spend another night on her sofa. He hadn't wanted to, anyway, and seemed happy to offer her a friendly, non-obligation, non-romantic dinner instead.

Lise agreed without hesitation; a free meal was a free meal. They chose a restaurant neither of them knew and talked office politics until the waiter brought after-dinner coffee.

"You know, Lise, I think that maybe you do belong up there."

"Up where," she replied, not entirely sure of his meaning.

"In your apartment. God knows I wouldn't have thought so at first. You look like one of your typical well-scrubbed faces from the wide open spaces but—I guess you do sort of belong up there. It's like having puzzle pieces that don't fit together until you realize you've been following the wrong picture.

"You still look and act like the last person I'd expect to find in the occult, but you take it all so matter-of-factly. I wouldn't believe that just yesterday you were one of the walking wounded. You've even convinced me you've got your problems beaten. You must be one fearless woman—a regular Joan-of-Arc."

"Well, in all fairness, nightmares haven't really been my biggest problem up there," Lise replied. "I have troubles but when I wake up with the screaming terrors it's not because I've been dreaming—usually the Phenomena are at it again."

"See, there you go again. They terrify you; I've seen it, but you can talk about them like they're nothing worse than the occasional cockroach you find in the refrigerator."

Lise struggled with the compliments, wondering as they drank their coffee if Alan remembered that Joan-of-Arc had been burnt at the stake for witchcraft.

"I'll see you home," Alan said as they left the restaurant.

Lise stiffened. "I thought we'd been through that already?"

"We have, but if it's all the same to you, I'd like to retrieve my toothbrush."

She laughed and strode along with him toward the subway.

"I'd offer you another cup of coffee," she said when they reached her building, "but I'm not sure I want to do anything that might keep you awake."

When Alan didn't answer she looked up and saw he was absorbed by something happening in Sam's office. From her position Sam was reading the sports page of the *Daily News*: hardly noteworthy. She walked around him, and could see without asking what held his attention.

In the far corner of the none-too-large room a tall, lean black man studied the intercom system. He was dressed in a cutaway black suit with velvet lapels and a satin stripe down the pants. A bonafide top hat sat on the narrow ledge in front of the intercom. Baron Samhain had come to pay a call.

Lise pulled Alan away and led the race up five flights of stairs. They could smell the incense after the fourth floor.

"Lise, you gotta go down and talk to Sam. Find out who that guy was and how often he comes here."

"No," she said, sweeping the half-burnt cones from the sill with a towel. "I know he's there. I know who he is and what he's doing. I don't want to involve Sam."

"Then I will. That man could be dangerous."

"I'd rather you didn't."

But he was already bounding down the stairs and she could only follow him. The stranger was gone and Sam was thoroughly surprised when Alan burst into his office.

"That guy who was just in here, where'd he go? Who was he? How'd he get in here, anyhow? He's the one putting the incense in front of Lise's door; when we got up there just now the cones were hardly burnt."

Sam folded his newspaper. "Mister, I don't know what you're talking about. Except for you and Miss Brown, there's been no-one in or out of this lobby in the last half-hour."

"He was right over by the intercom. Big, tall man, dressed to the nines—even had a top hat," Alan pushed past Sam to examine the intercom himself. "You saw him Lise, you tell him."

"It looked like there might have been a rather strangely dressed gentleman in here when we came in, and there was fresh incense around my door when we got up there. I did think there was a connection," she complied.

"Now you see here, Mister," Sam ignored Lise, "there's never been anyone in the building carryin' a top hat. An' you don't belong at that intercom anymore than he would—if he existed. So you just go on about your business. An' Miss Brown," he looked her in the eye, "you start being more careful who *you* bring into this building."

Lise took Alan's hand and pulled him away before he could heat up the situation further. She headed back toward the elevator. Sam had to be lying, though for what reasons she couldn't guess. If he wasn't lying then the Baron had stood less than five feet away and Sam hadn't seen him. And someone had definitely been at the intercom. An ebony walking stick had been left tucked against the wall. It was a weapon-like piece of wood with a brass skull for a hand-grip and bright red stones for eyes.

Chapter Twenty

Edith sat with her back to the rest of the hotel diningroom. Though the airline would pick up her bill she had ordered a plain filet of fish, fearing that the rich sauces of the more expensive entrees would upset her already jittery stomach. Between sips of sherry she glanced at her wristwatch and supposed that with better luck she'd have been well past the Irish Sea on her way to America by now.

A heavy, cold January fog had rolled in and shut Heathrow airport down indefinitely. Elizabeth, who had driven her to the airport, had offered to take her back to London when the first of many delays had been announced, but Edith demurred. Two days in the tiny flat Liz shared had been quite enough for one used to a rambling country house. She'd take her chances with the airlines; they at least promised a private bath.

Edith had dressed sensibly for the journey wearing tweedy-plaid slacks and a matching cardigan. Now she found herself underdressed for the dimly-lit restaurant and its attentive, foreign waiters. In the end, though, this was only one more distraction to shut out of her mind. She was alone for the first time in several days and she relished the solitude.

The journey had been fraught with unforeseen complications. She had reserved a flight for the fifteenth of January; it was now the thirtieth. There had been problems with her passport, then the airline had rearranged its schedules and cancelled her flight. Finally she'd caught a flu and been grounded for an extra week. Fog was a surprisingly predictable inconvenience. She seemed destined not to reach New York City and the Riverside covenstead until the very day of the Imholc celebration on the first.

Nonetheless when the filet arrived she put even those thoughts from her mind and enjoyed the meal. Bert had insisted she fly first-class since he could not accompany her.

The airlines equated first-class with Ruritanian royalty; the food and accommodations were superb.

"Madam?" her waiter interrupted. "A young couple is asking for you. Shall I tell them to wait in the lobby or shall I bring them to your table?"

Edith swivelled about in her chair, catching sight of Elizabeth's auburn hair. Liz would not have returned through the fog unless it was important.

"Yes, show them here." She took another spoonful of custard before pushing the plate aside.

"Mum, I've been trying to find you since four. The airline had no idea what hotel they'd booked you into."

Liz set her coat over the back of the chair, allowing her mother to see the other guest clearly for the first time: Hector Seymour, the psychic who sought Arthur's spirit not three month's before. He was carefully and conservatively dressed but nothing could conceal the wild look in his eyes; the price his talent made him pay when he moved among the people.

"Mrs. Brompton," he greeted her, taking her hand firmly. "I'm so sorry to disturb you, but when Elizabeth said you'd been delayed again, I knew I had to see you before you left."

Edith sat back in her chair experiencing an uncomfortable sense of déjà vu that would make most of his forthcoming story redundant.

"May we talk here?" Hector looked at the still-active diningroom and Edith understood that he could not talk comfortably here at all.

"No, I'll settle my bill and we'll go upstairs. There'll be more than enough chairs for us. I think my one room's larger than your whole flat, Liz."

Edith led the way to her room. The walls of the building were thick enough to dull the noise of the nearby airport and, apparently, also dampen the thought-maelstrom that habitually buffeted the psychic. He closed his eyes and rested while the women waited.

"Where to start?" he began. "I didn't start to suspect something was wrong until a good time after you'd visited me, but finally the jogs began to have a pattern and I wanted to talk to you. A journey to Cornwall is out of the question for us. I wanted you to come up to London, but I had so little to go on. So I've waited until I was certain, only to discover that your flight had been providentially delayed."

He hesitated until Edith nodded, then continued. "In the last few months the other side has seemed to have a different texture: spongier, as if the boundaries between Here and There were less firm than they'd been. It didn't affect me at first and I assumed I had changed, which has happened before.

"I continued my work without interruption but suddenly there was a tremendous change—about Yule. Since I was a child I've explored my past lives—I go back to a tribal shaman with a cave. Or I had done; within a few days of Yule I'd broken past even that life."

Edith wondered if he'd come upon Caer Maen or one of the other High Covens. The shadows which hid the Otherworld had been thought to shield the High Covens as well. It was clear Hector was no longer protected completely from the Otherworld, what else might be revealed to him. Hector would have to be brought into Caer Maen before he could inadvertantly cause trouble for himself or anyone else.

"I decided I could push myself back to the very source of humanity. I was a damn, bloody fool!" Hector exclaimed with bitter emphasis.

"What did you find?" Edith asked in a quiet voice.

"I got sucked right out of the ether—the silver thread back to my present was gone and I can't forget what replaced it—though I wish I could. But, it really wasn't unfamiliar. When I'd fought off the first panic I knew I'd seen it all through different eyes. Then I found your brother-in-law and remembered I'd seen it when he had been searching. What he'd finally found was worse than the last circle of Hell."

Edith recalled what she had felt at Yule and could only agree.

"I drew away from him and IT," Hector continued. "The Gods alone know how I did. I heard voices I couldn't understand and brushed up against spirits that were never part of this world. I didn't resist and they didn't notice me. After a while I began to understand, in a way.

"They were forging an escape route from that terrible place. They meant to invade our own here-and-now. I saw their wormhole which looked out into what appeared to be a normal room somewhere. The wormhole was still too small and they were building something that would enlarge it. I, on the other hand, was small enough to slip through. I was in New York City! I was certain I'd passed beyond reason. The Lady stood there in that New York room holding a silver thread in her hands. I touched the thread and woke up, five days later, in my own bed."

Edith brushed her hair back from her forehead and went to the fog-clouded window. She'd have to bring him into Caer Maen; he'd survived the Otherworld.

"You've been through the Otherworld," Edith said while watching his reactions on the glass. "Don't expect logical explanations. What you've learned is the truth, even if your memory won't let you remember all of it and the details change."

Hector nodded as if he understood. "And you—your daughter says you're going to that room?"

"Yes," Edith admitted. "The room contains a Rift, a guarded place where we send the dead and call the living through the Otherworld with our Samhain rituals—and all the while we're keeping *them* out of here. We've been the Guardians since the morning of time. But now my brother-in-law's death has left that Rift unguarded."

"There's more, Mum," Liz interrupted. "Tell her what you told me, about the Lady and the rest that you felt."

"It's simply that you're not the only potent force interested in that room. Before I picked up the silver thread, the Lady pointed to the window where somebody'd put up warding—not Wiccan warding, not anything I'd seen before. You've got allies—or rivals."

Edith wondered if it were possible for the Otherworld to have allies. For all that Arthur bemoaned New York, it did not seem credible that the City harbored something so cut off from life and death as to join with the Otherworld. But—did rivals have to be Otherworld allies? Hadn't she told Liz that Riverside must be guarded by native magick? Still, if the warding wasn't Wiccan, how would she deal with it? How could she contact its makers. How would she know that the Rift was guarded again and guarded properly if the magick was not similar to her own?

"They were going to push something through the wormhole soon. I'd guess Imholc, if I had to guess," Hector spoke into her reverie.

Edith's thoughts were as thick as the fog outside and less likely to clear by morning. If something should crawl out of the Rift she might know of it at once but it was equally likely that her mind would rebel against such base Otherness and she would not know until it was too late.

"Mum, I'm afraid for you. Shouldn't we all be going? What if you can't close it by yourself?"

"If I can't close it myself then we've only lost me. We can't risk any more of Caer Maen than that. I'll have to find people there to help me."

"We don't have any idea who's left from the Riverside coven. You shouldn't be going alone."

"Riverside is dead!" Edith said firmly. "I won't be looking for it. The Lady grant that there is someone waiting in Arthur's flat for my help. We may not be allowed even this second chance."

"You're speaking *ex cathedra* again, Mum," Elizabeth chided.

"Supposing though," Hector entered into the conversational lull, "that you can't tell the difference between what's valid and what's not. Supposing what they send through is a Trojan Horse? What then? How will you know who to train and who to oppose?"

"I'll know; of course I'll know," but Edith didn't believe herself and didn't expect Elizabeth or Hector to be reassured.

They sat in silence. Edith would have preferred if they had left her alone to arm herself for the journey and the trials ahead, but she was not so needful of isolation that she would ask them to leave. After a short while the room became so gloomy that she improvised a small altar upon the desk and sought the Lady's peace and clarity.

Hector followed Edith's lead gracefully but there was no peace-of-mind and little clarity for her daughter who sobbed softly throughout the improvised ceremony.

"I might never see you again."

"Try not to think like that, dear." Edith asked. "You'll only make me more nervous than I already am. You know it's what I've got to do."

With a louder sob, Elizabeth wrapped her arms around her mother's shoulders. "Then let me come with you," she begged. "I don't want to think of you alone over there."

"I need you here much more," Edith replied, gently stepping out of Liz's embrace. "With Riverside left unguarded, all the High Covens have been weakened."

"What about me? What can I do to help?" Hector asked as Liz sought her handkerchief.

"Protect yourself. You may have escaped unnoticed, but the taint of the Otherworld lingers. Elizabeth will teach you the basic personal warding rituals, since I know you haven't used any before. Protect your family as well—the taint spreads."

Hector looked like a small boy being scolded. "But, isn't there anything I can do for you?"

"Have faith in me, and—yes, let me get some rest now. They're going to call us at five AM if the fog's lifted."

Her guests acknowledged the command and after another half-hearted round of protests gathered their coats. Edith wanted to tell Bert what had happened and wanted to hear his supremely practical voice tell her she was equal to the challenge before them all. Instead she settled herself into the vast king-size bed. If they could bury the lines she'd have that phone put it; maybe even if they couldn't bury the lines. If she got back.

Chapter Twenty-One

Edith noticed little improvement in the overall visibility when she was bused back to the airport later on in the morning. Their jet, however, was waiting for them and the ever-solicitous, terribly apologetic flight crew saw that the first-class passengers were quickly escorted to their seats.

She dug into her shoulderbag for the same piece of needlework she had worked on during her last visit to the States ten years back. It had been for Gwen's next birthday; she tried to forget that as she sorted the yarn and covered the design with neat, tiny stitches.

A red-brown ridge ahead of the wing announced their approach to New York. The smog was worse than she'd remembered, but then it was worse everywhere; even Saint Ives had days when the air wasn't as pure as it could be.

Kennedy International was a nightmare of lost travellers struggling with their luggage and harried customs officials struggling with the travellers. Edith let herself be herded from one line to the next. She was confident she would sail easily through the obstacle course, if she didn't fight with it; Bert had arranged all her papers. But once the customs officials stamped her passport and waved her on toward the exit she was beyond Bert's careful preparations.

No-one was there to hug and kiss her or take command. She followed the crowds to the taxis on her own, looking the wrong way as she stepped off the curb and narrowly missing one of the speeding cars. No-one noticed.

"Where to, Lady?" a young man in a garish satin flight jacket called out to her.

Confidence, Bert had said: act as if you know where you're going and it won't seem worthwhile to cheat you. "The Grammercy Park, in Manhattan—via the tunnel," she recited.

"Okay, Lady—hop in."

She didn't, but waited to see that all her luggage was on board, too, before settling into the back seat. It seemed he was barrelling to destruction on the wrong side of the street, so she closed her eyes.

Her mind and body were utterly unaware of the proper time of day; it looked like noon and felt like evening. She was certain she only wanted to get to her room and collapse once she was unpacked, but even that resolve faded when she saw the high, fluffy bed. Kicking aside her shoes, she uncovered a pillow and expected to be asleep in moments. Instead, within a few minutes of stretching out, she was wide awake, listening to the sounds of the traffic below and anxious to be about her business.

Her suitcases could wait a few more hours until she returned from an inspection of the Riverside building.

Ten years had not done much to change the neighborhood. There were more signs in Spanish, but the buildings were the same and she didn't get lost. Her thoughts would jump ahead as she walked the almost familiar streets, remembering Gwen and the tasty dishes she prepared in the cheerful kitchen without a view. She could taste the savories, then reality would crash in and she would recall that everything she could remember was irretrievably lost now.

"Who're you visitin'?"

Edith studied the short, swarthy young man whose tone of voice brought her up short in the lobby. It was Sam's day off.

"Who you wanna see?" he said more slowly.

"I was wondering if I could see number 647?"

"S'not for rent. We don't have apartments for rent here. You gotta go to the agency." He turned away from her.

"You don't understand," Edith called after him. "I don't want to rent an apartment. Number 647 belonged to my sister—I'd just like to see it again."

"Just an old man lived there, no sister—an' he's dead too." He handed her a wrinkled business card. "You call that number. They tell you when we get apartments. I don't rent no apartments."

"But I just want to see number 647," Edith persisted,

wishing she had rested longer before adventuring in a foreign country. "I want to see the apartment where Arthur Andrews lived, not rent it—just see it."

The man tapped his finger against the brass mailboxes. "Andrews's dead, Lady. He don't live here or anyplace. Got it? A. Brown lives in 647 now—A. Brown."

Edith nodded and folded the business card into her pocket. At least she had a name to work with. A. Brown might have gotten her letter, might know what had happened to the Riverside Coven's ritualware and might, if luck were very strong, know who had been at the Samhain ritual where Arthur was stricken.

With considerable negotiation Edith convinced the man to ring the apartment but there was no-one home and a sixth sense told Edith she'd pressed the unwilling man as far as he would go. It was half-past three, local time, and if A. Brown worked for a living he or she wouldn't be home for another few hours. She had walked up to Riverside Drive and felt all the tiredness she hadn't felt back at the hotel. Reluctantly she hailed a taxi again.

It was after five when she had her things unpacked and the room arranged to her liking. Directory assistance had yielded a phone number for A. Brown, but there was still no answer. Though the clocks said it was dinner time, her body finally believed it was time to sleep. She set candles on the plastic-topped desk and celebrated Imholc quietly. She didn't even consider trying to close the Rift though she had come four thousand miles for that purpose. Instinct said she was still dangerously ignorant of the true situation at Riverside and unadapted to New York City. The Gods would have to understand.

She dreamt of the Riverside apartment building and of Arthur and Gwen who waited for her in the livingroom. There was suddenly, as happens in dreams, a black disk suspended in the center of the room. It became more real than the room as Edith's dream-self watched it. The disk spun slowly on its axis: a circle, an ellipse, finally a knife-edge and the cycle would reverse itself. Three times the disk went through its phases until Edith was synchronized with it and floated around the dark circle. Within the dream she felt danger—Arthur and Gwen were calling her, but nothing could weaken the attraction of the black disk.

Beyond the disk was the Otherworld, but she had been terribly wrong about the Otherworld. It was beautiful, not ugly. It was a place of shimmering color and eternal life. The disk spun faster. Edith could see the expressions on Arthur's and Gwen's faces. She was drifting into the disk regretting nothing except that the Otherworld was cold and she seemed to have forgotten a sweater.

"It's too cold for me in there—" she mumbled, waking herself up and thus dispelling the hypnotic power of something that had been more than a dream.

She was indeed cold; the blankets were all to one side of the bed. Her bare feet felt like ice. Hobbling, she made her way to the bathroom and shoved her feet under the bathtub spout.

It would be possible, even easy, for the Otherworld to create allies on this side of the Rift; she had learned as much. Whoever lived in apartment 647 would have succumbed, she supposed, to the constant temptation and could hardly be blamed for it. But the Gods had not forsaken the High Priestess from Caer Maen. She had no worse than tender, red toes to show for her brush with disaster.

The towels she used to dry her feet had been laundered at the Sutton Place commercial laundry. The name lingered in her thoughts well after she had replaced the towels on the rack and returned to her bed. Slowly, in the darkness, the face of a woman Edith had met just once, more than thirty years before; a woman she had never liked but who was Gwen's confidant. A woman named Marjory Sutton who had taken the circle name Rowen. The face of Sutton's constant companion floated free without further effort: Glasfryn—Rob Hynes, a dark furtive sort who had struck Edith as both ambitious and weak. No, the Gods had certainly not deserted Caer Maen's High Priestess.

It was almost midnight—too late to call the unknown A. Brown but not too late to call a High Coven Priestess on High

Coven business, if the phone books would reveal the number. She would recognize the address even though she couldn't quite remember it. There were several Suttons and one at an address that was familiar the moment her eyes passed over it. She dialed the number, but Marjory was not home.

No matter, Edith was determined and ready to face the streets and meet Marjory on her doorstep. She retrieved two tapering hardwood sticks from the closet and snapped them together. Back home the walking stick discouraged stray dogs, sheep, pigs and chickens; she expected it would be no less effective on the wildlife of New York City.

The hotel doorman stopped just short of physical restraint to keep her from going out into the night. It was Imholc, Edith told herself as she swung into stride on the sidewalk: a good time—the quickening of spring, by tradition the moment when buried seeds began to sprout, when leaf-buds swelled and when the wombs of domestic animals came alive; a night of life and joy in the dead of winter. In practice, Imholc was often one of the coldest nights of the year and that alone was enough to discourage all but the most ardent worshippers and criminals.

Marjory Sutton lived in a small, private building. A single row of mailboxes outside the curtained, triple-locked inner door showed that Marjory lived in 2A while J. Robert Hynes lived in 2B. Edith pressed both buzzers and held them until whomever was in either apartment would realized that the caller would not go away.

Marjory hadn't changed all that much. Edith recognized the strained, pale features as the woman peered anxiously around the lace curtains.

"Go away," Marjory rasped and folded the curtains back.

"Rowen, I am Camulac from Caer Maen—Morwedd's sister. I've come to talk to you about Riverside. Let me in," Edith commanded.

"Camulac? Gwen's sister?" Marjory repeated, studying Edith and reluctantly unlatching the door.

"I've come to help you," Edith announced as she stepped into the foyer.

Whatever sign Marjory needed Edith had finally provided.

"Yes, Camulac—Edith? Come in, please. We do need you." The tiny woman's change in attitude was as sincere as it had been sudden. The fear hadn't left her eyes, however.

Rob Hynes was propped up in a chair, an elastic bandage visible under the blankets wrapped around his right leg. A pair of crutches leaned against the wall behind him.

"Camulac?" he whispered in surprise and awe. "Here? You found us? I can't believe it. So much has gone wrong. Anerien's death, Branwen and the rest. It's hard to believe it's you in the flesh."

Fear was the most real presence in Rob's apartment; it was more alive than either of the people. Edith had to remind herself that she and they were contemporaries and that they had been the pillars of Riverside. She draped her coat over the back of a chair when Marjory made no move to take it from her, but only sat beside Rob looking up at the Caer Maen High Priestess.

"It's so good to have you here," Marjory said, her eyes filled with tears. "Since Anerien's death I've needed someone to talk to, and there was no-one but Rob; there hasn't been anyone since Gwen died. I've missed her—she was always the older sister I never had."

Edith was nonplussed and very tempted to say to the cowering woman that Gwen was the older sister she'd never had, too. But there would be no point in bickering, especially not with the true despair etched into their faces. If Edith needed any confirmation of the scope of the disaster, their expressions provided it.

"Tell me what happened to you, to the Coven and to my brother-in-law."

"Samhain was bad from the start. He had uninitiates in the Circle! That would have been enough in itself," Marjory began quickly and bitterly.

"Oh, no—those children didn't stay. It was the police who broke in after the invocation and frightened Anerien into a heart attack. They drove us out of the apartment before we could even try to close IT and they never let us back in," Rob explained.

"You did try to close the Rift, then?" Edith asked.

"Even before we knew Anerien had died we tried to close the Rift. We went to Branwen's apartment—Marjory tried to undo the damage, but too much had been disrupted—" Rob was reliving, not remembering, and the pain was clear in his face.

"I failed—IT came back later that night and killed Branwen," Marjory admitted in a whisper.

"Yes—well, no, not really. She was hit by a car on her way to work the next morning. Still, it couldn't have been coincidence, not really."

Edith remembered her mother's handwritten notes and agreed silently with them. "So you don't believe that you closed the Rift on Samhain. Have you tried since? This is Imholc, would you try now?" Edith asked, though she was fairly certain of the answer.

"There is only one Time—we didn't dare try again. We wouldn't dare try now, not even with you to guide us," Marjory stated with a finality that sent a chill down Edith's back though she'd expected the answer.

"You had the Riverside Grimoires, at any rate. You could have contacted Caer Maen. No-one told us anything, even about Arthur," Edith told them and there was bitterness in her voice as well.

Marjory shook her head. "Anerien had the only complete grimoire and that was locked up. We had our street-clothes and nothing else. I had a key; I was sure I'd get in the next day. But the police had put extra locks on the door and we never had a chance. The landlord rented it out right away and wouldn't talk to any of us who had been there on Samhain. Everything happened so fast—Riverside was gone before we knew it. Somehow the girl qualified and we were locked out. We went to talk to her but she wouldn't let us in—had her boyfriend in bed with her. I could see the furniture was as we'd left it—but she wouldn't let us in. There wasn't anything we could do."

"We haven't been back since," Rob added.

"Well, how could we? First there was Branwen, then I got

sick myself. The doctor said I needed sun; that I had to get away from New York, so we took a cruise over the holidays. The day before we docked back here, Rob fell and his leg hasn't been right since. They had him in the hospital a while, but it's not healing properly. It's so cold it's no wonder we're both sick."

Something was making the couple keep the apartment warm enough that Edith was already drowsy while they were bundled up and shivering. Edith recalled the cold of her nightmare, but said nothing. Let them believe, if they could, that the cold was only winter.

"This girl who's taken the apartment—can she get in touch with you?"

"We left a card with Marjory's number. We listen for the phone, but it's difficult to hear through the walls. Of course, if she'd found the grimoires it would be different—"

"It's been too much to bear alone, Camulac," Marjory interrupted. "You can smell IT in the air. Even when we were away I couldn't get IT out of my mind. Knowing the Rift is open and there's a clear path—it's not our fault, of course, but just the *knowing*."

Edith wasn't impressed. "And what of the girl? She, presumably has no experience or training. She's been left alone in the shadow of the Otherworld. What have you even tried to do about that?"

"There was nothing we could do. I could cry when I think of her—she was wearing Gwen's last Beltane gown as a bathrobe! She didn't want our help; didn't want us. It's never been our way, the High Coven way, to force ourselves, you know," Marjory concluded with a flourish of indignation.

"It's not our way to leave our burdens beside the road, either," Edith said in what was intended to be a calm voice. "You could have lied your way in—done whatever was necessary to get into the room and held the Riverside covenstead."

"That would be against the law," Marjory sniffed, without noting which law, Wiccan or civil, that she referred to.

"How much do you know already, Camulac? You knew how to find us—have you already been up there? Have *you* closed it?" Rob sat forward in his chair, letting the blankets slip to one side.

"No, I know about the condition of Riverside the same way Ravenna knew it was there fifty years ago. I only got here this morning. I remembered Marjory's name a few hours back. From the look of things I'm way too late." Edith gave vent to her discontent.

"No, you can't mean that," Rob chided her. "Surely with all of Caer Maen behind you—after all, *Caer Maen.*"

Edith wondered just what legends had been sown about the English coven. "I've got the girl's phone number, but not much else. As you say without the grimoires it is more difficult. I'll talk to the girl tomorrow, I hope, then I can make plans—" she tried to sound confident. She meant to keep an open mind about the Brown girl, but her own experience and the fate of Marjory and Rob did not allow her to believe that she would find an ally living in apartment 647.

She might have been scolding children for the way the couple pouted at her. What dreams had they shared to bring them to this condition? Had they already slipped through the black disk? Edith had little patience with fear, especially when it left undone everything that a High Coven ought to have done or tried to do. She had always had her doubts about Riverside; and, yes, even doubts about her sister. Gwen had been destined for Caer Maen; she was a maintainer, not a builder. Riverside had never become self-sufficient—the fact that the one copy of the Grimoire had apparently been lost was testament to that.

Edith purged her mind of thoughts of the past and concentrated on the future. She couldn't afford bitterness any more than fear. "Well, come now—it can't be that bad. You did open and close the Rift from that room every year for over a half-century; there's a fair amount of High Coven magick there to rub off on her as well. She needn't have slipped over the edge. It's not truly the first time something's gone wrong—it took us a year to find Riverside and close it the first time and the world survived. I'll talk to Miss Brown and we'll get a solution together."

The couple relaxed when they realized that Edith would do the work without them. They offered her a cup of coffee. The cold fear had retreated for a moment but it would return once she had left again. The Otherworld had crushed this section of the Riverside Circle. These two were like early-born lambs who die in the snow for the simple crime of being born at the wrong time.

Edith had a headache and went to the bathroom to daub cold water on her temples. They whispered in her absence, but she couldn't make out the words. She removed an earring and massaged the swollen skin; the throbbing subsided.

"It's completely out of the question for Rob to drive, but we'll call you a cab. You shouldn't be out walking at this hour," Marjory announced.

Edith did not bother to disagree.

Chapter Twenty-Two

Lise lay awake in the curves of Alan's body. His breathing was soft and regular; she had become accustomed to its warmth on her shoulder. Since they had seen Baron Samhain they had been inseparable, though they did not discuss the apparition. It was better that way; there were virtues in silence. So long as they travelled the same path at the same speed there was no need to talk about where they were going or who was leading.

The heating system was no match for the last night of January. Lise rearranged the blankets and snuggled into the protection of his arms. It might have been warmer at Alan's apartment; that building was newer and his apartment overlooked a sheltered alley instead of the Hudson River and all New Jersey. But that was another subject they had never discussed. Alan accepted that she belonged in her apartment and never suggested she relocate.

The clock in the livingroom clicked loudly. Lise used one finger to pull the blankets away from her face and confirmed that it was now February first. Culpeper's would be reopening later in the day. Ms. Hirshhorn thought Hynes might be back at his office. It would be noticeably warmer in just one month. Lise released the blanket and waited for sleep.

They were awake, both of them raised to one elbow. Alan's hand rested lightly on Lise's shoulder. With the curtains drawn the apartment was pitch black; the street sounds were muffled and distant. Yet they were awake and Lise knew by the pounding in Alan's wrist that he'd heard the sound too.

With her eyes made useless by the dark, Lise examined the room with her ears. She used the livingroom as a reference—if she could hear that, and she could, she would hear any sound in the apartment, even a footfall on the carpet. There was nothing. Alan's hand had begun to relax. Probably it had been an odd noise in the street—maybe one ring of the telephone. Whatever it had been, it was not going to repeat itself. Lise slid back under the blankets. Her heartbeat slowed but she kept the blanket away from her face and stared at the black quadrant wherein lay the bedroom door.

It came in silence; a finger of translucence wiggling through the doorway, retreating again. Hallucinations, Lise told herself. It came again, testing the air like a hunting snake and rising some four or five inches above the floor before disappearing back into blackness. Lise found Alan's hand and squeezed it.

She moved slowly within the bed until she was sitting up. The thread of light reappeared and retreated. Even now she couldn't be sure. They had waited for disaster for so long that it was impossible to be certain that it had, at last, arrived. If Alan had relaxed she might have done likewise, but he sat beside her with equally tense fingers and shallow breathing that matched her own.

—Okay, come through that doorway again—Lise thought, leaning forward. —Now, when I'm looking right there, let me see what you look like.

Blades of light flickered along the floorboards. Lise's heart pounded in her ears. If it had been recognizable at all, if it had fallen into those classes of Phenomena she had already named, she would have believed the whole episode was self-induced. But she could not imagine a natural origin for the pale flickering light nor an unnatural one for the luminous snake.

She heard sighs that drowned out the sounds of the living-room clock yet her instinct said that the source of those sighs was very far away—not in the next room.

Lise moved her left hand; the bedcovers rustled and she froze. One scream might have broken the spell, released her from terror and driven the Phenomenon back but Lise could not breathe much less scream.

A large self-luminous snake-head broke the plane of the bedroom door at about chest height. Alan quivered and she could no longer feel his breathing.

—This is the terror that kills.—She forced herself to breath so that death would not be her own fault. Her fingernails dug deeply into Alan's palm, but he did not react at all.

The snake moved slowly, testing each mote of space before it advanced. It was hunting. Lise would not get out of bed to meet it. She willed herself to disbelieve in the phantom, but now she could hear the bellyscales rubbing on the wood floor.

The serpentine rope of light pushed further into the room, bobbing its head in the direction of the bed. The tongue, forged of a redder luminescence than the rest, darted in counter-point to the weaving of the head; it could taste her panic. It was all snake now, yawning, dislocating its jaw in anticipation of a feast.

Lise closed her eyes; the image of the snake was unchanged in her mind. Her chest hurt from the pounding of her heart; her throat was tight with unescaped screams; her eyes burned and her ears rang.—Let it be quick—she prayed; the interminable fear, the fullness of her horror was worse than death. But the balance swung again. When her mind surrendered to the paralyzing fright, her body was freed. She found her pillow and heaved it into the illusion. She screamed and barred her teeth in rage.

The sighing faltered and the snake retreated. Lise followed it with a predatory ease all her own. Medusa—a sickly yellow, undulating ball of light, awaited her in the livingroom. It sprouted snakes from its surface, sent them slithering toward her and drew them back again.

"Spiders," Alan whispered beside her in the doorway, "drawing us into their web."

There were no spiders, not in the scene she saw at least, but she didn't ask questions. It was no harder to believe that he saw spiders where she saw snakes than to believe in the snakes themselves. She tried to imagine the spiders and broke the illusory spell. The thing at the center of the livingroom was not Medusa sprouting hair of snakes, nor was it a spiderweb. It was a shimmering globe with projections of pure, indescribable light.

"Omygod," Lise repeated in mantra-chant. She was cold,

numb, nauseous and drained. She looked away from the globe and forced herself to look back again. It had to be real—irrational but real. She saw a mottled amoeba of darkness growing within the eerie yellow-green light. It couldn't be—but her powers of disbelief were long since exhausted.

"Run," she whispered as the dark blob grew. "We've got to get out of here. We've got to warn them." Not that her churning stomach and liquid knees would let her run.

Alan was pulling her backward. The mottling had obscured most of the glowing globe now, and was starting to penetrate the constantly writhing coils of light. Appendages bubbled out of the sphere and were absorbed again. IT would break out at any moment. IT was unstoppable, irresistible. IT was infinite in its Otherworldly terror and evil, but Lise past beyond her ability to feel or fear; she no longer cared about fate.

Her eyes were open but she didn't see all Hell break loose in her livingroom. Concussive sound threw her against the bedroom doorjamb, only Alan's grip and raw reflexes kept her on her feet at all. He shouted something and began dragging her down the hallway. The livingroom overflowed with a blinding, oozing radiance. Spirals of darkness wound through the light: the arms of a new-born demon whose cries rattled the walls of the building.

"Open it!" Alan ordered as they came against the locked door at the end of the hall.

Lise obeyed. The light from the bare bulb over the landing disappeared into the darkness emerging from the livingroom. The menace surged for them and freedom with gutteral salverings and insect-like buzzing both at the same time.

In excruciatingly slow motion, Alan released her hand and lunged back at the still open door once he had shoved Lise to relative safety. Mark Ratner and two other men had appeared to help him. Rachel Ratner held her hands by her face and screamed, but the sound was lost beside the birth of the demon.

The men could not latch the door. The demon exploded out of the corridor, sending them to their knees in agony as the seething cloud sent exploring tentacles of darkness over their bodies. Lise took another step backwards, crashed down the stairs and into unconsciousness.

A ringed woman's hand with dark nail polish held the ammonia-soaked cotton that burned and choked Lise back to consciousness. The sharp odor unlocked a torrent of uncontrolled, hysterical tears. She had survived, somehow. The memories were locked in her mind, frozen by the fall. She moved her thoughts carefully lest the memories come unpleasantly back to life.

"What happened?" she asked hesitantly.

Rachel's bloodless face swam in front of her. "IT happened."

Lise sank back on the very cold, very hard, very real stairway and cried in powerful sobs that twisted and contorted her into a small, fetal ball. Rachel smoothed her hair and spoke in soft calming tones.

"Where's Alan?" Lise choked out through her sobs.

"Gone," Rachel whispered.

Lise stopped crying to look into the other woman's eyes. She waited for the rest; she was not about to ask the fatal question.

"That—that THING held onto him. It let the others go—but Alan went with it."

Lise was seized by a shivering fit.

"She's turning blue," Rachel announced in a voice Lise could barely hear anymore. "Help me get her inside."

Strong hands lifted her up. They turned her until she could see the open door of her own apartment. "No, not in there!" she protested, stiffening and bracing her arms and legs against them—but no-one intended to set foot in her apartment.

Rachel unlocked her door. "She can stay here until—"

There were ten of them crowded into the Ratners' living-room. Everyone was quiet and solicitous as they brought extra blankets to the sofa and inquired if she were feeling better—but no-one would look directly at her. Rachel handed her a tumbler of amber liquid. The brandy hit like fire; her nose and eyes watered; she coughed helplessly but the shivering subsided and the worst of the panic was memory.

"I had a nightmare," she confided to Rachel. The entire room heard her whispered remark. Whispered conversations among neighbors came to a halt as they stared away from her and each other.

"I got here as soon as I could," a man called from the open doorway. "Is this my patient? What's the problem, Rach?" Rachel nodded and took his coat. "Looks like shock—a few bruises. What happened? She fall?"

"Dave, you won't believe this," Rachel hesitated, "but something came out of her apartment; something unreal—"

Everyone took a chance describing the apparition, but the effect was cumulative not contradictory. When not talking the neighbors nodded to each other and shuddered. On the sofa, Lise trembled unnoticed. She whimpered when the doctor pulled her wrist toward him.

"Any injuires then beside fright?"

"She did fall. She fainted and fell down the stairs."

Dave counted Lise's pulse, grimaced and turned to face his sister again. "If I didn't know you better," he whispered to her, "I'd say this was an elaborate plot to get me to make a housecall on the coldest night of the year."

"Dave—" Rachel protested.

"No, don't start up. I said I knew better. You all think you've seen something frightening, but the woman might have a concussion as well. You should have taken her right to the hospital—you surprise me."

"I—I don't want to get downstairs, or outside. Dave, we're not putting you on. That thing was not from this earth."

Dave turned his attention back to Lise. "I'd like to give you a sedative, a mild one—very mild. It'll help you calm down. You've had a bad scare and a nasty bump on your head." He loosened the blankets and pushed up the sleeve of her nightgown. "Rach, can she stay here. Will you be able to keep an eye on her if concussion symptoms start to develop?

I'll leave a number for the hospital, in case she starts going down. Where's Mark, anyway?''

''Mark's out chasing the other victim of this—this put-on.''

Lise ignored them. She looked away from the needle and toward her apartment as the needle pricked her skin. The door to 647 was still open. The little hallway table was overturned, the rest was lost in darkness.

''Alan—you said that it'd gotten Alan,'' Lise said as they pulled the blankets up around her again.

''It held your friend—sort of carried him down the stairs past you. Mark and some of the other men followed; we'll know better when they get back.''

The tranquilizer took effect. The rigid muscles in Lise's neck unlocked and her thoughts were sheltered behind a layer of benign unreality. Whatever happened, and no drug could conceal the knowledge that something had happened, no longer seemed quite as ominous. Alan would return with Mark and all would be explained; Alan would find the correct explanation for everyone, even Rachel's doubting brother.

Lise waited silently, lulled into unmoving calm by the injection. The neighbors returned to their own apartments and all doors were closed, even her own. Her mind had drifted into unfocused nothingness when a key rattled in the lock.

''Mark! What happened to you?''

''I'm okay, Rach. Dave! Glad you got here. Give me a hand with this fellow. He should have frostbite over ninety percent of his body. I must have chased him around that damned park three times.''

''Is he okay?'' Rachel asked, ''Should we get him someplace?'' She clearly wasn't as worried about Alan's cuts and contusions as she was about his vacant, glazed expression.

''The police didn't think so. God protects fools, remember? He was doing fine until we got off the elevator—''

''And what about the thing?'' Rachel interrupted.

Mark shrugged.

''It got away from me,'' Alan said in a distant voice. ''I

couldn't stop it in time." He pounded fist against palm and winced from the pain.

"It was just a dream," Lise added but Alan stared hard at her and she retreated into her blanket cocoon. There were things in his eyes that no tranquilizer could shield her from. After a moment's consideration she reached out and touched his battered, cold hand.

"He was there," Alan whispered to her alone. "The Baron was there. I saw him come out from under the trees laughing like a skull. He was there. IT went right to him." He shook his head, jarring tears from the corners of his eyes. "That laugh. Ogod, that laugh! I tried to get between them; I tried to be there—I gave it everything I had and all they did was laugh. The cloud came down and hid him from me but he kept on laughing until the cloud swallowed him." Alan put his hands over his ears and groaned.

Chapter Twenty-Three

Edith awoke on the wrong side of the bed. The sunlight hit her face from the wrong angle. The entire room was aligned in the wrong direction. She recognized the hotel room slowly. Her heart settled down and the moment of waking panic passed.

American coffee made her feel equal to the list of tasks she had set for herself. At the top of the list was finding and speaking with A. Brown. With any luck she'd have seen the Riverside apartment by dinner time. Marjory had assured her that Sam was still the regular doorman; Edith was certain he could be made to understand her situation. And for relaxation, of a sort, she'd go back to the Hynes' apartment and retrieve her sapphire earring.

New York City was experiencing a break in its winter weather. Rising temperatures and a southerly wind made the streets feel of springtime. It was reassuring that the Imholc holiday should be so closely followed by the promise of fairer weather. Edith dressed as she would for a walk on the moors: thick-soled oxfords, a servicable cardigan with deep pockets and, of course, her walking stick. This time the walk up Manhattan did not seem to take so long.

"Sam?" she inquired, unbuttoning the cardigan and pulling off the matching stocking cap.

He hadn't changed much in the many years since she'd seen him last though he no longer wore a uniform and his hair had gone steely-grey. Bert often assured her that she hadn't changed much herself but she was surprised when Sam came out of his office with a broad grin of recognition.

"Mrs.—Mrs.? Why I've forgotten your name as sure as I remember your face. You're the image of your sister, Mrs. Andrews. You've come all the way from England—" The smile faded suddenly.

"Edith Brompton, Sam—you've got quite a good memory. Gwen's been gone these five years now. Sometimes I can hardly remember her face myself."

"Can't say as I remember everyone, Miz Brompton. Both of the Andrews went back to when this was a real home—a place where people knew each other. There aren't many of those left. You know, don't you—about Mr. Andrews?"

"About Arthur? Yes—well, not as much as I'd like. It was very sudden, there was no chance we could even talk to him before he died. There was so much left unknown—that's partly why I've come over. He'd been entertaining, hadn't he, when it happened?"

"Entertaining? He had an odd group over every month or so. The new neighbors didn't like it. They called the police this last time. It was too much for him.

"They sealed the apartment up right away. It was terrible—with the rumors and all. A disgrace to their memory and all the years they'd been here. The things people were saying—"

"Spare me," Edith held up a hand in protest. "What I'm interested in is what happened to the furniture and his personal belongings after his death. Are they in storage? There are a few things—sentimental mostly—"

Sam shook his head and was plainly ill-at-ease with the question. Edith affected a look of modest surprise.

"They haven't been destroyed or sold, have they?"

Marjory said she'd seen the furniture, but that was no guarantee everything was still intact. Arthur had made the necessary legal arrangments to insure that the apartment was leased intact—but the new tenant could possibly not have been told why 647 was a package deal.

"Not exactly," Sam explained, "no, not at all. Mr. Fine left everything as it was once the police were finished. Everything's signed over to the new tenant—just like it was supposed to be. Miss Lise Brown, she didn't have two sticks to rub together when she moved in but she might not have kept everything. These sentimental things, Miz Brompton, you know: one man's treasure's another's garbage."

Edith accepted his comment in silence. She had to believe the Gods would watch over the altar which Riverside had used. Although she herself had recently used a hotel desk as an altar she balked at facing the Riverside Rift without the Riverside altar. And if she could not imagine success then she would not achieve it no matter what else might happen.

"Miz Brompton, are you okay? Here, come inside and sit down."

Meekly Edith followed Sam into his office. The morning's confidence had vanished. She knotted her fingers together and let Sam think she was some silly old woman who grew faint at the loss of family snapshots; let him think anything while she sifted through the remnants of her pride-blind plans and adapted to harsh reality.

"I should like to see Miss Brown, at least—if she's here. I'd like to talk to her, just in case."

"She's most likely at work, but I'll try."

No-one was home in apartment 647. Edith wrote herself a letter-of-introduction and gave it to Sam trusting that he would give it to Lise as soon as possible. She borrowed his phone to call downtown to the Hynes. The phone was answered at once by an unfamiliar voice and a rush of slurred American syllables.

"Is this the Robert Hynes residence?" Edith asked hesitantly.

"It is," the man replied in what she felt was an unusually guarded tone.

"May I speak with Mr. Hynes, then?"

"I'm afraid that can't be arranged, Ma'am."

"Oh, is Marjory there? May I speak with her?"

"Un—no, Ma'am. There's been an accident."

Edith caught her heart beating in her throat. "An accident? To whom am I speaking?"

"Detective Joseph Berrens."

Images of the frightened couple in their overheated rooms flashed across her mind. There was other images too, none very pretty. She had felt the warning while she visited them—there had been no accident.

"Ma'am, we don't know exactly what happened—" the man began.

"—But, they're both dead, aren't they?" Edith blurted out. She was all alone and seeing the world as a more cohesive and malignant entity than it had ever seemed until this day.

"Yes, Ma'am, they're both dead. Are you a friend or relative of either of them?"

It was the Burning Times again; a time for carefully worded questions and even more carefully worded answers. She must know whatever the authorities knew or suspected, but they must never suspect her. They must never know of Riverside High Coven and its failure.

"Yes, a cousin from the UK," she dissembled quickly. "I've come over for a vacation. We were together last evening; I was calling about dinner tonight. This, this is unbelievable—" Edith paused for dramatic effect—it was all too believable for her. "Dear me—my earring, I left it there last night. I was going to pick it up at dinner—" she let her voice trail off.

The detective covered the phone then said that if she could come to the apartment they would be able to give her the earring if she would show them the second one. Edith agreed and the conversation ended.

There would be time later, she hoped, for the shock and grief she so rudely thrust from her thoughts. Events had speeded up precipitously and she had no alternative but to heave herself into the riptide after them.

Two police cars were parked near the brownstone but there was nothing else to show that two people had recently lost their lives to violence. The street door had been opened so she had no need of the bell. A faintly repulsive odor filled the stairwell as she climbed up to the second floor but it was not until she stepped through the demolished door to Rob's apartment that she recognized the scent.

It had been some time since the accident. The bodies were gone, but not the blood that had been splattered across the room with a gruesomeness Edith labelled inhuman. The space-heaters had been on when the murderous accident occurred and had been covered with gore like everything else. They were turned off now, but the charred smell lingered. She remembered the smell from the fires and destruction of the Blitz.

"Ma'am?"

The young detective startled her. He brought the horror of the room into sharper focus: here and there amid the bloodstains were wisps of hair, clothing and tiny lumps of humanity the forensic teams had somehow failed to collect. For the first time in her life Edith felt truly faint and staggered toward the nearest chair.

"Not there, Ma'am," the detective informed her as he grabbed her arm and steadied her. "Not in this room at all, Ma'am."

The dark shadows on the upholstery were damp spots of blood and worse. He gently guided her back into the hallway and interposed himself between her and the ghastly tableau. "You're the lady with the earring?"

Edith nodded and produced its mate. She wanted not to imagine what had happened but her thoughts were drawn toward that speculation with morbid irresistability.

"I think we've found it for you. If you'll just come with me into the other apartment over here. We'd like to ask you a few questions: just routine, then we'll give you the jewelry."

Edith followed him quietly into Marjory's apartment. She'd expected this. A second, older man introduced himself and she answered his list of questions with scrupulous honesty. Yes, she supposed she had been the last person to see them alive and yes, she did remember the number on the taxi-cab. No, she knew of no-one who might have killed them; she knew nothing about Hynes' business and very little of their personal lives—the family was not close. But she had thought they seemed obsessively frightened. Blackmail? Maybe—they had never married and no-one knew why.

The detectives were polite and recorded her answers but it was, as the younger man said, strictly routine and Edith ventured to ask a few questions of her own.

"The livingroom—I've never seen anything like that and I drove an ambulance during the War. Do you have any idea who did it?"

The younger man turned away from her, but the elder began speaking with tightly controlled emotion. "Madmen! There's an eyewitness—the woman upstairs—in shock at the hospital. And a cab-driver saw someone break the front window and climb onto the roof. A madman, a psychotic. He didn't kill these people, he tore them apart. Forensics didn't know where to start. There wasn't anything they could identify outside a lab—" He caught himself saying too much and shook the conversation out of his head. "We'll find him, Mrs. Brompton," he assured her. "I hope to God we find him before he kills again. He'll go to ground a while but he'll be back—they always are. We'll be waiting for him, I promise you that, Mrs. Brompton."

Edith answered him with silence. No Caer Maen reference to the Otherworld was complete without mentioning its hunger, but she had always thought in spiritual metaphors. Imholc had seen the spawning of some denizen of the Otherworld and it fed on the bodies of two Riverside witches who had felt its coming. But to tell the earnestly outraged officer that his promises were worthless and that security lay in an age-old ritual and a sixth-floor livingroom miles away would be more foolish than any High Coven Priestess could ever be.

She had one last glimpse of the apartment as they escorted her to the street. Her eyes would not see the blood but they saw Rob's crutches still leaning against the wall. Those bits of wood, unmarked, unmoved, brought the violence into her thoughts in a way that stayed with her well after she had left the building. The foul air of fear shrouded her like a cocoon. There was no-one with whom she could share her fear except the gods and what she had seen in that apartment had shaken her faith in the Gods.

People hurrying home on the crowded sidewalks had no time for a distracted old woman. Edith was jostled and sworn at more than once before she found herself back in front of the hotel, drained, exhausted and with nothing but shattered hopes to show for her day.

Though it seemed reasonable to assume that Sam would have told her if some unnatural horror had overtaken his building, Edith found it almost impossible to believe that Lise Brown could be alive, much less safe. Whatever had hunted Marjory and Rob had undoubtedly been hatched out of the Riverside Rift in Arthur's livingroom. Edith knew better than to second-guess the Otherworld, but it would not likely spare those who dwelt by the Rift however innocent that frightened young woman might have been.

Edith drew the curtains and cleared off the small excuse to a table the hotel decorators had planted under a dim ceiling lamp. She took a pair of silver candlesticks and green beeswax candles from within the mounds of lingerie in her dresser. Other hiding places yielded incense and a black-hilted athame—the knife Wiccan initiates used in the working of magick.

Within hours of erupting the Otherworld had found two of those who had been its keeper and guardian. Edith supposed it would be able to find her just as easily. Wiccan rituals offered the hope of protection from even the Otherworld, but Edith placed a call to Bert's office, just in case.

She spoke the traditional words of warding to seal the cracks of the windows and doors, the pipes and drains in the bathroom and even the electric fixtures and telephone against vagrant evil before the phone rang. She heard the voice of Bert's anxious clerk telling her that Bert had not come to the office and that he was planning to drive up to Caer Maen after hours to learn if something had gone wrong.

Edith held back her tears until she'd hung up the phone. Then she knelt on the floor by the table and let her forehead rest against the plastic-wood tabletop where the candles and incense still burned.

"Dear Sweet Lady of the Night—whatever shall I do now?"

Chapter Twenty-Four

"You're looking much better," Rachel said to Lise.

Lise wasn't certain she agreed. When she had last surfaced from her drugged sleep she had succumbed at once to hysteria and been given a second shot. A tranquil dizziness lingered and it took exhausting concentration to recognize Rachel and piece together the events of the past days.

Recent events had not been kind to her favorite nightgown. Several inches of lace hung loose from the sleeve and half of the embroidered roses had fallen off. But, in expectation of her guest's eventual resurrection, Rachel had provided fresh towels and a new toothbrush. She had also procured, laundered and ironed the clothes Lise had left on the bathroom floor of her own apartment before all this had started.

"Just how long have I been out?" Lise asked.

"Two nights, one day. Your boyfriend, Alan, left yesterday morning. I tried to get him to go a doctor but he'd have nothing to do with the idea; some people are like that. I don't think there was anything physically wrong with him. He left a note for you across the hall."

"Across the hall? You mean in my apartment?"

She should have guessed, if her clothes were here, that they had gone into 647 already. Alan would have wanted his clothes— She imagined herself unlocking the door and got a case of the shakes. She'd have to go over there sooner or later; the Ratners couldn't be expected to shelter her forever. It was an unexpected miracle that they'd helped her at all.

"How about something to eat?" Rachel asked when Lise had emerged from the bathroom. She was already gathering up Lise's discarded nightgown and the once-used towels. "C'mon out to the kitchen."

Lise settled into the Swedish-modern breakfast nook.

"I should warn you: we keep kosher," Rachel explained before she opened any of the cabinet doors.

A Mid-western upbringing had provided Lise with only the barest details of Jewish domestic customs and, while Rachel cooked, Lise's curiosity was lured out into the open. It was a half-hour before Lise suspected that Rachel was teaching her the particulars of an Orthodox household rather than discuss anything else.

"What was it like over there?"

"To tell you the truth, Lise, I didn't go over. Mark explained just enough to Sam to get the keys from him; He and Alan went over yesterday. Apparently there's been no major destruction. I probably shouldn't say this, but I expected everything would've been reduced to kindling. It bothers me to think we could have seen that *thing* and then find out it hadn't disturbed anything but us."

"I should go home, then," Lise said aloud to herself. "If there's no damage I should just go back; tell myself it didn't happen, even if it did. I'm okay; the apartment's okay. I shouldn't be taking up your space. Pick up the reins and get moving—as my grandfather would say." But the Michigan farm had never seemed so distant or irrelevant.

"You don't have to go," Rachel reassured her. "At least wait until Mark gets home and we can all go over. Maybe he was wrong and something has been damaged. Anyway, you shouldn't go over by yourself and I'm not going over with you without Mark. Another few hours won't hurt."

Lise was persuaded. The Ratners' apartment offered isolation and grace. Rachel went back to her legal papers and Lise read the newspapers she'd missed. The *Times* had lapsed into lurid reportage in response to the latest criminal psychotic loose on the streets; a pair of unnamed, dismembered and partially devoured corpses had been found in a quiet East Side neighborhood. The elegant words conveyed what a *Post* photograph never could. The overall story, however, reassured Lise that her personal traumas had not interferred with daily life in New York City.

When Mark returned home the three of them went to Lise's apartment. They stayed close by as she investigated, poking into all the corners and cabinets. She conceded that, except for the now-righted hall table, nothing had been moved, much less damaged during the night of terror. The lingering malice of the livingroom was gone too—as if the room had finally purged itself.

"Will you stay here again?" Mark asked as Lise pulled the blankets over the unmade bed.

"Well, I guess there's no reason not to— Well, maybe I could call Alan. He'd understand. Just for tonight, of course; I've got to come back home sooner or later."

"Give us his name and number, then—he didn't leave it. If the place stays quiet for another night or so we can tell you and you can think about coming back then—" Rachel's voice trailed off as if there were things she wouldn't say.

"Or, you could just call Bernie Fine now. He's got other buildings," Mark suggested.

"No, Mark, if it stays quiet then everything will get back to normal. It's never good to run. Once you start running you can't ever stop. If it's quiet tomorrow, Lise can come back."

Rachel willed herself to walk alone into the livingroom as she spoke. It was all well and good for her to say it was time for Lise to come back; she lived on the far side of a different locked door. The Ratner's were probably cured of an interest in living in 647 themselves.

"Don't forget Alan's note," Rachel called. "It's here on the table."

"Dear Lise," it began. "Forgive me for running out on you like this but I can't face you, this apartment or anything. I've talked to the office and cleared everything for you to take a few days off—I said your apartment'd been broken into. Everyone understood that you'd need a few days to recover. I'm going out-of-town myself. We'll decide if we can put the pieces back later."

He'd signed it with his initials; the same way he signed his memos. Lise folded the paper and dropped it into the wastebasket.

"He was wrecked, Lise," Mark explained. "He reminded me of the guys comin' back from 'Nam."

"But what about me? Aren't I pretty wrecked too? We could have helped each other," Lise complained bitterly.

"If you got together what would you say to each other? All you could tell each other is how frightened you were and still are. You'd both wind up locked up for good. You'd be better off to stay with someone you know but who doesn't really *know* about your apartment. Get away from anything that'd remind you of the other night. Maybe you could visit Michigan."

But Lise called Maria and in a voice that could not be denied asked for refuge.

"Are you hurt?" Maria asked when Lise had provided the barest details.

"No, not where it shows, anyway. Alan's taken off. I've been over with Rachel and Mark Ratner since it happened," Lise explained, mindful that though the Ratners were still in the room with her, Maria would guess how extraordinary the situation must be.

"Can you get here on your own or should we come and get you?"

"I'll take a cab down as soon as I pack up a few things."

The Ratners stayed while she grabbed the minimum overnight survival kit and stuffed it into a canvas bag along with her knitting—this last in hope that the demanding tedium of knitted lace would draw her away from her darker thoughts.

Maria responded to the SOS in the traditional Agnelli way: a glass of wine was waiting for her and the spaghetti sauce was bubbling on the stove. Bob had been dragooned into exemplary behavior. But it wasn't enough. Simple distance did not make the terror retreat. As the tranquilizers wore off completely Lise was consumed by pacing fretfulness.

She finally convinced Maria to go to bed after the late news. The television offered up a raft of progressively older movies; Lise knit error-filled inches of lace but, finally, a costume-epic crone hovering over a skull-shaped candle jarred her memory back to usefulness.

If nothing else it was February: Culpeper's should have opened; Hynes might be back at the bank. It was four AM but Lise achieved non-drugged sleep.

"There really was no need for you to take a day off," Lise

said as she and Maria headed uptown for Culpeper's the next afternoon. "Now that I've gotten some real sleep I'm feeling a lot saner."

"You didn't look particularly sane when you found out Hynes'd been murdered," Maria grumbled.

"I saw that article in the *Times*—who'd think it could be someone I sort of knew, that's all. It took me by surprise. And, anyway, it's not as if I'd struck out; Culpeper's reopened on time."

Maria muttered something under her breath and Lise had the sense not to discuss the matter any further. Suzanne Hirshhorn had broken down into tears when Lise called the bank. Lise had shared that sense of loss for a moment, but not very much longer. She hadn't known the couple, certainly hadn't liked them. It was terrible that they had been murdered, but she was just as glad to cross them off her list of options.

A new coat of paint graced the front of Culpeper's building. Art Nouveau scrolls curled around the doorframe; a painted fairy held the words Culpeper's Herbal in her hands. The smell of fresh paint overwhelmed all the old aromas in the now-bright stairwell. Another fairy pointed to the door-buzzer.

"Hi, Lise," Jason greeted them. "Sally's in the back acquainting our newest employee with the mysteries of the mail-order files. I'll tell her you're here. Look around; admire the power of white paint and window cleaner."

The basic layout of the store was unchanged, but that didn't diminish the transformation. Dusty and ominious mystery had been replaced by a lighter sort of magick. Everything had been cleaned, polished and displayed in an airy, almost ethereal, way. The friends were still exploring the endless array of oddments when they were summoned behind the black velvet curtains.

"Sally's waiting," the unfamiliar voice repeated.

His sudden appearance from behind the curtains caught Lise in panic. She looked in the direction of the voice and was momentarily blinded by the strong sunlight as it bounced off a new mirror. The Otherworld globe had blinded her the same way, and the memory chilled her.

"Go on back," he said. "Is something wrong?"

Lise pulled her attention away from memory. She blinked and stared before seeing the stranger as a pale-skinned young man, dark-haired and quite attractive in a way completely opposite of Alan. By then Sally had come out from the other side of the curtain.

"Lise, what did you see?" she asked matter-of-factly.

Though she had come to Culpeper's for help, Lise was tongue-tied. She looked away from the man but couldn't bring herself to speak of the Phenomena in his presence. He smiled and it became a bit easier.

"Memories," she stammered. "The mirrors reminded me of what I came here for—brought it all back home, as it were."

"That's the first complaint we've had about the redecorating," Jason added and laughter swept away the awkwardness. "We'll have to buy some dirt. Nigel, can you watch the store while I head to the bank and Sally talks to Lise?"

Nigel walked silently to the cash register while Lise and Maria followed Sally behind the curtains. Sally had seen the Phenomena and was disposed to listen to Lise's tale without disbelief. Maria had seen the Phenomena too, and she muttered that nothing, now, would get her back in those rooms again. When Lise was finished, Sally poured tea.

"Even if you don't go back there to live, Lise, you should try to cleanse the place. It's like a cancer up there and it will only plague the next tenant—however quiet it seems now."

"I've decided I'm staying up there," Lise said firmly.

"You can't," Maria exclaimed. "It's getting worse all the time. You could be killed!"

"I know—and, believe me, I'd sort of like to leave," Lise said without looking at her friend. "I feel like that kid with his finger in the dike; if I run then everybody'll run. It's a pain to be the one whose finger's stuck, but that's the way it is. The Phenomena are bigger than me, but in some ways I'm the one with power over them. I can make a difference up there.

Does that make sense to you, Sally?"

"Only if you protect yourself from that power. It's a good idea to be grounded before you decide to be a lightning rod. You're up against real power and you've already got some idea of the real damage it can do."

"Can I just learn to ground myself, as you say, or do I have to accept witchcraft and everything connected with it first?" Lise demanded slowly.

Sally sat back in her chair, sweeping her cloud of hair into one hand. "I could teach you to protect yourself but I'd rather not. The Craft *is* the best protection you could have. It's a positive alternative to all that's happening to you and it can help you avoid the temptations that power always brings. Besides, after what happened to Jessica, you'll need more than individual power."

"I was afraid you were going to say that," Lise admitted. At four in the morning she'd told herself she'd pay any price for Culpeper's help; becoming a witch, considered at two in the afternoon, did not seem like a rational price.

"We're starting a Pagan Way class here," Sally continued when Lise said nothing more. "We'll be teaching the Wiccan traditions but none of the mysteries: no-strings witchcraft. The Old Religion is strong enough again that we can think in terms of a congregation as well as a priesthood. I look at Pagan Way as something for the sincerely curious. You might think about it; the class runs for six weeks starting next week."

"What've you got with strings? I don't think I've got six weeks to spend satisfying my curiosity," Lise sighed.

"You especially should be sure of your commitment," Sally warned. "If you don't feel it's right— The Craft magnifies your intentions and if they're bad we'll all suffer."

"I'm ready," Lise replied.

"Well, I've got a Dedication class at four-thirty on Sundays. I've got novices from over a half-different covens coming together once a week to learn the Craft. I'm not kidding around with them; I expect everyone in Dedication to take the Craft seriously. I told Nigel I wasn't sure about him because, frankly, we hired him to bail us out of our mail-order backlog, not to become a witch, but if he can try, you can too."

"I'd like to sign up, too," Maria said suddenly, "I've been doing my homework. I know what I want."

"Sunday's our Dedication Class, as I've said I'm reserving it for novices sponsored by covens or people I know something about. I think you'll be better off coming to the Pagan Way." Sally was polite, but firm.

"My mind's made up. Maybe you don't know me, but you know Lise; more important, you know her apartment. I think she might need me before this is over. She'll vouch for my character." Maria was equally polite and firm.

"Well, yes—" Lise stammered. "But I didn't think you were interested in any of this."

"Yes, friendship is admirable, but it's not a good reason for taking up the Craft," Sally argued.

"It's good enough just about everywhere else," Maria complained. "I've been terrorized in that apartment, too. I want to help get rid of it—isn't that a good enough reason?"

Sally didn't challenge Maria further. Lise accepted the tangible support with as much grace as she could muster and didn't ask questions until they were signed up, paid up and back on the street.

"First off," Maria began with a trace of indignation in her voice, "Father Britey laughed when I told him what happened. Then I talked to my mother and she told me about the *strega* and an aunt of mine I never met. I've thought about it a lot and whatever your Phenomena really are it is my Christian, Catholic duty (just as Father Britey would say) to become a witch and do something about them.

"Besides, the church and the Craft aren't completely incompatible. No-one's going to ask me to recite the Lord's Prayer backwards. I'll admit, though, I decided between the Pagan Way class and the Dedication class when I realized Nigel might be in the Dedication class."

"I saw him first!" Lise laughed. "Besides, you're a happily married old lady now."

"I know—and I'm not attracted to him. That's the problem; I didn't like what I felt when I looked at him. I don't like his smile—it reminds me of your Phenomena; witches're supposed to trust these odd hunches, you know."

Chapter Twenty-Five

One emotion set the tone of Edith's life in New York City: loneliness. Loneliness that gripped her whenever she thought of Gwen or Arthur or of the blood-spattered walls in Rob Hynes' apartment. Loneliness that kept her in her hotel room in empty despondency doubting herself and all that she had ever trusted. She wrote, and mailed, rambling letters back home and all but gave up eating. The Brown girl had never returned her calls or messages. A second trip uptown had coerced from Sam the information that something "odd" had happened early in the morning of February first. He hadn't seen the young woman since then and didn't know if she even intended to return.

Powerful, frightening nightmares seethed through Edith's sleep with such intensity that she could not escape them even during the day. Even the good news that the Imholc rite at Caer Maen had gone very well rather than poorly and the coven had stayed together an extra day for companionship's sake did not lighten her spirits but pushed them down further.

Her loneliness continued to deepen until the first of her letters reached home, setting off a flurry of concern that forced her to bolster herself lest all of Caer Maen fly to her in panic. Edith Brompton, Lady Camulac, High Priestess of Caer Maen smiled at the sunlight until she was glad it was light; she conversed with the hotel staff until she was glad there were people in the world; she restored herself. Armed with a page copied from the yellow pages, she went out to visit the occult supply houses; kindred spirits must exist in this metropolis and she intended to find them.

Culpeper's Herbal topped her list; it was in the best neighborhood and was large enough to purchase a small ad instead of a single line of print. She approved of the fresh, clean paint, the graceful fairies and the well-lit stairs and climbed to the second floor with increasing confidence.

"Are you the proprietor?" she asked the dark-haired young man behind the counter.

"No, I just work here," Nigel answered.

Their eyes locked a moment, clearing away Edith's depression and replacing it with a shivering edge of fear. Neither bothered with subtlety as they took the measure of each other. Her thoughts formed the words of a common self-defense spell as she battled with his intense black eyes. He broke away first.

"Sally's in the back, if you want to talk with an owner," he said as if the encounter had not occurred.

There was no victory surge; Edith was not able to go on as if nothing had happened. Her nerves had been suddenly, violently abraided. The menacing force she had seen in the man's face had vanished without a trace, but she was not at all convinced it had disappeared.

"Yes, I must speak with her," she said stiffly. She was halfway to the black curtains when she pretended something had caught her eye and glanced backwards. But even the truer sight at the corners of her eyes did not reveal the inner spirit of the man. She lifted the curtain to one side and steeled herself for the worst.

Sally looked up and this time the moment of strangeness passed in a moment. Edith's doubts faded, even the fear she had felt in the outer room; she had found someone to talk to. They established their credentials; trading names and places while Sally steeped fresh herbal tea.

They found the common touchstones of their beliefs: age-old Celtic Wicca and modern poly-cultural paganism. They understood each other's Craft.

"And you've come all this way just to see what sort of Craft is being done over here?" Sally asked with gentle disbelief.

"It's more than that," Edith conceded. Ironically she was less inclined to speak of the Otherworld with someone who would understand its dangers than she would have been with someone completely ignorant of magick. "My sister died over five years ago; my brother-in-law last Samhain. Since then three more members of their coven have died; actually, there might be more deaths—I don't know the names of everyone in their coven. At one time they were a full third-degree circle."

Sally frowned. "I can understand your concern, but, honestly—I don't know of anything mysterious happening on such a scale and, while I don't doubt you, I think I'd have heard of a third-degree circle's problems."

"It would surprise me. Riverside kept the old ways. I'm sure there was never any knowledge of the coven. They didn't think very highly of your American neo-paganism, I'm afraid."

"Riverside?" Sally interrupted, twisting her fingers through her apricot hair. "Was the coven named Riverside, or was that its location?"

"Both," Edith said, watching the lights of recognition glow in Sally's eyes. "They lived on Riverside Drive and the coven took its name from the address."

"I know it. They never came to us and I've no idea who they were; I've learned what I know since Samhain." Sally spoke softly. "The girl who moved in after your brother-in-law's death, Lise Brown, she's part of my first-degree Dedication Class."

Edith smiled with happiness: Lise Brown had resisted; she wasn't part of the Otherworld—yet. "This Lise Brown, I've been trying to find her. I've wondered about the altar and the Riverside ritualware."

"From what she's told me, she took the apartment over lock, stock and pussycat. I've been there and it has the mark of a covenstead—she hasn't changed much. She's not there right now, though."

Edith sensed the change in Sally's mood, the very real concern in her voice. Sally would not break confidence, but Edith could see that Lise was having problems.

"Riverside coven did ritualwork of importance; they were part of a very old tradition. I believe the untimely deaths are not outside pressure but the result of a—a failure in their Samhain ritual." Edith's memory focused not on the Riverside apartment but on Rob Hynes' crutches.

Sally shuddered as if she shared the vision and revealed

what she knew of the Phenomena. In the end she produced Maria DelVecchio's phone number, assuring Edith that Lise was staying there. With exquisite irony Edith knew she might already have seen the woman; Maria lived less than two blocks from the hotel.

"There is one last thing you might help me with," Edith said as she folded Sally's paper into her wallet. "I'm having dreams about a black man, a few years younger than myself. I see him being beaten to death. I don't suppose you've seen a very tall black man, thin and bald? In the dreams he has a top hat and a walking stick—"

Sally shrugged. "Our voodoo notwithstanding, you can count the number of blacks who come here on the fingers of one hand. I'll keep my ears open. Everybody in the City's heard about those Eastside murders. If they were Craft, I'll start hearing rumors pretty quickly."

They went out into the store. Sally played proud-parent and Edith made appreciative noises as she looked at the array of neatly labelled esoterica. She took time to browse through their herbs and gathered a selection that would remind her of Caer Maen without unduly alarming the maids at the hotel.

"Did Sally tell you how to find Lise?" Nigel whispered behind her back.

Edith turned around without answering. She did not like silent moving people, though she was one herself.

"I hear she's with friends. Hard to say how long *that* will last—staying with your old boyfriend and his new wife might almost be worse than living at home—don't you think?" he confided.

"I've a phone number," Edith said icily. He must have been eaves-dropping—and she'd said more than she should have. The shadow of malice was back in his face—simple, petty malice, she prayed. Without further comment she dumped her purchases on the counter and waited while he took her money and placed the herbs in an unlabelled sack.

Edith marched straight to a phone booth and dialed Maria's number. In turn she got Lise's office number and finally heard Lise Brown's voice.

"You're the English lady, aren't you?" Lise asked bluntly. "I recognize your name. I guess if you've tracked me down through Sally, she's told you my secrets. I'm at my office and I don't talk about these things here. I guess you know that I've been driven out of *my* home."

Edith couldn't miss the bitterness in Lise's voice, but she was not wholly discouraged. The young woman had formed a strong attachment to Riverside; that could only mean that she had been as influenced by the lingering High Coven magick as she might have been by the Otherworld. Edith said nothing of this, however, and only mentioned her desire to meet Lise. She suggested they meet for dinner.

"I guess if you've come all this way, the least I can do is eat with you. I'm not going back uptown for a while yet—but there're places around here."

"That will be fine," Edith allowed, although she had hoped to get inside Riverside.

Lise rattled off a list of restaurants. Edith fastened on one name and parroted it back. She memorized the address Lise gave her and rang off. There were four hours before she was to meet Lise and she spent most of them planning her questions and explanations.

The young woman was already at the restaurant when Edith arrived fifteen minutes early. Edith assessed her from a distance; Sally's physical description had been both complete and accurate. Lise was attractive enough, though she didn't compare with Elizabeth—but that might be maternal pride. Neatness and inconspicuousness seemed to be the hallmark of her business personality but her face had some of the marks of a strong, almost stubborn, person. All of which was good. Her movements were nervous, which, in light of what Sally had related, was not surprising.

In their first awkward hello Edith felt both Lise's exhaustion and her wariness. She abandoned any hope of luring Lise uptown. The young woman needed help and reassurance first. Edith channelled her energies into breaking Lise's barrier of fear and preparing her for the knowledge she would eventually need if she were to survive in Riverside.

"I thought getting out on my own would make things better," Lise insisted, "but I guess I put too much faith in the material world and didn't look inside enough. I've thought, really, that the Phenomena are, well—extensions of my own problems. At first I did—so many people've been affected now, I'm not sure any more. On some deep down level I just don't believe that what's happening is happening, or that it's magic and witchcraft."

"It's hard to say, Lise. If you hadn't moved into that apartment, perhaps getting out on your own would have done everything for you. You don't seem all that undirected and unsettled to me, even now," Edith replied as she set down her wine. "You remember, though, the legend of the Seige Perilous?" Lise muttered that she didn't. "The Seige Perilous was the last seat at the Round Table and it called its own knight. Some people are drawn, fated if you will, to be in places they would never consciously choose."

"Are you trying to say I was pulled to that apartment? I've heard *that* theory too," Lise stated. "I backed into the lease—nothing called me. Maybe I wasn't exactly tricked, but I didn't know what I was getting into—and I wouldn't make the same mistake again."

Edith let the conversation slide into benign subjects for the duration of the meal. It was not until the dinner plates were gone that their conversation took an occult turn, and to Edith's surprise it was Lise who turned it.

"If it's not unforgivable to be curious, since you've met Sally and you already know so much about me—can you tell me just what sort of a witch your brother-in-law was, say, compared with what Sally's teaching me?"

Edith automatically judged the distance to the nearest occupied table before speaking. "I really think that it's only when you take lesson in the Craft that you can think of competing products. But, if you need a label you could say we're hereditary witches. We learned our Craft within families and covensteads that go way back before the time when your witchcraft, or Sally's witchcraft, was concocted. Though—this isn't to say she's any the less a witch—"

Lise nodded abruptly as if her question had been answered and she needed no additional information. "Okay, so far, so good. Your brother-in-law died on Hallowe'en, Samhain, after or during a ritual that got raided by the police who thought it was a drug-orgy. I can understand that much—

"Don't get me wrong. Everyone assures me that your brother-in-law was as lily-white as they come but it was his death that set all this in motion. I find it very hard to understand how such a *good* person came to be messed up with such monumentally evil things," Lise concluded defiantly.

She laid down her fork and stared past Edith.

"It was his obligation, his *droit,*" Edith stammered. Four thousand years of tradition was too strong; she could not talk of the High Coven in a public room. At Riverside with the Gods, perhaps even in Culpeper's—though she had taken excessive risks there—but not here. "We failed to do what we must do each Samhain—that is the root of the evil and why I've come this far to set it right."

"You're going to set things right? Mrs. Brompton, I've tried very hard to understand you, please try to understand me—"

Edith felt her back stiffen. Lise was not one to be reassured by strength, as Rob and Marjory had been. The young woman's jaw was set in a hard line—the only question left was how far had Edith overstepped?

"Something's escaped from my livingroom. I think it's damaged a very close friend's mind. You've said it killed two people. You also tell me that this could be just the beginning if I don't let you set things right. Now, six months ago I could have laughed in your face, but you seem sane enough and rather than laugh I would have let you play your games in my livingroom. But it isn't six months ago and I can't let you—or anyone else—do something I don't understand or don't truly believe in my livingroom.

"So, you'll say I believe the bad in what you say but not the good—and I'll have to agree with you. I'd like to trust you Edith, I truly would; I'd like nothing better than to drop this mess in your lap—but I don't trust anyone and yet *I'm* responsible for that occult pollution. If I let you try something and it didn't work— You might be one-hundred percent honest and I might be making a terrible mistake, but if I have to choose between fighting the Phenomena my own way and making that mistake I'll choose the mistake."

Edith swallowed her despair. She was being defeated not by Otherworld malice but by the carefully nurtured secrecy and obligation the High Covens wove into their covensteads. Were she in Lise's place her reaction would not have been disimilar—but she would have the power of Caer Maen beside her and this woman only had her stubbornness and whatever latent talent had made her compatible with the covenstead of Riverside in the first place.

"Then I won't come to your home," she said. "If you wish me to stay away; if that will increase your own confidence and strength then I will stay away. I won't leave New York, and if you change your mind I will be waiting for you to help you, but Lise, I do trust you and I pray that whatever you do will be triumphant."

Lise fidgeted, unprepared for Edith's capitulation. "I don't want your prayers—I'm not familiar with your hereditary magick. I can't turn to you. Sally can teach me—I'm taking her class."

Edith wouldn't shatter Lise's illusions. Sally was a conscientious desciple of the Old Religion; a woman the Wiccans could be proud of, but she was no High Coven witch and the Otherworld could flick Sally aside more easily than it could touch Lise herself if it took a notion to.

Chapter Twenty-Six

It had been a week since Lise moved back into her apartment; two weeks since she had barred Edith Brompton from it. She was afraid of the livingroom as she had not been afraid before, though the room was Phenomena-less, but she lived with her fear. Sally's Dedication class was underway and she carried the Wicca before her like a shield when she went through the French doors.

She knew the place was only resting from the Imholc event. She used garlic and honey, frankincense and rosemary as Sally had taught her to confine the terrors in their eventual return. Her ability to face the future faltered only when she thought about Alan.

Wiccan magick was most often, and most successfully, performed by a man and a woman working together. Alan would have nothing to do with the Craft now that she was involved with it. He'd returned from his family's suburban home before Edith met Lise for dinner and had been in the fast-lane to a nervous breakdown since. He had asked her out each Saturday night since his return and cancelled out at the last moment each time. Despite his promise of reform, Lise was sure he would cancel again sometime before he was expected at seven-thirty.

She thought she knew who was calling at six-fifteen, only to hear Nigel's voice.

"Hey, I know it's *tres gauche* to ask a woman to dinner on fifteen minutes notice, but I don't think I can face another hamburger alone. How about dinner for two? I got paid today; you can even have french fries! Even if you've already eaten, you're invited just for the company." He was oozing charm. Lise thought of herself, dressed for dinner, and of Alan who most likely would not show up to take her out.

"That sounds nice," she said slowly.

"But you've already got plans?" he said wistfully.

She thought again of Alan. These days his company was grim, his conversation both limited and morose. Nigel offered a pleasant evening, but she owed something to Alan.

"I'm waiting for a phone call."

"Take the phone off the hook. Anyone who'd keep you waiting longer than me is definitely not worth it."

"He's an old, close friend. We need to talk—"

"Okay, okay—I'll tell ya what: I'll buy our dinners and bring them with me. If he calls, I'll vanish. What kind of wine do you prefer with your Big Mac?"

The words—no thank you, maybe some other time—were primed on her tongue, but she said "Lafite Rothschild 1972," instead. Unpleasant and self-imposed obligations could not always prevail. It would take Nigel and hour to get uptown; Alan should have shown up or bowed out by then. If Nigel arrived to find an empty apartment he'd understand and probably kid about it at the Dedication Class. He wasn't the sort of person who ever seemed to take offense.

He had thick, black hair that barely covered his ears and an elven grin that carried him through each outlandish act. He'd taken Culpeper's by storm, adapting quickly and adding his own style to everything. No-one knew much about his past or his ambitions; he talked as if he'd been everywhere and done everything already, though he couldn't be over thirty.

It was past seven; Alan had not called and in embarrassed, ashamed desperation Lise had tried to call him. There was no answer and she remembered why, for so many years, she had shunned the path of reckless pleasure. She got her coat out of the closet, in case Alan showed up and they left in a hurry; she rinsed her wineglasses, in case Nigel had taken her seriously. She paced from one window to the next.

"Oogod, don't let them meet in the lobby—"

Nigel pounded up the pavement like a street-tough. No matter that he had only just arrived in the big city; he had naturalized with an ease that left Lise openly envoius.

"Oogod, don't let Alan show up now!"

Not Alan whose sophistication had vanished that black night. Not Alan who couldn't handle a challenge right now. But, if he didn't show up—and he wasn't at home—then where was he? Had his roller-coaster finally jumped the tracks? A tide of genuine concern and fear swelled up then ebbed as the intercom announced Nigel's arrival. She finger-combed her hair; adjusted the waist of her sweater and waited anxiously by the open door.

"So, how's life, liberty and the happiness of pursuit?" he asked, kicking the door shut behind them and enveloping her in a hug that was a bit more than friendly. "Your friend call in yet?"

"No, I'm still waiting."

She paused but he was heading down the hall to the livingroom. "Nice place. The wine has to breathe at least two minutes or a million irate Frenchmen come out of your glass and assault you with over-ripe brie."

Lise relaxed anyway as he followed her in her search for a corkscrew. He had made himself at home: shoes off, feet on the sofa pillows. Lise shed her own shoes and curled up discretely at the other end of the sofa, enjoying his chatter, reminding herself that this was, indeed, the way she'd expected life alone to be and only occasionally looking out the window or listening for the elevator cables. Her thoughts were far from Alan when the fates brought him to her door.

"Hi," she said through a forced smile. "I'd stopped thinking you were coming," she continued and wished at once she hadn't.

Alan's eyes were hollow and deeply shadowed. They swam with thoughts that never surfaced into speech. "We had a date, I thought," he said simply. "It took me longer than I expected; I had things to do. I'm sorry, but at least I did make it."

Alan's coat wore him instead of the other way around, emphasizing the weight he had already lost. For a moment Lise hated him for the weakness the Phenomena had placed on him.

"When you weren't here—after the last few times like this— Well, the point is, Alan, another friend of mine called and came over for dinner. I was hungry. I didn't really expect you."

"Can I join you? I'm not terribly hungry anyway." He did

not retreat from the doorway. "Or is your friend another man?"

"Nigel called, we're in the Wicca class together. We've talked; said we should get together sometime. I couldn't see spending another Saturday night here worrying about you and feeling guilty over everything."

"Oh," Alan stared at Nigel who was now in the hallway at the French doors. "I guess the conversation's a bit too private and secret for outsiders?"

"Not really, we haven't learned any secrets yet. We're just talking about the Craft in general," Lise lied, but Alan's disinterest in the Wicca had been stated many times.

"But, no skeptics allowed?"

"I don't see any point in arguing the Craft with one more person, Alan." Lise's voice filled with frustration.

"Okay," Alan muttered. "See you on Monday, then." And he headed down the stairs without looking back. Lise held the door open until he reached the third floor landing then she locked it.

"Was that your friend?" Nigel asked gently.

She nodded.

"Your friend needs help, I'd say. A few problems there."

Nigel led her back to the livingroom where he installed her against the pillows and refilled her wineglass.

"And what about you? Would it do you any good to talk about it. From what I overheard this isn't much of a friendship you two've got going."

Lise stared at the wine. "I guess it's not all for friendship. I owe him. He's like this because of me."

"Ah," Nigel nodded knowingly, "so he's the one?"

Lise nodded. She hadn't spoken about the Phenomena at the Dedication class but Nigel, as an employee at Culpeper's, knew more about her problems than she had directly told him.

"He got run over, literally, on Imholc. I didn't see it—I fell down the stairs and blacked out—and he won't really talk about it, but something snapped; he's wrecked now. He was one of the ones who told me about Culpeper's in the first place and now he practically goes nuts when I mention the

Craft. I think he's been having dreams; I know he's taking too many pills."

Nigel was properly concerned and outraged. He drained his glass and emptied the bottle refilling it before he spoke again. "Maybe he needs special help?"

"I've tried everything I can think of."

"But what about the Craft itself, Lise? A little proverbial white magick to help him find the light?"

"No," she said firmly. "I wouldn't feel right about it—and certainly not here. The first thing I'm going to do once I'm initiated is clean out this apartment—and I'm not going to do anything else in here until I do."

"I know I haven't experienced any of these Phenomena, Lise, but I honestly don't feel anything all that evil here. Maybe just by living here you've purged the evil away?"

"I haven't," Lise said, turning away from his smile.

Nigel took her hands. "Hey, I don't know. I don't want you to be upset. I was just putting my clumsy fingerprints all over things—But, if it's that bad why don't you just *do* the room. We must have twenty different room-blessing rituals in stock at C-P's."

"I'm not ready. Sally hasn't taught us."

"Lise, you've got it *all* wrong. Magick isn't something you're taught; magick is something that exists inside you. If this room bothers you; if you need to cleanse it, then you can—right now. We can do it right now!"

Lise wriggled free. "No, really. I'd be too nervous. I don't know what might get out. One of Sally's friends tried magick in here and it wasn't very nice."

The wine had gotten to him. He vowed to meditate and purify the room if only she'd show him the most offensive spots. He'd do almost anything to help her be rid of her fear of the room. Lise laughed but he persisted with a quiet intensity.

"What about here?" he asked, standing on the very spot where all the horrors had begun. Lise was speechless. "Ah! So this is the spot! Out damned spot—out I say!" he exaulted. "But, seriously, Lise. Sit beside me, we'll beat this thing for once and for all."

"No, Nigel."

"Then I'll try to do it myself—but it won't be as convincing."

He spun down into a full lotus position: arms extended, palms on knees, fingertips touching thumbs, and, as Lise watched, he plunged into a profoundly visual meditation. His facial muscles were slack and his breathing barely noticable. She watched in discomfort, amazement and finally awe through the passing of twenty minutes. He left the meditative state with a ripple of tension ending as his eyes opened already focused on her.

"There's nothing here, Lise. Join me and see for yourself."

Lise sat down in front of him. A full lotus position was beyond her, but she wriggled her back, shook out her arms and let her hands flop, palms down, on her knees. Nigel turned her hands over and held them.

"Come with me—there's nothing to fear in this place."

She doubted him almost enough to pull her hands back. His fingers grew colder but their firm hold did not weaken. His relaxed breathing was contagious; her mind did wander through literal images of warmth and peace until it achieved a state where she no longer thought at all.

"There, see—that wasn't so hard," Nigel chided, squeezing her hands.

The clock showed another twenty minutes had passed.

"Whatever else happens on Beltane, May-eve, we'll meet here and remove whatever fears remain in this room and in you."

He spoke with confidence and this time she did not doubt him. She had never before gotten to the legendary plateau of ecstasy in her meditation attempts. She held his hands tightly in silent gratitude and looked into his eyes. Without breaking the visual thrall, Nigel guided her hands to his thighs and pulled her forward against him.

"Not here," Lise protested as he wound around her with feline adroitness, undoing her clothing with ease.

"Why not?"

"I'll be cold?"

He laughed. "I'll keep you warm enough," and ran his fingers along her ribs as he gathered her beneath him.

Lise felt nothing but the warmth of him around her. Once, as she felt hard, hot teeth behind his kisses, she knew that she could not have resisted him, much less stopped him—but she had no desire to either resist or stop. At first she kept her eyes open, but there was a daunting nakedness in his expression and she shut them for privacy.

There seemed no limit to his capacity for passion. He teased her to orgiasmic heights, indulged her languor then began again. She complained once, when a handful of hair got caught beneath them. For a moment sharp claws dug at her shoulders, then he lifted her slightly and she slipped back into rapture.

When she awoke it was Sunday afternoon. Her clothes were scattered across the carpet beside hamburger cartons and the empty wine bottle. But for that, and the unmistakable listlessness above her thighs, it might all have been a dream. Nigel had disappeared leaving her warmed by an afghan and her discarded coat. It was too late to get to the Dedication Class.

A radio broadcast the usual baker's dozen of good news: the Eastside Slasher had struck again killing at least two. There was something unique about this one. The police needed at least an extra day to know how many bodies they were working with. She hoped they'd catch him soon; she was already starting to think twice before going outside after dark.

Chapter Twenty-Seven

A grey Indian Winter had returned after a glimmer of spring at the beginning of February. Raw, mid-forties temperatures persisted until late March when Lise committed Spring. The brighter colors boosted her morale enough to offset the constant need for a sweater. Still, it was not the company's drafty lunchroom that made her pull the bulky knit tighter across her shoulders.

A month and a half after his chase through the icy park, Alan Porter was still profoundly wounded. He had returned to his office a changed and perhaps destroyed man. His membership in the elite corps of rising-young-men was tacitly revoked; he'd been outcast by those well-tailored Young Turks who had been his friends and competitors. Lise was his last companion.

Alan's studied, conservative appearance deteriorated to a malignant casualness—though Lise had not needed to remind him of the virtues of toothpaste and soap for almost a week. His shoes were often mismatched and he seemed to always sleep in his suit jacket. Lise could have ignored these lapses; the company itself was willing to ignore most eccentricities, but the surface changes were a symptom of the deeper emotional problems the Phenomena had created within him.

Lise wouldn't meet his eyes when he talked anymore.

"Krozier dropped the big one today," Alan was saying. "I guess they talked with Doc Dudley and got everything arranged before they talked to me: officially I need a rest. Old-school Krozier undoubtedly thinks I should be replaced by someone with a better image. I get eighty-percent disability for eighteen months—the executive benefit package, I guess the work drives everyone crazy. Maybe I'll have things taken care of by then."

"I'm sorry, Alan."

He laughed silently, his ill-dressed body bouncing up and down with unshared mirth. Lise looked away to the WPA murals painted on the cafeteria walls. They were sitting in the

Wizard of Oz alcove, right under Dorothy's house and the Wicked Witch of the East's ruby slippers. There were lots of Munchkins but the Good Witch of the North had been replaced by an air-conditioning vent.

"My ex-wife says she's sorry; she thinks now she was unnecessarily cruel to me—not that she's coming back, you understand. She's offered alimony, though. My family's sorry for me—but not as sorry for me as they are for themselves. The Porter escutcheon hasn't been this badly blotted since Henry the Eighth. But, Lise—you shouldn't be sorry. Doc Dudley'n'I've been doing dreams. He's got me back to that night. I can remember stuff now!"

Lise nodded politely. Alan wasn't as wild-eyed as he'd been at first. Maybe Doctor Dudley with his unorthodox therapies and bottles of pills was on the right track, but though she'd listen to Alan's adventures she'd never solicit them. He waited for her to ask about his memories and didn't seem to notice her silence.

"I saw Samedi come out of the bushes. He had that walking stick in his fist and he used it to attract the demon. They built a glowing wall around themselves to keep me away. The cloud flowed down the walking stick and Samedi was gone. That's when the laughing started. The cloud shrank until it was maybe four feet all around and looking like a cat—sort of.

"It had funny ears—pointy things—and a muzzle that was all teeth like a crocodile's. I tossed something at it—a can, I think—and it ran toward the street, changin' as it went. By the time it was out of sight I knew it was running on two legs. It's laugh reminded me of your friend, Nigel." Alan's hands gestured independently as he spoke. Beads of sweat had come out on his forehead.

"And how does Dudley interpret all this?" Lise asked. She pretended not to notice when he mentioned Nigel and would not feed whichever of Alan's delusions connected the Phenomena with the dark-haired man.

"He's a sneaky old fart—plays games and doesn't say a thing. But the cat's still following me; we know that. I see it in my dreams. Lately I've seen it around here. It was on the roof of the building across the street yesterday."

Lise stirred her soup. Insanity was relative. She had seen what Alan called the demon-cloud. Mark had seen Alan throw a beercan into it. But only Alan had seen it turn into a cat. Mark was still sane; she was still sane but Alan was rapidly losing his hold on reality.

"Not a real cat, Alan," she suggested softly.

"You're a fine one to be playing doubting-thomas. Of course it's real. It's as real as anything else in your damned apartment is."

"Someone else would have seen it."

"Someone else has seen it—but they're all dead now!" he said with chilling enthusiasm. "What do you think's been killing all those people on the Eastside?"

"Alan," Lise said in a patient, frightened monotone. "I know the police always hold details back, but if they thought it was a *cat* then they would be treating this very differently—and I think that they can deduce the difference between a knife wound and a bite or claw wound."

"Not these claws!" he smiled. "Nobody but me understands yet, but I'll be ready."

"I'm not really hungry, Alan. I think I'll take a walk down to Maria's boutique and see what's new—" Lise retreated from her uneaten lunch, unable to cope with Alan any longer.

"I'll walk you as far as the corner, then. I've got to get some film for my camera. You're sure you don't want anything to eat?"

Lise put her tray on the service cart. "It should be pretty up near your family's place." She hoped to change the subject; it didn't work.

He looked at her with undisguised amazement. "I'm not going to leave the City now. I'm going to photograph that cat."

Lise felt something freeze within her and said nothing until she was alone again. It was Maria's day off, despite what she'd told Alan and she headed for a nearby vest-pocket park. Alan had never blamed her but she was numb with self-inflicted guilt nonetheless.

Alan did not return to the office after lunch. Lise shut her ears to the rumors that raced among the desks. Midway through the afternoon James Krozier, Alan's erstwhile boss, called her into his office. Krozier had a reputation for openness in the company; the closed door conference was not part of his usual style.

"Porter's not coming back," he said without looking at her; the statement had a ring of finality to it. "Damn shame—damn wife." He unfolded a newspaper clipping with a picture of the ex-Mrs. Porter. It must have been quite a promotion to merit a picture in the *Times*. "Careerwomen they call themselves—unscrupulous bitches's more like it. Broke his back. Alan had potential, but not when she got done with him. Now, don't get me wrong. Life's a two-way street. I don't say a woman shouldn't live her own life or that a man should walk all over her— But, damn! We needed Alan Porter and she didn't—

"Anyway, you should know how I feel about this; how *we* all feel about this because we want you to take over theYear-End Analysis project now that he's gone."

"A level-10 clerical is hardly qualified for that—" Lise heard herself say. She hadn't been complimented by his frankness, but she hadn't expected herself to quibble over the extra work.

"We're not unaware of that. You've been here three years; it's time we took a closer look and examined your potential. You did a fine job on the first round and we know who's been heading the team since February—be sure we do. And we know your wife won't leave you."

It was a joke and she laughed. You laughed at all their jokes when they owned you and with the salary Krozier quoted he owned her. She waited until after the office had emptied before piling her belongings on her chair and wheeling everything into Alan's deserted office. Mandala-like sketches covered every inch of paper in sight. She crumpled them all into the waste-basket. After cramming Alan's unsorted effects into a file drawer and locking it she left the building and took a cab uptown to Culpeper's.

Sally had asked them to come to a special seminar on the preparation of essential oils for the festivals of the Wiccan year. The class, having been told often enough of Sally's determination to create a true priesthood of the Old Religion, knew that if they wanted to be initiated at the end of the course they'd best attend all her extra sessions.

The store was still open for business when Lise got there, with Nigel manning the cash register and several of the other novices milling around. There was a line of customers so Lise simply returned his smile and looked for seats for herself and Maria.

Surrounded by purposeful activity in which she did not choose to take part, Lise fell victim to her morose thoughts. She didn't look up when Maria arrived carrying a pillowcase stuffed with the robes she had run through a sewing machine and which were now ready for the hours of embroidery Sally insisted on having.

"You look like you've had a terrible day," Maria greeted her.

"I've gotten a promotion. I've got four walls on my own now, even if they don't go all the way up to the ceiling," Lise announced flatly, taking out one of the robes and holding it to her shoulders.

"You're kidding!" Maria took the robe back. "That's status stuff, isn't it? Should be worth four or five thousand a year, at least. Are you in shock or something?"

Lise shrugged her friend's enthusiasm aside. "Nothing's official yet but—Oh, dammit, Maria, I'm getting Alan's job. I've got his office now the raise comes in two weeks. They've put him in mothballs."

Sitting down beside Lise with a noticeable thump, Maria fished a Kleenex out of her purse and offered it to Lise who had begun to cry. "What happened? I thought he was snapping out of it? You said he'd been a lot less space-y lately."

Lise blew her nose. "He's gone quietly crazy. Now he sees cats following him. He's convinced the Eastside Slasher is a cat and it's just waiting for him. But he'll be ready, he's going to take its picture. It's obviously all very real for him but it's beyond me."

"So they gave him the old deep-six?"

"They're calling it temporary disability, but the emphasis

Chapter Twenty-Eight

The over-sized deck of cards was carefully wrapped in antique cream-colored silk. Edith refolded the cloth gently and tucked it back in the leather box before showing Sally the tarot cards Elizabeth had sent from Caer Maen. Elizabeth would not have travelled across town without her deck and when she'd come upon her mother's neglected cards had sent them along air-mail in the hope that they would help end the loneliness. They hadn't; they wouldn't. No matter how troubled she became, Edith never peered into the future. But the little package had given her another excuse to visit Culpeper's.

"They're lovely," Sally agreed, "and different. I've never seen designs like these anywhere." She extended a finger to touch the jewel-like analyne colors and the braided celtic borders, but then she hesitated and withdrew her hand.

"No, go on and handle them. They've just come by post from London and I've never been one to use them much anyway."

Despite the reassurances Sally handled the seventy-eight handmade cards nervously. She slid them past one another until she uncovered the arcana of the High Priestess which was different in style from the rest. "Did you draw this one too?" she asked.

Edith laughed. "I didn't draw any of them; drawing isn't one of my talents. They're all copied from other decks in the coven—took me the whole of my sixteenth summer. Most of them are my grandmother's design; she was a true artist. Except the High Priestess—" Edith stared at the card which was a portrait of Gwen. It had been made from a black-and-white snapshot and the colors weren't quite right, but the likeness was there.

Sally held the card carefully, striking a pose similar to Gwen's but without her unearthly regalness. "It must be a tremendous source of strength to have that much tradition; to do things because that's the way they've always been done. New Moon coven is over ten years old and we're one of the older ones. I think the Old Religion's truly rising again—but for us it won't go back much before 1960. You grew up with it; you never had to change your mind about anything. You probably don't find yourself missing the Christmas carols—"

"Not to disappoint you, Sally, but we're not so open in the West-Country. We Brits may have a fine tolerance for the strange, but only within limits. We still go to church on Sundays; in fact the parish church has an altar stone that was once one of ours."

"Thousands of years," Sally sighed and slipped the card back into the deck. "If half our covens survive more than two years we think we're making progress. That's why I'm so excited about this Dedication Class; it seems like the time has come for the Old Religion again. Incidentally, the class is going to stay together as one unit and not go back to the other covens. Nigel has become the focal point for them—Lise Brown will be his H-P if I have to make a guess."

Edith had heard that Lise and Nigel were in the Dedication class together but this was the first she had heard of any relationship, social or magickal, between them. The young man had never shown the dark side of his personality again, but Edith had never stopped watching for it; never felt comfortable in his presence—and he knew it. She shuddered at the thought of such a flawed spirit coming into contact with the Otherworld.

"Isn't it a bit early for that? None of them has been initiated yet. A year and a day plus another year and another day before they can start thinking High Priest and Priestess—or isn't that the way over here?" she chided.

"No—you're absolutely right. I'll work them up through all the degrees, but when the time is up there won't be just one woman or one couple at the heart of things—we've gotten some pretty tyranical covens over here—this coven will think of itself as a circle of equals.

"But Nigel's got extraordinary power and rapport—Jason and I saw that from the first; it just needed a channel. I thought you'd be pleased to know Lise has moved to the center of things so quickly. I would imagine there will be a continuity of sorts at the Riverside apartment. Maybe they could be pursuaded to adopt the Riverside name—if that would please you."

"She's bringing him to Riverside," Edith whispered to herself, forgetting that Sally could hear.

"No, not so far as I know. Lise's no fool; she knows what sort of problems she's got up there and that she's not ready for any magick until she's cleansed everything. She's said, though, that it's been quiet since she took up the Craft."

Edith nodded. She knew about the quiet. It was the middle of April and nothing had happened since Imholc. Bert had suggested she return to Cornwall until the situation deteriorated further, but Edith still hoped Lise would call. She had moved to a YWCA residence; she was thinking of getting a job if she could find one that didn't violate her visa. There had been nothing to do but wait for almost two months now. The needlepoint picture was long since finished and three others besides.

"Will you join Jason and me for Beltane?" Sally asked. "It's New Moon anniversary. I'd like to have you there."

Edith had no desire to sit at another coven's circle yet neither did she look forward to spending Beltane alone or in the company of the young, displaced women at the "Y" who always assumed she was the grandmotherly type.

"In Brooklyn? You'll have to give me step-by-step directions. I haven't left this island since I landed."

"I'm glad you'll come. It'll do you good. The maps are out by the cash register. I'll give you a general idea and have Jason make up the detailed instructions."

Nigel was talking with a young woman at the cash register. Their conversation halted as soon as Sally and Edith were in ear-shot and seemed unlikely to resume. Edith smiled to herself; it was likely that Lise was not the only woman to succumb to Nigel's charms. They might easily go their separate ways.

"Oh, Maria—it's good to see you," Sally acknowledged the woman.

"Hi—I'd rather tell you myself, anyway. Lise got a call from her brother last night. They've taken her father to the hospital—they're supposed to operate sometime today. It's his stomach, I think. She's gone back home until he's out of danger. There wasn't time for her to call you, but she wanted to be sure you knew why she was missing classes."

So, this was Maria—Lise's friend and confidant. Edith watched the plump, olive-complexioned woman unobtrusively. As Sally asked all the polite questions Edith decided that Maria didn't trust Nigel either.

"I don't suppose she left the keys with you?" Nigel interrupted. "I loaned her a few books and I'd like to get them back. If you think she'll be out of town for a while I can borrow the keys and get them back myself."

Edith wanted to shout against the possibility of this odd man alone near the Riverside Rift, but Maria spoke first.

"If you'll tell me what books, if any, you've really left up there I'll see what I can do for you. If Lise wanted you to have the run of her apartment she'd have given you a set of keys long before this."

"Maybe she would have—if she knew she wasn't going to be around," Nigel said, imitating Maria's inflection and posture with devestating accuracy before turning his back on her.

"I guess we'll hope it's not too serious and that she's back with us soon," Sally interceded, laying the map of Brooklyn across the counter.

Edith set the tarot case aside and plunged deeper into her purse for a notebook.

"Is that your tarot deck?" Maria asked.

"It is," Edith agreed, trying to be friendly with Maria yet stifling Nigel's ever-ready curiosity at the same time.

"I was showing the class some of the standard decks we carry a few weeks back. Of course we don't have anything as unusual as yours. Would you let them see it?'' Sally urged.

Edith had been out-maneuvered. She undid the silk and left the greater number of cards still within the leather box. Sally cocked an eyebrow at the omission but Edith felt no need to explain. Maria looked at the cards with open-faced awe.

''They're magnificent,'' she said, without trying to touch the cards.

Nigel went at once to the cards Edith had left in the box. He had the silk unwrapped before Edith could voice her protests.

''Nigel,'' Sally scolded. ''That's rude—you should know better than to handle someone else's tarot. If Edith meant for you to touch those, she would have handed them to you.'' She squared the cards Nigel had handled and returned them to the silk.

''Everyone's awfully touchy all of a sudden. If Lise didn't want—If Edith didn't want—'' Nigel complained. ''It's just a game, really,'' he continued, catching Edith's eye. ''There's no power to the cards, no aura. They can't tell you anything about the future you don't already know—can they?''

''If you think it's a game then it's a game. If you think you know everything then life itself is a game,'' Edith averred and he turned his back on her.

The atmosphere had become stubborn though Edith was not exactly sure how she'd gotten locked into the duel.

''Game or not, I've got to be going; it's getting dark,'' Maria discharged the tension. She faced Nigel but spoke loudly enough for them all to hear. ''With Lise out of town there won't be any extra Beltane circles in her apartment—do you understand?''

''I guess so,'' he replied with uncharacteristic pensiveness. ''I guess I can survive that, somehow. I wonder about her friend—it's Alan I'm really worried about.''

''He'll manage to take care of himself a little while longer,'' Maria replied sharply.

''Edith, Maria—you're both in the same part of town, why don't you travel home together?'' Sally suggested.

The increasing notoriety of the Eastside Slasher—who

now struck all over town—had led most women to travel in pairs or larger groups, though the Slasher really had no sexual preference. Edith didn't share the average horror at the crimes. None of the victims since Rob and Marjory, and there had been a half-dozen, seemed to have occult connections but she remained convinced that the crimes were being caused by Otherworld influences. She doubted that travelling in groups of any size provided protection, but went along quietly with Sally's suggestion.

Maria said nothing as they walked along the rain-swept blocks to the subway. She was, Edith reminded herself, Lise's closest friend and Lise had not been pleased to meet her.

"How about a cab?" Edith suggested, "If you think we can get one in the rain."

"I'm on a tight budget this month," Maria replied.

"Two ride as cheaply as one, I think. I haven't mastered the subways yet; I have this terrible fear I'll wind up in the middle of nowhere."

"Then you'd probably be in Queens," Maria replied in a friendlier voice. "I grew up with trains but I can live without rush-hour this once." Maria stepped off the curb to wave at a speeding yellow cab which ignored her. "You're not at all what I was expecting," she added bluntly as yet another stream of occupied or off-duty cabs rolled by.

"Your friend and I didn't hit it off too well."

Maria nodded. "We'll do better at this down at Fifty-ninth Street." They started walking. "You don't even seem the right type to be involved with witchcraft—that is, the type of witchcraft that's rooted in Lise's livingroom. Though, looking at her furniture doesn't warn you either."

"Perhaps there's just the slightest bit of exaggeration going on here?" Edith lured.

"I've seen it once—I won't let myself see it again—and I don't think I could exaggerate it. But, from everything Lise says, the Phenomenon I saw was nothing compared to what rolled out over Alan at Imholc."

"She doesn't talk about it much, but she was terribly frightened," Edith agreed. "I had tried to assure her that I wanted to help her shut the Phenomena out, but she couldn't believe me."

"There's an evil in that room."

"For the time-being let's call it a family curse; something that came over with my sister and her husband and is our responsibility. When my brother-in-law died, it escaped." Edith tried a new and carefully rehearsed explanation.

"At this point I'd believe a curse; it's getting very hard not to believe anything. Alan believes that some sort of cat came out and that the Slasher is one-and-the-same with the cat. Alan is not rowing with both oars—but he might still be right. Edith? You look sick—are you all right? Don't tell me your curse *is* a four-foot-high cat?" Maria shook her head as she held Edith's arm.

"No, no—" Edith regained her composure quickly. "No, Alan—if he was touched by something from within Lise's livingroom is right. That cat is real for him, and a very real danger to all of us because it is real for him. You'll want to use all that Sally's taught you to insulate yourself from it."

Maria shrugged. "I was frightened, but I don't live in fear. Alan's the only one who's been permanently damaged. Even Lise doesn't really seem to be all that affected. She's different, but I wouldn't say it's just the result of your curse. She's had other changes going on."

Edith was impressed by Maria's staunch defense of her friend and by her unemotional approach to Lise's Phenomena. Maria embodied loyalty and trustworthiness—and she had already brushed against the Otherworld; Edith had located a person who could be told the truth about the Otherworld. She explained as much as she could as they sat on a bench out of the rain.

"So, you see—it is because the task was unfinished that these things continue and will get worse," Edith concluded, shaking the water off her raincoat as she stood up.

"You haven't told Lise all of this?"

"No, the time and place weren't right. I could have told her but she wouldn't believe me, and she's safer not knowing than not believing."

Maria bit her lip in thought. "But Lise's not unreasonable; she'd help you. If you explained everything to her the way you just did to me, I'm sure she'd let you finish it."

Edith shook her head. "The more I learn the more I'm convinced I don't have the power to close the Rift anymore—the power belongs to her and that's one more thing making her suspicious."

"I don't know. Lise doesn't want to have that kind of Craft in her house, she wants to put everything behind her," Maria warned.

"But the Beltane circle you mentioned at Culpeper's—"

"That's Nigel. He wants to play at magick. He knows Lise has all the paraphernalia and he knows about the Phenomena. He's using Alan as an excuse. I really think he's caught up in the Eye-of-Newt, Toe-of-Frog Syndrome."

"You don't like Nigel, do you?" Edith forced herself to ask calmly.

"I seem to be the only one who doesn't," she admitted bleakly. "Lise has me convinced that I'm the one who's being irrational about it. But, then—I irrationally don't trust him."

Edith said nothing as Maria finally hailed a cab. The young woman had the good sense to talk about her passion for Italian cooking during the ride. She invited Edith to dinner some night. Edith responded in the same casual way, though in her heart she was cheering.

"I can get out here with you," Maria announced when the cab pulled to the curb at Edith's residence.

For a moment Edith thought she was short cab-fare, but a quick glance at Maria's face told her that wasn't the reason. The rain was falling hard as she led the way into the small, spartan lobby. The concierge called Edith before Maria could explain.

"*Man* to see you, Miz Brompton."

"Oh?" Edith replied, genuinely surprised.

The woman's face was a mixture of curiousity and disapproval. "A *black* man. He was dressed funny and had one of those down-island accents. He hung around so I asked him to leave. You do know our rules, don't you?"

Edith muttered something, she didn't remember what. Her thoughts were instantly with her nightmares, and the oddly-dressed black man who frequented them. She had almost forgotten Maria beside her.

"I'd like to come with you to the Beltane ritual at Sally's next week. I've been invited too, but I'm sure it's just because I'm Lise's friend—I'm not the light of the Dedication Class the way she is. It'll be a fair trade: you don't know the way and I don't want to go alone."

Edith nodded. The next of the great lunar festivals was upon them. Life was speeding up again and, as the Chinese would say, becoming interesting.

Chapter Twenty-Nine

New Moon coven gathered at Sally and Jason Star's half-renovated house down a Brooklyn side-street. Edith would not have found it for love nor money but Maria, who had grown up in a nearby part of the city, found it with ease and led the way up the cracked, cement steps.

"Blessed be, my sisters!" a gentle-seeming man greeted them and pointed the way upstairs where they would change.

The house was a fitting extension of the Culpeper style: vast projects of interior decoration were in various states of incompletion but the shelves of books and bottles were in perfect order. Carefully cleaned brick-work gave way suddenly to fifty-odd years of plaster and paint midway up the stairs. Some two dozen people wandered through this intriguing maze, most dressed in costumes as eclectic as the decor.

Like the Yule ritual at Caer Maen this Beltane ritual was a reunion more than it was a purposeful magick circle. No one person knew everyone else and soon Edith and Maria were no worse off than the rest.

"Will you show me what to do?" Maria whispered as Edith adjusted the filet band of gold-braid on her short, curly hair. "I've read what I was supposed to, but now I can't remember a thing. I know I'm going to foul things up."

"Don't forget than since you haven't been initiated yet they won't expect you to actually sit in the circle. If you can make your way through a regular church service you'll have no trouble. Anyway, the purpose of ritual is not to embarrass the celebrants. Everything will be very clear, but if you'd like I'll stay outside the circle with you."

Maria, resigned but not reassured, followed Edith into the room where the ritual would be held. Beltane, like all the other Celtic festivals, was primarily a celebration of nature and the outdoors. It centered around a bonfire made from debris left by the previous winter and heralded the return of spring to the fields. But, in practice, Beltane could rarely be celebrated properly by a modern, urban coven.

Sally had disguised the indoor setting of their rite with displays of plants and flowers. The furniture had been removed except for a large straw mat on which, instead of a bonfire, they had a flame-colored altarcloth.

Edith took her turn slicing strawberries and dropping them into plastic wineglasses while Maria filled the glasses from bottles of chilled May wine.

"It's more like a pot-luck party," Maria said. "I was expecting whispers and people huddled in dark corners."

"This is as it should be," Edith explained. "The great Esbat festivals are different from an ordinary sabbat circle which is smaller and more attuned to magick. I'm surprised Sally hasn't stressed that more with you. In our day the Wicca tended to the needs of a whole society—their mysteries, their leadership, their justice and their drunken parties. So don't skimp on the wine!"

Maria was silent and kept any other objections and comments she might have had to herself. Finally the curtains were drawn shut, the candles lit and the music begun. Shuffling into the crowded room they found empty spaces at the edge of the straw mat. Sally, Jason and the four other third-degree initiates of New Moon emerged from the kitchen with candles in each hand: the ritual had begun.

Each High Priestess casts a distinctive circle. Edith's circles were solid, practical and likened to the trunks of stout, old trees. Sally cast a circle that was airy, open and, if it were depicted in color, pale yellow-green; less a shield than a gentle breeze of magick wafting around them. New Moon's High Priestess captured the light promise of Beltane and lulled her witches into the illusion of a warm spring night despite the walls and the omnipresent street noises.

Edith tested the gossamer web of power, casting her thoughts beyond the light. It would be better to learn the circle's weaknesses, if any, at her own initiative than to wait until disaster threatened. She was quickly drawn back into harmony with the rest of the gathering and was able to relax knowing that New Moon was strong despite its lightness.

The Beltane celebration was a commemoration of New Moon's past. They lit white tapers for those members of the coven who had departed for whatever reason; Edith thought of the creamy candles Gretna had forwarded on Arthur's behalf. Jason gave each of New Moon's initiates a crown of white flowers. They sang, passed around the lemon cakes and wine and Edith wished she were back in Cornwall; the celebration was so much the same that she could only see and appreciate the differences.

Sally swept down on Edith once the ritual was ended and introduced her to the local Wiccan community. Maria was left to fend for herself until it approached ten-thirty and, as a veteran subway traveller, she sought out Edith and insisted they head for home before the dangers became unconscionably high.

"It's too bad Lise couldn't have been here for that," Maria said when, once again dressed in street clothes, they were waiting for the train. "It might have gone a long way toward convincing her that there's more to ritual magick than fighting Phenomena. I wasn't expecting anything special—but there was magick; I do feel more aware of life and growing things even here in Brooklyn." She hesitated a moment. "I even thought I could feel the baby," she confided. "I only found out yesterday for sure, so I can't—not really—but I was so sure of her a few hours ago."

"Perhaps you did. I was most aware of my daughter Elizabeth when I was drawing down the moon for Caer Maen."

"I think, maybe, I will feel comfortable with the Craft. It seems warm and personal—at least right now. When I've been at the classes with Lise there's been a grimness to everything. Did you know Elizabeth was going to be a girl? Bob and I decided that we hoped it would be a boy; we want to have two, a boy then a girl. But now I'm sure she's a she."

The train roared into the station sweeping loose newspapers and idle conversation in its path. By the time they reemerged into the night air of Manhattan the magick of the evening had almost vanished.

"You must be lonely here in the City," Maria said as if she had read Edith's thoughts. "Why don't you stop upstairs for a few minutes before you go back to the "Y." Bob'll be glued to the TV watching the playoffs, so you won't be intruding."

"I'd be glad to," Edith replied. Until that moment she hadn't realized how much she wanted to avoid her barren little room.

They walked in a proper New York City cadence moving fast enough to seem purposeful but not fast enough to draw anyone's attention. The sidewalk was spotted with dog-owners exercising their pets after the late news. There was a curb-and-leash law, but a prudent walker always watched the next few sections of pavement, especially at this time of night. Edith had naturalized enough to watch the pavement and the approaching corner without seeming to be in a permanent daze. She saw the teenagers slouching in a doorway; the dark-coated man who wasn't too steady on his feet and the couple getting into a parked car. At the limit of her attention she saw the silhouette of a rangy man, a cape flaring out behind him and the distinctive lines of a top hat adding to his already considerable height. He headed down a side-street as she watched.

"That man," Edith said, tilting her head but not committing the urban sin of pointing at a stranger, "do you see him around here frequently?"

" 'Fraid I missed him. What did he look like?" Maria asked as they approached the now-deserted corner.

"He seemed to be dressed like my gentleman caller." Edith stared down the empty street.

"Oh, how could I have forgotten? I was going to tell you first thing. I saw *that* man in our lobby as I was getting off the elevator on Wednesday. He was talking to someone else from the building, I think, but they were both gone by the time I got there. You still don't have any idea who he is or why he wanted to talk to you?"

"No, he hasn't come back. I thought that might have been him."

"Another of life's little mysteries—still unsolved," Maria joked. She pressed one of dozens of identical buttons in the lobby to warn Bob of her return. "At least he doesn't wander the street shouting that the devil's in league with Macy's—we had a screamer like that for a couple months last year—around Christmas."

If Bob was surprised or upset by Maria's sudden hospitality he recovered himself quickly enough not to show it. He turned off the TV without being asked and listened attentively while Maria described the ritual. Edith was pleasantly surprised by how much her companion had remembered.

"So, you've made New York City safe for spring," he said when she was finished, managing somehow not to sound disrespectful. "Should we celebrate by eating candied daffodils? Or would everyone be satisfied with ice cream?"

It was agreed that ice cream was preferable to flowers and Maria insisted on preparing it and coffee. Bob and Edith were left alone in the livingroom.

"Don't go adding any pickles to ours, Mari!" Bob shouted into the kitchen. "Did she tell you," he returned his attention to Edith, "the next generation of DelVecchios begins this September?"

"Yes. She seems very happy about it."

"Mari's almost always happy—she doesn't let the unpleasant things take over. Like this witchcraft stuff—she's enjoying it. She's been talking about this ritual-whatever you went to all week long, but with her it's nothing like it is with Lise." He tapped the side of his head with his forefinger and shrugged before continuing. "That girl's gone 'way overboard. I've lost count of the number of times she's moved back here. Lise's got a real bad case of something—and now she's gone back out to Michigan! She got thrown out at Christmas and vowed nothing would ever get her back. She wasn't figuring her father going under the knife. We'll be lucky if she doesn't come back in a body-bag."

"Do you worry about Lise?" Edith asked, almost casually, though she was poised to remember every nuance of his answer.

"Yeah, sure—I worry. Hell, I wanted to marry her back when we were both young, naive and still in college. I guess sometimes I feel bad that it didn't work out. But, Lise's always had this in her. She's always been deep and moody. Everything's fine and suddenly Lise's off in another world getting hysterical over something. I guess you'd say she's one of those who march to the beat of a different drummer. There's nothing wrong with Lise—she just doesn't live in the same world we do; it's not her fault.

"Like I said—this whole witchcraft-thing. For Lise it's a crusade against evil in her apartment: total commitment. She's had dreams about huge snakes and spiders—"

"But Maria's said she's seen them too," Edith interrupted. She was glad to hear someone talking openly about Lise, and discounting his words for that very reason.

"Edith, if you were with Lise and she said pink elephants were hitch-hiking down Madison Avenue you'd believe her. Annalise Brown, five feet, four and one-half inches of unquestionable sincerity. You can't not believe her."

"No, Bob, I meant that Maria saw the same things Lise saw and they've frightened her as well."

Bob pushed himself back against the sofa cushions as though they would shelter him from Edith's stare. Then he straightened and leaned forward. "Okay, something happened up there one night; something's probably happened every time she's come running to us. But, consider Lise's imagination. Forget about the pink elephants; say there was a loud noise on the street and you didn't know what it was. Maybe Lise'd say it was a car backfiring, maybe she'd say it was a gunshot and maybe she'd say it was Godzilla come from Tokyo for a vacation: no matter, you'd believe her."

"Have you ever been in her apartment to *not* see what everyone else seems to see?"

"Nope," he said without apology or hesitation. "I helped her move in, so I've seen the place but I've never thought it was necessary to check out her stories. I know I'd believe her, if I was there. Hell, I lived with her for a year and a half at school—I know her powers.

"Anyway, Lise and I don't belong in the same room alone, really—too many memories and frustrations. Frankly, it's just not that important to me. I'm trying to get my MBA in June so we can be settled in a house by the time the baby gets here. You know: fight, fight, fight—claw your way up the ladder of success," he concluded in a broad English accent which brought Edith to laughter—though she had not found the greater part of his monolog all that amusing.

"Coffee'll be ready in a minute. I'm bringing in the ice cream now," Maria announced as she entered the livingroom with much-embellished dishes of ice cream. "Was I interrupting something?"

"No, Bob was just telling me how he hopes to move out of here before your baby's born," Edith answered quickly.

"Yeah, an apartment like this's no place for kids and I don't want to try to move when she/he's a year old. We're thinking about Brooklyn or, God forbid, Queens. Maybe even a house—we've only just started looking." Maria smiled and headed back to the kitchen.

Bob was silent as if a new and unpleasant thought had crept into his head. 'You aren't in New York just because of Lise and her apartment, are you? She hasn't managed to convince you, somehow, has she?" he asked with narrow-eyed suspicion.

"I have always known that the untimely death of my brother-in-law could result in just those sort of things Lise and your wife have seen. I didn't need anyone to convince me. I came because Arthur's death left many things undone. I won't go back home until they are all done," Edith answered in the same tone.

"And I won't let Mari get involved with it—not now, not with the baby coming. I don't want her hurt or frightened. Witchcraft is okay so long as it's just making the world safe for spring—but nothing more."

"You're scowling, Bob," Maria chided as she came back into the room.

His face relaxed at once and the subject was dropped not to reemerged even when he walked Edith back to the "Y." The streets were middle-of-the-night quiet then; the lobby of the residence deserted even by the ever-curious concierge. They said good-night unnoticed by anyone. But a message for Edith had been tacked on the small cord board outside her door. The black man had been asking for her earlier in the evening. He still didn't leave his name—but he had said he would be back.

Edith was more tired than usual and looking forward to a night without dreams, but sleep had to be postponed a bit longer. Once safely behind her locked door and closed curtain she got out her candles and incense. It was a familiar pattern: protective wards at all the cracks and crevices in the room; a soft prayer of thanks that she had survived so far and a plea that she survive until she finished what she had to do.

She waited for sleep in the dark room, thinking about Lise and what Bob had told her. He had listed most of the requirements for a High Priestess, prerequisites she had only hoped for in the young woman. If she could trust Bob; if she could trust anyone who had been in the Riverside apartment and brushed against the Otherworld there, then there was hope. An uncorrupted, well-trained Lise Brown could form a High Coven equal to its task around herself. Then Edith thought of Nigel, and of him as the High Priest beside Lise and rather than think any more she willed her mind into a blank, fitful sleep.

Chapter Thirty

When Edith finally found restful sleep in the early hours of May first, she surrendered to it completely. Her hall-mates and the concierge banged loudly on the door before she conceded wakefulness and groped for the light switch and her slippers.

"What is it?" she asked, still fighting back yawns and leaning heavily on the half-open door.

"Miz Brompton, you got a phone call—an emergency," the concierge announced.

Mindful of the dark stares of everyone her emergency had awakened, Edith draped her robe over her shoulders and followed the heavy-set woman down to the lobby. She was still half-asleep when the concierge thrust the sweaty phone in her hand.

"Edith? Edith—is that you?" a man's voice asked.

"Yes, this is Edith," she said before she was absolutely certain. "Who is this?"

"Bob DelVecchio. Edith—wake up!" he shouted. "Something's happened to Maria—one of Lise's things. She's hysterical. I can't do anything for her; she keeps calling for you."

The sleep-fog cleared; she didn't need to be asked twice. The implications of Bob's words burned through her thoughts like desert sun. Without any explanation to those who waited around her, Edith hurried back to her room.

"You leavin?" her next-door neighbor asked.

"Yes, just for the night. I'll be back tomorrow."

"Okay—we won't call the police until sundown."

Edith nodded. A single psychotic murderer had made more changes in the social life of the City than any dozen public relations campaigns. The women at the residence paid close attention to each other's movements now and Edith was caught in the general concern.

"I should be back well before sundown. I'd like to be home for breakfast."

A wind had risen since midnight. A few delivery vans rumbled in the distance. A black man was sleeping in a doorway. Edith stole a side-long glance but it wasn't her ominous caller. The nameplates above the ranks of buttons in the DelVecchio's building were defaced to the point of illegibility. She pressed a likely looking one and waited for the explosion from the speaker.

"Edith?" Bob's voice asked and the lock chattered open. "Thank heaven you're here," he continued when she reached the door.

He fairly wrenched her coat from her arms after shutting the door, but by then Edith was already caught in the crisis and didn't notice. Maria's moans could be heard throughout the apartment and probably beyond it. She had pulled the blankets off the bed and huddled herself under them between a bureau and the wall.

"Do something for her!" Bob demanded, climbing over the bed to be near his wife. He retreated when his approach drove her deeper into hysteria.

"Maria? Maria can you hear me?" Edith lowered herself to the floor and reached tenderly for the quivering mound.

A wrongness pervaded this corner of the room, not a wrongness of odor or sound but of something more subliminal. Edith perceived it only after she had been rebuffed and Bob's frantic encouragement was turning hostile. Ignoring everything else she tested the wrongness, letting it approach her like the incoming tide until a symbolic wave lapped at her and she recoiled in shock. Gentleness and caution vanished. She grabbed a handful of blanket and wrenched it away from the terrified girl.

"Get the rest!" she shouted to Bob before he could question her. "Get her free of these blankets!"

Edith hauled and tore at the cloth with a violence she had never before brought to bear on something living or dead. The fibers reeked of the Otherworld; they felt rotten in her hand.

Maria's nightgown had torn away from her shoulder and was spotted with blood from dozens of self-clawed scratches.

She clutched her arms around herself and cowered, pressing her fingers against her face until the nails drew beads of blood. Edith and Bob shouted and got in each other's way in their efforts to remove Maria from the cramped corner. In a blind panic himself, Bob finally got both arms under her and carried her, crying but not resisting, from the room.

"Put her in the livingroom," Edith commanded. She opened her purse and upended it. Everything she would need was certain to be in there. The tiny white-handled knife in its silk-wrapped sheath—she used that to cut two lengths of twisted silk thread from a battered spool; the cellophane wrapped candlestub that reeked of sandlewood; a package of salt from an airline dinner tray; a badly bruised clove of garlic. After a few moments of ransacking the kitchen as well, Edith was ready to describe a circle of protection around Maria who was curled up and crying on the living-room floor beside Bob.

"Once with salt; leech it out!
You cannot stay; you cannot cross!
Twice with cloves; drive it out!
You cannot stay; you cannot cross!
Thrice with water; wash it out!
You cannot stay; you cannot cross!
Last with fire; burn it out!
You cannot stay; you cannot cross!

Now that the circles were complete Edith went to work on the spasms that kept Maria's fingers drilled into her face. As Bob watched with disbelief, Edith dipped the thread in the hot candle wax she had collected in the palm of one hand. Her hands shook but not from the heat of the wax. She tied the still-flexible string around Maria's wrists and sealed the knots with more wax. Then she massaged the terror-ridden woman's forearms, always stroking toward the string. The frantic tension eased out of the cramped muscles but long minutes passed before Maria's fingers were still and recovered her sense of self with a rushing purge of tears.

"There now, there now," Edith comforted, "just go

ahead. Let everything out. We're here now with you."

"May I touch her too?" Bob asked, despite his earlier skepticism he was not eager to cross the invisible lines Edith had made.

"Yes," Edith nodded and turned her attention back to Maria. "It's safe now," she said to both of them. It wasn't, of course, not really, but the rings of protection should hold until Maria got her strength back.

"It crawled all over me, like hot roaches." Maria sagged into Edith's arms as she spoke. She gagged, but there was nothing in her stomach to expel.

"Mari? Darling, are you all right?" Bob asked lifting sweat-matted curls from her forehead and kissing her.

"Get my robe, please? I'm cold."

He looked at Edith who sent him on his way to the closet. Maria forced herself to breathe deeply. They helped her into the robe but Edith would not move her out of the circles until all symptoms of the attack had faded.

"Then I'll be here a long time," Maria said in a cold voice. "Another six months, at least."

"The baby?" Edith sighed, putting the pieces into place, knowing that the Otherworld had found the child. The Wiccans themselves didn't know when a child accepted its karmic burden or, more precisely, when its name was called from the Summerland—if it was a reborn soul—or when its karma was fixed if it were truly newborn. Where the Wiccans, and the High Covens, could not agree there were bound to be weaknesses the Otherworld could exploit.

Maria pressed wide-spread fingers against her belly. "It's not ours anymore."

"Mari, that's our baby—our little girl Anna," Bob whispered as he knelt beside her.

"No, it's not ours anymore. Our baby's gone. I felt *it* change."

Edith watched in silence. She did not want to consider what the Otherworld could do to the unborn, but she didn't doubt that Maria had endured it. The mouth could lie; the mind could lie but beneath Maria's fingers her gut writhed with the inhumaness within it.

Believing Maria didn't make anything easier. Edith was faced with additional and onerous tasks. The child, the Otherworld child, must not be brought to term. If Maria wouldn't agree then Edith would contact Caer Maen and Elizabeth would go into the warrens for the dusty apothecary books with their faded recipes for potions that might kill the mother with the child. Edith didn't want to spend the rest of her life in an American prison, but she would if it would keep the Otherworld out.

"Poor child," Edith whispered aloud.

"The baby's going to be fine," Bob insisted. "If you two will just quit talking this way. Tomorrow you'll go to the doctor and he'll tell you that the baby's going to be fine."

"No," Maria said, pulling the robe taut over her belly. "I'll go to a doctor, or a clinic—whatever. It's early enough—they won't ask questions. They can get rid of it right away—before IT grows!"

"Maria!" Bob shouted in shock and outrage.

"Edith?" Maria asked, "I should, shouldn't I? For us all? It's what you've been afraid of, isn't it—a beachhead? And I've been with you and Lise; I've been in that apartment. It knew about Anna, didn't it?"

"I believe it must have. I don't know what we could have done to prevent it. You couldn't know exactly when you conceived, but it would have been around Imholc, I think, and the baby would be born near Samhain, I'm sure—"

"Maria, what is all this?" Bob demanded. "You're having our baby! Don't talk like this!" He turned to Edith. "I brought you here to help. I told you how I felt about all this. I thought you understood. I won't let some witch-y notion destroy my child!"

"Robert DelVecchio, witchcraft did not destroy your child—something else did that, something that almost took your wife as well while you watched," Edith lowered her voice, "and might just come back for her. By all the gods ever worshipped—her only hope is within the Craft."

Bob sputtered angrily but he was not unreasonable and after what he had witnessed only an unreasonable man would dismiss Edith's warnings out of hand.

"There'll be more," Maria said, looking to Edith for confirmation.

"I'm sure," Edith said without certainty.

"Then I make the arrangements tomorrow." She shuddered involuntarily. "You can't offer another way, can you?"

"I have nothing safer," Edith admitted.

"Then it's as good as done." And with that Maria allowed the tears she had fought back to overwhelm her. Edith shifted the burden of her weight and sadness to Bob's waiting shoulders. She left the apartment at dawn when pink light brought a moment of innocence to the city streets. She had not stopped to say good-bye.

Peggy Brown sat in the kitchen of her sub-division home in the automotive suburbs of Detroit. Morning sunlight softened the lines of her face. It was one of the few times Lise could see her own face in her mother's. Peggy Brown showed the strain of her husband's illness in the same way that Lise revealed the trials of her apartment. It was their last quiet moment together before Lise would go to the airport with her brother.

"I'm glad you came," the elder woman said with a thin, but sincere, smile. "It was good to have you home."

Tom Brown was out of surgery and out of danger now. He would be in the hospital a few days longer but his prognosis was good, if he slowed down. He had heeded pre-surgery warnings and reconciled himself with his incomprehensible daughter.

"Who knows," her mother continued, "we might even come to visit you sometime this summer. Your father's going to have to take his time now. We'll travel a bit more—while we can afford it. We'll take those vacations we never took."

"New York City's hardly a place for a rest, Mom," Lise said with a laugh. Now was not the time to have them visiting her apartment, not until she could be certain the Phenomena were over. "Maybe we could meet at the ocean. That'd be fun, and better for Dad.''

''But, your vacation time, Lise. Haven't you used most of your two weeks?''

''RHIP, Mom—Rank Hath Its Privileges. This isn't a vacation and, anyway, I get four weeks now.''

It was a simple statement, not intended to make her mother's eyes widen with surprise and pride. Lise was doing well in Alan's job; she'd keep it even it he did come back—but that didn't lessen the guilt she felt whenever she thought of it.

''Your father worked twenty years to get four weeks off—and then he could never take them. You're doing well, Lise: a home of your own, a fine job. You've always said you knew what was right for you, maybe someday we'll learn not to argue.''

''I've never had anything to prove, Ma—I've never gone out of my way to be difficult. It just seemed to happen to me.'' Lise was not merely embarrassed by her mother's sudden, wistful pride, she was moved to tears.

There was a sound in the street, just possibly her brother driving up. She raced into the diningroom to watch a strange car pull up at the stop sign at the end of their street.

''Have you joined a church yet there in New York,'' her mother called from the kitchen.

This was her first chance to admit or deny her witchcraft. It was May-day, maybe a good day to talk of the Craft? ''No, Mom, New York just isn't a very church-y town. There's nothing to draw me into a parish or anything.'' She hesitated and added, ''I'm sorry,'' without saying for what.

The Browns had never been church-goers except for Christmas and Easter. Lise's apostasy had never been a source of contention before.

''I worry about you,'' her mother said, raising one hand for peace and quiet, ''not *that* way, though I worry about that too, but we've got violence here. I have this feeling that you don't have enough roots. I see you adrift in the City—but not just the City. I really don't know what I see—but I think a church would help, somehow.''

It was Lise's turn not to answer, though she'd never have a better time to share her secrets with her mother. She would never have suspected her mother of latent psychic talents—not that bastion of single-minded practicality. Her mother wasn't talking about Sunday choirs or quilting parties but of those fundamental mystical strengths of religion that the Browns had never felt the need to call on—not even when Tom had been in intensive care.

"I'll think about it, Mom. I'll do that much, but you know," Lise warned, "if I think about it and I decide to do something I'll do my own thing—"

"It won't matter as long as I don't have to worry about you."

Chapter Thirty-One

There had been Phenomena in the apartment while Lise was gone. The livingroom was in complete disarray when she got home from Michigan just before suppertime on the first of May. One of her geraniums had been overturned on the sofa—but only recently because the leaves hadn't withered much and, with luck, the plant would survive. The top bookshelves had been swept clear of books, one of which lay on the floor beside the glass goddess which it had knocked over but not broken. Lise was replacing the last book when there was a knock on the door.

"I saw you were back," Rachel said. She hesitated and looked down the hallway before crossing the threshhold. "I thought I should come over and tell you what happened last night—in case you're not here when Mark gets home."

"It was pretty exciting, I take it? I've just about got things cleaned up. Don't sit on the sofa though—I haven't vacuumed my geranium yet," Lise warned as they walked down the hall.

"Everything had been quiet up to a few days ago when the incense reappeared. I looked for that colored man you talked about, but there never was any sign of him. We were warned, though; we were watching. Someone downstairs remembered that April thirtieth is Walpurgisnacht. He said we should wait here until midnight and see what happened. Nothing happened *at* midnight but not long afterward we started hearing things from over there. Mark and I still have our key but we didn't have the courage. It was quiet again in about five minutes. I guess we could have come over and checked things out this morning—but we were running late ourselves and I'm a coward through and through."

Lise was not about to cast judgment. There had been times when she would not have entered the apartment if there had been somewhere else to go.

"No problem," she reassured her neighbor. "I've got it under control. My glass statue got knocked over but it didn't break. The plant looks like it's going to survive; there's no permanent damage. All seems to be quiet on the western front of the building."

Rachel summoned a wan smile. "There was incense there in the morning, but nothing since. Maybe it is quiet again. We got three months of peace—almost to the day. Do you think we'll get another three months?"

The question seemed to be rhetorical; Lise ignored it anyhow. Someone in the building had stumbled upon the memory of Walpurgisnacht—which was only another way of saying Beltane. How long before they notice the other coincidences. Then she noticed the *mezzuzah* Rachel always wore and decided it might be a while.

"Coincidence," she said aloud.

"Probably," Rachel agreed. "Is there anything you need? I should be getting back. Mark'll be back soon."

Lise heated up a can of soup, sliced some cheese onto crackers and called the combination dinner. Watching the evening news while she ate she slipped back into the rhythms of the City, putting Michigan back into the seldom looked at portions of her mind. There was none of the lingering malignance she expected to feel after an outburst of the Phenomena—despite the dirt on the sofa. She should have gotten the vacuum out before eating, she'd never get to it now.

The dirt was still there two days later when she got home from a long day at the office. She thought, again, about vacuuming and decided to call Maria instead. She'd been unable to catch up with her friend since her return from Michigan.

"She can't come to the phone," Bob replied when he answered the phone.

Something was seriously askew at the DelVecchio's; Lise felt a slackness in her gut. It wasn't the same slackness she'd felt when her brother had called and told her about her dad, but it was enough to make her freeze.

"What's wrong?" she asked.

"She's napping; she can't come to the phone, that's all."

"But she's okay, isn't she?" There was desperation in Lise's voice. "Nothing's happened to her?"

''No, not yet.''

Lise relapsed into silence. Whatever was actually wrong with Maria it was dwarfed the the coldness in Bob's voice. While she held her breath she sought phrases which might unlock his trust. He was blaming her for whatever had happened. Maria was indisposed and Bob was angry, not with his wife, but with Lise herself. There was no way to unlock his trust.

''Well, maybe I'll call her at work tomorrow,'' she suggested.

''She won't be at work tomorrow.''

''Well, it's not terribly important. I just wanted to tell her about Michigan this time around. Tell her I hope she's feeling better, will you? I'll call her again—or have her call me when she'd feeling up to it, okay? Maybe I could drop over after work tomorrow?'' Lise forced banal amiability into her voice and waited for his response.

''Don't'' was all he said before slamming the phone down.

Lise was up to the fifth digit of their phone number before caution overcame her. She hung up the phone and paced the room. A stifling panic grew and doubled with each step she took. The need to know what had happened became all-consuming and to get around it she had to talk to someone else.

Sally's phone was busy; Nigel didn't have a phone wherever it was that he lived and Alan was either out or not answering his phone. Rachel and Mark across the hall? Her hand was on the upper lock before she rejected them. The Englishwoman—but Lise couldn't remember the name of her hotel and Sally was still on the phone. She started to dial the DelVecchio's and stopped again before completing the process. Vestiges of pride and reasonableness finally triumphed over her ranpant emotions; she could wait. There was nothing terribly urgent—as she'd told Bob. She would wait until time made things clearer.

As Bob promised, Maria was not at the dress boutique the next day. The shopowner knew nothing more than that her employee wasn't feeling well; she guessed it might have something to do with Maria's newly confirmed pregnancy. This was the first Lise had heard of that.

Back in the office she wondered if Bob's erratic behavior couldn't be traced to the same cause. Her concern faded as she dug into the pile of work that had accumulated in her absence. She worked late, returning home a little before nine—hungry, tired and willing to forget everything but her own comfort. The phone was ringing.

"Bob said you wanted to talk to me," Maria explained. "What's up?"

She's been sick, Lise reminded herself, she's apt to sound unenthusiastic. "Oh, nothing very much. Dad's going to be okay—they've told him to slow down and I think he's going to listen. I've been reaccepted by everyone—"

"That's nice."

"Actually, I'm more worried about you. Bob sounded pretty upset when he said you were sick. 'Course I didn't know about the baby then—Congratulations—what's the date?" Lise continued trying to fill the gaps in the conversation.

"I wasn't sick."

Lise retreated from the conversation, reassured herself that she couldn't be at fault and confronted the issue. "Maria, what's bothering you and Bob? If I didn't know better I'd say you were angry at me."

Maria sighed. "No, I guess it's not your fault. It's hard to think straight now. There were problems with my pregnancy. I went to a doctor—No," she paused and drew a ragged breath. "Lise, I just can't talk about it now."

The frantic tightness returned. "I think I've a right to know, if you think, somehow, I've done something to interfere—" Lise said in a voice that revealed the turmoil within her.

"You haven't, really. I'd like to explain, but not now."

"Tomorrow then? Lunch? Twelve-thirty—as usual?"

Somewhere in the sobs that erupted from Maria's end of the line came the words yes and that's fine. There were no good-byes, just the sound of the phone bouncing as it was hung up. Lise, too, burst into tears.

She would have apologized for the sun rising in the East at that moment and by the time she reached the appointed restaurant the next day she had uncovered a myriad of neglected, unatoned-for slights she did intend to apologize for—if Maria was there. She had meant to arrive early, but Maria was there before her, looking pale and shaken.

"I'm sorry I'm late," Lise began before she sat down.

"You're not late; it's barely a quarter after. I didn't go to work again so I had plenty of time to get here."

"Have you ordered yet?"

"I don't think I'll eat anything."

Lise continued with the moribund conversation. "I'm not terribly hungry either. Why not just walk around? It's a nice day out. If you're up for it."

Maria grimaced. "No, I think I'll have a glass of iced tea. It'll be easier sitting down—I think."

"Maria—what've I done to you? What can I do to undo it?" Lise pleaded.

Maria's eyes misted over. She blotted them with a tissue and shredded it in her hands. "The Phenomena aren't just in your apartment anymore. They've moved—they followed me." Maria shrugged as words failed to convey her memories. "Friday night, after the Beltane ritual at Sally's, they came after me. They changed the baby. Yesterday I had an abortion—I had to; there wasn't any other way."

The ice in her water-glass chattered against the sides as Lise sipped from it. Maria was explaining what had happened that night, how Edith had been the one to break the thrall of the invading Phenomena but not in time to save the baby.

None of that mattered to Lise anyway. All that mattered to her had been said right at the start: her apartment had spawned some hellish Phenomena that had caused Maria to go against her upbringing and abort the child.

"It's over now, Lise—it can't be undone. There's nothing you or I can do now."

The balance had begun to swing the other way; Maria was comforting Lise.

"It's evil. You, Alan, Jessica—even the old man. It reaches out and takes people, Maria. I'm part of a curse. It lives with me, but it doesn't want me—it wants my friends." Lise berated herself.

"Lise, you're not part of it. We were wrong. None of this

is your fault. You never knew it was going to happen. You couldn't stop it."

"I knew. I told you right from the start that there was something wrong with that apartment—with the whole set-up."

"Then, it's my fault as much as yours. We talked you into moving. Bob and I practically pushed you out the door. And for what? You could afford our place now and we need a house—"

They both hesitated, both realizing that there was now no need for Bob and Maria to get a house; there was no baby crowding them out of the Twentieth Street apartment.

"I'm sorry, Maria—so sorry," Lise repeated. The waiter came for their order; Maria got her iced tea but Lise clung morosely to her water. "I don't know what to do."

"Wait," Maria advised. "Everyone's telling me to wait: the doctor at the clinic, Edith—Mostly Edith. I don't know what we'd have done without her. She brought me back after It touched me, when I didn't think I'd keep living. She's got the power to make the Phenomena go away, Lise."

"Then I'm glad she was there when I wasn't," Lise mumbled bitterly.

"She came as soon as Bob called her. She's staying here just to help us deal with the Phenomena. She thinks you could learn to control them—"

"I'm glad she helped you," Lise repeated, though she wasn't glad at all. She couldn't share Maria's enthusiasm for the woman any more than Maria seemed able to share her liking for Nigel. Edith had come on the scene too conveniently for Lise's comfort. She couldn't yet separate the woman and her dead relatives from the Phenomena and the notion that they were all tied together in a profoundly malignant way.

The women left the restaurant professing that their friendship could survive anything the Phenomena could throw at them. Throughout the afternoon Lise manipulated the abacus-stones of emotion and rationalization until she could believe that it was Edith and not herself who should feel the guilt. Edith's relatives had failed to control the Phenomena in the first place, then Edith had been late in getting to the States and finally Edith hadn't gotten to Maria in time to save the baby. After all, by Maria's words, Edith did have the power to control the Phenomena.

Edith Brompton, curse-bearer, who had been so accessible to the DelVecchios when they wanted her; who had known about the Phenomena from the beginning; who might have wanted the child as much as the Phenomena did. They had only the Englishwoman's word and Jessica's impression to vouch for the Riverside coven's benevolence. And, as Lise considered further, there was a lot more to be said against the coven than for it.

There were facts that didn't square with the emotional package Lise constructed in her mind; she discarded them. Her need to be free of guilt was greater than her need for the truth.

At the end of the day Lise went uptown to Culpeper's intending to warn Sally about Edith and to take Nigel into her confidence. He would surely be willing to use magick for Maria and against Edith and now she was ready to practice ritual magick on her own.

She opened the shop-door and stopped cold. The Englishwoman was sitting behind the cash-register where Nigel usually sat; Sally was talking comfortably with her.

"Lise?" they asked in unison.

"Where's Nigel?"

Edith looked to Sally and Sally hesitated before answering. "To be honest, Lise, we don't know. He left work early last Friday and no-one's seen him since. Edith's taking his place for the time being. It's good to have you back—"

Lise fled back down the stairs without waiting to hear anymore. The scope of the betrayal overwhelmed her; the English witch had usurped Nigel's place at Culpeper's. She had wormed her way into Sally's confidence as she had done with Bob and Maria. Nigel had disappeared the same night that Maria had been attacked—but no-one had gone to look for Nigel. No-one listened for his cries of help.

She was alone now against the Phenomena, its allies and all that they could spawn.

Chapter Thirty-Two

"Seventy; seventy-five; four; five and five is ten—" Edith counted out the change from a ten dollar bill. Change-making in unfamiliar currency was the worst part of her work at Culpeper's and even that was becoming easier. She had more than enough background knowledge to answer questions about the store's supplies and neither the American nor the British governments had been much concerned about a foreign national working for an occultist once they realised an occultist had nothing to do with eye-glasses.

Her salary barely covered room and board but she hadn't taken the job for the money. After Nigel's sudden and complete disappearance, Jason and Sally had genuinely needed a knowledgeable but cheap clerk and Edith had needed something to do lest she wither away from boredom.

"How's it going?" Jason asked as he returned to the store with a sandwich for her.

"Quiet but steady," she replied.

"It could get exciting this afternoon. I'll stay out front here with you just in case," he said, unfolding the afternoon paper and setting it on the counter.

"Voodoo Priestess—Slasher Victim," Edith read aloud.

The story was meant to be read aloud; the copywriter had surpassed himself in describing the gory, alliterative scene. He was, after all, competing with the equally graphic work of the staff photographer. The pictures showed the blood-stained coat the woman had worn at her death and which the police had not hidden quickly enough.

"I should think this would discourage people from paying us a visit," Edith commented.

"In a perfectly sane world I'm sure you would be right," Jason agreed. "But this isn't a perfectly sane city."

He took a third sandwich to the back room and Edith read the rest of the article. Odile-Marie Toussaint, an immigrant from Haiti, had been twenty-eight at the time of her death. She had owned a delapidated store-front on the Upper Westside that catered to the needs of her voodoo devotees. Most of the article was on the crime itself which followed the Slasher's by now familiar pattern: brute strength had torn the door from its hinges; the police would not describe the wounds on the body.

Edith shut the paper without reading the mayor's latest promise to end the crime-spree or the side columns on the psychiatric profile of the killer. The tiny article the paper had included on voodoo had been wrong where it wasn't hopelessly vague. Edith had already explored Culpeper's library enough to know that there was a connection between voodoo and the black man who still haunted her dreams. She'd uncovered a lot about the Baron and retailored her room-warding rituals to his presumed prejudices. But despite this she didn't believe Odile was anything more than another random victim—it shouldn't have taken the Otherworld seventeen tries to locate the *mambo*.

She got out a map of Manhattan and marked the address of Odile's storefront on it.

"Planning to get lost?" Sally asked from the opposite side of the counter.

Edith laughed nervously. "No, just seeing where that poor woman lived."

"Starting to get worried? It's hard not to," Sally answered her own question. "What was she—seventeen or number eighteen? It makes you queasy to realize that the police aren't doing any better with the Slasher than they did with Jack the Ripper."

"There are unfortunate similarities. We can only hope and wait," Edith said as she folded the map and stared into nothingness.

"Have you made plans for dinner, yet?" Sally asked, snapping Edith out of her reverie. "I've got a friend I'd like you to meet."

Edith arched her brows in a physical expression of inquiry.

"Jessica was at Lise's apartment last December with me. She had a bad psychic experience there—bad enough for her to back away from the Craft and almost all of her friends. She called this morning to say that she wanted to talk to you if you were still in town."

Edith agreed to the dinner but the plans for it were almost swept out of her mind by the arrival of a gaggle of curious teenagers. Jason's prophecies were coming true: any mention of the occult in the papers brought an odd lot of customers to their door. Edith answered the inane and often rude questions with the calmest intelligence she could.

The afternoon tide had washed up some two-dozen curiosity-seekers and these were enough to leave Edith in total silence at the end of the day. She rode the subway with Sally without attempting to conquer the constant noise with conversation. They were silent on the short walk from the station to Jessica's home.

Edith knew immediately what Jessica's talents were. Her dark eyes had Hector's wariness and her home was insulated against forces which the rest of the world knew nothing about. Edith extended her hand and was unsurprised when Jessica held it tightly for a few extra moments.

"Welcome," Jessica said, releasing Edith's hand and leading the way to a back room where fruit and cheese were already laid out and handmade quilts covered the walls.

"You couldn't have picked a better day to invite us," Sally affirmed after nibbling a handful of grapes. "This latest Slasher victim brought out the fruits-and-nuts. It's always so quiet here—peaceful, like a garden."

Edith felt the calm of the room but was not yet ready to partake of it. She perched on a rocking-chair and was immediately joined by a calico cat.

"Musli's my official greeter," Jessica said of the cat. "It's her job to keep everyone in the right mood. She really owns this place."

Edith continued to pet the cat. It wasn't time for her to speak yet. Sally could guide the conversation while she observed.

"You said something made you change your mind—made you think about coming back to New Moon," Sally began and the cat jumped from Edith's lap to Jessica's.

Jessica watched Edith rather than Sally as she spoke. "You knew him, didn't you? You're related to the man who died in Lise Brown's apartment. You knew his coven?"

Edith nodded.

"I can still feel his pain—even this far away in time and space. I'm afraid of being drawn back to him so I wouldn't work at all. But, now I'm convinced I don't want to be alone any more, whatever the price I'd have to pay."

Sally started to speak but Edith cut her off. "You have contact with my brother-in-law Arthur Andrews here?"

"No, not with him, with the place where he is."

"We almost lost Jessie to another world that night," Sally added for Edith's benefit. "I couldn't blame her for what she decided and for backing away."

"It's more than that now, Sally. Something is happening here. I can't quite explain it but the same things I felt around Arthur Andrews I feel in this city. There are holes in the past and the present and things keep disappearing."

Edith recalled Hector's story and compared descriptions of the essentially indescribable. The stories meshed well with each and with what she herself had encountered at Yule—but she could scarcely send Jessica to Caer Maen for safe-keeping as she had with Hector.

"Do you know of Hector Seymour?" she asked, taking a change that coincidence was dominant in the occult.

"Hector Seymour? Yes—I've heard of him. He does work for the British police, I think. Do you know him well?"

"Well enough. He has felt the same things you have. He was telling me about them just before I left London. I'd asked his help in learning the details of Arthur's death and, like you, he found that finding Arthur on the Other Side changed him."

"Then he's told you? You know already?" Jessica asked with relief.

Edith swallowed hard. "No, Hector said things were—spongy. I haven't heard from him directly since the end of January."

"There's a psychic horror loose among us," Jessica said quickly. "Something right out of the Saturday afternoon movies—and I don't want to be alone to face it. The covens might have power against it, but no one person would."

"Lise's Phenomena?" Sally guessed.

"Well, maybe there's no connection, but this thing feels a lot like what I found at Lise's. I went back up to her building—as an experiment. I couldn't get within a block of the place—it was that bad." The cat butted her mistress' hand.

"What about Lise, then—she's alone and *in* that building," Edith asked into silence.

"She'll be alright for a while longer. There's something in the apartment that will protect her, I think. But only her—the rest of us are in danger."

Edith knew all she wanted to know. If she were lucky she wouldn't have to learn more, but she wasn't lucky.

"The woman who died last night," Jessica began. "She was performing a ritual just before she was attacked. She was drawing water from the dead—it's a voodoo ceremony to rid a place of restless spirits. The ritual went bad. I don't know what went bad, or how—my sources at the police department don't remember details they can't understand—but she got everyone else out of her place in time. She faced *it* alone and it killed her. That's why I don't want to be alone any more, and also why I had to talk to you first; I could bring it with me."

"Do you really think the Slasher is pure psychotic evil? Not human?" Sally asked incredulously. Edith sat back to hear Jessica's answer.

"No, not really," Jessica admitted. "It must be a man; someone who's gotten caught up in this. He's incredibly strong—he'd have to be to do what he's done. But psychotics can be, you know, when they're in the grip of psychosis."

"Friends of mine, members of my brother-in-law's coven, were the first victims," Edith offered for consideration.

"I hadn't known that. Well—I don't know much about the first cases. The police have to be pretty much up a creek before they call me," Jessica admitted.

"You've actually—" Sally hesitated, "—worked with these murders?"

"Only since about the tenth. My detective called me and asked me to take a look, as he puts it, at the evidence. There wasn't very much—scraps of cloth. When I touched them I felt the danger. I lied and said I couldn't feel anything." Jessica looked beyond the walls of the room for a moment. "If I said what I feel when I touch those things it wouldn't help. The police can't cope with the Slasher.

"But even a psychotic makes mistakes, sooner or later. They'll find a fingerprint or a blood sample. Something they can work with,'' Jessica concluded as if trying to convince herself.

''They've found nothing so far?'' Edith remembered the two detectives at Rob's apartment and their determination to solve the case.

''Nothing—absolutely nothing. No motives, not much of a pattern to the victims—except for how the crime is committed. They know they've got one nut to crack. He's a cannibal—for one thing—the ears, nose and eyes are never there; a woman's breasts, a man's penis—''

''Jessica, please,'' Edith interrupted. The images were too powerful—not when she saw Rob and Marjory instead of anonymous victims. Musli came and sat beside her.

''No wonder you're frightened,'' Sally said in a cracked voice. ''New Moon's waiting for you, though. We wouldn't leave you alone to face this.''

Edith withdrew from the conversation; she could not extend the protection of Lise's nonexistent Riverside High Coven. Only a High Coven could possibly insure safety against what Jessica had described and there wasn't much time left for the formation of a Riverside High Coven. Over half the ritual year had passed and the Otherworld was growing stronger. The murders were coming more closely now—at least one a week.

Jessica might have been a gourmet cook, Edith didn't remember. She ate the meal set before her without tasting any of it. Only the cat, Musli, seemed aware of her wayward thoughts. It never left her side; its purr reminded Edith of the warrens at Caer Maen and set her thoughts in useful directions.

Lise Brown would have to be made to understand the dangers—and led to understand that if she couldn't control the Rift herself, if she couldn't bring a High Coven into being around her, then she would have to step aside and let others try—perhaps Sally's New Moon coven. The Riverside circle should include Jessica, but the psychic could never undertake the closing; her rapport would make her too vulnerable to Otherworldly temptation. It took a special durability to guide a High Coven and Edith prayed that Lise would find it within herself.

Chapter Thirty-Three

The grey police barriers set up around Madame Odile's voodoo shop seemed more imposing than similar barriers used to mark parade routes. However many curiosity-seekers had been by the store-front during the afternoon, the street was empty now and Lise studied the dark, broken windows by herself—save for the two policemen who ignored her.

She wasn't normally one to gawk at tragedy. The notion to take the train an extra stop after the unsettling visit to Culpeper's had been sudden: an action accomplished before it was questioned. She reached the barricaded crime scene without knowing what she expected to find there. She walked around the cordon to the waiting policemen—thought better of talking to them and headed back to Riverside Drive and home. She didn't really want to know more than had been printed in the papers.

"I'm sorry," she whispered to the warm May air. "I can't help it. I can't control it—not for Maria or her baby or Alan or anyone else. I know I should have—but I don't know how."

There were tears running down her cheeks so, of course, Sam was in the lobby staring right at her when she came through the doors.

"Miz Brown, whatever's wrong?" he asked, scurrying toward her.

"Nothing Sam, nothing really." She sniffed loudly and caught a teardrop on her sleeve. "I don't know what came over me as I was walking up the block."

"Maybe you need someone to talk to—to find out what did come over you."

"No, Sam," Lise protested, though she followed him into the cubicle. Acute embarrassment had contracted her stomach to the size of a walnut that rattled uncomfortably beneath her ribs. She did need someone to talk to but however he smiled or cajoled it wasn't going to be her doorman.

She escaped to the elevator without checking her mailbox. Not that there was anyone she could talk to upstairs either. She closed the door of her apartment and slid the bolts into place. She took refuge in the bathtub, as was her custom when things got the better of her. There, fortified with bubbling bath salts, she stripped herself of the day's events—though not of the need to share them.

She sorted through her reactions to Odile's death and Maria's abortion—two lives for which she felt personally responsible, but by then the water had gone tepid. She had all the questions with none of the answers. Wrapped in a nightgown and robe, Lise curled up on the sofa and stared at the glass goddess.

"It was better when the Phenomena were just here—wasn't it?" she asked the statue. "I didn't get much sleep but there weren't any murders or crazy people either. It was my inconvenience—correction, my madness when it was here. And no, I don't forget how terrified I've been. But the Phenomena weren't so dangerous then. I'd rather they were all back here—if only for Alan's sake. It's worse to be crazy like that than to be dead. But it's too late now—even for Alan—isn't it?"

Lise stared at the glass, holding her breath, waiting for a miracle. Those outstretched arms might open, the cloudy drapery of her gown might shimmer with life. The Wiccan goddess might have the answers she sought. The goddess said nothing but while Lise waited the phone rang.

"Hello?" she said, still watching the statue.

"Lise is that you? It's Alan."

A chill raced down Lise's back: to expect a goddess and get a madman! She turned away from the statue. "Where are you? I haven't heard from you for weeks."

"Keeping busy. I've run at least twenty rolls of film through my camera but I haven't caught that cat. I don't get anything more than a shadow. Now I've gotten my own developing and processing gear."

"It must be very expensive."

"No problem, my ex-wife's paying for it. I wanted to be sure you were okay, though. I've been worried all day."

"Worried about me?" Lise sputtered. "That's nice of you, but silly. I'm fine. Keeping myself busy, too."

"Yeah, I heard you got my job. Don't let Krozer get to

you; treat him with the contempt he deserves and he'll leave you alone. But that's not why I was worried. I know you can handle it—I trained you. I was worried on account of that voodoo woman—you've heard, haven't you? She's the one you saw, wasn't she—back when we thought it was voodoo?"

"Yes," Lise admitted. "I visited Madame Odile's back in January. And the truth of it is that I'm taking it hard. She's the third—"

"Third what?" he interrupted with interest.

"Third victim: Odile Toussaint, Maria's unborn baby and—and—" she caught herself, "and Nigel," she improvised.

"Nigel?" Alan replied, drawing out the name. "Ni-gel? What's happened to ol' Nige-baby. Phenomena aren't on his side any more?"

It had been a singularly ill-inspired improvisation. "He's disappeared."

"Ol' Nige-baby? And you think the cat got him? No way, my lady-fair, no way. Old Nigel's safe from anything except maybe you witches. The Wicca's a castration cult, you know—"

Lise wondered, despite her annoyance with his taunts, if he'd actually been following Nigel; he might know what had happened to him, But it would be morally reprehensible to encourage the demons that lived in Alan's imagination.

"Can't find him?" Alan asked into her silence. "He hasn't disappeared. He was up in your neck of the woods last night—in the park across from you. You could have seen him if you'd looked out at the right time."

"Alan, that's enough. You don't have to like him, but lying isn't going to prove anything," she scolded.

"What 'lying'? I've got his picture."

Alan's voice took on that lilt it had when he was in the grip of his obsession. Lise closed her mind to the insanity of his voice and sought a verbal end-run that would get Nigel out of their conversation. "Then I stand corrected—Nigel wasn't a victim."

"No, ol' Nigel isn't a victim. He was up there walking

down Odile's street, whistling away. But, he hasn't seen me; he doesn't know what I know. I've been too careful for that. Old Nigel hasn't seen me."

"Alan, this is ridiculous," Lise said, twisting the cord nervously. "You don't like Nigel—fine. Maybe you're jealous—not so fine but understandable—" she brought the discussion to an abrupt and unplanned end by twisting the cord once too many times and knocking the phone off the table. The connection was severed.

After righting the phone she stared at it, defying it to ring again but wondering if she shouldn't call him. It was only as the minutes went by in silence that she thought at all about what he had said and what, if anything, she should believe of it. In the end she believed that Nigel was alive and well, although not interested in picking up the threads he'd dropped at Beltane. The rest she discarded.

"I can't cope," she said to the statue. "Nothing makes sense. I'm out of place; Nigel's out of place; even Alan's out of place. I need a sign, something that will tell me what to do next—"

She was trapped in the bad habit of looking for omens but not waiting for them. She could see the guiding hand of fate in the slightest riffle of a curtain but when, for all her wanting, nothing happened she could not see that for what it was and went to bed nursing her sense of being out-of-place in the grand schemes of the universe.

She moved through the next few days like a person surrounded by wet paint. Nothing moved naturally; she was aware of the awkwardness of every gesture she made. But the world took no notice of her anxiety. Sunday came and she did the *Times* crossword puzzle in an open courtyard at the Cloisters, far from the Dedication class.

It was not that she had returned to traditional religion. The Cloisters might be magickal but they were also nonsectarian. If Lise had abandoned anything it was the traditional Wiccan pathway Sally was offering in measured weekly doses.

With her livingroom the source for things that destroyed other minds and bodies Lise found little relevence in Sally's lectures on herbs and moon-spells. Or she had convinced herself that it was Culpeper's irrelevance that kept her from class not the fact that Nigel was missing or that Edith might be there now.

She stopped at the deli for a roast-beef sandwich and ignored the phone as she worked her way through the three locks on her door. Whoever it was, if they really wanted to talk to her they'd call back, as Maria did an hour or so later.

"We missed you at class today," Maria said.

"I don't think I'm going through with it."

"But, why Lise? Edith was there—she wanted to talk to you—on your own terms."

"My terms are that I deal with this myself. I've said that all along and I mean it—especially after what's happened to you. I don't want anyone else involved."

"But we already are involved. What about the Thou Shalt Not Witch Alone rules? Don't you think it's risky to deal with the Phenomena by yourself? You might do the wrong things; everything might get turned on you. Why won't you work with Edith? She's had experience with your Phenomena?"

"I've thought about it and I'll take the responsibilities for my own mistakes—if I make them. But, if I did want help she'd be the last person I'd ask. I know she's got something to do with the Phenomena but I don't know what and that strikes me as a whole lot more dangerous than facing the Phenomena alone."

"I know that Edith's desperate to talk to you," Maria insisted. "Her daughter's been hit by Phenomena—"

"She's got a daughter over here too?" Lise cursed this additional complication.

"No, her daughter's in England but she's linked to the woman who lived in your apartment. Anyway, the daughter was leading a Beltane ritual in England and a Phenomena tried to tear out her throat. She's in the hospital and Edith thinks that if she doesn't get to your apartment soon we're all going to be in real danger."

'She's making up stories," Lise answered quickly, unable to believe that her Phenomena could reach to England and a woman she didn't know. "How long is it going to take you to see through that woman, Maria? Do you really think a person could spend a lifetime working with Phenomena and not be corrupted?"

"Isn't that what you think you can do?" Maria asked softly.

Lise said nothing.

"Lise, you're making me choose," Maria continued. "And I've got to choose Edith. She believes you can control the Phenomena, but you'll need training first—her training. Lise, she explained it all to me. There's a special network of covens whose rituals control the Phenomena all over the world. Without those covens things go wrong, like they've started going wrong around you. Either you take over the burden of the High Coven of Riverside or you've got to step aside and let Edith do what she can."

Lise looked at the disconnect button; it had happened with Alan by accident, it could happen a second time and she could say it had been an accident. "I think she's sold you a bill of goods, Maria. I can handle it by myself. I'm sure of my intentions. I'll write out everything beforehand, nothing will backfire on me. Once they're gone, when I'm sure I'm in control, then Edith and I can talk and if there's something I can do for this daughter of hers, I'll do it. I don't want her trying to teach me anything."

"I give up, Lise. You think you're protecting us—we're not asking for your protection. You're so willing to suspect Edith—to think the worst of her that sometimes I've got to wonder a bit about you—"

That was all Lise could take. She slammed the receiver down and refused to pick it up again when the phone rang seconds later. While it continued to ring she dragged the altar from the end of the sofa and set the glass statue on it. She jimmied the cabinet open and retrieved an *athame* along with incense and candles inherited from Riverside.

Nigel said it was only will that mattered. If her spirit was set in the right direction then everything else would fall into place. No-one, not friend nor enemy—would doubt her attitude toward the Phenomena after tonight. No-one would blame the stupidities of some witch she didn't know a half-world away on her and her apartment.

"Guardians!" she commanded with the knife held high in the candlelight. "Draw near! There's work to be done!" The flowery pseudo-poetry of the rituals wasn't for her, either.

She paced out the circle in silence, pausing only to make a pentacle salute at each cardinal point. In her haste she had forgotten to pour a glass of wine for use within the circle. Imagination came to her rescue while she knelt before the statue.

She's use blood; that was what the wine stood for, after all. The Christians weren't the only ones to realize that. Blood would be better than wine; stronger. Still kneeling, she composed her thoughts and expressed them silently.

—I want Them out of here. Out of *everywhere*. I don't want the responsibility for these things anymore. I just want them gone! Do you understand me?—

Now for the sacrifice—that part of herself which would seal the bargain. The knife was sharper than she'd thought; it opened a deep gash on her palm that bled more than she'd expected. She held her dripping hand over the out-stretched arms of the goddess. The blood filled the cupped glass hands then dribbled onto the altar.

The bargain was sealed and the blood should have stopped flowing; she'd willed it that way. There was a good sized puddle on the altar now and nothing stopping the blood that leaked from her clenched fist. She had a vision of herself kneeling before a bloody, leering goddess: a barbaric, primitive image filling her with shame. The universe laughed.

Lise broke her circle without ceremony; bandaged her hand and cleared away the mess. The vision of herself kneeling before the bloody Bitch wouldn't fade but it was only later, in bed, that she realized that the universe had laughed with Nigel's voice.

Chapter Thirty-Four

Lise studied her palm. The athame cut had healed without infection though it had seemed to take forever to do so—perhaps because she had never before watched the healing process so closely. She'd kept it bandaged long after it had scabbed over, when air might have done it good; even after she'd invented legitimate-sounding excuses for the perfectly straight gash. Each morning she had hoped it would be gone. Each morning it seemed she would have a permanent scar—an idiocy line, an indelible reminder of the laughter of the universe.

Sticking a band-aid over it, she went on with her morning routine. Out of sight, out of mind—if she was lucky. She enhanced her luck by immersing herself in her office work until nothing could distract her.

Since the abortive ritual Lise had shut out most of the world. She had had to exclude Maria for reasons too numerous to count. They saw very little of each other. Alan had no time for anything but his demon-cat and the sophisticated techniques with which he hoped to capture it. Nigel had never reappeared, not even to claim his final paycheck from Jason. So, Lise submerged herself in her work and told herself it was all that she wanted. She had success, respect and opportunity—and at twenty-five she could still kid herself that there'd be time later on for the things she was missing now.

"Consolidated liked the table you did for them, Lise," Krozier was saying from the chair beside her desk. "They said you saved them almost a million dollars. Next time they go into union negotiations they want you specifically on-site with them. Everyone here is very pleased.

"There's a retirement reception for Harm Harington next Friday, Lise," he continued in the same tone. "You should be going. I noticed that your name's not on the list."

It was gentle, sincere concern—the kind Lise disliked the most. She shuffled through the ever-changing piles of paper. "Next Friday," she mumbled, "Midsummer's Eve—I have to go out and dance with the fairies that night," she said with bantering truthfulness that most often stopped further inquiries into her private life.

Krozier was not amused. "Lise—it's not for Harm. You don't know him; he doesn't know you. But you've got to have a few more rungs under your feet before you start bucking the tide." Krozier wasn't old enough to be her father but that didn't stop his paternal advice.

The Dedication class was having a dinner that night and initiation the next—not that Lise was going to be initiated after missing the last six weeks of class. But Maria had invited her to a private dinner beforehand, the first meal they would have shared since Beltane and its attendant disasters. She had faced a choice between much-needed fence-mending and business. Krozier promised money and status. Maria promised? Lise had acquaintances and coffee-machine comrades in her new business stratum but not friends.

"I'll see what I can re-arrange. In the future I'll keep my priorities straight," she mumbled.

"See what you can do. If you want to bring someone—go ahead. The men do. Bring a girl-friend, if you want—there're never enough women—if she'd fit in, of course."

Lise nodded as Krozier left her office.

Like Alan before her, Lise used the higher salary to avoid the pretense of cooking. If she didn't eat out she brought food in—this time an aluminium plate of shrimp scampi that had leaked and left her chunk of Italian bread a delightful, buttery, garlicky mess that she licked eagerly off her fingers. There were at least ten hours before she had to breathe on civilization again.

The intercom buzzer went off.

"Gentleman to see you, Miz Brown," Sam said to her.

"Who?" she asked, listing the possibilities: Alan depressed, Alan obsessed or Alan manic.

"Says his name's Nigel. Shall I send him up?"

"Yes! please—go ahead."

She crumpled the tin plate into the trash, sprayed the kitchen with air freshener that added the aroma of sandalwood to the garlic and rummaged through her purse for a mint. She found her shoes just as the doorbell rang.

"Long time; no see," Nigel said, putting a bouquet of flowers in her hand, slipping past her arms and heading for the livingroom.

"One could say the same of you. I've at least been where I usually am—and you haven't." She paused in the kitchen to fill an inherited vase with water.

"Then where were you on Beltane when I needed you?" he accused.

In all her imagined reunions with Nigel there had been nothing to warn her of his bitterness. She had her back to him, putting the vase on the table as his anger hit her. He'd changed in the weeks he'd been gone—hardened. The planes of his face stood out in sharp relief, there wasn't an extra ounce on him. His posture was tense even though he was lounging on the sofa.

"I was in the waiting room of the University of Michigan hospital. My father was in surgery." She leaned back against the table rather than sit beside him.

The hardness faded. "Okay—I guess he's got the right. I shouldn't hold a grudge. I should've believed Maria. How's your friend Alan—the one we were going to help that night."

"Still chasing cats," she answered, feeling her pulse rise. "In his own way he's become very consistant."

"I'd like to talk to him someday about his cats."

"They're figments of his imagination. Talking to him about them will only reinforce his belief that they're real—and that's not right."

"Maybe they aren't figments of his imagination?"

Her pulse was racing now and the more she tried to hide the fact, the dizzier she got. "I don't want to talk about Alan or Alan's cats. Tell me what you've been doing this past month and a half. Sally and Jason were worried sick when you didn't show up back at Culpeper's. We even thought the Slasher might have gotten you."

Nigel shrugged. "Things just got to be too much. They had plans for me; they were always on my back." He stared past her as he spoke. "Everything's got big plans for me—big plans. Nigel do this—Nigel do that. It got out of control at Beltane. I wanted to see you, Lise. I wanted to come up here and be with you that night.

"I like it up here—it's like home to me. Your friend Maria got on my case—as if she thought I'd come in here and steal something when all I wanted was a peaceful place for a while—"

"But I've been back over a month," Lise reminded him.

"When I put something behind me—" he paused, making a fist that brought up the veins on the back of his hand. "Right then, after Beltane it was just as well I didn't see you. But I couldn't get you out of my thoughts so I've come back. Even if it means Culpeper's, I've come back for you."

He was confessing to her and to her apartment; that much she could understand, even if the reason for the confession eluded her. "Well, it won't mean Culpeper's," she said carefully. "I've done a bit of dropping out myself. I guess you could say things were swarming over me too." She tried to create a sense of empathy between them. "I guess if everyone's going to blame me for the Phenomena I'll have to take care of them my own way."

"They haven't been bothering you again, have they?" he said, jumping out to the middle of the room.

"No, not me—but just about everyone else. I was getting to feel very guilty. I remembered what you said about how personal magick should be, so I figured that if I had to, I could do what needed doing myself."

He relaxed and she didn't tell him how haunting her attempt at magick had been, how her palm still itched, as it itched now, or how the universe had mocked her with his voice.

"I was right," he said, taking her in his arms and squeezing her until her back popped. "You were strong enough.

No-one can push you around. I need you, Lise. I need you very much.''

He went limp and she struggled to keep them both upright. ''Nigel, love, we're going to fall over—''

''Do you really mean that?''

''Yes, you're not as light as you look, and I'm not that strong—''

He straightened and stood inches away from her. ''No, that you love me. I don't think I've ever been loved—not truly loved.''

Lise took the opportunity to retreat to the sofa. ''Yes, I could love you. Why not? There's nothing inherently unlovable about you. I'm not saying I love you—or anyone else—mind you—''

''But you called me 'love' just now?''

''A figure of speech; a cheapening of the word. I enjoy your company and I've missed you. You're a fantastic lover,'' she admitted, reddening slightly. ''But I'm not ready for or interested in falling in love.''

''Love isn't something you plan—like planting seeds. It just happens. I belong to you already. You're a part of me—somewhere that I return to. But, it'll only work if you let yourself feel the same way.''

She could only see his eyes—a startling shade of blue that captured all his intensity and yearning then shot it into her. His craving held her motionless. His pupils seemed to grow larger as she watched until everything was a uniform, luminious black.

She could love him. He fitted nicely into all the physical and emotional contours of her desire. The idea got better the longer she considered it—but it wasn't her idea. Closing her eyes, Lise freed her arms from his and pushed him back. He could have resisted and she'd have been in trouble, but she was able to create an arm's length between them.

''I don't know how things work where you come from, Nigel, but I won't be conquered by some sort of sexual charisma. Maybe you don't think that love grows like seeds but that's exactly how I think it grows. If you really want to find out if I'll love you you're going to have to give me more space."

He stared into nothingness again. "I don't want to leave," he whispered. "This is the only place where I feel comfortable."

"I didn't say you had to leave," Lise took his hand. "I said you can't force me to love you. We'll just have to see how it goes."

He lapsed into silence while Lise reminded herself how little she knew about this man who spoke so desperately of love. He had changed so much in just the short time she'd known him—though she couldn't define all the changes or what had provoked them.

"Just what *have* you been doing for the last six weeks?" she demanded.

"Odds and ends. Getting to know the city better."

"But what have you been living on?"

"I get by; I don't need very much."

Lise sat back perplexed. Usually Nigel made a story out of everything; reticence was not his style. Perhaps he wasn't in love himself, just in need of a place to stay. Perhaps it wasn't emotional intensity but some drug-induced personality aberration that made him watch her so closely then stare into space. He hadn't lost much weight but he did look hungry.

"Let's go to bed now," he announced suddenly.

She realized, with a sense of foreboding, that she didn't want to share his passions, not now with so many questions in her mind about him. "No, I've got to go to work early tomorrow. It'll be a busy day and I need my sleep. God—doesn't that sound awful? When I put it that way, I mean—but it's the truth. Business before pleasure these days—dammit." She tried unsuccessfully to laugh.

"I have to leave?" he asked.

"Well, yes. You must have someplace to go, don't you?"

"Lise, I can't leave here." He gripped her hands tightly.

"Why not? What's happening to you, anyway?"

"I made enemies, enemies of the worst kind at Culpeper's. Not Sally and Jason, but others—you know who I mean.

They're looking for me and they won't stop for anything. They follow me everywhere." He paused and Lise thought of Edith and Alan with his cameras, though Alan certainly had nothing to do with Culpeper's. "No, Lise, it's not my imagination. I'm not Alan or his cat. These are real enemies and real attacks. But they can't reach me here because of you and the magick here."

"I might be susceptible to flattery," she replied, "but not like this. Really—it's getting late. Listen, I've got a business party next Friday—how about coming with me?"

"I'll do anything next Friday, but let me stay here now."

He lunged forward and there was no mistaking the power of his emotions—even if Lise couldn't be certain which emotions were driving him. She had known since that first night with him that he would not take a simple no for an answer and, as she suspected, he was unaccustomed to defeat. His fingers were kneading the tense muscles of her back. She could play these games, too—if she had to. She went rigid with icy disapproval.

"Don't turn me away, Lise," he warned. "My enemies are your enemies. If they destroy me they'll come after you. They won't believe you if you say you're innocent of me. Our only hope is to stay together and fight them on our own terms."

He wasn't brutal, just overpoweringly strong. The pressure of his embrace warned her that she would have to yield or be injured.

"Nigel!" she snarled as the buttons of her blouse popped open.

The hall doorbell rang and they froze in mid-struggle. Lise glared at him and he released her. Her visitor had to be someone in the building—maybe Rachel. Or maybe Sam had gotten suspicious; she wouldn't complain this time.

Nigel must be high on drugs, she thought, straightening her clothes and releasing the first lock. Drugs did things like this. He certainly wasn't himself, certainly not someone she should make a habit of entertaining. She turned the last knob and swung the door open.

Lise would have screamed, if she could have found her voice.

"Good evening, Miss Brown."

He was tall, maybe six-foot-six, the color of brown mahogany and dressed in clothes that belonged in a vampire movie. His richly accented West Indies voice rippled with power.

"I heard your call for help."

There was a crash in the livingroom, the sound of a window slamming open and footsteps on the fire-escape.

"May I help you?" Baron Samedi asked.

The hall light reflected off his bald head. It reflected off the brass skull that capped his walking stick. The eyes of the skull glowed the same dark red as the lining of his cape. A familiar scent of incense clung to him and tendrils of smoke curled around his shoulders.

"Who are you?" Lise demanded in a quivering voice.

"I am the Baron Samedi," he said, light playing off his luminous teeth as he smiled. "I heard your call—but he is already gone. Lock your doors and windows, Miss Brown—and be quick about it!"

He bowed to her then turned and raced up the stairs. Lise needed no special urging to do what she'd been told to do, though the security grate over her fire-escape window had been torn from the wood and the glass itself was cracked from the panic of Nigel's escape.

Lise picked up the phone to notify the police, then thought of what she would have to explain to them and hung up. The unbelievability of her entire life these days struck her as she sat down next to the glass-statue and prepared to keep a night-long vigil beside the broken window.

Chapter Thirty-Five

"So, by the time everything was finished it cost me a hundred dollars to put fifty cents' of plastic wood in my windows and spend five minutes getting the security-grate back up. They wouldn't touch the broken glass. I've got duct-tape over the cracks now because everything else sweats off in the rain."

"And you think Nigel ripped the grate out when he realized you were talking to Baron Samedi?" Maria asked with a laugh.

They were enjoying a quiet dinner together; Lise had decided friendship was worth more than a promotion. A tangy German wine and the balmy evening breezes that blew over the rooftop restaurant had healed many of the wounds between them. That Lise was complaining about Nigel didn't hurt.

"The grate was definitely pulled out of the wood and no-one but Nigel was there to do it. Between that and the Baron leaving packages of incense in my mailbox—"

"I'd think you'd be a nervous wreck—but you seem to be bearing up rather well."

"I've learned to take these things in stride."

There was truth in what she said—not the whole truth, but enough. She coped better than anyone who had seen her in January might have expected. After one night's vigil by the broken window she'd forced herself back to normal sleep patterns. She didn't mention the price of all this will-power: *déjà-vu* nightmares that struck if she relaxed too much while awake.

"I guess we've both recovered then," Maria lifted her wineglass for a mid-meal toast, "though with Nigel and the Baron on the streets it's a bit difficult to stay relaxed."

"Or to know who to trust," Lise added. "You know I'd rather believe Nigel—but he was acting so strangely. The

Baron was a gentleman—not that that would matter. It's the lesser of two evils, I guess."

"Just draw a line in your life and put both of them on the far side of it. I don't understand why you think one of them has to be right and the other wrong."

"I don't think they'd stay on the other side. They'll come back, just like the Slasher comes back and the Phenomena come back. They're going to make me choose and I'd like to think it over first."

Maria nodded and ate trout almondine in silence. "What about Edith? She's never disappeared; she's never behaved strangely at all. Maybe you could trust her now?"

"I'll admit it sounds less distasteful than it used to, but it's still far from appealing."

Maria had learned not to press her luck where Edith was concerned and took off on a tangent about the latest arrivals at the boutique. Lise followed and their discussions remained innocuous through dessert. They parted in good spirits on the street outside the DelVecchios' building. Lise wished Maria well at the next night's initiation ceremony.

The evening was young enough that a subway trip to Riverside Drive seemed a reasonable risk. A variety of people still waited on the platform and she was not dressed well enough to attract unwanted attention. After looking around a second time she dropped her token in the slot. The trains were less frequent at night. She leaned against a grafitti-smeared pillar with an unfocused stare that allowed her to be alert for movement without actively watching for it.

She became aware of being watched. He was on the other side of the platform and grinned the instant she glanced his way. Then he disappeared into the underpass that connected the up and downtown platforms. It might have been Nigel, but, again it might not have been. Whoever it was, she hadn't liked that smile. Trust your paranoia, the urban native said, it could save your life. Lise decided not to take the subway after all.

She pushed quickly, but not too quickly, through the exit gate and thanked the ambient Gods when an empty taxi rolled to the corner. Without a backward glance out the windows to see if she had been followed, Lise huddled into the back seat of the cab. She radiated fear—and knew it.

"Problems?" the woman driver asked as they turned onto Seventh Avenue.

"Don't really know. A watcher—you know the type," Lise shrugged and sank further into the seat. "Better safe than sorry."

"That's the truth. Even when they catch the Slasher, it's going to take me a while to relax on the streets. Every time I pick up someone who's a little weird it kinda gets to me.

"I've been drivin' this cab for five years; been robbed a dozen times or more but, damn, this guy's got the town tied in knots. I had a guy—professor-type—in back the other day an' he said he's an avatar. So, I sez—what's an avatar an' he sez a living thing of a kind that shouldn't really be alive—like the Slasher's all the violence and craziness of the City come to life. Then he sez they'll never catch him 'cause being an avatar he's—ya know, one step beyond—"

In the back of the cab Lise ground her fingernails into her palm to keep from shaking.

"I was thinkin' he's some kind of nut," the cabbie continued, weaving through traffic and ignoring the passenger to whom she spoke. "Then last night I was down at the Battery just after they found someone. The place was crawlin' with gore-freaks so I stayed—they usually got money for a cab home. I even got out to look around myself. Jeez—never seen anything like it—

"There was a booodstain that went ten feet up the wall, if it went an inch. Heard 'em say he musta ripped the heart out while it's still beating to get the blood up so high. These plainclothesmen was lookin' around with baggies, pickin' up bits'n'pieces and dumpin' everything into plain old garbage bags. I was gonna be sick myself. Christ, the whole place smelled of puke, I wasn't the first. I was walkin' to the curb when somethin' went 'squish' under my foot.

"Jeez-o-pete, I got out of there, I tell you. Maybe the egghead was right. Maybe this Slasher isn't human. Damn, you couldn't prove it by what I saw."

Lise left the cabbie with a generous tip; she was too nauseous to wait for change. She bolted to the elevator which, fortunately, was waiting for her. She calmed her stomach with bicarbonate of soda but she had nothing to soothe her nerves with. For once she was too uneasy to retreat to the bathtub and sat, fussing with her yarns, in the living-room. Her frazzled, overextended senses strained at every sound in the building and simple will-power was not enough to force her to sleep.

Twice she was out of bed and armed with her silver mirror only to hear familiar voices leaving the elevator. By two-thirty the building was silent enough that she could hear any sound it made. By three it had started to rain—the first huge drops clanging against the fire-escape.

Generally there was security in storms; your average street criminal didn't want to get wet any more than the next urban citizen did, but the footfalls Lise awaited in the thunder weren't likely to be detered by dampness. By four-thirty, disgusted with herself and still awake, Lise resigned herself to Maria's often-voiced advice. She wasn't going to get through this fear-seige without help and Edith Brompton did have a telephone number. As soon as the regular switchboard opened, her call went through.

"Mrs. Edith Brompton, please? I don't know what room she's in," Lise said to the concierge at Edith's residence.

"It's six o'clock in the morning," the woman complained.

"She'll understand, I'm sure. It's an emergency," Lise added. Minutes passed before the phone was picked up again.

"This is Edith Brompton speaking."

Lise recognized the clipped British accent and the sleepy edge of anger. "Mrs. Brompton, Edith, this is Lise Brown. I need to talk to you."

"I'll be dressed and on my way in five minutes." All trace of anger was gone.

"No, not yet. I want to meet someplace else, someplace neutral," Lise hesitated. "I want to talk to you, hear what you have to say, then maybe we'll come up here."

"It would be just as easy for me to come to you—I do

know the way."

She was pushing again; Lise found herself mentally backing away. "Edith, I'm scared," she warned. "I'm exhausted; I haven't slept all night. I want to meet you away from here. I'll be at the restaurant on the corner of Twentieth and Third as soon as I can."

"What about right here instead? I'll have coffee and rolls waiting for you and we can talk more privately?" Edith offered.

Leaping to the conclusion that nothing too dreadful could dwell in a YWCA, Lise agreed. She dressed quickly, stuffing her hair under a pink, floppy hat and covering her eyes with sunglasses. It didn't matter that she looked like someone trying to hide, so long as no-one guessed who she was.

"You look like a refugee," Edith commented when she let her into her room almost two hours later. "Never matter. Leave your coat and that hat on the clothes-peg and tell me what to put in your coffee."

"Sugar, cream—whatever you've got. I'm not fussy."

The institutional room with its battered furniture didn't show much personality, but the desk was piled with air-mail letters, the small radio was tuned to a classical station and three bedraggled daisies were stuffed into a bottle on the window-sill. The room did not inspire fear.

"It's instant, I hope you don't mind, but that's the only way you can have coffee and I have tea."

Lise burned her tongue on the steaming liquid. The rain had stopped after she left her apartment. Edith had the window open and the solstice gave the impression of being in the middle of August rather than the middle of June. She could hear her hair friz and her sinuses close from the humidity.

"Edith," she began grimly. "I'm here because I'm giving up. I don't trust you any more than I trust Nigel or Baron Samedi, but Maria trusts you—so you're the one I'm surrendering to."

"They say the end makes the means. I'm glad you 're here and that we can talk to each other," Edith said gently. "To begin with, I don't trust Nigel and while I've not met the Baron my inclination is not to trust him either. So, you see, we do agree on somethings. We're both afraid of what lurks out of sight in your flat and, unless I miss my guess, we've both thought that we were the equal of the Otherworld and we've both had our noses bloodied rather badly."

"I thought you *could* control it?" Lise groaned. "Everything Maria's said—the letter you sent me. I didn't come here now to find out that you were a fraud."

"I am Camulac—High Priestess of Caer Maen High Coven, Guardian of the Curtain. I bear the knowledge of generations. If I do not know immediately how to heal the Rift, how to banish the Otherworld, it is only because never before has it befallen that we failed." She spoke, as Liz would say, *ex cathedra*.

Lise held her breath. She didn't doubt the woman for a heartbeat. At that moment the "Y" could easily have been the center of the universe.

"How do I fit into all this," she asked in a small voice.

Edith slipped out of her majesty as she broke a sweet roll. "Arthur was preparing to pass the burden on. He was unhappy with Riverside and himself, and meant for the Gods to choose the next Guardians. I trust he had a plan; I assume it went awry when he had a heart-attack. If this is so, then by a process I cannot guess, you were chosen as the keystone of the new High Coven of Riverside."

Lise sighed and picked up her cup. Maria had hinted at all this; it wasn't a surprise though it only made sense if fate and Gods always had the upper hand—a notion she'd discarded along with original sin back in high school.

"Even if you cannot believe that your karma has always led you this way," Edith suggested, "surely you acknowledge that since you moved your life has not been the same. You couldn't leave now if you wanted to—which you don't."

"You certainly don't kid around, do you?" Lise remarked acidly. "Okay, I'm stuck with 647. I should have been suspicious when they told me the rent."

"Rent?" Edith's eyebrows straightened. "Rent, why, my dear, Arthur's will makes you part-owner of that building. I'm sure he covered every contingency of inheritance—even though we never expected this. No, with the Otherworld anchored in your livingroom fifty years (and why there no-one knows for sure. Arthur and Gwen tried to relocate it but they never could, so they did the next best thing). The building and the land under it belongs to the tenants of apartment 647. The covenstead belongs to the High Priestess; the building which houses the Riverside Rift belongs to the High Priestess of Riverside."

Lise's protest faded before it found words. She resigned herself to the idea. After admitting defeat at four-thirty in the morning she wasn't going to quibble over terms now. She was only half-listening as Edith continued her explanations, and Edith noticed.

"You're not ready for this, are you? Of course not—how could you be? I grew up knowing—I don't remember not knowing. Well, while we don't have much time, we'll make time for you to get used to the idea."

"I appreciate that," Lise muttered.

"Sit and think about it. Let your mind wander across the idea. You can take the day to think about it. I'm not going to work; I've already called Sally. When the idea doesn't seem so strange—and it won't for long—we'll go uptown and have a look-see. I'll be more help after I've seen Riverside again."

Edith was as good as her word, reading in silence while Lise argued with herself. The explanations Edith gave did have a hypnotic power all their own. But Lise simply could not imagine herself as High Priestess of anything much less of the tradition and power Edith described.

"But I'm not even a witch!" she blurted out. "I quit the class—"

"Since we've no precident for the failure of a High Coven nor much precident for the forming of a new one it seems no surprise that you are untrained for your role. We shall simply have to proceed blindly," Edith replied in a pragmatic way that reminded Lise of her mother. "But, don't let that worry you, Lise, let that worry me."

For the time being Lise was willing to do just that. She didn't even argue when the older woman announced that they would walk the length of Manhattan to get back to her apartment—though all she really wanted to do now was sleep.

"You're not ready to sleep—you need physical exhaustion," Edith explained as she removed her staff from the closet. "The mind behaves better when it's in tune with the body."

She set a mean pace through the growing heat and humidity. When they first left Edith's room, Lise had asked questions about the Otherworld and the High Covens. After she was too tired to ask anything, Edith talked about herself and the farm at Caer Maen, of Elizabeth and the economy of Cornwall, of the Blitz and the death of her fiance. It wasn't until they were inside 647 and Edith was moving confidently through the kitchen that Lise realized she knew Edith better than she knew her own family.

"You're very good at what you do," Lise admitted. She rested against the sofa cushions, mindful as ever of the disarray, but too tired to do anything about it.

Edith handed her a glass of iced tea. "I trust the gods and believe They know what they're doing." Her voice was sharp and not to be argued with. She admired the glass goddess. "Have you set the Lady upon your altar for a personal ritual yet?"

"Just once," Lise replied and told Edith about the ritual that had given her the scar.

"Well, let me see your hand."

Lise extended her arm reluctantly and cringed when Edith touched the hard line of the scar. "I'll initiate you tonight," Edith said.

"Just the two of us? I thought it was dangerous to work alone or in small groups?" she said, rubbing her palms together.

"It is, but not as dangerous as leaving you outside the Craft. No, we'll present you to the Lady this evening—Midsummer's. It's Her ascendance—as good a time as any—But we've got work to do. I'm sure you've got everything we need but, Lise, we really can't initiate you with cobwebs on the altar."

By nightfall the apartment was spotless and Lise knew the

stories behind the ritual objects she had inherited. The Phenomena lurked in the shadows, riled by the bustling presence of the High Priestess. Yet at the same time the benevolent power Jessica had noticed was also rejuvenated. The battle lines had been drawn at last. Lise washed, robed in one of Gwen's gowns and returned to the livingroom quickly—her home was no place to be alone in tonight.

"Sit there," Edith commanded, pointing to a corner of the carpet that had lately been under the sofa. "I won't do anything fancy; you don't have to watch or pay attention. I'll bring you in and acknowledge Midsummer with you. Right now I'd like you to find the name by which you wish to be known to the gods."

As she had done throughout the day, Lise obeyed quietly. Sally had lectured them about names and Lise had already chosen one—Sybylla—because she liked the sounds. She waited for some hidden, truer name to rise in her thoughts, but none did. One name was probably as good as another; she hadn't chosen Lise and it fit her well enough.

She was distracted from her futile quest by Edith's purposeful movements at the altar and her march around to the cardinal points.

"Guardians of the sunset and departing souls," Edith said as she approached the west where Lise sat. "Home of the Goddess Diana—we beg Thee be strong in Thy watchtower this night. Hold the western elements within our sphere as we raise this our circle of Midsummer joy and celebration."

Three times Edith made the circuit of the watchtowers, sprinkling salt, wine and swinging the censer. Each time Lise was doused by the element, but Edith seemed not to care—if she noticed at all.

Lise couldn't hear the invocation, though magick became alive in the room. The candle flames all bent toward the altar and outside the circle, Lise felt her scar prickle. She had begun to scratch at it when Edith reached through the circle to take her hands.

"Join us now; tell us your name."

"Sybylla?"

"Sybylla, be welcome to the Goddess and Her Consort."

Edith guided her to the front of the altar where she stared at the familiar statue whose eyes were at last alert and whose hands reached out for her own.

"They know you, already, Sybylla. You, Sybylla have been brought here to act for Them and for all of us. You, Sybylla are charged to honor and serve Them as They have honored and served you."

Lise looked into Edith's eyes and looked away quickly. Despite the last rational strongholds of skepticism, the Gods were here—and there in Edith's eyes. No, not Edith—what had she said her Craft-name was—Camulet, Camul-something? Whatever, she was the High Priestess and she had felt Lise flinch. She laid firm hands on Lise's cheeks and stared into her eyes.

"You, Sybylla, will not take the Degrees as will your friends and companions; no-one shall know your measure. You, Sybylla shall be set apart. Your path will be your own and no-one else may safely walk it. You, Sybylla shall become a Guardian of the High Covens for the alternative is the Otherworld!"

Lise saw it then, stretching before her—the Otherworld: cold, empty and hungering. Her understanding of it deepened beyond words. It held her hand while the High Priestess held her head. It touched her with temptation and power; laid them in her hand and caressed her fingertips into a loose fist. Close the fist and It would be hers forever: not Guardian but Goddess—

"Sybylla!"

The voice burned and battered; tore flesh from her bones. Assaulted her spirit with wild, white fire.

"Sybylla! Make your choice!"

Sybylla screamed from her soul, fell to her knees as her hand was engulfed with the white fire. She pressed her hand to her belly and the flames caught there. She folded her head and shoulders into the flames; drew her feet and legs up as well and the voice tossed her like ash on the wind.

"Sybylla! Sybylla! Your *choice!*"

Chapter Thirty-Six

The High Priestess gripped the screaming girl's arms and hauled her to her feet, calling her newly chosen name, Sybylla. It was not that the High Priestess expected the stricken Sybylla to respond to that name, or to any other; she meant to remind the Gods, should their attention have wandered, of the battle being fought before Their altar.

The girl had inordinate strength. She snarled and fought tooth and nail to escape the circle. The High Priestess was filled with inspired strength herself and equally determined to keep Sybylla within the sanctifying rings.

When she had the girl, Sybylla, braced between herself and the altar she continued with the Midsummer ritual, thanking the Goddess for ripening fruits, acknowledging the height of summer and praying for a good harvest in all human endeavor. It was a short and perhaps perfunctory recitation of the rite, but the High Priestess held the girl within the circle throughout it. Then, because Sybylla was not yet dispossessed of the Otherworld, the High Priestess took the purified elements she had used to create the circle and anointed the new witch's face. Nothing more could be done within the magick sphere; she banished the circle and gave her attention to the gasping, writhing young woman.

Lise had been physically and emotionally exhausted before the start of her ordeal; she lacked the strength for a long fight with friend or foe. Her eyes opened when Edith touched them with an ice cube.

"So tired," she complained, moving awkwardly. "I just want to sleep, please let me sleep, Edith."

Well, at least she was still able to recognize people; Edith took that as a good sign. "I think you'll be more comfortable in bed, Lise. Come on now, try to get up. It's only a few steps."

Lise was slightly built but Edith could not possibly move her onto the high bed without cooperation. She urged, cajoled and used the ice to get Lise into her bedroom. Familiar surroundings would make a difference when Lise woke up; a few moments of disorientation could give the Otherworld all the opportunity It needed for a second attack.

"You'll stay with me, won't you? You won't just leave me here?" Lise asked.

Edith tossed the light coverlet back and let her slide onto the sheets. "Of course," she replied, not adding that there was no force in any realm which could have driven her out of that apartment before she knew for certain on whose side Lise/Sybylla had landed.

Lise dropped into motionless sleep and Edith could examine the scar on her hand without fear of disturbing her. The area was blistered and blood had collected under the skin. Whatever had happened at Lise's one, impulsive solitary ritual, it had enmeshed her with the Otherworld. If the swelling wasn't down by morning, Edith resolved she would open the blister and drain off the bad blood.

She left the night-light on while restoring the livingroom to its mundane condition. Lise had not yet moved in her sleep by the time the last candle had been stowed and the last chairleg set back in its carpet-cup. Edith checked Lise's vital signs: the pulse had gone up and her breathing was shallow. She was running a fever. The swelling in her hand had not gone down at all. Edith rearranged the light blankets around the unprotesting body and went into the kitchen for tea and thought.

Winter in New York City had been cold and raw but not unbearable. The summers here were something else. No air at all stirred in the apartment; the Midsummer incense was a stale blight in all the rooms. Edith finished her tea and settled into a fragile boudoir chair in the bedroom. One eye was on Lise and the other kept track of the universe.

Save for the quiet Gods Edith had no-one to turn to herself. She had initiated Lise because she believed it safer to get the girl properly within the protection of the Craft; she had not expected a full-scale struggle for her soul. In retrospect she had made the monumental, inexcusable blunder of working under the open eye of the Otherworld. Lise would have been better off at the initiation of Sally's Dedication class.

What if Lise did not awaken to her right mind? What if she did but had been subverted by the Otherworld? Edith thought of the athame tucked in her belt. She would use it if she felt she had to but she knew that if she did she would never know for sure which one of them the Otherworld had subverted.

The weight of years had never seemed so great. Sometime in those featureless hours before dawn Lise began to move under the coverlet. Edith roused herself from hazy half-sleep and felt the girl's forehead. The fever had broken, the swelling her hand was almost gone and the subcutaneous blood had been reabsorbed. She gave Lise's hand a gentle squeeze and the girl muttered something in her sleep.

Safe, for the moment; Edith dozed off herself. She awoke to Lise's alarm clock, but Lise did not, nor did she rouse to the sounds of Edith finding her way around an unfamiliar bathroom. The aroma of fresh, strong coffee, however, supplied the necessary incentive to awake.

"I feel like I've been run over by a truck," she complained and sank back onto the pillow after an unsuccessful attempt at sitting up.

"That bad?"

"Worse. One minute I was standing there listening to you—the next minute—ZAP! If I've got a muscle or tendon that isn't strained—I'm gonna make it, though. You must've been worried about me, but I'll be okay."

"You're sure?" Edith asked, the question not as lighthearted as she made it sound.

"I'm awake—that was the hardest part. I wasn't sure I could do that much. Now, if I can sit up, drink my coffee and get to the john I'll not only be on the road to recovery, I'll know the gods love me."

As it turned out she needed Edith's help to get from the bed to the bathroom. She had several more recurrences of fever during the day, each accompanied by listlessness and swelling in her hand. Though Edith watched each episode with due concern and doubt, Lise seemed to snap back on her own, aching but with a wry humor Edith could not believe was an Otherworld deception.

After sundown Lise's relapses were more serious. Her fever shot up and in her delirium she tore at her scarred hand. Edith thought of calling a doctor, though she knew of no-one over here—certainly not one who treated Craft-related symptoms. She thought, also, of her room at the "Y"; the few things that were her home-away-from-home and which were now, again, separated from her. Lise could not be left alone until she were free from relapses.

"Talk to Rachel across the hall—she's nursed me before and she's usually home days," Lise suggested the next day when it appeared the cycle would start again.

Having no better option except to call Sally or Maria who was currently guarded by an unsympathetic husband, Edith knocked on the Ratners' door and explained the situation to Rachel with as little detail as necessary. Lise was resting and would likely sleep the whole time she was out getting her clothes and more food for the nearly empty cupboards in the kitchen. She checked out of the "Y," loading everything of value or sentiment into her suitcase, packing the rest to the post-office and England, and returned to Riverside Drive by taxi several hours later. Even if Lise recovered quickly, which Edith doubted, they should be spending a lot of time together now.

"She slept the whole time," Rachel confirmed when Edith came through the doorway. "She hardly moved at all."

"I thought she might not."

"Does this have something to do with all the screaming we heard? I don't know how much Lise has told you, but this apartment is not normal. Back when Andrews lived here we thought it was him; now we think it's the place itself and I'm very worried about Lise. I think she should get to a doctor, and get out of here for her own safety."

Edith ignored the latter part of Rachel's suggestion.

"Do you know a doctor who believes, as you do, that it is this apartment that is the source of Lise's trouble?"

And so Rachel's brother David, who had attended Lise after Imholc, looked after her again. He wanted to put her in the hospital, citing a list of slow developing diseases that started with prolonged delirium and fever, but once he was reminded of that cold winter night he relented. He would call her ailment a fever-of-unexplained-origin for the medical reports Lise's company was certain to require but he left her in her own rooms to recover under Edith's arcane guidance.

That recovery took longer than even Edith expected. The woolly plush of the sofa had ceased to bother her and the apartment was as much home as the "Y" had been by the time Lise was past danger. She set new protective wards around the apartment as she had done in her rented rooms and conducted a week-long purging which heralded the last stages of Lise's recovery. By the Fourth of July holiday, her patient was ready to venture out into the sun again.

"Have we beaten them?" Lise asked as they sat on a bench in the park. "I'm well again. I know which path I'm on. The apartment is sealed against malevolence—"

"I wish it were," Edith replied. "No, we simply haven't lost the war. Only one thing counts as victory—the closing of the Riverside Rift. Until we do that we really haven't done anything."

"But the apartment is sealed and the Rift is *in* the apartment. Isn't that almost the same thing?"

"I should think we're safe from accidents or little things like your mobile pillows but nothing big—nothing like the Imholc incursion."

Lise frowned and watched the river in silence. "They could come after me again, couldn't they? The scar's still tender—"

"If they wanted to, but perseverance doesn't seem to be the mark of the Otherworld. They ignored me when they approached you and they might ignore you now that they've failed with both of us. It would seem they don't give their plans a second chance."

"What about the Slasher? Alan would say he, or it, is Otherworld."

"Oh, I agree the Slasher is Otherworld; it came through at Imholc, but somehow they've lost control of it. It's just a taste of what will live here if their plan succeeds. If it were a part of their attack, though, it would have struck closer and more frequently."

Lise nodded and they began a slow walk along the pathways, stopping to watch a dog playing frisbee with a group of teenagers.

"Odile, Rob and Marjory," Lise ennumerated. "They were all afraid. Maybe it tracks fear and can't find us?"

"Speak for yourself. I'm still quite frightened."

"Yeah, me too."

With her initiation ordeal behind her, Lise had become a student of Edith's vast knowledge of the Craft. She listened carefully and plunged into obscure philosophical arguments at the least inconsistency. Edith recorded this as a sign that the Otherworld still dwelt within the new High Priestess—weakened but ready to exploit any opportunity for doubt. Accordingly, while Edith never lied, there were many important things Lise did not know and would have to learn on her own.

Edith had forgotten herself in daydreams of the cool breezes of Cornwall when Lise halted abruptly and Edith followed the girl's line-of-sight to a pile of leaves meshed in a dying bramble bush. Emerging out of the earth-colored leaves was a fist-sized grinning skull set on a pole of weathered wood.

"A rather gruesome little souvenir, isn't it?" Edith remarked. "Makes you wonder about the man who used it."

"It's the Baron's," Lise said in a whisper. "It was with him that night before Midsummer when he came to my house—when Nigel broke the gate off the window and went down the fire-escape to get away from him."

Edith used her staff to clear the debris that covered the stained wood and metal. Her consecrated staff would also ground any vagrant malignance that might still cling to the object. Over Lise's objection she picked it up and examined it more closely.

"The eyes glowed red when he held it," Lise mused without daring to touch.

Closer viewing did disclose a faint redness to the dirty material backing the metal skull. Edith touched one of the black areas of the metal, then moistened a finger and touched it again. "This was burned, or very near a fire," she decided.

"I wonder what that means? Did the Baron catch up with Nigel?"

"If he did then I'd say he got the worst of it. The wood's got char marks as well. See here?"

Edith held the stick for Lise's examination, but Lise turned pointedly away. Her complexion had paled. Edith realized it was time to head back to the apartment if they were to forestall one of her less frequent but still ominous relapses into lassitude and fever.

"Please leave that here. I don't want it in my house," Lise pleaded as they headed back along the path.

"No," Edith said firmly and they walked the rest of the way in silence.

Though Lise remembered seeing the Baron at Midsummer, Edith's thoughts returned to those nightmarish first days in New York and her dreams about the black man chased through this park. She wasn't a seeress or psychic like Hector or Jessica; she couldn't read the past in material objects, but this wood had lain under those withered leaves for more than a month.

They paused in the lobby while Lise checked her mailbox. Sam wandered out of the cubicle to say hello but stopped short when he saw the skull-capped stick.

"Hello, Sam—quiet day, isn't it?" Edith said, watching him watch the stick.

"Yes, Miz Brompton, it is. Wherever did you get that ugly thing?"

"Under the bushes in the park. It has a rather odd charm to it, don't you think? I thought the brass might polish up and convert to a paperweight. The wood's burnt."

"Were me, I'd finish the burning. Stick the whole thing down the incinerator."

Edith nodded and followed Lise to the elevator. Once again she had the feeling that Sam was no stranger to the occult spheres but once again she had no tangible evidence to base the feeling on.

"No-one shares your liking for that thing," Lise said as the elevator cables snapped, whined and hauled them upward.

"Our enemy has left something behind," Edith replied sharply. "One studies the effect when the cause is hidden."

"It could be the Trojan horse of the Otherworld."

"There are no Greeks; I've seen to that. No, I'll study it for a while. Maybe in the end we will be no wiser and we'll just let it melt away as Sam suggested."

"There's no incinerator in this building," Lise corrected. "That's an euphemism. Two or three times a week they cart everything into dumpsters and it gets hauled away. It's part of Sam's job, I think, to see that everything gets hauled away."

Edith said nothing but thought of Sam and everyone else who might be interested in the Baron's cane. There might be a second Baron, if Lise had indeed seen him before Midsummer; perhaps the first hadn't been killed as he had in her dreams. Someone was interested; there was incense above Lise's door—the first placed there since Edith had moved in.

Chapter Thirty-Seven

The skull-cane rested inside the front door of Lise's apartment. Edith had cleaned the brass and ebony as best she could. They had not learned anything from the object. The incense had appeared just that one time when they had brought it upstairs. There was no need to keep the dubious artifact, yet Edith made no move to dispose of it and Lise, not wishing to dignify the subject with discussion, managed to ignore it.

She had recovered her health and equilibrium to the extent that she was back on the job, but her private thoughts were not yet secure enough that she wanted Edith to leave. The Otherworld still had its dormant handhold within her and she needed the High Priestess.

"Are you ever homesick?" Lise asked one night after they had eaten and Edith had placed a phone call to Liz in London.

"I have trouble remembering all the curves and slopes on the road down to Saint Ives anymore. It's been almost six months. I've never been gone from Caer Maen this long."

It had been a foolish question; she knew Edith would return home as soon as she could. "Will I be strong enough without you, or will I always worry about succumbing?"

"You'll always worry, but you'll be strong enough. I won't leave until you are."

"Sometimes, Edith, with the quiet and the waiting and the learning I feel I'm going to burst apart. I want to deal with Nigel, the Baron—even Alan's cat. Whoever our enemies truly are, I want to meet them and finish our battles," Lise said with sudden passion.

"We'll finish on Samhain and either we'll bring back what has always been or we shall simply and completely be swept away by the Otherworld."

Lise believed what Edith taught her, but she preferred not to think about that duty which set a High Coven apart from the rest. Despite all that she had seen and felt; the scarred hand that ached and sent sharp pains into her heart—despite all that she could not really believe they might all be dead November first. She could emphasize with Edith's moments of brooding silence but not share them.

They approached Lammas, the night before August first—and Edith grew even more taciturn on the subject of the Otherworld. Lise began to suspect there were things her teacher was not telling her, but then Lammas was an ambiguous holiday—a bit of winter's darkness in the midst of Summer.

"Since there was writing," Edith explained, as the July evening breezes blew in from the river, "there have been eight esbats—Great Festivals—at six- and seven-week intervals through the year: a solar quarter-day cycle and a lunar one. But, before there was writing, when people told time by the moon alone, there were only the lunar festivals. Lammas was the moon at the height of summer. It marked the time of weaning and drying off the crops—which are the foreshadows of death.

"As Imholc marks the spark of life at midwinter so Lammas is the chill of long night and death at the height of the goddess' power.

"The church, I believe, ascends the Virgin Mary bodily into heaven on the first of August; they deny the crone, the aged, infertile woman within us all. In parts of Ireland, though, they still take off their shoes and dance on rough stones until their feet bleed; that was the climax of our Lammas—"

"Edith," Lise interrupted, "is this your roundabout way of saying we're going to have trouble?"

"It is my way of awakening the images of the past within you—since I intend for you to grope your way through the ritual. You might start looking for your own images if you don't like mine. You might start thinking of who will be in your coven. You can get by without the thirteen, but you should have one person for each full moon as soon as you can."

"I've thought about that," Lise said, proud that for once she had anticipated her teacher. She got a worn brown envelope from her briefcase and spread its papers in her lap. "I don't have thirteen and they aren't balanced between men and women, but it's a start. First there's me—I don't have a partner yet, but I don't absolutely need one if I'm the High Priestess—any consort will do. Then Bob and Maria—Maria thinks she's got Bob talked into it. Then there's Rachel and Mark across the hall. They're Jewish now, but they saw everything at Imholc. Wouldn't you say we've got an obligation to take them in—since they've touched the Otherworld? And, of course, you'll be here—" Lise concluded with an implied question.

"For Lammas, but not much longer. Caer Maen needs me—I must go home. Elizabeth is still recovering, as you are, and I must be at my true place of strength for Samhain. Without me you'll have only five for Samhain—that's dangerously small. Your fingertips will barely touch when you stand in the circle."

"Well, I've thought about Sally and Jason, but they're so committed to making paganism a recognized religion that I'm not sure. In some ways I want Alan here, but he wouldn't bring any strength even if he'd come. I'd take Nigel—" Lise noticed Edith's face darken but continued, "—if I didn't have so many doubts about him now. I could steal half of Sally's Dedication class."

Edith shook her head. "Weak as a five-witch circle might be, it will still be stronger than a larger circle that is simply plugged with bodies. You must take Jessica as well—she'll give you six."

"Jessica—she's New Moon—"

"She's psychic—she'll be a link to the other High Covens. Besides, she's felt the Otherworld. A coven, any coven, needs a balance of elements in its members; without Jessica you'll have no air."

Lise grunted and set her lists aside. The Gods were supposed to provide the nucleus of the High Coven—or so Edith promised. They hadn't served Gwen and Arthur and Lise doubted they'd help her. She ran through her mental lists of friends and acquaintances; she doubted that the New Riverside would ever get up to strength.

She had decided to keep the Riverside name. It seemed fitting since she had to keep the Riverside location. Edith had raised any number of objections but in the end Lise had held firm and Edith accepted her defeat.

They cleaned the apartment again on the rainy afternoon of Lammas Eve and baked dozens of cookies—more than seven people could possibly consume. Edith insisted that magick would make them hungry.

Maria arrived during a thunderstorm, promising that Bob would join them after work and growing visibly nervous as six o'clock came and went without any sign of him. Then, with more hostility than apology, he arrived just after seven.

"We've made a mistake with him," Lise whispered to Edith when they were alone in the kitchen. "I'm surprised Sally let him into the initiation—"

"Perhaps—we'll wait a bit longer. His disbelief is a brittle shield. Once in the circle his skepticism will break easily. Remember—he doesn't know our strength, only our weakness."

Lise was not as sublimely confident as Edith appeared to be. Ducking into the bathroom she washed her hands carefully for at least the eighth time. The scar was a thin line and had given her no trouble all week. For caution's sake she rubbed a few drops of frankincense oil into it then rejoined her coven as it gathered for the first time.

Rachel had brought her own cookies, wine and glasses; the Ratners would accept High Coven magick, but they would not surrender the rituals of a lifetime. As no coven should ask a Christian to debase the sacraments, neither would they hesitate to make room beside the altar for a second, kosher, plate. When Jessica arrived at nine they were ready to begin.

Visions of the bloody-goddess taunted Lise as she took the long white taper and lit it from the altar candles with her good hand. The scarred hand had begun to ache and she dared not look at it. She walked to the northern candle behind Edith.

''Guardians of the watchtower of the North,'' she whispered. ''Draw nigh and attend the rites of this solemn circle.'' She walked carefully to the east and repeated the invocation, then to the south. A draft caught the taper as she approached the west. She reached out to shelter the flame and watched with horror as a drop slid from her palm.

''Guardians of the West—of the watchtower of the West, draw nigh and attend the rites of this circle—'' she could feel the moisture on her skin. Bending over, pretending to adjust the candleholder, she wiped her hand on the sofa and winced with pain. Edith smiled as she returned to the altar; her weakness had gone undetected.

She traced the nine-foot circle four times—with salt, wine, incense and finally wheat, since this magick circle was for the harvest to come. Her left hand was numb now and it left a dark stain on the wheat stalks where she had chanced to touch them. But she'd created a circle and the world hadn't ended. They all held black-handled athames and prepared to welcome the goddess.

''Blessed and bountiful goddess, mother of the summer—'' Lise chanted.

They had rehearsed this until the lines flowed easily and there was no need for written words but Lise could not remember now. The bloody goddess and not the Wiccan Lady crouched on the altar. The circle she had cast became a bell-jar trapping Otherworld laughter.

''Mother of summer we ask your presence here with us—''

There was a law, and old Wiccan law that said the left hand must not use a consecrated tool. Lise's numb, bloody left hand was moving toward her athame; not reaching but being drawn as if the Otherworld within the open sore commanded her movements.

''Edith,'' she called in a penetrating whisper, ''Lady Camulac! Help me!''

Camulac was already at her side, restraining the hand, frowning at its bloody wound and beckoning Jessica, who was also a witch of the third degree and able in such emergencies to help a faltering High Priestess.

"Take her north and hold her there," Camulac commanded.

She had been so certain of Lise's recovery, so untroubled by the tiny scar on her hand. The power of the half-invoked Otherworld pressed hard against the High Coven circle. Lady Camulac called upon the oldest magicks, the power of names, to strengthen the coven before it was too late.

"Bright Ceridwen, Silver Diana; Hathor, Isis Selene
Be not set aside by this intrusion of the dark
but abide with us.
Join us in that place which is no-place yet all places,
in that time which is no-time but all time—
Share *this*; a celebration of the harvest of life!"

She raised her hands in imitation of the crescent moon. Her arms were filled with the malice of the Otherworld. The noxiousness of the emerging Other crippled her, but there was a glimmer of the moon-goddess, silvery and gentle, behind the darkness. Camulac found the strength to continue.

Turning away from the altar she told the story of the corn-god who grew through the first half of summer, stopped and was long-dead by harvest. She recited a few verses of an old version of *John Barleycorn* when her senses tingled and Lise screamed.

They were not alone anymore. Chittering and skuttling noises scraped down the altar. Rachel clung to Mark as something invisible chittered out of the circle beside her. Edith faced the altar and was covered by a stream of odious black smoke. The altar candles went out with two small popping sounds; the Guardians candles went out next. The frightened coven pulled closer to the altar and each other but the stench overwhelmed them. It sickened and paralyzed; it brought the body of the High Priestess Camulac to its knees, but it had no power over her mind.

She reached out the other High Covens—Caer Maen, Gretna, all of them—imploring their power, setting herself to be the channel of their strength and dedication. The blackness lifted. She could feel its weight above her as she crouched on the floor where the air was now tainted but no longer alien.

Within her mind, Camulac heard her daughter: "We cannot hold!" and with an explosive shock the black cloud burst through the Riverside circle, shattering the apartment windows, knocking Lise's plants to the sidewalk but letting the cleansing rain into the room in its wake. The witches gagged and groped their way to the window; there was no circle left to ritually banish.

"There it is," Bob said, pointing at the cloud which was visible and distinct in the rain.

They said nothing as it settled out of sight. The first scream came some five minutes later. The second was cut short in a way that said death—even to these sheltered children of civilization. They took each other's hands.

A young man was seen entering the now-quiet park. His heels struck hard on the wet pavement, his thumbs were stuck in his belt. He whistled of John Barleycorn's death as he walked. Those who did not know the young man felt fear for him. Those who had recognized Nigel felt only wariness and fear. No-one moved; they waited but there was only the gentle patter of the rain.

Screams finally ripped through the silence. A couple staggered out of the park; the man hauled his companion along by her wrist. She was screaming, stumbling after him, taking the pavement in lurching, off-balance strides.

"We've loosed the Otherworld," Edith muttered and pressed white knuckles to her lips.

Someone rang the doorbell. Rachel went to handle the first of the inevitable complaints, but she found only a tissue-wrapped package of six cones of incense when she opened the door. By the time she brought the incense back to the livingroom Lise was clinging to Edith, crying disconsolately. The rest were watching a tall, black man in a cape and tophat march into the park. The street light made the top of his cane glow like red embers, even at this distance.

Chapter Thirty-Eight

Edith stood apart from the young people in Lise's living-room. Rain from the shattered windows dampened her hair and robe, but the discomfort was not enough to make her move from self-chosen isolation. Her thoughts had not congealed into words; any interruption would send her back into confusion.

The Otherworld cloud was gone. The park was quiet. Neither Nigel nor the Baron had come out through the stone-and-cement gates, but she wasn't reassured.

Edith had attended a Wiccan healing during the war when the Gods' peace had brought back a young soldier's senses. Caer Maen had drawn rain down from thin clouds and banished storms that threatened the fishing fleets. The High Priestess had never doubted the existence of Wiccan magick but she had never before met with magick that did not obey the Wicca.

The memory of the Otherworld taint—its unbreathable air, its unholy smell—was fading. The mind healed itself against such horror, but there was no doubt that the Otherworld was loose and that its power was darker than anything ever misattributed to witchcraft. The might of the combined High Covens had halted the flow of the Otherworld ooze, but it had not been able to reverse it; the Rift was still open and could erupt again.

"Where do you lead us from here?" Bob asked her.

"We're as far beyond the Wicca as we are beyond ordinary coincidence," she admitted. "Would you call it sorcery? Demons? I don't know. We'll wait; hope."

"Should we go over to the park? Mark's offered to go over with me—Should we call the police?"

"No," Edith said quickly. "Not now, we can't divide our strength. Maybe when it's light." Primal fears had caught her thoughts and she led them along the path of fearfulness. She *was* afraid and could lead no other way—if they looked to her.

And who else could they look to? Lise? Lise had recovered and was rescuing her possessions from the storm. She used both hands without hesitation now, but her magick was tainted. Jessica? No, no sensitive could command a High Coven. For now it was Camulac and her fears or no-one.

No-one made the decision that the newborn coven would remain close by. Jessica went across the hall with Rachel and Mark. Both apartment doors remained ajar; for once the greater danger was not crime and safety did not lie with multiple locks. Maria and Bob closeted themselves in Lise's bedroom. Lise moved about the livingroom, a silent ghost setting the furniture to right and protecting it from the rain as best she could.

"It wasn't your fault," Edith murmured when the cause of the ceaseless activity penetrated the heaviness of her own thoughts.

"If thy hand offend thee; cut it off?"

"Don't be foolish. What you did, you did well enough and when you couldn't do any more you turned to me and I turned to the other High Covens. When the Rift is open it seems no one person is strong enough."

"Is it closed now?" Lise asked softly.

"No, only quiet. We've had another skirmish. We haven't lost the war—again."

"That cloud is going to make the Slasher seem mild-mannered," Lise said calmly, putting a plastic sheet over the sofa with Edith's help.

"I should expect you're right," Edith replied.

"What do we do now—hire an exorcist?"

"If there are exorcists, they'll come on their own. The Otherworld should be alien to us—albeit tempting; it ought not thrive here just yet. I think, though, one of us should always be in this room from now on."

Lise shrugged. "Funny, I'm almost more afraid of leaving it."

The room and the park remained quiet the rest of the night and into the morning. Before dawn the rain stopped and the sun rose into a blue, cloudless sky. By eight Edith had awakened from an aching sleep to the smell of Lise's powerful coffee. She took a steaming cup to the wide open windows and studied the park with Mark and Bob.

"Strangely enough, the police haven't been through,"

Mark informed her.

"No," Bob agreed. "We went over and checked it out just after dawn, but there's nothing. We must've been hearing things."

Edith did not dignify the supposition with a denial.

"We'd like you to go back over with us," Mark continued. "Maybe we're not seeing everything that's there."

It was another hour before Edith felt sufficiently composed for amateur detective work. The day promised to be hot but less humid than many in August. New Yorkers thwarted in their pursuit of a tan for several rainy days abandoned their offices and flocked to the parks. The Wiccans would do their searching amid the capricious curiosity of sun-bathers, ball-players, joggers and ordinary loafers.

"After the thing with Alan you could tell something had happened. There were broken, burnt branches. But this time—" Mark let a branch spring back to its normal position, "—nothing at all. You'd think someone came through and cleaned. There's not even the normal garbage."

"Perhaps they did." Edith used her rowen staff to poke through dead leaves. The area had indeed been scoured but there had to be something left behind. Nothing could be perfect, not even the Otherworld. With her eyes out of focus, she let the rowen guide her. By the hollowness in her stomach and the sudden cold air around her, she knew before she saw. "I've found it."

On the ground lay a gnarled man's finger, severed below the third knuckle and seared like a piece of meat. The tip of the rowen staff trembled. Despite nearly fifty years of reading, movies and one major war, despite countless fictionalized catastrophes and injuries, the sight of a part of the body utterly separated from the rest of that body was a compelling, surreal experience far more upsetting than the Otherworld. This time the memory would not fade.

"Don't touch it," she commanded, letting the ghastly remnant disappear back under the leaves.

"But—a murder's been done. The police—" Mark protested.

"We cannot afford to attract attention! You and I know it wasn't a conventional murder. Do you think the police can lock that cloud in a cell?''

Mark said nothing but was the last to follow her back to the building. Though she had said the right thing, the only thing, Edith would have been glad to be rid of the responsibility and the knowledge. But there was no occult army to fight the Otherworld crimes—only the High Covens. She searched her mind for a way to tell Lise and the rest without terrifying them into uselessness.

The necessary words were in her mind as she opened the door, and lost immediately to the conversation emmanating from the livingroom. She strode down the hallway leaving the men behind.

''What's wrong now?'' she asked as gently as she could.

''Alan—'' Lise began, but tears shut off her voice.

''Doctor Dudley's secretary called to say Alan was dead. He'd been murdered during the night. There's a box of his stuff for Lise at Dudley's office. Apparently Alan'd been expecting this and Dudley'd gone along with his fantasies. Now Alan's dead just the way he said he'd be. Rachel's gone down to get the box,'' Maria explained.

Alan, the young man who had been touched by the Otherworld at Imholc, dead a half-year later. Lise had been concerned about him but not enough, Edith judged, to account for the despair that had taken her. Perhaps her affections had been deeper than suspected; perhaps she had never lost a loved-one; perhaps she was not, in truth, deeply affected by *his* death but overcome by everything and his death simply the most recent outrage to endure. Whatever, nothing was going to get done until Alan's box made its appearance.

''He took too many risks,'' Lise said to Edith when they were momentarily alone.

''You seem certain,'' Edith cautioned.

Lise nodded. ''He was always following Nigel. We saw Nigel last night—and the Baron. I'm sure Alan was out there somewhere. Maybe we heard his scream.''

Edith thought of the finger but said nothing. Lise had not asked if they found anything; the information did not demand to be shared. There was no reason to suspect a connection between Alan and the previous night. A half-crazed man hung with pawn-able cameras could easily have fallen prey to the City's naturally occurring criminals. His death need not be entangled with the Otherworld. Edith sighed and surrendered; pure random coincidence did not happen near the High Covens.

Rachel returned in the afternoon with a small, taped box labelled with Lise's name. Lise ripped through the nylon-reinforced tape and unfolded the cardboard. He'd put a note in the box, printed in block capitals that slid down the unlined paper.

"If this reaches you—my luck has run out. This is my proof—use it wisely."

Lise set the paper aside and everyone crowded around her as she lifted out a set of enlarged photos. The first showed a mist-shrouded intersection; the second a dark, irregularly shaped shadow in the mist. The remainder were of a cat, or rather a fanged, furred creature; it was no feline spawned in Earth's primordial soup. Its muzzle was like a wolf's but with evenly spaced fangs interlacing outside its lips. The forehead was high—like an ape's—or a man's and the eyes were like nothing they had ever seen with fiery spots instead of pupils.

There was one last photo, wrapped in black paper. Lise unwrapped it and looked into Nigel's face. That camera couldn't have been more than a few inches away and had taken him by surprise. He must have moved because the image was blurred, only the midnight eyes were in focus. It might have been a double-exposure as well, for the longer they stared the easier it was to see the cat too.

"He wasn't crazy," Maria said, breaking the silence first.

"Cover that up," Jessica requested.

Lise did with no further urging. "I can't believe it, no matter how hard I try. I cannot believe these pictures are real." She had lost too much that day to face losing her affection for Nigel as well. "I could just possibly believe there won't be a tomorrow if some crazy presses the wrong button—but not because a few people didn't finish a Samhain rite—"

No-one disagreed with her, not even Edith who had seen in the picture how easily the Otherworld could slip past them. She had not liked Nigel, but she had never doubted his humanity. He was handsome, personable, elusive and possibly unstoppable—and he had a strangle-hold on Lise's affections.

"Did they tell you how Alan died?" Maria asked Rachel.

"There'll be something in the papers. It wasn't the Slasher; they think it was suffocation. They found him in an alley not far from his building. He'd been frightened. Dudley's answering service got a garbled message from him and Dudley tried to reach him about two this morning. Dudley called the police and the police found him about five. He hadn't been dead long—"

"Suicide?" Bob asked.

"Apparently not. Don't ask me how they can tell—I've never seen a dead body outside a funeral home." Rachel did not see the grimace on her husband's face.

"What should we do with the pictures?" Lise asked.

Edith tucked the box under her arm. "Be thankful for the warning. Whether this thing's the Slasher or not doesn't matter. Our first task is still to get the Rift closed before anything more evil, more powerful comes through."

"You didn't do that last night?" Jessica asked.

"Think of us as the little Dutch boy. The Otherworld's still pressing and the dike still needs repairs."

The afternoon sun was streaming in now, making the room uncomfortably hot. It didn't seem important to get the windows repaired, but Edith set them to measuring for the glass.

The pale glimmerings of a plan began to form after she'd spoken words of warding around the box and set it safely aside. Ideas for warding the new glass, for chants before the goddess to keep the Otherworld from popping out again. The Gods would have to provide the greater plans and power, though, or lose their worshippers—not just at Riverside but at Caer Maen and elsewhere. Elizabeth had had a relapse; Bert had taken her to the hospital again. The Gods might judge that a witch at Caer Maen was more expendable than one right beside the Rift, but Edith wasn't a God and Elizabeth was her only daughter. If Caer Maen perished while she aided Riverside the gods would get nothing more from Camulac.

She called the airline and made her reservations for home. She would leave at the end of September whether Lise was ready or not.

Chapter Thirty-Nine

The crisis brought its own rhythms to Lise's life; she throve in the environment of co-conspiracy the Otherworld forced around her young coven. It could be added that she was thriving on the sheer excitement of being at the center. The rising tides carried her through Alan's funeral and her meeting with his parents without forcing her to share their bleak sense of loss. She lived a life of disguise and concealment, working diligently, sharing the latest gossip about the Slasher and then giving each evening to the grimoires that Edith taught from memory.

She copied the Wiccan laws onto fine vellum paper that Jessica had made into books. Most evenings, there were others to share her lessons in the livingroom—learning, waiting for the unexpected and the unwanted. But some nights Edith herself would have to escape, and Lise would have to fidget away the evening with her coven.

"I wish it would hurry up and storm. I can't breathe," Rachel complained.

"It won't make any difference; it's August," Mark reminded her.

The Ratners were taking their turn Other-sitting with Lise. Edith and Jessica were cooling themselves at a neighborhood movie. A thermal inversion had settled over the summer-baked island, reducing life to pure discomfort and bringing the aroma of ripened garbage as high as the sixth floor. Consolidated Edison warned against the excessive strains on the power-grid caused by air-conditioners; the Board of Health urged everyone to breathe only filtered air.

"It'll be better once the sun goes down and it's dark," Lise apologized as she poured more iced tea; none of them had wanted dinner.

Riverside Coven was taking the electric company's advice. Arthur's fan had wheezed its last and the City was out of air-conditioners until Christmas. Lise scratched her legs where the sofa plush had raised a rash. It was too hot to knit; the yarn stuck to her fingers and her sweat corroded the needles.

"Sometimes a breeze comes in off the river—if you don't mind the smell," she added.

Mark managed a weak laugh and helped himself to more tea. They waited for a sunset, a storm or a breeze and Edith's eventual return.

"Lise!"

Three heads turned toward the fire-escape but only Lise had recognized Nigel's voice.

"Lise, I've got to talk to you," he insisted from the shadows.

She told herself it was her imagination—the room hadn't gotten cold; the only smells were those of garbage—not the Otherworld. "Nigel—where did you come from? How'd you get out there?"

"You know him?" Mark asked, not recognizing him.

Lise walked around to the end of the sofa. "Yes, but I—"

"I told you I had enemies," Nigel whispered loudly, ignoring the Ratners. "I warned you they'd come looking for you after they found me."

"Enemies?" Rachel asked.

"Nigel, these are my friends—"

"Send them home. I've got to talk to you."

His hands were clenched around the steel grate—the same grate he had torn from the wood once before. Despite the heat he was dressed in heavy black clothes. His pale face and hands reflected the fading light. Lise knew, without giving the matter a second thought, that she wouldn't send the Ratners away nor unlock the gate.

"Nigel, you can tell us all what the problem is—"

"I don't trust them."

"They're my friends; they've shared a lot with me. I'll tell them what you say, anyway."

"Lise, it's not safe for you to be here alone anymore," he said watching the Ratners rather than her. "There is a gateway to tremendous power within this room. Your Phenomena are only the glimmer of that power. But there are those, our enemies, who would use that power against us—against you and me; you know who I'm talking about. Unless we harness that power ourselves, they'll blast the defenses

Sally's taught you and destroy us both."

His fingers raced along the grate as he spoke. Lise leaned against the sofa and judged his fingers still fell several inches short of the key. "We've seen this power, Nigel," she said grimly; she could admit that much without compromising the coven. "It's not something I'd ever use."

"Lise, unlock this gate and let me explain!"

"—even if I had enemies I couldn't use the power here against them. I'd rather be defeated than use it. I'm not alone anymore, either. You don't have to worry about anyone—your enemies or anyone else—trying to use the power in this room."

Nigel chuckled. "What do you know about enemies? The Baron will be here soon—he can't resist. And you can't resist him. You've put your Wiccan wards on the glass and the grate—you've played right into his hands, Lise. The power will seep and ooze until there's an explosion that will make Lammas look like a popgun."

Lise heard Mark rise out of his chair and prayed he would have the sense to stay back and stay quiet. She wasn't surprised he knew about Lammas; they'd seen him enter the park that night. Nor would it take special imagination to guessed they'd put wards on the new glass.

"We have everything under control, Nigel," she said quickly.

"And when the Baron comes to your door? What will you tell *him*? I'm your *friend;* let me show you the wards that will keep the Baron out. Let me bind the power so it will never hurt you." He lunged forward and caught both her hands through the grate. His fingers dug into her scarred palm. "I gave you my word they wouldn't hurt you—I can't keep it if you won't let me in now," he whispered.

"Lise," Mark stepped forward and placed his hands on Nigel's and Nigel looked at him with atavistic hatred.

She saw the demon-cat's eyes for a second, then the reflection of a traffic light as it went to green. "I'm all right, Mark." She folded her own fingers around Nigel's wrists and held him as tightly as she could. While her thoughts invoked the protection of the Goddess, she spoke softly to him.

"Nigel, if you'll come to the door—like anyone else—if you come to the door you can wait with me and I'll share your wisdom."

"Don't use me like this, Lise—" His grip went weak. "The Baron is our enemy; he's waiting for me. Your High Coven ritual won't bind him. He'll take possession of your body and your coven and everything else in this room. He'll use it to his own ends and nothing will be the same."

Surprise passed from Lise like a spark; she let go of his wrists and stared into his blue-black eyes. The Baron, and not Nigel, was the Otherworld minion? Nigel knew of the High Covens? A hundred more questions leapt into her mind and she throttled them all.

"How do you know about the High Covens?" Mark demanded.

A faint smile played across his shadowed face. "There are more Rifts than High Covens, aren't there, Lise? Don't you think that if Caer Maen knew, others would know? Do you think the secret is Wiccan? Do you think there is agreement on how to confine the Otherworld, or if it should be confined?"

Lise stared at him without speaking.

"Do you believe we have enemies, Lise?" he asked gently.

"Yes," she answered, fighting panic, "and so we'll need allies. Come through the front door, Nigel and we'll talk. Come through the front door," she repeated. "I can't afford to fix the grate again."

He muttered something she couldn't understand and scrambled out of sight. She listened to the sound of his feet going up the fire-escape.

"Is the elevator-shaft door locked?" Rachel asked.

"Lise, my god, why did you invite him in?" Mark asked.

"He can't," she answered in a distance voice. "If he could come to the front door he would have already."

"Whatever makes you think that?" Mark replied sarcastically.

Lise reached within herself and found Sybylla. "I know when to trust my instincts," she answered forcefully. "He can't pass through the front door." Raw authority swelled out, taking command of the situation and surprising them all.

"All right," she said seconds later in her normal voice, "he's probably right. There *are* more Rifts than Covens, Edith's told me that. He *could* be from another coven—or even another type of magick—"

"Do you honestly believe that?" Rachel asked. "After Alan's pictures?"

"He probably is Otherworld. But I believe; I'm convinced it's not just us and the Otherworld around this Rift. We could have allies; we've got enemies—just like he says we do."

"And if he does come to the front door?" Rachel pressed.

"We'll let him in and burn our bridges from there," Lise answered in a whisper.

He couldn't come through the front door. Silent lightning flashed over the Jersey hills offering the hope of a break in the weather. And if Nigel did try the front door he'd have to go past Sam first. And Sam would call upstairs; she'd be warned. Lise began to relax when there was a knock on the door.

"Shall I let him in?" Mark asked.

"No, I will." Lise stood up carefully, lest her knees buckle. She went to the triple-locked door. She held the peephole cover tightly so it wouldn't click as she spun it away from the dot of glass in the door. He stood too close—there was just a mass of blackness. The cover-clicked shut as she worked the locks.

"Good evening, Miss Brown," the Baron said as he bowed.

Lise's hand slipped off the doorknob; the world tilted at odd angles. She grabbed for the door but instead of pushing it shut, her falling weight pulled it open. The Baron caught her shoulder, dropping his skull-cane in his hurry, but he wasn't enough to keep her on her feet.

She was out for a second, just long enough to crash to the floor and bring Mark and Rachel from the livingroom. It was a living nightmare; she was weak, speechless and unable to turn away from him. A brilliant flash of lightning was followed by painfully loud thunder. The lights flickered and faded away—but she hadn't fainted again.

"Great god, help us," Lise whispered.

"And what more would you have me do?" Baron Samedi, lord of the dead, whispered in return.

"Go away? "

He released her. The aroma of incense had faded by the time Mark had brought a candle down the hallway from the livingroom.

"Lise? Lise, are you akay? Where is he? Was that the Baron?"

"I told him to go away," Lise muttered.

The open door drew a draft down the hallway from the windows. Mark shielded the candle, but Lise felt her strength return in the cooler air.

"Did he attack you?" Rachel asked in hysterical concern.

"No, he just scared me—I wasn't expecting him." Lise rested her head against the table. "I should have. He's done this before; he scared Nigel out the window. Nigel really can't come to the front door. He's more afraid of the Baron than I am—and the Baron used the front door," she mused.

Thunder continued to reverberate around the building. There was no interlude between the blinding light and the concussions of the thunder. They got more candles and waited for the natural violence to end.

The storm, the fainting spell and possibly the incense had left Lise detached from the chaos of reality. After the Baron and Nigel there was nothing that simple storm could do to upset her. She wasn't even ruffled when Edith appeared in the doorway to the livingroom during a cacaphony of overlapping thunderclaps, though Rachel's yelp could be heard over the storm.

"A bit of panic when the lights went out," Edith explained. "Didn't mean to scare you—we've been scared enough ourselves tonight."

"We were lucky not to get trampled to death," Jessica added.

The last thunderclap had exhausted the storm. Longer periods of silence descended on the group and Edith was able to perceive the tension.

"What happened while we were gone?" she asked Lise.

"Well, first Nigel showed up on the fire-escape. Then the

Baron came to the front door. I guess there was enough commotion to ground this storm right on top of us. I fainted and cracked my head on the table—'' The insulation which the storm had provided faded as Lise saw the concern on her mentor's face.

''And?'' the Englishwoman demanded.

''No disasters; the war isn't lost,'' Lise's voice had lost its steadiness. ''Nigel knows about the High Covens and what happened at Lammas. He tried to bargain with me—'' Edith did not interrupt, though Lise had hoped she would. The lights flickered and came back on. ''Nigel says the Baron's our enemy, but he couldn't come to the front door.

''The Baron can come to the front door whenever he wants. He puts the incense there. He came again right after Nigel disappeared. I can't decide which one's against us,'' Lise wondered aloud.

''They're all against us,'' Jessica announced.

''I'm not even sure of that,'' Lise admitted. ''Nigel knew that there were more Rifts than High Covens. He made a convincing argument that if Edith knew our Rift was open, so should some of the other Guardians. He'd like me to believe, I think, that he's a Guardians from someplace else. The Baron acts as if he were a voodoo Guardian— What do you think Edith?''

Edith towelled her hair vigorously. ''Arthur and Gwen failed, and they were High Coven. Since the beginning I've known that we might not get a second chance; the powers and fates that move around us might decide that since the Wicca had failed some other mystery should guard this Rift.'' Edith paused. ''Still, I wouldn't give up to anyone without a fight and I'd never compromise myself with allies.

''But, Lise, you're the High Priestess of Riverside; you'll have to decide if you need allies and who they should be. You could surrender the Rift to anyone, anything who wants it. I'm going home in a month—you won't always be able to rely on me for your decisions. You shouldn't anyway; I'm not right for this place.''

It was not what Lise had been hoping to hear.

Chapter Forty

"But it's your last chance to get out to the beach, Lise. Bob and I got away for a few days but you never got out of the City the whole summer." Maria made a final attempt to convince Lise to join the rest of the coven for a Labor Day outing to Jones Beach.

"No, really, I'd rather stay behind. The two of you go and enjoy yourselves for me. I'll be fine here by myself for a few hours." Lise locked the door behind her friend.

They wouldn't believe she wanted to be alone in her own home—because none of them would even consider the idea. The very real dangers in the livingroom notwithstanding, Lise had had almost all the polite companionship she could tolerate. And getting out of the apartment while someone else babysat the Rift was not the answer. Edith had understood; she'd suggested the picnic, claiming she wanted to see the other side of the Atlantic just once.

Lise celebrated her privacy with a long, lazy bath then lounged in the sunspots on the livingroom rug to dry her hair. The open Rift still commanded respect but Lise's fear of it had lessened since Lammas. Nigel had been right about one thing—when you were busy fighting your enemies you didn't have time to fear them. She could almost see the shimmering filaments of High Coven magick around her; the livingroom was a tangled web of warding spells and protective chants. She never entered or left the room without adding another knot to the Otherworld's prison.

Had it been night or dreary she might not have felt so free-spirited. Sunlight masked the latent malice that oozed past the wards. Lise hadn't intended to let her thoughts slip into darkness and didn't notice when they had.

She mourned for Alan now that she was alone. He had named her beneficiary for his insurance—making her heiress to a substantial sum of money that his parents could not be induced to keep. The money would go into the bank along with the papers Edith had secured from Fine that named her co-owner of the building. In a modest way, Lise Brown had become wealthy and the shame of it filtered into the sunny afternoon when she had been alone not more than three hours.

Edith assured her it was the Gods' way; the Guardians had enough responsibility so they didn't suffer materially. But Lise could not accept that fate brought her fortune through the mortality of her friends.

The crossword puzzle remained more space than letters. She shoved it aside. For two weeks she had wanted nothing more than to be alone. There had been so many things she wanted to do—hadn't been able to do and now she wasn't doing any of them. Her thoughts wandered downward until she felt the tendrils of the Otherworld and knew she had been seduced.

Getting up from the carpet slowly, she backed away from the Rift. You could know fear, have it within you and yet not allow yourself to obey it or feel it. Thinking of the skein of magick around the Rift, but not of the Rift itself, Lise kept her thoughts slow and methodical. She gathered the High Coven's power strand by strand without panic. Edith had taught her well; she could do it. Her human mistakes were not irredeemable errors.

The Otherworld could not learn from its errors as she could. For all its power it was trapped outside the karmic cycle, unlinked to the Great Chain of Being. It was, after its fashion, an inspired genius creating malice from chaos time and time again—but it did not learn. The very fact that she could make mistakes and correct them proved that she could be redeemed. Lise wove that knowledge into the wards.

The balance between the confidence necessary to maintain the wards and an over-confidence which the Otherworld could exploit was razor-sharp. Lise visualized it and set herself on the edge, lest she lose her alertness.

Smoke began to curl from the puzzle book she had left on the rug. Her other senses confirmed the impression; she could smell the smoldering paper, hear it crackle as the first amber-edges flames appeared.

"It's not real," she whispered. "I should ignore it—"

The terror of the Otherworld could be denied through her Wiccan training, but nothing could redirect her fright at the sight of a fire in her home. Lunging for the watering-can, Lise heaved the liquid onto the charring book and, by accident, propelled herself into the Rift.

Its embrace was obscene: moist and clammy, oozing with notions of snails and slugs. Retching, Lise staggered to the bathroom.

She'd left the Rift when it was aroused; a violation of all the rules Riverside had made for itself—that she insisted it make for itself. But she could not have remained in that room and fought the Otherworld. There were scraping noises and the Gods-only-knew-what heaving into reality in the next room, but the spasms of her gut would not be denied. Lise gripped the cold porcelain and felt her stomach churn.

She saw herself an inverted mess of muscle and viscera smeared over the bathroom, growing, taking on life as the retching continued. What had been within Lise Brown was now a pulsing horror that boiled over the porceline and grabbed her fingers. What had been the facade of Lise Brown had become nothing. It was the daylight reality of her nightmares—but she could not wake up.

Hands—open your eyes and look at your hands—fool, she raged at herself. You'll see them; feel them. They're real. No blood, no guts.

She gasped, catching her balance against the tank, exerting will-power to see the world as it was supposed to be: white knuckles, white enamel, an insignificant amount of yellow-pink froth on the water. She could swallow again, breathe—get back to the livingroom.

She screamed.

Every neuron of human sensibility within her seized that scream and froze into negation: the bloody mess that had chased her across the landscape of her nightmares; that had emerged with the vomitus from her stomach now throbbed, sprawled and extended skeletal fingers at her as it dragged itself across the carpet. Otherspawn—oozing down from an aperture above the carpet; oozing out from the bathroom behind her—vile slime that snared her ankle in hot, sticky claws.

"Bylla—Ybylla—Sybylla!"

Her vision streaked with red. She was within the slithering apparition, seeing with the pathetic, revolting thing's eyes. It was all that remained of the Lise Brown from whom the High Coven had carved a new High Priestess. That priestess—the goddess toward whom she crawled—had no mercy. It kicked her tortured hands away and backed out of the room.

She didn't remember unlatching the locks. She didn't remember shutting the door behind her thus locking herself out of the apartment. She did know she was out on the landing. Lise was Sybylla; Sybylla was Lise. It was only the Otherworld that made it seem otherwise. The Otherworld had created the creature in her livingroom and induced her to share its vision.

For a moment the sense of being in one piece, one personality, within her own body was enough. She tried the door a second time, rattling it on its hinges.

"I can't be locked out. The damned door doesn't lock without a key. If I got out I'd have to have my keys in my hand!" She peered through the slits of light at the edge of the door. "Damn! The dead-bolt's on."

This last was a whispered protest as she pounded on the door. It was locked from the inside; she was outside. Who, or what, was she if Annalise Brown's apartment was locked from the inside? The Otherworld could deceive, could it also make a doppleganger?

She rattled the doorknob with all her strength. Everyone else who had a key was at the beach, but with the dead-bolt thrown, even a key wouldn't help. She kicked the door.

"Miz Brown," Sam chastized as he came up the stairs.

"Oogod, Sam, something awful's happened. I'm locked out. I've got to get back in—quick."

He looked her over carefully, taking her measure from

head to toe noticing, as Lise noticed, the blotched, red ring around her ankle.

"We'll go downstairs and get my keys, then, Miss Brown," he said.

She followed, not truly knowing why—the deadbolt was thrown, a key couldn't help, but maybe Sam knew things about these doors and locks she didn't.

Sam lived in a neat, threadbare room. Pictures of Sam Jr.'s triumphs were stuck in the mirror; a Columbia University graduation tassel swung from a lampshade. In all, it was a safe place to sit while he sorted through a drawer of keys. She almost didn't notice the angular motifs stenciled on the windows—if he had found the keys quicker she wouldn't have noticed. They were similar to those on Madame Odile's shop and the long-since vanished markings on her windows. Sam saw her staring.

"The Other—they prey on your imagination, Miss Brown," he explained. "They take your worst thoughts and twist 'em back to you."

"You know?" Lise whispered.

"Many years ago, Miss Brown, Missus Andrews came to me when I needed someone. Her husband never knew; no-one knew. They'd been eating at me, you see, twistin' me. She told me whitefolks' magick, whitefolks' truth—it don't matter wheres she was wrong—she showed me a path—" his voice droned softly as they rode the elevator upstairs.

Edith's sister had told this man about High Coven mysteries? That seemed barely imaginable. Had Gwen tried to bring Sam into Riverside? Lise could not imagine the original occupants of her apartment taking an ex-sharecropper into their lives.

"—and when he died," Sam continued, raising his voice slightly, "I waited to see who would be next—if it'd be his guests. Can't say as I expected you to make it, Miss Brown." The elevator rattled to a halt on the sixth floor. "There was plenty of others who looked—some were more likely than you. But you're the one the apartment took. You've been here comin' onto a year now, you can't go letting Them eat your fear."

"What about voodoo, Sam? You must've known about the Baron?" Lise asked.

"Blackfolks' truth," he grumbled and wouldn't say anything more as he worked the first key in the lock.

The door gave a quarter inch and clanked loudly against the steel bolt. Sam's eyes widened as he stared at her. She knew exactly what thoughts were going through his mind; the same thoughts still haunted her. But if she couldn't explain it to herself, she couldn't explain it to him.

There were footsteps coming up the stairs.

"Maybe we can both push on it and pop the screws. I've got to get back inside," Lise pleaded.

"That's a metal door, Miss Brown. We'll never push through that."

"Maybe with one more shoulder?"

Lise didn't need to turn around; she recognized the Baron's voice. Sam shared her moment of awe-struck surprise when the aristocratic fingers clutched the knob firmly. She wouldn't look at him, so she looked at the leering brass skull, the twin of which rested on the opposite side of the door.

He tried the door once without success. She heard him sigh and dared to look at his face. His brow was furrowed, teeth showed through his frown; he looked like his brass death's head. Then he smiled, a slow-growing smile that focused on the dead-bolt. Gesturing them aside he raised his cane and brought the skull sharply against the door. Nothing. He hit it again. The third time brought sparks and the sound of the bolt-housing falling to the floor. The door swung open.

"Miss Annalise Brown, will you invite me into your home?"

Vampires, Lise remembered, needed permission to enter a home. Simple enough—she'd say no and re-lock the door. She couldn't remember if voodoo loas were also vampires. His teeth were very white but they weren't pointed.

"I don't know what we'll find," she said in a small voice.

"We won't find anything until we look for it."

The Baron led the way down the hall, Lise followed but Sam decided against having anything more to do with the lord of the dead. The livingroom was quiet. A wet spot marred the carpet where she had emptied the watering can on an otherwise unmarked puzzle book. The blood ring around her ankle was gone as well.

"It's vanished," she murmured.

The Baron stood by the water mark, speaking in a lilting foreign language. His hands wove through the air where the Rift was and where the High Coven wards should have been. Lise was still too upset to narrow her eyes and visualize the shimmering web—if it were there at all.

"You must light these when I go," the Baron said, making a pair of candles appear from nowhere.

She wouldn't take the twisted, dark candles from him so he put them on the writing table. "Lise Brown, listen to me—so far your ways have held their magick. Whatever was here and sent you through the door is gone; it failed. But they will try again. They know us all very well now and we must work together. They will not expect to find my magick here, so—light these when I am gone!"

She couldn't imagine doing what he asked—but she couldn't lie outright to him either. "I don't trust you, Baron Samedi. The way you come and go; the incense you leave behind; the chicken—even the way Nigel fears you. I don't know whose side you're on."

He frowned. "I've answered your calls. I have helped you when you needed help without asking if you were worthy. Time and time again you destroyed what I brought, endangering me as well. Now, I ask you to burn these. Do whatever else your way demands, but burn these!" He waited through her silence. "Lise Brown, I have no more time—will you help me?"

"Yes," she whispered.

He left without saying anything more and she didn't go back down the hall until the door had swung shut. She slid the dead-bolt into place; the sound of it falling to the floor had not been real.

The Baron hadn't said where to burn his ugly, little candles. Lise set them on two inexpensive spikes and left them on the windowsill where their smoke might drift out of the room.

She got her hairdryer and removed the wet spot. The puzzle book was beyond salvage; she hid it in the garbage. She had learned from her mistakes: she would not daydream near the Rift; she would not insist on privacy within these walls; she would watch Sam with new respect. And, if no-one guessed something had gone wrong, she would never speak of this day to anyone.

At six-thirty the coven trooped back to the apartment. They brought soda and pizza and suspected nothing. Lise felt their sense of security and relaxed herself. It was not until late in the evening that she remembered the Baron's candles again. The windowsill was empty. With the grate bolted in place she couldn't see where the candles might have fallen to. They were inexpensive candleholders, anyway.

Chapter Forty-One

The steel-drums and congos of a street-combo slipped into chilly silence. The tallest of the drummers, a young man who had lately visited a voodoo Houngan, split down the broken cement steps to the tenement's basement with unseemly quickness. His companions, none of whom shared his passion for Island magick, simply stared at each other, acknowledging the discomfort that had occurred for no apparent reason and was now passing.

Baron Samedi had emerged into the Caribbean enclaves of Manhattan's Upper Westside after wandering from the somewhat respectable area of Riverside Drive where the Rift was guarded, erratically, by the young, white Wiccan High Priestess. He smiled into the basement darkness, but he had no time for the young man's dreams.

The Baron had no enemies here. He practiced simple, but effective, mind-control—a necessary talent for one who was not a God but whom the faithful expected to see only at the time of their deaths. He could feel the tensions of the Riverside Rift this far from it, knew of the Slasher's hunger and movements and knew that for some small time he was still safe.

The barricades in front of Madame Odile's shop that been removed and the windows boarded over with half-inch plywood. No-one saw the Baron drift to the back of the building, spring the police-lock and enter the ground-floor establishment. The Baron had ways to be certain of his privacy.

He lit incense and candles in no particular order, then sat in the brokendown armchair to sift through waves of thought and memory. This body had had its own life before he took it; it had its own memories and those memories were now his. Samedi had lived a supernaturally long life on his own, but it was the extra memories from the lives he had assumed which made it seem unbearably longer. When he had been forced to change bodies frequently, as he had since January, the memories overlapped.

His long, tapering fingers concealed his face as he saw Lise with many minds. He was not omniscient, regardless of what Odile had believed; he could only trust that the Wiccan Priestess would burn the candles.

He knew more about the High Covens than they suspected about him. They were a closed society with traditions creeping back to the mists of man and the first Otherworld incursions. He had begun his own guarding less than five hundred years ago. His Rifts were newer, smaller, more easily controlled—as Riverside should be. The High Covens manipulated the Rifts with group magick. They stored their power in the circles, not in the people who raised them. Witches lived and died, but the High Covens went on. If he died— The Baron moaned softly and refused to think about his own death.

High Coven magick was strong and passive: stout walls against the Otherworld. They were utterly reliable and difficult to destroy; he would never have thought of Riverside if the coven were strong. But Wiccan magick moved too slowly; one mind must take this challenge if the Otherworld were to be bested in time.

The Baron had come to New York when Arthur's Riverside Coven failed. He had watched through Sam's eyes, through Odile's eyes and the eyes of a dozen unsuspecting other people. He had intended to add the Riverside Rift to his protectorate and place Madame Odile over it. She had been no more reliable than Lise and now, three bodies later, he found himself preparing for personal battle with the Otherspawn calling itself Nigel.

Late summer heat filled the smoky chamber; the air was thick enough to stifle a man, but it was the wrong heat for a native of the Caribbean. Baron Samedi was as homesick as the High Coven woman Edith Brompton and in considerably less comfort. He slipped into fitful unproductive sleep. When he awoke the sun had set and it was raining. The streets were empty, the park where he would issue his challenge should be deserted; magick had not failed him yet.

"Come to me, Otherspawn Nigel," he thought to the mists as he walked down the street to the park. "We've waited long enough, haven't we?"

Empty wood-and-concrete benches watched as he followed the macadam pathways. The skull was living-warm in his grip; its dull, red eyes watched the rain. He stepped off the pathway and hid in the shadows as an intrepid runner splashed by. When the park was silent again he continued.

"Don't waste our time, Otherspawn. We both have much to do when this is finished—and I'd prefer to do it alone."

The young man stood beside a fog-entwined lamppost out of sight of any passerby. They were not far from where they had met at Imholc, three bodies ago. Samhain hesitated, glancing toward the Riverside building. Had she lit the candles? It was raining, but perhaps it had been supposed to rain?

"You are insistent," Nigel said calmly. "For one who has tasted my world, you might be called overinsistent."

"You would not have it any other way," the Baron replied, adjusting his gloves and raising the skull's eyes level with his own. Otherspawn—there could be no doubt.

"Do you want me so badly, Samhain? My body won't suit you. The changes you'd have to make to this flesh would drive even you mad. Or have you decided it is time for your own death? You will *die*, truly, you know. You aren't immortal. Nothing that lives and breathes is immortal. I could stop your heart before you shed that flesh. I do learn from my mistakes—even if my makers do not."

Samhain was unmoved. They would both use some time to test each other before the duel; it was to be expected. At Imholc they had battled blindly, without a sense of each other's power and, of course, they both still existed. It was not a tolerable situation.

"You are Otherspawn, expelled through the Riverside Rift at the Wiccan rite of Imholc. Your makers used the High Coven circles as a lens to force you through. You have slain among the Wiccans; you have slain among my people but you must slay me and you must slay the new High Priestess before your task is complete. Why deny it, Otherspawn—your masters impel you whether you will it or not."

Nigel's composure wavered; the Baron smiled. Had the Otherspawn breathed long enough to remember an unredeemed life in some other maelstrom of existence? Did he realize he was enslaved? Did he rebel against the power which had made him? Or, had he not realized that the girl was High Priestess—however inept.

"She knows you, Otherspawn. The Wiccans are not swift but they are ageless and persistent; their power is not mocked. Your Rift is no longer unguarded."

The young man was distracted. The Baron seized the advantage. The skull-cane whirled in his hands, battering Nigel with blows that should have crippled a man but only raised the Otherspawn's anger. Nigel launched his own attack, capturing the ebony cane in one fist. Samhein lashed out with steel-tipped boots. The Otherspawn reeled before the onslaught of *savate* learned generations ago in Marseilles and forced into the sinews of each body he took.

Nigel collapsed against the lamppost, breaking his fall with his wrist, grimacing as the bones splintered. Flecks of red appeared at the corners of his mouth; he shook them loose.

The Baron tightened his grip on his cane. He had heard the wrist shatter but Nigel's masters would not allow him to run for cover. The Baron had barely enough time to raise the cane before the Otherspawn lunged. The ebony was scored by the jagged marks of teeth that could not fit in any human skull and would have torn out the Baron's throat if the Baron had not defended himself against the Otherspawn's true form. The brass cracked against the visible, human teeth.

"You have not wasted your time," Nigel acknowledged, wiping blood from his mouth. "But you've made a new mistake. I've no masters. I'm free of them. I want that Rift no more or less than you. My purposes are not so different—who could resist the power of life and death?"

The Baron closed his mind to the spawn's words.

Truth-twisting was a gift of the Otherworld—given enough time and the fertile garden of a near-immortal mind, It could destroy truth utterly. He would not listen nor bargain for an Otherworld alliance that was certain to be worthless—even if Nigel did not know it. He swung the skull with deceptive speed, cracking the spawn's neck with a thunderclap.

Nigel snarled blood and grabbed the cane, twisting it and the Baron far to one side. There was nothing human left in the Otherspawn's face. Its eyes had rolled back to reveal smoldering orange embers of malignance. His shadow shimmered in the lamplight, creating the shape of his spirit, but not his body. The Baron fought for his cane and his sanity.

"I have not wasted my time either," Nigel spoke within the Baron's head. He raised his hand and it vanished into darkness. The Baron knew the salt-metal taste of fear in his mouth. He twisted his cane, pouring desperate strength into each movement. Nigel lurched in the opposite direction, his hand slip out of darkness. It was furred for an instant, with multi-jointed fingers ending in crystaline claws, then it was human again—a closed fist opening to reveal two half-burnt candles.

The Wiccan girl!

"She failed you, Baron Samhain," Nigel gloated. "She left these for me."

Samhain cursed Lise Brown forward and backward in time then, knowing he had nothing left to lose, he abandoned himself to the dark, deathly aspects of his own evolution. Though he might die and his Rifts be left open, the spawn Nigel would know that unique taste of hell which it was the voodoo lord of the dead's privilege to provide. His cane and curses poured on the Otherspawn, battering its face to a featureless pulp that shifted with the rain. The Baron's shadow grew as Nigel's lessened.

Though by all rights wounded beyond repair of regeneration, Nigel fought back. He resisted the agony of crushed bone and cruelly exposed nerves and found that darkness that was his to command since Lammas. The Baron in his death-lust did not see the opaque cloud which flowed from Nigel's mind.

"Feed," Nigel urged through partially regenerated lips. "Feed on our enemy—our blundering but not immortal enemy."

Darkness surged and covered the Baron. The Lammas Plague, freed from the prison of Nigel's mind, raged with a hunger even Nigel himself could not duplicate. Cell by cell it ate through the Baron's clothing and into his skin. The voodoo loa blazed with his own power, disrupting the cloud and revealing a half-flayed mortal to the Otherspawn Nigel who cringed now against the lamppost.

But the Baron was not about to effect a transfer of spirit nto the spawn's unspeakable body. He used the moments of strength his power gave him to raise the ebony and brass cane one last time and smash it into Nigel's brow.

"Otherspawn! I have marked you. You shall be seen by all who have the power to see. The Wiccans shall know you. The masters you deny shall take you back!"

Darkness closed in on the Baron again; he did not see Nigel lying helpless in the lamplight. The agony of losing his flesh to the ravening plague was insignificant beside that of losing nerve, muscle and bone. The long-dead voices of those whose memories were his exploded from a score of mouths newly opened in his dying body. He who brought a single death felt the death of thousands and which would not end. Samhain would surrender his spirit to the Otherworld, but the Lammas Plague was not the Otherworld. It ate past anatomy and into the essense of the Baron's being-without-end.

The screams faded, but did not die.

Nigel rested against the lamppost, gasping moist air through restored nostrils. He felt his skull where the Baron had marked it and molded new flesh over the brand. Samhain was gone; the plague the Otherworld had sent at Lammas buzzed around his head.

Flaccid with exhaustion, the dark-haired, pale young man roused himself and forced the cloud back into his mind. Its hunger and anger seared his thoughts. His erstwhile masters had intended the plague for him, but he had mastered it, instead. It would destroy him if his control ever weakened.

He could not make it disappear; he had already tried after it killed the tiresome, but harmless, Alan Porter. The cloud was a drain on his own strength when he could least afford it.

He was numb. His senses were keyed to the supernatural and he did not know of the addict until rude hands ripped open his jacket and probed his pockets. He groaned and the addict flashed a saw-tooth filet knife against Nigel's neck.

"You don't move, man. You don't scream or I'll kill you."

Dazed from the duel, Nigel lacked the strength to challenge the addict; he lacked a wallet and money as well. In drug-roused anger the addict pummelled the tender, regenerated flesh of Nigel's face and shoulders. Pain, and the realization that he, too, could be mortal, broke the Otherspawn's stupor.

He could not send this menace to the plague—he lacked the strength to reconfine it afterward—but he could send him to the Otherworld. His hands closed around the addict's neck, squeezing with steel-sharp talons that slit soft, human skin. The addict died silently, collapsing on Nigel's chest.

The compressed plague-cloud whined but he would not release it to a feast—nor would he feed himself; gluttony had never been his vice. With the last of his strength he heaved the body over a distant railing then he lapsed into uncaring sleep.

The yellow sunlight burned, forcing him from a rest which should have been many times longer. He groaned and shielded his eyes. His recovering mind wanted a blood-orange sun, cool and filling an eighth of the sky. It wanted muted, rotting colors and the tang of a dying world. Nigel gagged on his own memories and sat up, staring at the clever appendages which in this life replaced his claws.

He was, undoubtedly, more intelligent this time and they hadn't counted on that at all. The Vastness of the Otherworld remembered very little of life and death; They certainly hadn't considered the variety of life that lay beyond the Rifts, or the results of transplanting bits of it. They never should have chosen him; never should have tempted him. It had been

Their folly to distill from Themselves the complete essence of one exiled being and spit it out whole into this bright, young world.

Nigel clambered to his feet and looked for the addict's body. There was left down on the roadway, not even a bloodstain. Nigel felt his stomach; he wasn't hungry and wasn't a carrion feeder in any event.

His makers should have begun with the plague—with a mindless minion that would devour in Their name until, in time, a large enough area had been devastated on this side. They had thought an entity with what these beings called "free will" would do the job quicker and more thoroughly. They should never have sent him. He had mastered the art of learning; he felt ambition. Lise would fall to him despite, and because of, her High Coven initiation. Without the Baron's interference he could call back the seeds he had planted within her. With the High Priestess' aid he would have his way. He hadn't lied to Samedi, he rarely lied—that wasn't his vice either—he acknowledged no masters.

Chapter Forty-Two

New York phased out of summer and into early autumn filled with the racing sickness of paranoia. Neighborhood, block and building security associations blossomed. The Slasher claimed at least one life every seven to ten days. City and police officials clung to their tersely worded, sanitized accounts but rumor was rampant and rumor contained much of what Jessica had said was the truth.

Almost as often as a mangled victim was discovered an alleged perpetrator was produced to account for the crime wave. The City held its breath and counted the days. They never got past ten before the Slasher struck. The citizen's patrols were remarkably effective. Crime, in general, was down and the Slasher's depredations were all the more noticible.

It did not seem possible that the massive dragnet yielded neither clue nor sane eye-witness. None of the routine coincidences upon which policework was based had surfaced. Naturally then the rumors became darker; the people drew upon their primal fear and came close to the truth of the matter.

Culpeper's business had increased steadily since Madame Odile's death. There were days when a crowd waited when the store opened up. Jason grappled with cost and supply problems his marginal operation had never envisioned. They worked long hours packaging herbs, answering questions and relating bits of folklore. Edith believed that telling the truth would solve nothing, but she added to her burden of guilt each time she answered a fear-filled question. She was counting the days to the twenty-eighth when she would go home.

"Jason's rented a Xerox copier," she explained to Lise who was heating up nine o'clock leftovers for her. "Unless we know the people we won't sell a book anymore; they can make copies of the spells. Our shelves are almost bare as it is—and we're not the only ones. Weisner's downtown has been using copiers for a week."

"Jason and Sally must be thrilled."

"The blush will be off the rose some morning. They'll find Culpeper's burnt out with any change in the winds of fortune. Even if Nigel doesn't make a mistake, sooner or later people will realize what we're selling won't work against the Otherworld."

"Have Sally and Jason ever suspected that Nigel is Otherworld—that he probably *is* the Slasher?"

"No. Oh, they believe the Slasher is occultly mismotivated, like everyone else, but they'd welcome Nigel with open arms."

Lise sat forward in her chair. "Could they ever find out the truth? You once said the High Covens and the Otherworld were always hidden—even from other occultists. Well, with the Otherworld out—how vulnerable are we?"

"I should imagine if you can ask the question you already know the answer."

Lise got up and paced the length of the room "Then I've made up my mind: Sally and Jason are coming into Riverside. Like you said, they'll welcome Nigel with open arms. I'd rather have them in the circle than outside it." She waited for Edith objections.

"You're the HP, Lise. I won't tell you what to do with your coven. A coven can only have one High Priestess and Sally's not used to sharing. Riverside can't withstand a power-struggle—"

"It's my coven. I want her here."

"I would too—even with the risks."

It was settled that quickly and Lise was left to the task of bringing her decision to reality; convincing the rest that the vocal and visible Stars were right for Riverside and convincing the Stars that there were more important things than the pagan revival.

Lise spent the better part of a week campaigning and in the end got not only Jason and Sally but two more couples of their choosing to bring the coven's strength up to twelve. Edith wrinkled her brow when Lise admitted strangers to the circle, but having warned Lise against it, she was not the one to begin the power struggle.

"You have all you need now," Edith agreed when both she and Lise were out of the apartment, a feat more easily accomplished now that Riverside was larger and its members better trained. "You seem to have been right to get Sally and Jason; the people she's brought should be used to ritual and restriction. You'll be ready for Samhain."

"I'll be nervous without you. I wish you would stay."

"My own coven needs me more now, Lise. You should get away from my habits anyway. You'll be better off on your own; your talent will go into decision making, not into asking: what will Edith think?"

Reluctantly Lise agreed. She had begun to exercise her leadership prerogatives and what she judged appropriate for New York was not always the first thing to occur to Edith. These days she only presented conclusions to Edith, all but demanding approval yet still awkwardly dependent on her teacher.

The train-ride uptown after work was noisy, dirty and yet generally safer than it had been a few months before. Travellers watched each other carefully, even conversed occassionally if only to exchange the latest rumors and suspicions.

"They're leaving poisoned meat at twenty-five locations in Manhattan," the bespectacled matron confided to Lise as they rattled out of Forty-second Street.

"Have they said why?" she replied; not to reply would invite suspicion.

"He's drawn to the smell of blood!"

Lise nodded, grateful for the screetching wheels of the train. Nigel wouldn't be caught by poison. Whatever formula he used to select his victims she was certain they were in good health immediately prior to their deaths. Lise still thought fear had something to do with it; a special fear which, because of the love-hate she felt for him, he might someday sense in her.

A cool wind, one of the first of the season, was blowing off the river. Lise buttoned her sweater and hurried home.

"Miz Ratner said to leave word: she had to go out to Queens," Sam called while she checked her mail. "Slasher got her mother's neighbor. She left a few minutes ago."

Lise grimmaced and felt a knot of cold fear in her stomach which did not rise from sympathy. It was the first time one of her witches had abandoned her post. And why Rachel—who had promised and could handle the warding of her own—of all of them she was the most conscientious. Lise headed silently for the elevator.

"There's no problem up there, Miss Brown," Sam interrupted. "She didn't want to go but it was better than bringing her mother here. I been keeping an eye-out up there. Everything's quiet."

Lise wasn't reassured, but didn't let it show. Sam might not be a member of Riverside but he knew the dangers of the Otherworld. If he said it was quiet, it probably was—still, she'd feel better when she was there herself and had gotten a fellow babysitter.

The apartment was calm and quiet when she entered it but the phone at Culpeper's—her most likely source of assistance—was busy. After several attempts she was convinced it was off the hook. It was six-thirty already, with Edith expected back no later than eight-thirty. Lise eyed the livingroom warily. She hadn't broken her vow never to be alone in her apartment since she had made it. Maria and Bob would come if she called, though they'd be in the middle of dinner and probably couldn't get uptown much before Edith did. Everyone else was even further away.

In the end she dragged the altar out into the center of the room, set the goddess-statue upon it and lit her favorite incense. She wouldn't leave the room—until the doorbell rang and her hopes soared thinking that Mark had come home early and didn't know Rachel had left. She opened the door and stared into Nigel's smiling face.

"I've come to the front door."

He reeked of sincerity and contrition. She'd given her word to talk to him if he came to the front door—believing he could never do it. "There's no-one else here," she said awkwardly, blocking his path.

"That's all right—I'll feel more comfortable if it's just us."

She stepped aside and closed, but did not lock, the door. "Things are different now," she asserted, looking at the altar. "Maybe I agree there're enemies—but I deal with them my own way—and it works."

"You've conquered your inhibitions about bringing Craft into this room, I see. I like the incense." He inhaled the smoke and sat on the sofa.

He was attractive, enormously attractive, when he chose to be—and the gods had never offered Lise a cure for her emotional loneliness. It was an effort to keep the need for love out of her mind, but Lise did by thinking of the black-wrapped portrait.

"If you had let me, we could have avoided all this," he said gently.

"No, Nigel—this is a High Coven Rift, and whatever you are, you aren't High Coven."

"No, I'm not High Coven," he conceeded, "but I'd like to be."

Lise thought she had been prepared for anything—but not for this. In the depths of her heart she still wanted him as a partner—in the Wicca and elsewhere. All his Other-ness stood in the way—but if he were to renounce; if it were possible to renounce— She watched him take the glass statue in his hands and study Her face.

"Or, don't you accept the once-tempted?" he asked. "None of us has had a second chance before."

She swallowed hard. "I don't know, Nigel—I honestly don't know. If you know so much then you must realize—I can't know." But her inner voice said she did know and she should get him out of this room, this apartment by whatever means necessary. He was Other; he was irredeemable and she loved him.

Nigel affected not to notice her dilemma. He put the statue down and went to the geraniums, examining the scarlet flowers with his eyes and the soft touch of his fingers. "We had no flowers; the ground had already died. Maybe it was like this once—we didn't have legends or history either. Maybe we killed it once when we were stronger, or smarter; maybe my ancestors succumbed to some great temptation and that's why the Annihilator came for us. No-one knew then; I don't know now. Our sun was amber twilight, thick shadows and the smell of death. Can you imagine my world?''

Lise shook her head. His voice was mesmerizing, though he only looked at the flower and not at her.

''We lived off the rot; I wasn't any different. Then, there was nothing to remember until February first—but my world's long dead. I don't remember being chosen for this world. Do you remember when I said too much was expected of me?''

His fingernail severed the flower from its stem. Their eyes met and Lise expected him to crush the flower in his fist. She didn't doubt his Other-ness. He spun his fingers and laid the flower in her hand.

''You were terrified that night I came from the Other-world. Your terror was alive—I followed it, but you disappeared and I couldn't find you. Maybe it was hunger—maybe it was love. We would have made no distinction.

''I took a little from everyone I met that night, until I was rooted in your world and had this form—but by then I was lost. I followed what I thought was your trail and found the old ones. I was weak; I did what I'd been made to do. A man chased me—I rose to challenge him, but I didn't know how to change. Imagine your legs turned to clay, the air choking you. Imagine reaching for a kill and finding this,'' he held out his hand, flexing the fingers as he stared at them, ''—where you had claws of living crystal?''

Lise felt her dinner rise to her throat because she could imagine, just as she could see the shadows of razor-like claws on the carpet. She looked at his face, expecting to see the cat, but it was still Nigel. He raised his eyes to meet hers.

''I was beaten by a nylon warm-up suit. I fought with it until these flesh-fingers were wet, frozen blisters and the man sprayed my face with tear-gas. I've felt pain, Lise—who hasn't? But nothing like that. What are you? You swarm under a bright, living sun, you waste everything—including each other and yet the Annihilator," he pointed at the Rift, "finds not one in a million who fails its test."

"We're human; we have striving souls. We're moral and improve from generation to generation," Lise recited.

Nigel gave her a look that spanned disbelief and disgust. "You're clever—that's all; weak but agile. Your minds are like your hands. You made rituals to bind the Annihilator. You give your so-called souls a thousand chances to pass its test; we had failed before we were born. You've warped and evaded until your world is an over-ripe fruit. Your rituals will fail; They will come after you. The Annihilator will claim all it has been denied. The sun will fail; the ground will ooze death." He grasped her hand and forced the images of his mind into hers.

Lise cringed and struggled, but he held her to his vision. His world flooded past the rational barriers of her mind. A synesthesia of corruption and degeneration crushed down upon her. His reality bore down on every nerve ending until, with an explosion of nausea, it *was* her reality too. The corruption smelled sweet; she was hungry.

Three pairs of opposable, crystalline claws locked over her arm, immobilizing her hand, which was no longer a hand but a clawed appendage like his. Nigel—no earthly photograph had captured him. No purely human mind could hold him in memory: compelling, charismatic, sensual, the epitome of his kind and yearning for her.

"Ours, ours alone—beyond the power of the Annihilator," a blue-black snake tongue caressed her. "Ours forever when we seal this Rift."

The inhuman face of her lover faded in and out of focus before her own red-pupiled eyes. A scarlet stain appeared at his temple and grew sharper with each polarizing shift.

"You shall be seen by all who have the power to see—" the Baron's voice floated between them. Lise saw the bloody imprint of the skull-cane illuminated by the light in her livingroom.

Nigel released her with a groan of agony. Human hands

covered the gaping hole above his eyes; blood streamed over his fingers. The stench of her own vomit pushed Lise further away from him. Her mind formed a plea to the Baron who had always aided her.

"Witch!" Nigel snarled, making the word a curse. "You could have had it all." The bloody hand slashed in front of her, she dodged and felt nothing but a faint tug. Three parallel stripes—deep, long and red, raced down to her wrist; he was going to kill her as he had the rest.

She was beyond panic; able to realize she had no defense against this creature who phased from one body to another faster than her eyes could absorb the change. The gaping wound on the side of his head did not affect his speed. She dodged another sweep of his hand; a second set of stripes crossed the first. She began to feel the pain as well as the fear.

"You think I'll kill you, High Priestess?" his voice was velvet with malice. "I won't; I need you against the Annihilator. What you could have taken freely will be forced within you. You *will* share my future."

He feinted for her face; Lise raised her bleeding arm and felt invisible claws lock on her shoulder, pulling her to him, stripping her clothes from her.

"You'll learn—"

His lips closed over hers. She tried to bite through his tongue and the claws paralyzed her with pain. If she could die—but he wouldn't kill her. The two tongues, human and Other, swelled within her mouth as the claws bent her backwards over the altar she had so conveniently placed beneath the Rift.

Her mind reeled as he forced his way between her legs; not a human rapist but a profanely alien lust tearing into her belly and working an exquisite torture on her mind. His senses overcame hers—the sight of her body writhing against the altar—against him. He let her drown in the shame and degredation then he stripped even that from her and forced her to experience the rape as he experienced it—the sating of an eon of lust. Her screams were trapped beside her in the web of his mind as she saw her pain-wracked body rise to meet him for the dazzling instant of mutual orgasm.

"You'll learn—"

He let her back into her own body, her own conscience. There was only agony and aching shame—and the brilliant memory of pleasure he brutally burned into her life. A piece of an alien mind had been grafted into her own where it grew with unseemly vigor. *She* had been attacked; *she* had fought—it had been rape but the rape of her body was nothing compared to the rape of her mind.

He was Nigel again, the human Nigel unmarked and whole, cradling her fouled body gently in her arms. He loved her and that love, strange, cold and unimaginable, lived within her now blocking her own purely human hate and rage. She willed her teeth to clamp down on the vulnerable flesh of his neck; her swollen lips brushed softly against him.

"You could have loved me freely; instead it will be like this. I am saddened—it makes my victory bitter. But I had to win, Lise—some day I hope you'll understand that."

She screamed and raged against him, but the sound and the movements were sealed ineffectually in her mind. She would never understand; never accept the outrage. With strength that came from all the High Covens and all their Priests and Priestesses she opened her mouth and closed her teeth on his neck as his passion rose again.

Chapter Forty-Three

Everyone at Culpeper's—customers, owners, workers alike—had fallen victim to the City's foreboding. A cloud had hung specifically over Edith since late afternoon; she had to leave the shop early or explode in omnidirectional anger. She hailed a taxi at Lincoln Center.

Traffic was snarled near the Riverside building. Flashing red lights and milling crowds halted the cab. Edith paid off the driver and elbowed her way to the front of the mob.

"Let me through—I live here!" she commanded, intimidating the block-association guard.

There were green-garbed ambulance attendants outside the lobby but no sense of emergency. Once inside the wood-and-glass doors no-one seemed particularly interested in her. She wormed closer to Sam's cublicle, hoping to learn what was going on. The old man sprawled in his chair; Edith couldn't see his face but she could see what remained of his neck. A burst of hysteria announced the arrival of Sam Junior. Edith slipped out of sight up the stairs.

The elevator was resting at some other floor. She pressed the button but could not endure the waiting. She grabbed each half-landing bannister and propelled herself up the stairs like a woman half her age; yet she was barely winded when she reached 647.

She fought with the keys and instant before realizing the locks weren't set and that a moaning could be heard beyond the door: Lise—her voice a disconcerting blend of lust and agony. Things were different in this country and these times; a single woman did what Edith would never do—and it was Lise's home.

But, no—those sounds were utterly wrong. She would not ring the doorbell in warning but brace herself for the worst and confront them. Disgust and outrage washed over her as she stared at the desecration occurring on the altar. Precious moments passed before she believed that the obscenity was compounded because Lise was not a comprehending partner to the act.

Blinded by her own tears Edith stumbled down the hallway and retrieved her rowen staff from its resting place by the door. The feel of its smooth potent surface restored her.

"Get out!" she screamed, punctuating the syllables with two-handed punishment from the staff. "Go back where you belong!"

Nigel rolled his head to see Edith, but he would not abandon his passion. He swung once with his inhuman strength and Edith toppled backwards. Soft, human lips spread from blunt, human teeth, but the warning growl he emitted came from another place and time.

Edith raised herself up with the staff and closed with him again. She no longer held the wood like a thin, but not terribly effective club. Her hands divided the staff into thirds. It had been many years since she and the other children of Caer Maen had played knights-and-friars—but if the Goddess still abided in this room then she would remember how.

The knobby staff flicked out with a thud against Nigel's shoulder. His arm snaked out. Edith twirled the staff and brought the knob-end into the soft hollow under his arm. In her day not a cousin had crossed Friar Tuck's bridge. His arm whipped back in pain. She put the ferrule into his ribs like a billiard cue.

Letting Lise drop to the floor, Nigel finally gave Edith his attention. The demon-cat's pupils glowed, the rest of him remained human—and the effect was all the more horrifying. Edith looked only long enough to realized the hypnotic danger and willed herself to look away. She struck with impugnity and came to know he was toying with her. Her swift assaults did not injure him, but they tired her. She changed tactics and began circling the altar.

His goal was simple: destroy Caer Maen's High Priestess and work his way on Riverside's—but simply staying alive would not give the victory to Edith. She must vanquish him as thoroughly as he could vanquish her. Lise had managed to drag herself out of the way; Edith dared not notice more than that. She hoped the young woman would rally but it was a fleeting hope sent on to the Gods with the rest of her panicked entreaties.

Whatever advantage surprise had given her was gone now as he adapted to the situation and worked his deceptions on her. Edith felt the alien presence in her mind and the man she fought was no longer Nigel but Bert—then Elizabeth and finally Gwen—red-haired, blue-eyed.

"Don't 'E'—you're hurting me," her sister's voice said, using a nickname Edith had not heard these past five years.

Knowing it was Nigel was not enough to keep one surge of emotion from freezing the rowen-wood in her hands—and that was all he needed. Gwen's face broke into a thousand decaying holes and the red-eyed demon laid his crystalline claws on the staff.

There would be no more—just the time for a last prayer to the gods. His lunge pressed her back to the sofa, the rowen-wood ineffectual between them. His breath was hot and foul; his serpentine tongue uncoiled and lashed her throat as a garotte, pulling her closer to the claws and the shimmering teeth.

"My Gods, I have tried!" Edith croaked and closed her eyes.

"Bastard!" Lise screamed, and the choking tongue unlashed itself. "Scum! Slime!"

Hope returned. Edith opened her eyes to see Lise wielding the Baron's charred cane; the grinning brass skull inflicting the damage her rowen-wood had not. The creature still crouched over her. Edith drove her knee into its groin and smiled with pleasure as Nigel doubled over and the claws slid away from her staff.

Two fighters are rarely as good as one, but Edith had to strike at the Otherworld. The Gods were with them for they were able to hurt their foe and not each other. But it was Lise, fighting with a crazed ferocity, who battered Nigel with injury rather than annoyance. Edith did no more than to keep him from retaliating—but that was enough.

"Why are you doing this to me?" The question exploded in their minds. Half the cat-fangs were broken and that creature that was both Nigel and the cat was trapped in mid-transformation. What had been awesome strength was now easily avoided awkwardness. He protected his battered head with half-furred arms. Human fingers bled where the crystal claws emerged from them. His moans filled the room and their thoughts, but they pummeled the crouched form until it lay still against the altar, then they rested.

"What now?" Lise asked between gasps.

Edith shook her head and pointed with the staff to Nigel's healing arm.

His second attack came as a mental onslaught, warning them of the Lammas plague within him which would begin an unchecked rampage unless they cooperated. When they did not, he released the plague and the women batted the buzzing mote away, fully aware of what it would become. They had begun to understand the extent of his treachery against his masters. It was impossible to imagine the tortures which awaited him in the Otherworld, and they pressed their attack all the more determinedly.

When arrogance and intimidation had failed to secure his freedom, Nigel grovelled before them, offering the Wiccans his power for eternity if they would spare him.

"We'll make a circle," Lise whispered loudly. "You and I, opposite each other; we'll make a circle and drive him back through the Rift."

Forcing herself erect and calling on unsuspected reserves of stamina, Edith took position on the opposite side of the altar. She held the staff horizonally as they began the slow, circular movements; Lise copied her stance with the Baron's cane. They were too exhausted to compose a chant and too winded to recite it even if they had—but their desperation-borne thoughts had a profound effect on Nigel.

The Otherspawn drew himself up on shaky, unequal legs. His anguished disbelief and terror penetrated their thoughts as raw emotion. He felt the reality of their Wiccan magick and the yawning hunger of the Otherworld calling him back. A flood of temptation washed over Lise but it lacked the precision of his earlier attacks; she knew they were winning.

Their circle had become a decreasing spiral, pressing

against a palpable force. That which had been Nigel screamed from a perch atop the altar. The cat-form was no longer stable and seemed more spidery than feline. His head, if any remained, was hidden by shaggy, blood-matted fur. His pleading was the outward force against which they braced the staffs. The room had begun to reek of the Other-world and above Nigel the black, spinning disk Edith had seen in her nightmares evanesced.

Edith lost track of time as they wound the spiral tighter. The disk blocked her vision; she had barely enough strength to place one foot past the next and none to call to Lise. She thought of the Goddess as the Rift spun in front of them and told herself they would succeed—even if it took to eternity and the building collapsed around them.

The outward pressure dropped suddenly. They both stumbled and Edith's mind cleared barely in time to see a shifting, ethereal malice where Nigel had been. The disk had intensified; its blackness receded to infinity. Keening sounds swirled around the room; both women trembled from the vibrations.

"Bring the staffs together!" Edith called to Lise.

The apparition elongated and was drawn into the disk with gnashing rebellion that rattled the apartment's windows. Lise's face was drawn—as if she had aged a thousand years since morning. Perhaps it had been that long. Sparks passed through the malice as it faded into the disk. It was over with a thunder-clap.

Lise roused herself from floor-bound stupor first, flexing her stiff, aching arms then crawling to Edith's side. Her mentor had fallen into a deep, relaxed sleep. The taint of the Otherworld was faint in the air—but other evidence proved the reality of their struggle. The varnished surface of the altar was puddled with thick blood; the eyes of the brass skull were caked with the same substance. The carpet was probably beyond cleaning. And, of course, there were her wounds and her tattered clothes.

Her hands shook as she gathered the cloth into a bundle and shoved the lot into a paper bag. She'd have to dress before she could take the bag to the incinerator chute; she'd have to bathe before she could dress. The lingering pain of rape and panic crippled her and made the walk endless. She closed the door to the bathroom, locked it and let hot water pour into the tub.

"I'll be all right," she told herself as she sat on the hamper, removing the knee-socks Nigel had somehow missed. "I'll wash; rest. He's gone—I can hear him from the Rift, in my mind—but he's not getting out again."

She stood up and caught her reflection in the mirror. A throbbing bruise had risen on her cheek. Clumps of vomit matted her hair. Her mouth was rimmed with blood and saliva that cracked and fell to the floor when she raised a hand to touch it. She watched the flakes collect on the floor and recorded the blood, sweat and vomit that had marked her during the ordeal. But mostly, irresistibly, she saw the rope-y, blue scum that wrapped around her thighs and disappeared upward between her legs and into her body where she could feel its lingering warmth. There wasn't anyone to share her pain, only herself—violated, groping across the floor to the bathtub.

She scrubbed until her fingers were wrinkled and the skin of her inner thighs was a raw, burning red. She resurrected a dusty douche-bag from the closet and injected herself with hot water and stale vinegar—not caring what harm she might do herself so long as that unspeakable semen were seared out. When the mirror was hopelessly fogged, she contorted herself on the clammy grey-white tiles, searching for any last trace of shame, knowing she had not removed any of it from her mind.

"Lise, Lise—are you all right?" Edith called through the locked door.

She didn't answer, but Edith heard her moving.

"Lise, come out now."

Reluctantly, Lise unlatched the door and stepped into the dark bedroom. The Englishwoman handed her a soft, fleecy robe that, by the smell of roses, must have come from deep in Gwen's wardrobe. Then she sat down with Lise and held her hand in the darkness.

"Spit it out—don't let it take root within you," she suggested.

"I can't," Lise protested. "It's too late."

"You must, dear," Edith squeezed her hand then held Lise's damp head against her shoulder, "before the scars are too old."

Lise shook her head but the tears had begun to fall. "I can't go on. I want to die. He was inside me; he is inside me." It was not the rape which shamed her, though that was bad enough, but the knowledge that the alien sharing of his lust remained within her and could not be banished. "He's defiled me; made me garbage. I'm only fit to be thrown out—like him."

"No, you're the High Priestess of Riverside. You don't have the power to remove yourself for crimes you imagine you've committed."

"Edith—he didn't just rape me. If you hadn't come when you did he would have possessed me—even now *he's still here!*" With thoughts of him, the part of her mind which he had changed came alive; he was beside her, inside her and as much as she hated him she longed for him. "Let me go!"

"You're letting the Otherworld win, Lise. There's nothing wrong with you—you let the perversion live," Edith told her.

"Will you understand," Lise screamed, "right now—it's not you beside me—it's him. I'm full of him. My body lusts for him; a part of my mind *is* Nigel and will never, never go back to the Otherworld. I carry him with me—we're one person, one thing!" She fell into hysteria and the knowledge that she would never dare to take a lover—and always have Nigel within her.

Edith pinched Lise's shoulder. "You are Sybylla," she yelled over Lise's sobs, slapping the bruised cheek. "You are the High Priestess. You could never be enslaved to a man's flesh—not demon nor lover! Whatever you felt when he raped you—even if you still feel it now—you sent him back. You've redeemed yourself before the Gods and nothing else matters!"

"Leave me alone!"

Edith slapped her again. "Not until you will yourself to live with the obligations laid upon you. Do you hear me, Sybylla? You may have your outrage, your shame, your demon-within you but you are forged from the god's own steel and you *may* not break nor surrender."

"No," Lise said in a smaller voice.

"No what?" Edith demanded. "No I shall not be defeated by the Otherworld in any of its guises'?"

"I could be pregnant, Edith," Lise protested. "What of that? Do I have the obligation to bear an Otherworld child? Maria didn't."

"I've seen your pills. There's no reason for you to be pregnant; Nigel works on your mind—not your womb."

"I can't face the coven—never. I won't know what to say. How can I tell them *he's* a part of me? I can't be their High Priestess."

"Tomorrow, when they're all here for the Equinox you'll tell them you are the High Priestess; you have been tempered in the blood of the Otherworld."

"No, Edith—tell them for me. Help them choose someone else. I'll move."

"And live with both your shame and Nigel still inside you? No. You'll have to solve this one yourself; this time tomorrow I'll be in Cornwall." Lise froze in mid-sob. "While you bathed I changed my flight. I suspected all you've told me. I called the airline; there'd been a cancellation on tomorrow's flight. I don't argue with omens. You can see me to the airport but you must go the rest of the way yourself."

"No, Edith—not when I need you so much!"

"You've been greatly violated. But, if I help you now it will only confirm your everlasting weakness to yourself. If I deny you the time to experience your shame, to move around it, you might not adapt to it at all. If I don't leave you now I'll deny you the chance to recover; I'll have done the Otherworld's work and not the Goddess'."

Then Edith's voice softened and she hugged Lise tightly through her own tears. "I'd stay with you; I'd leave Caer Maen far behind. They've tempted me into leaving both of us weakened—two High Covens without their rightful leaders. I should be grateful the Gods have made my path so clear—but I'm not."

Slow moments passed before Lise could see that the gods had left her a narrow, twisting path up from misery. The struggle would offer less solace than the depths of despair, but then the Gods might have chosen her because she was just stubborn enough to do things the hard way.

The two women held onto each other until sleep caught them both.

Chapter Forty-Four

There was a morning. Twelve hours of sleep all but insured that Lise would survive; she had missed the appointed time for self-destruction. With each passing iota of time it was easier to keep going than to stop. She ate, laughed and put the rape out of her mind for whole minutes at a time.

A dose of aspirin had dulled the aches and pains of the previous night. She stood alone in the kitchen caught up in habits that carried her safely from moment to moment. Edith was packing and re-packing her suitcases.

She had decided on the going-away gift weeks before. Once, when she was ten and her favorite aunt was returning home, Lise had tucked her penny-bank in the aunt's suitcase—trusting that such a valuable object could only be returned in person. Two weeks later a large package had arrived for her: the bank, wrapped in newspapers, filled with extra pennies but without her aunt. Lise didn't expect Edith to return the pearl she wedged into the lid of the Wedgewood box, nor even to know it was stuck there but she herself would have to go to Caer Maen one day to retrieve it.

She brought the box into the bedroom where Edith was looking at the overflowing mess.

"I'd like you to take this with you." Lise held out the gift.

"Thank you. You know—"

"That it was Gwen's? Yes. I guessed when I saw you looking at it. You haven't asked for anything; the least I can do is give you this."

Edith smiled and made a nest of her handkerchiefs to protect the treasure. "And, wisely, you chose something small. I thought I was being so careful. I sent my winter clothes back months ago—souvenirs too—but I've still got twice as much as I started with."

She shrugged and the two worked in near-silence, rearranging, compacting, reluctantly discarding until, with an effort, the suitcases could be locked securely. There wasn't much to say and that could wait until they were at the airport.

Just before one Sally and her sister-in-law, Eileen, arrived for an afternoon of watching the Rift. They looked at Lise's bruised face, her bandaged arm, the damp cloths still strewn across the carpet and took the news of Sam's death and Edith's departure badly.

"There were problems last night," Lise reiterated, as Edith would say nothing. "Sam's dead—and for all practical purposes, so is Nigel." She felt the crabbed beginnings of orgasm in her gut whenever she spoke his name and remembered that Sally had never thought ill of Nigel. But Sally said nothing. "We've held things steady—you won't have problems. But, well—Edith has her own coven to worry about."

Sally shrugged. "Is this a good time for Edith to be leaving? When the Otherworld's striking so close? Nigel, Sam—both in one night. Wouldn't it be better if she stayed?"

Lise bore the meandering spasms of pleasure in her groin. Standing in the livingroom she could almost see her lover/rapist; she could certainly hear his agony. His torture weighed heavily in her thoughts. "Caer Maen needs Edith," she said with more finality than was necessary.

Sally turned to Edith for more information, and getting none, bid the Englishwoman a somewhat disgruntled goodbye from herself, Jason and everyone who knew her from Culpeper's and would be unable to say goodbye in person.

It was Eileen, the newcomer from another of Sally's covens, who clasped Edith's hand tightly and pleaded for the most experienced Guardian to stay.

—She's weak—Lise thought—too weak. She'll never make it. I shouldn't let other people choose my witches.— She surprised herself not only with her certainty, but with her acceptance of Riverside.

It was later than it should have been. At Edith's insistence they hailed a cab—and tried not to notice the detectives prowling through Sam s office. The cabbie, recognizing the address from the morning papers, assaulted them with questions. When they provided no new answers, he offered his own theories: a mixture of Communists and mafiosi so far removed from the truth as to inject humor into an otherwise grim day.

The check-in process went quickly. Edith's ticket had been

waiting for her. Her bags rumbled down the conveyor without over-weight tags. They exchanged hope and reassurance and watched the slow progress of the clock. With an hour left before flight-time, Edith asked Lise if she'd rather return to Manhattan now . .

"There should be some great symbolic gesture I could make right now," Lise mused as she shouldered her purse. "Cymbals, choirs—something like that. I'd like to wish you something more than—have a good flight."

"I'd appreciate a good flight—I'm not one for roller coasters. Just knowing you're the High Priestess is gift enough."

Lise paused and realized that the shifting softness in her gut had abated. "Getting out of the building helped a lot. Nigel is just a memory this far from the Rift—but I've got to go back. I wonder—at the end, what he was or if we misjudged him. Could he have redeemed himself?"

"I doubt he was ever anything but a part of the Otherworld," Edith chastised softly. "His entire being might have been created to tempt you—even his memories and his rebellion. We'll never know for sure; it's best to believe he was ever a pawn. On Samhain you'll close the Rift and it will be over."

Lise looked away, not wanting to see how much of Edith's confidence was just last-minute politeness. There were still the Lammas Plague in the City and six weeks until Samhain. The mood of parting had been broken; Lise was thinking about Samhain and being alone. It would be better to be gone from the airport.

"You will," Edith repeated, speaking to Lise's fear. "Remember you owe them leadership—not explanations. Anything less will be your destruction."

Lise didn't understand what Edith meant but didn't stand around waiting for clarification. She waved a last time and headed out the doors to the bus-stop. A passing glance caught a tall, well-dressed black man disappearing into the terminal and for a moment Lise saw the Baron. She had taken the first steps back when the crowd parted for an instant and she saw clearly that the man was a stranger. The bus wheezed into sight and she made her way to a window seat.

It was just past five when she opened the doors of her building. The police had padlocked Sam's office and there was, if she used her imagination, a lingering trace of death in the lobby. She would eventually have to contact Fine and discover what these events meant to her as an owner of the building—she already knew what they meant to her as High Priestess. Her gut was churning again but with hunger and not orgiastic torment—she hoped.

"You're back early?" Sally said with ill-concealed concern when Lise had reclosed the apartment door.

"Neither of us like long-drawn-out good-byes," Lise explained. She felt like a child expected to do an adult's work. Sally seemed larger than life, Eileen was a menacing stranger on the sofa. Pre-orgasm tremors wracked her then turned to knife-edge pain as she listened to Nigel's screams—screams no-one else could hear.

"Lise, you look sick," Sally said, shifting back into her customary role of caretaker.

Lise let them fuss over her, though the spasm had passed. It was ironic: the memory of Nigel within her could dispell any other influences the Rift had on her. He kept his promise. So long as she retained her gnawing, tortured attachment to Nigel no other Otherworld artifice could effect her.

"I think I should lie down and rest before everyone gets here," she said.

"Lise, what's wrong? Twice while you were gone we thought we heard someone screaming. Now you're acting very strange—like you're talking to someone we can't see—" Sally did little to veil her suspicion and fear.

"The screaming is coming from the Otherworld—and I'm acting strangely because we almost lost the whole ball of wax last night and I haven't recovered." She felt another twinge in her gut and didn't fight the pain.

"But—you're all right?" Eileen asked. She did not say: but you're still one of us—though from the expression on her face these thoughts were obvious.

"Of course I'm all right," Lise snapped. "I'll rest, then when everyone's here I'll start at the beginning and go through it all just once. You'll just have to trust me until then.'' Her voice was crisp—as Edith's usually was when she was not in a mood for nonsense.

Lise slept, though she hadn't thought she would and awoke refreshed. Rachel and Mark were whispering with Sally in the livingroom. Lise rolled over and saw it was just past seven. Her first impulse was to rush to the other room and interrupt their worries with self-justification.

The Ratners were certain to understand and she would have allies when the rest arrived. She would also divide her coven between those who had known before and those who hadn't. Tucking the pillow back under her bruised cheek, Lise pretended to sleep a while longer.

She covered the bandages on her arm by the sleeve of a loose sweater and concealed the bruises under make-up as best she could when she did get up. She tried to act as if whatever had happened was completely over, but they a-voided her when she came out into the other rooms. Lise accepted the growing sense of apartness; she should have expected it as well. Even without the rape the coven expected her to be different; Edith had said no-one else would walk her path. She put water on for coffee by herself and did not ask anyone to share it with her.

''Lise?'' Maria walked into the kitchen. Lise had not noticed she had arrived. ''What happened?''

''Like I've said to everyone else, we almost lost the Rift—''

''I've heard all that. Sally called while you were sleep-ing.'' Maria took an extra cup down from the shelf and set it beside Lise's. ''He hurt you bad—didn't he?''

Lise brushed her fingertips over the livid bruise. ''I guess that's obvious.'' She poured the water into her cup but not into Maria's.

''Nigel—he's the one we're hearing—isn't he. And he's the one who raped you?''

The words were soft and compassionate, but they only whipped up Lise's anger. ''I haven't said that—no-one's said that,'' she warned.

''Lise, I know. Remember me—remember what happened to me at Beltane? You don't have to say anything to me. I can see everything I remember in your eyes—*everything*—''

Lise held the coffee-pot, not knowing if she would set it on the stove or, in one wild, irrational act, spill the steaming water on Maria's concerned face. She'd have to have one friend—one person who could know the private self she would have to hide from the coven most of the time. She poured the water into Maria's cup.

''I'm planning to tell as much of it as I can to the coven tonight—emptying my shame: a sort of confession instead of a ritual. I don't want to be doing any magick at our altar until Samhain.''

Maria studied her coffee. ''I don't know, Lise. I can see the part about not having a ritual—too dangerous—but even the Pope confesses in private. I *know* what happened because of how you look and act; I'm not sure I want to hear you *tell* me I'm right.''

''I've got to get it out of me and you have to know, like you do, and then still accept me, knowing everything—''

''You want to share your shame with us,'' Maria accused.

It was Lise's turn to stare into her coffee. But it was what she wanted: public confession then public exoneration. Maria very plainly felt that was somehow wrong. The silence lasted until Maria broke it.

''They'll have other things on their minds soon enough.''

''How so?'' Lise asked.

''There's been an accident on the subway—we heard about it coming up here. A train stalled under the river. They wound up sending transit people down after the passengers—but when they got to the train everyone had disappeared.''

''What of that? The motorman could've led them in the other direction.'' She had more important problems than the aging subway system.

''There's more, Lise—there's got to be more. The story wouldn't have been on the news at all if there weren't more. They said the people had disappeared—not that the train was empty. Anyway—when I heard about it my stomach curled, Lise, like it does when I'm near the Otherworld.''

Lise felt her own stomach churn and set down the coffeecup. Nigel had warned them. Twelve hours before she could have rushed into the livingroom and consulted Edith—and Edith would have said there was little the High Coven could do with the Lammas Plague except hope it disappeared after Samhain, if not before.

"We'll wait," she said to Maria. "We can't go chasing rumors. Our obligation is to the Rift not the rest of the world. If we do our job the rest will take care of itself."

"—But I thought you should know."

"And now I know. Nigel released the Lammas Plague when Edith and I cornered him. If what you say is true then I know he was telling the truth—but he usually did."

Maria stifled whatever resentment she felt, but Lise saw the marks of it in the way her friend wrapped her fingers around the mug. She couldn't beg Maria to understand; in time she would or she wouldn't. Nothing would be the same. Since her initiation she'd been adapting to larger changes—it was the smaller ones, the ones that cut through friendship, that took her by surprise.

Everyone except Jessica had arrived for the ritual. The sounds of people donning long robes reached the kitchen. She couldn't put it off much longer. After filling her cup with water and leaving it in the sink, Lise went down the hallway.

"No, don't bother to change," she called as she passed the bedroom door. "We're going to be talking, not chanting, this evening."

Sally disapproved; she had re-arranged New Moon's equinox celebrations because of her commitment to Riverside, but if Lise wasn't going to live up to her basic obligations as High Priestess—

"My obligations say that with Nigel bottled up in the Rift we don't want to tamper with the balance around the altar until Samhain."

"Nigel?" Rachel asked, pulling her sweater tight.

Lise groaned. She was into it now—without benefit of the careful preliminaries she'd evolved. "Yes, Nigel. I don't know if he was the one who slashed your friend out in Queens but I'm certain he killed Sam in order to get up here after you left. He wanted to join Riverside."

A ripple of concern and rebellion spread around the room. Lise wiped her palms on her sleeves. She had intended to have the initiative, to weave the story skillfully until, at the end, the agreed with her actions. She hadn't planned to be on the defensive, explaining the events in piecemeal response to bitter questions. She'd expected it would take the better part of the evening to reach Nigel's assault and everyone was supposed to be sympathetic by then. Jessica wasn't even here yet and half the coven was up in arms; the other half was terminally confused.

"You refused to talk to him, didn't you?" Mark asked.

"Well, of course, I—well, I was stalling for time. I didn't know about Sam but I suspected something was wrong. I told him I couldn't possibly make that kind of decision myself—"

"But you've said he was Otherworld, Lise," Jason interrupted. "What exactly was going on in your mind. Were you ever thinking of going along?"

"Let Lise tell it her own way? This isn't a trial!" Bob snapped protectively.

"I could say I was too frightened to be thinking straight—because I was. But the truth was that he made sense: I wasn't sure I could have refused him our protection—if he hadn't attacked me later." The knots coiled tight within her; a trickle of liquid raced down her thigh. It didn't seem possible that no-one else heard his screams.

"Lise?" Maria asked, noting Lise's physical distress.

Lise shuddered and escaped the orgasm. "Why're half of you here anyway?" she exploded. "The Otherworld had touched you and Edith and I felt you were safer in the Coven than outside it." They all glared at her, even Maria. "He put on quite an act; and he had the most to fear from the Otherworld."

They fidgeted, mumbled or sat and stared silently. It wasn't falling apart because of the rape and the degredation; it was falling apart because they questioned her judgment. Nothing she was saying was reassuring them, either. There was a knock at the door and an overlong silence before Lise went to let Jessica in.

"We're having a rather heavy session," Lise explained

when Jessica asked what was wrong.

"No," Jessica said simply, holding Lise's hand again. "That's not the first cause."

"A lot has happened—I'm trying to explain it but things aren't going well." Lise pulled her hand away. "If you'll join the rest of the crew in the livingroom. I'm trying to go through all this just once."

"Lise, you don't have to explain anything," Jessica said, taking Lise's hand again. "You sacrificed yourself. You were the lure, then the avenger; you don't need to apologize."

Lise couldn't say anything.

"You've taken the Slasher," Jessica continued. "He's been here; he's the one who hurt you deeply—betrayed you and lingers in your soul—"

"He—" Lise began awkwardly.

Jessica held up a hand in protest. "I don't want to know. If that's all you're going to talk about—then I'll leave."

It was Lise's turn to know complete confusion. "If I don't tell you everything, then how can you trust me?"

Jessica shrugged. "I trust because of what I feel—but even if I didn't have that I'd still trust you. If I couldn't trust you the gods would already have dealt with you. The rest should see it that way, too. I don't tell everything I see; you shouldn't tell them everything you've felt. They don't have the strength for it. Maybe you have the right to expose their weakness—I don't."

"All right, then, but don't go. I still don't think we should do the ritual, but it wouldn't hurt if we were together for a while."

If Lise had never tried to explain but simply told them there could be no ritual because of the Otherworld, there would have been no dissent. She had learned a bit more about the power of a High Priestess. They looked to her for focus and leadership, she understood, and when she reversed the process disaster followed quickly.

Chapter Forty-Five

Twelve days had passed since Sam's death and Nigel's capture. The police were never certain if the black doorman's death were the Slasher's last act and, of course, they never knew about Nigel. The several million inhabitants had counted the days. By the time they had reached ten, no-one was thinking much about the Slasher. Anxiety and nervousness had ascended into mass hysteria.

Maria had been right about the subway incident. One hundred and thirty-four people had vanished. There was no ransom or terrorist demand. None of the bodies had surfaced in the rivers; no-one wandered home with amnesia. The figure was an approximation for it remained impossible to know how many had been on the train when it stalled. Dogs had been led into the tunnel; they had whined in terror until returned to the surface.

But not until a pattern emerged, after about a week, did the social fabric of the City unravel. There were more disappearances: individuals who didn't make it home for dinner, work-crews that never came back. Then, before the horrified eyes of the staff of a small export house, two window-washers screamed and flung themselves off their scaffolding; the bodies were gone before they reached the ground.

Lise knew how the men had met their ends but that didn't stop her from avoiding the windows of her office, fearing something she could not describe but would not fail to recognize. Businesses all over town suffered from absenteeism, but she kept coming in.

"Lise, would you step into my office?"

Krozer stuck his head and shoulders around the open doorway. Everyone was jumpy these days but she thought there was an extra aura of distraction about him which was confirmed when he closed the door of his office.

"I've just gotten a call from personnel—now I don't know

what's going on, and I don't think you should be unduly concerned—but the police are waiting to talk to you in your apartment uptown."

"Maria, Jessica?" Lise said almost to herself as she thought of the catastrophes her apartment could unleash. "What happened?"

"I don't know that anything has happened—in fact I rather doubt that anything has. I didn't get *that* feeling from personnel. The police specifically want to talk to you, now. Do *you* have any idea what they could want?"

Lise shook her head and left the office, not much caring what he might think of her silence. Mundane authorities milling around the Rift could only mean trouble. It was raining and all the taxicabs were either taken or off-duty. She wasted precious minutes hoping her luck would change with the next traffic light before furling her umbrella and heading into the subway.

The tunnels were steaming. Expresses and downtown locals roared by frequently, but the uptown local she needed remained resolutely out-of-sight.

"Fine time for the gods to abandon me," she muttered and bought a newspaper for distraction.

At length the local screeched to a halt and absorbed the platform of people. Lise's synthetic silk dress clung to her; her skin itched in places she couldn't possible scratch and the beefy hard-hat who towered over her had garlic-and-onion breath.

She tried to lose herself in the comics until the car lurched and jolted to an unexpected halt and the lights dimmed. Someone at the far end of the car started shouting in Spanish. Her own shoulder had absorbed the sudden stop but the hard-hat had managed to step on her ankle, sending an inch-wide run up the side of her leg. Silently cursing the man, Lise blew her hair out of her eyes and stared out the grimy window.

They were in a wide, open part of the tunnels; there was another train stalled on the far side of the steel-girders, its lights flickered wildly. In the moments of brightness she could see pandemonium on the other train. A young woman directly opposite was beating on the window with her shoe.

Gas? A fire of some sort? The woman didn't seem to be injured. Then she stopped her frantic struggle and slumped against the glass. Lise felt her throat tighten, she didn't want to breath but what she saw was worse than gas—the woman was disappearing. A great red smear appeared where her forehead touched the glass, but it wasn't enough to obscure what had happened to the woman's face. Great black lesions appeared on her skin, peeled it back to the pinkish white bones and into the matter beneath that.

Panic erupted around Lise, but she was only dimly aware of herself as the Lammas Plague settled over the dead woman. The train she was on gave another lurch, the lights and fans hummed with power. The woman in the other train had subsided from view. Lise grabbed the steel-strap and hoped she wouldn't be the only person on the car to vomit.

She made the rest of her way home in a daze. She envisioned herself bursting into the apartment and telling the police what she had seen, though the authorities would know even by now. Surely the police were already swarming over that train.

The door to her apartment had been left open; anger burned away most of her panic. No sounds emerged from the living-room. She called to Maria and walked carefully down the corridor.

"Are you Lise Brown?" a uniformed man asked as he escorted her to a chair.

"Yes."

"Please sit down," he gestured toward the chair they had moved from behind the writing table. "I can inform you that there are no charges pending against you, nor are any specifically contemplated at this time. However, the nature of our inquiry is such that the answers you give could become relative to criminal prosecution that might possibly include yourself at a later time. You may decide that you would like to retain the services of a lawyer and postpone questioning until he, or she, is present. Strictly off the record—that could take weeks, Ma'am and we've got people dying all over this city because you haven't come forward before this to tell what you possibly know."

Lise saw the fear in Maria and Jessica's eyes and fairly

seethed from the idea that her witches had been subjected to heavy-handed pressure. Her urge to confess was gone, replaced by the endless memorizations on answering questions from the Inquisition.

"It has never been my intention to hinder the wheels of justice. Ask your questions; I'll answer them as best I can."

"Ms. Brown, did you know the previous tenant of this apartment?"

"No, the apartment didn't become available until he had died," she answered honestly—as the grimoires always advised.

"Did you ever know any of his friends, then?"

"No," she replied. Edith was a relative, not a friend—and she never truly knew Rob or Marjory.

"Do the names Marjory Sutton and John Robert Hynes mean anything to you?"

Lise paused, though the names were in the forefront of her mind. She warmed to the game. "They were the first victims of the Slasher, weren't they?"

"Yes, as a matter of fact, they were, Ms Brown," the officer allowed. "They were also here the night Arthur Andrews died. What about the name Alan Porter—does that name mean anything to you?"

Lise let herself blanch. If they knew to ask Alan's name, pretending ignorance was folly. "He was killed during the summer—not by the Slasher—just killed." She shuddered involuntarily. There were spasms in her gut again and Nigel's screams in the air. "I worked with Alan," she said softly.

"You did more than just work with him," the detective accused and Lise blushed. "You were the beneficiary of his life insurance—or have you forgotten that?"

"No, Sir—or, well, yes Sir. It's not something I like to remember."

"You don't think it's rather strange that so many people around you have died under mysterious, if not criminal, circumstances? It's obvious that you knew the doorman as well."

"Of course I think it's strange," she rebutted indignantly. "It's strange and frightening but there's not much I could do about it except get more locks for my door.''

''Ms. Brown, do you know this man?''

He showed her a police-sketch of Nigel. Her gut churned wildly; she thought she might faint. His screams were deafening; Jessica seemed to hear them, or something, but no-one else did.

''Or this man?''

The second drawing was of Baron Samedi. She held the pictures loosely in her hands and ransacked her mind for the right answers. It was written do not fear to say: ''There be witchcraft in the land'' for to deny it is to invite suspicion and the Question. The New York Police Department was unlikely to put her on the rack, but they were getting suspicious.

''I have seen these men,'' she answered, returning the pictures. ''Are they victims too?''

''Do you know their names?'' the detective asked.

''The white man's name is Nigel; he doesn't use a last name. I've never known the name of the black man.''

The man shrugged and tucked the pictures back into a clipboard. ''Ms. Brown, both these men have been seen around this building and around the scenes of several of our unsolved crimes. Any information you have about them could save lives.''

The unwanted empathy Lise had with Nigel became a nest of wasps within her. Stabs of hot agony threatened to crumple her where she sat and the harsh, unforgiving eyes of the detective did nothing to make her relax. Unwittingly she stared at the Rift when pain swarmed within her. She wouldn't have seen anything except for the movement; a dark drop coalescing out of the air and falling to the carpet. The agony redoubled itself.

''They're both a bit strange,'' she explained. ''They frighten me,'' she hoped that would account for whatever pain was visible in her face and her reaction to the next large drop that was forming from nothingness. The air seemed a bit foul already, though maybe it was only her fear. ''I wouldn't want to have anything more to do with either of them.''

''Have you seen either of them lately?''

''Nigel—almost two weeks ago. I told him not to come

around again. He frightened me."

The detective began to sneeze violently. His eyes watered copiously despite his blotting them. Jessica excused herself from the room. The stench of the Otherworld was unmistakable now, but the detective did not suspect the supernatural source of his discomfort nor had he glanced up at the right time to see the droplets of blood fall to the carpet. Lise found herself praying that the man would find a reason to leave before things got further out of hand.

His face had turned a dull red. "Ms. Brown," he wheezed, handing her a business card. "If you see either of those men again, please call this number. I don't know what's come over me—gotta get outside."

His basic suspicion remained; he had gotten a drop of blood on his coat as he headed for the door. If he ever noticed the mark on the dark fabric or, worse, ever thought to have it analyzed—. Lise made a show of offering him a glass of water or anything else he might wish for his discomfort but it seemed that once the notion to leave had settled in his mind, nothing would deter him. She locked the door firmly once he was on the elevator.

"Lise, what're we going to do?" Maria asked. Tears were flowing down her cheeks. "They're going to blame us. They're going to think we're responsible for all this: they'll bring back the death penalty if they think we're the Slasher or the Plague!"

"First we get a bucket," Lise responded with a calm she did not possess. She found a plastic tub under the sink.

Jessica had already lit incense before the statue of the Goddess and was kneeling before it when Lise slipped the tub under the steady trickle of Otherworld blood.

"Do you think he guessed?" Jessica asked as she fanned the fragrant smoke toward the Rift.

"I doubt it. He was suspicious, all right, but the Otherworld is not the sort of thing a sane person suspects." Lise replied, and froze as the first drop of liquid to reach the tub was not red, but a viscous blue. She felt her legs go slack beneath her and staggered backwards until she flopped on the sofa.

"Omygod!" Maria exclaimed as she examined the fluid. "What do we do now?"

"Nothing," Lise mumbled, getting her strength back as the wave of orgiastic torture passed. "The police aren't going to hold anything against us because we haven't done anything wrong. I would tell them if I saw either the Baron or Nigel again—but I won't see them." She remembered the scene on the subway and a delayed shudder ran down her back. "I guess we could try praying for ourselves and Samhain," she added softly.

The drops covered the bottom of the pan. There were both deep red and thick blue fluids oozing out of the Rift; they didn't mix but formed kaliedescope patterns on the bottom of the tub. Dangerous patterns should anyone stare too long at them. Gradually the flow tapered off and the angry snakes in Lise's groin quieted as well. She felt the exhaustion her efforts to control her expression had cost.

Nigel and the Otherworld were behind the Rift; the Lammas Plague was loose but there was nothing the coven or anyone else was going to do about it for another three weeks. The police could watch the building—in a way that was a comforting thought, no-one could mistakenly attribute the Lammas Plague's rampages to them if they were under surveillence. They were safe unless everyone started thinking in terms of magick—but she couldn't worry about that, yet.

Chapter Forty-Six

The nightmare Lise had witnessed in the subway never surfaced to public knowledge. It never even rose into the rumor network. The train itself had been found abandoned and more people were said to have disappeared. No-one seemed to have witnessed the fate of the commuters. Lise felt no temptation to step forward and enlighten the City.

She was certain she had seen the Plague in action and equally certain there was nothing she could do about it. Even Maria, who was also convinced the subway disasters were the direct action of the Plague, could not have conceived of what Lise had seen nor kept her courage once she knew.

During the Slasher's reign of terror, people had feared to be alone. With the mass disappearances the people grew wary of subways and buses, of crowded elevators and brightly lit discos. Children were kept home from school by parents who had stayed away from their jobs as well. Those who could leave the City, left—and were not particularly welcomed in their places of refuge. The daily accounting of New York's lost people had become a national obsession.

"They're making it worse," Jason complained as he turned off the television in Lise's livingroom. "The media creates the climate of hysteria then reports on it." His mood was, perhaps, impaired by the fact that Sally had taken herself and their children out of the City.

"Well, what are they supposed to do? More and more people *are* disappearing," Lise pointed out.

"They're going to discover a lot more than they bargained for, one of these days. The Otherworld's recruiting its army," Maria argued.

Lise said nothing to contradict her. It was almost too late to share the truth now that half of October had gone by and over a thousand people were reported missing. Riverside wasn't immune to its own rumors. The Otherworld army wasn't

Maria's idea; Mark had come up with it first. Remembering the disintegration of the woman she had seen, Lise personally doubted that even the Otherworld could make use of what the Plague left behind.

Although she had not requested the additional support, the coven sat by the quiescent Rift in groups of three or four rather than singly or in pairs. Sleeping bags regularly cluttered the abused livingroom carpet. Maria's boutique had shut its doors for the duration, leaving her with no better place to be. Both Ratners' were operating their much-curtailed law practices from their apartment. And, citing the near impossibility of restocking his shelves, Jason had padlocked the doors to Culpeper's when he sent his family to safety. They congregated around the Rift and Lise could do little more than be polite about it.

"You'd think that at least they'd stop watching us," Rachel complained. She was standing by the window and speaking about the police who watched the building with an ever-increasing lack of subtlety. "Whatever it is that they think we're doing up here it should be obvious, even to them, that we are not hiding missing people up here."

"Nothing is obvious to the police," Jason muttered. "They'll sit out there until Hell freezes over."

"They might not have to wait long," Maria commented bitterly.

"Look, folks," Lise began in her current interpretation of Edith's leadership style. "They do us a lot more good than harm. If anything happens anywhere else they're our proof that we weren't involved. And they'll also keep us safe if the anti-occult movement gets rolling."

"What anti-occult movement?" Rachel asked.

"Rumors," Lise admitted. She was one of the few who still travelled back and forth to her office and picked up the street gossip. "Garlic and rabbit's feet aren't working anymore. They've burnt their candles; said their prayers and people keep on vanishing. One suspects that they're going to start feeling betrayed. What I actually heard that some end-of-the-world type in the Bronx got beaten to death for claiming that this was the Great-They-In-the-Sky's way of purifying us. I don't think it happened—but I don't like the idea popping up in the rumor mill. Sooner or later, now, some little knothole of people're going to decide it's somebody's fault—or the fault of people like us—and they'll remember what they heard about up in the Bronx and they'll think it's okay."

"I don't think the police will protect us from that kind of riot," Rachel averred.

The coven knew about the dripping episode that had occurred while Lise was questioned by the police. They were all convinced the man had left because the Otherworld's closeness distressed him subliminally. Likewise they believed the stake-out officers were being affected. There was no consensus as to what the Rift had done, or was doing—only the belief that it had acted on the policemen's minds to make them unreliable.

"Well, we've only got to get through Samhain. Everything will come clean then, for better or worse. Once there's nothing happening they won't feel the need to keep paying attention to us," Maria suggested and the room fell silent.

They had not stirred to other conversation when the sound of a key in the locks got their attention. Lise walked in the hallway to greet Bob.

"You got the TV on?" he asked before she said anything.

"No, Jason turned it off—the news is rather hysterical these days."

Bob nodded and pushed past her to turn on the set. "Hysterical's not the word for it. Something's loose on the docks."

He ran through the channels until the screen filled with that particular confusion that marks the crisis-in-progress from any re-enactment of it. Red glare from police cars periodically washed over the abandoned buildings. For the moment there was no commentary.

"What's it supposed to be?" Jason demanded.

"If I'm overhearing things correctly, then they've stumbled onto the Lammas Plague while they were looking for the missing people."

A crisply dressed, earnest young woman stepped into the red glare. There had been, she informed her audience, no further word from the police-spokesperson on the scene; nothing to confirm the rumors that the initial search team had been found dead in the storage area or, indeed, anything to connect the derelict building with the missing people. "But," she added as the camera panned away from her to the jumble of squad cars and wire-window buses, "the police are here in force, not planning to leave for some time. They are proceeding with the utmost caution." She promised they would stay on-site until a conclusive story could be assembled. The picture flip-flopped back to the news-studio.

Bob began running through the channels again and Lise, looking down the street to a young man who looked uncomfortable as he tried to look inconspicuous, exchanged the picture tube for a subway window in her mind.

"Just what can this Otherworld Plague actually do?" Jason asked. "It's not really a disease, is it?"

But no-one tried to answer his question as Bob found another live broadcast.

"Let me repeat—for you and your audience—there is nothing in this building to indicate that any of the missing persons were ever, in any number or at any time, detained here," the obviously nervous spokesman for the City stated. "We think there might be some dangerous chemical concentrations in the building at this time—"

"What of the initial investigation team?" the reporter pressed.

"They're still inside."

"Then why," the reporter gestured and the camera followed his fingertips to the mass police presence, "are all these men here? If you've got chemicals, why are the men armed? Isn't this a job for the fire department?"

The spokesman never answered. The camera, which focused on the guarded entrance to the old warehouse, relayed the scene in eloquent silence. The doors swung outward and for a moment it seemed that nothing had emerged, then there were screams from the men closest to the building; they tore at their clothes, their skin. Men and women holding microphones gasped as the taint of the Otherworld reached their unprotected nostrils. One policeman broke rank and raced to shut the double doors. Lise was the only person in the City who knew what to expect, who flinched before the man reeled backwards, turned to the cameras and revealed a face of horror to the world.

"He's already dead," she whispered, but no-one heard as the cameras pursued the stricken man across the rutted pavement. The mini-cam operator, perhaps because things do not seem quite real through a view-finder, ignored the chaos around him and kept tight focus on the scene.

The anchor-woman they had seen on the other channel screamed—a scream so loud and powerful that all the microphones caught it clearly. Then even the mini-cam operator shuddered. The policeman, on his knees now, was decaying into nothing—live, on camera. The mini-cam operator refocused.

The dying man's eyes were black pits; the Plague destroyed eyes quickly. There was little blood, not enough to conceal what was happening from the millions who saw what the mini-cam saw. Dark lesions appeared, spread and deepened across the man's face. There was no nose; the mouth was an emptiness without tongue or teeth. As they watch a lesion crept down his neck and out of sight beneath his jacket. A dark stain spread across the fabric, but the Plague did not stop to destroy the less-appetizing clothing this time. In a coincidence of perversity the camera was focused on the man's hand as the lesions crept down and swallowed the fingers, one by one.

The mini-cam operator had seen enough. The picture bounced wildly and settled again with the horizon running from corner to corner. From that crazed perspective Lise and the rest watched as the first victim imploded with a blur. Another, less expert, hand steadied the camera and focused it on what had been the young newswoman. The Lammas Plague had her; lesions spread over her face and hands quickly merging into uniform blackness. She wasn't resisting, just staying paralyzed still until there was not enough left of her body to hold it upright.

"Turn it off!" Lise commanded—and when no-one responded she pushed the button herself and faced her shaken comrades. "All right—now you know exactly how it's happening and that anyone who's disappeared is not ever coming back. But there's *still* nothing we can do about it except prepare ourselves for Samhain."

"Couldn't we try going down there and making a circle around it? It might work," Jason suggested.

"And if it didn't who would perform the Samhain rite—the only rite we know has a chance of working?" Lise retorted. "The High Coven is pointed to Samhain. Even if that *thing* ate for the rest of the month, without stopping, it wouldn't justify leaving the Rift and risking our lives. If it came here, the way Nigel came here, I'd try something. But we can't go hunting for it; we can't set traps and we really shouldn't try to attract its attention."

They weren't happy with the decision, but they wouldn't openly argue with her. She had survived two weeks without Edith and was getting used to exerting her own, unsupported, judgment. It helped, of course, that none of them really wanted to confront the Otherworld-spawned Plague however vocally they objected to her conservative approach. The newswoman's dissolving face had been seared into their memories, giving some of them the first clear vision of the dangers they faced.

Lise's sense of timing had improved, as well, she knew how long to leave them with their thoughts and when to direct that fuming energy elsewhere.

"Okay, let's do what we *can* do: a couple more times through the Samhain invocation—" Their faces showed rebellion, but Lise went on. "Look, I want every last one of us able to run this Samhain ritual: first, second and third degrees—everyone. Now that you've got an idea what we're up against, I can't see why you'd argue with more practice. If that Plague comes calling while we're squeezing off the Otherworld we've all got to be prepared. The old Riverside lost because they were slow and they didn't believe they had power without Arthur. I can't let that happen to you. Now then: On this most sacred and terrible night of Samhain—"

They fell into ragged unison behind her. Even without the circle as a lens, the Samhain invocation brought a sense of the Goddess and the Consort to the room. Lise led them through the closing chants as well, just to be safe, before releasing them to thoughts of dinner.

Lise rarely participated in the nightly arguments over food. If she suggested something they all fell in step meekly; when she didn't the discussion could last an hour. Without the coven's active concern over food she would have skipped most meals as she drilled herself mentally for Samhain.

"Could we stop the Plague if it did come here?" Maria asked much later in the night when the dockside scene had been replayed so many times that its impact was lessened.

"If we didn't panic; if we kept our heads until the Rift was closed," Lise replied, not looking up from the embroidery she was putting on the hem of her Samhain robe.

"Do you think it will come looking for us?"

"Eventually. When we threaten the Otherworld—from its point of view, that is—the Plague will come to stop us."

Maria and Bob returned to their own apartment that night. Mark and Rachel went across the hall at midnight and only Jason remained with his sleeping bag unrolled on the sofa. Lise could hear his gentle snoring some time before she shut off her light and settled in for sleep.

Nigel, if it was still Nigel, broadcast his screams and temptations most clearly in those moments before she slipped into her own dreams. Lise expected his incursion into her nightly rituals and when no Rift-borne images assaulted her thoughts the result was not reassuring. She slept lightly without losing awareness of her surroundings and was upright in the bed the moment the light went on in the livingroom. She picked up the silver mirror and tiptoed to the French doors.

"I couldn't decide if I should wake you," Jason said from the sofa. The dishpan sat in the middle of the room to catch a steady stream of dark fluid. "I woke up when it started, I guess; that is—the carpet wasn't very wet by the time I got the bucket in place."

"Damn them!" she said, staring at the Rift. "I'm really

tired of this—more than anything else I'm just tired. I'm past being frightened but I don't know how much more my nerves will take. I never was one for your classic eyeball-to-eyeball confrontation."

"Well, not quite classic," Jason said with a little smile. "These were what actually woke me up. Another two inches lower and you would have had an ex-Guardian on your sofa."

He held out two crab-like objects which Lise had little difficulty in identifying: Nigel's hands, their crystal claws splayed outward to slash through soft, human flesh. She looked down at the stream of blood and listened for his screams. They'd cut off his hands—she held them almost tenderly. The beginnings of tears were filling her eyes.

"What should we do with them?" Jason asked.

"Purify them, I guess, then bury them someplace where they won't ever be distrubed."

She looked at the marks the claws had made in the window sills. If they'd touched Jason he would have been killed. If they had even been aimed at him.

The lights of New Jersey twinkled with a rainbow of colors; she watched them, thinking of their beauty until she realized they'd never shone with so many colors before. The Lammas Plague had moved, grown. It hung somewhere between herself and the Palisades and it was easily as large as the building in which she stood. Perhaps he had called it; perhaps he was still trying to protect her in his own fashion.

Chapter Forty-Seven

"Look up, fools!" Rachel complained as she looked down at the stakeout. The Lammas Plague shimmered above the treetops opposite 647 but though the men often stared at the windows they never looked straight up.

"Oh, just ignore them, Sally advised. "It's been quiet. If they looked up and saw something in the trees they'd be all over us.. We might not be able to perform the ritual tonight and we know what that'd get us."

In truth, they didn't know. The Lammas Plague had metamorphosized since Lise had witnessed its arrival. It was huge and appeared different from the apartment than it did when viewed from anywhere else. From the ground it was a barely discernable, wispy black cloud but from the living-room it was a swirling diffuse web of many colors and changing patterns.

If they didn't know why the cloud was changing, they knew it hadn't budged since its arrival; no disappearances had been recorded since the dockside massacre. Now it was noon on Samhain itself and if the Plague was going to do something it would do it in the next twelve to eighteen hours.

"Are you planning to do anything more with the windows?" Sally continued after she'd joined Rachel in staring out them.

"No," Lise looked up from the writing table. "We renewed the wards at new-moon. I can't see any point to doing anything now that we're passing the full moon. They'll be strong enough."

It was tradition to work strengthening spells at the new moon and debilitating spells on the waning moon. Lise had been unable to think of a way to use the waning moon's power and had decided to leave the windows and the Rift warding untampered with.

She had promised herself the necessary research into the Celtic calendars to recreate the real cycle of Samhain. She thought it should be a new moon festival—to take advantage of waxing magick. Its date shouldn't wander randomly through the moon's phases on the whim of an industrialized calendar. But over the years the Wiccans had internalized the Julian calendar and even if the day were wrong from the point of view of moon scholarship, it was correct for psychological power and magick.

Edith had called earlier from her husband's office in Saint Ives. She'd offered kind encouragement and the knowledge that both Caer Maen and Gretna would sit within their circles from sundown in Cornwall until sunrise in New York. The phone connection had been bad, but the message had gotten through: the older High Covens stood ready to share their power and experience. If Riverside, or the Riverside High Priestess, wished to use that power all she had to do was believe she could.

The corridor echoed with Jessica and Eileen's excited conversation. They were all at 647 today, all twelve of them—though with any luck they'd go their separate ways before the eleven o'clock news was over. Lise could look forward to having her apartment back—if she could avoid thinking about the rite that came beforehand.

"Package for you," Eileen announced, putting a battered, string-tied parcel on the table.

Lise got the scissors but examined the package carefully before cutting any of the strings. The postmark was smeared beyond deciphering but the stamps were Haitian and that roused her. The return address was a box in Port-au-Prince—but she wouldn't expect to see "Baron Samhain" neatly printed in the upper left corner. Of course, Lise didn't expect to see Baron Samhain at all.

Her attitude of apprehension had spread to everyone who gathered at the table as she began unrolling the brown paper. The cardboard box that eventually emerged and produced, in turn, several glassine envelopes of rust-colored powder and a half-dozen candles the like of which Lise had last seen on her windowsill did not seem to justify the suspense. Her hand did not betray her by trembling, but Lise would not touch any object in the box.

''What is it? Some kind of practical joke?'' Mark asked, but he did not touch the voodoo items either.

''No,'' Lise admitted.

Sally picked up a glassine envelope and sniffed the powder. ''Dragon's blood: voodoo.''

''The Baron sent this?'' Rachel asked.

''Then just throw the stuff out,'' Mark suggested.

''Yeah,'' Bob chimed in, ''we don't need any voodoo magick muddying things up. We never knew where he stood; we'd just be inviting trouble to have this stuff any where near here tonight.''

A ripple of nods and mono-syllables wove through the group while Lise gingerly picked up one of the oily, gnarled candles. It left a film on her fingers that had a dubious, rotting odor. ''I've got to think about it,'' she answered without looking at any of them. There was more paper in the box but none of it contained a message or instructions.

''What's to think about?'' Maria demanded. ''The stuff reeks almost as bad as the Otherworld. It's not witchcraft—it doesn't belong on our altar.''

''It's Lise's decision,'' Jessica reminded them. ''She's the one who takes the responsibility. Voodoo incense and candles have been used on Wiccan altars. Some of their magick is ours; some of ours is theirs. There's no necessary contradiction.''

''I don't think I could be comfortable or confident if I thought the Baron was in the circle with us,'' Maria announced, creating a focus for all the dissent and malaise in the group.

Lise could have cheerfully taken her long-time friend out of the room and rattled her teeth. ''We'll wait,'' she said evenly, staring directly at Maria. ''I'll know what I want after I've thought about it a while.''

''He was an evil man—I'm just as glad he's disappeared along with Nigel. Edith never trusted him,'' Maria would not be cowed.

''Well, Edith's not here now—you'll have to abide by my decision!''

Lise was angry and let them know it as she left the room for the privacy of her bedroom. The package remained open and untouched on the writing table throughout the afternoon, gradually filling the room with the scents of rampant vegitation. More than once Lise was tempted to take the easy way out and dump the lot in the incinerator. But the knowledge that she had failed the Baron with these candles before would stop her. She searched every inch of the wrapping paper and box in private, seeking a clue that would make her decision for her. She had failed the Baron—did he seek revenge or did he offer her yet one more chance to accept his help? By the end of the afternoon she knew what she had suspected from the start: it wasn't meant to be an easy decision.

She was saved from making the decision at that moment by the simmering of the ubiquitous stock-pot which Maria had transferred to Lise's kitchen. They were to eat early, as Lise insisted that everyone partake of the traditional salt-water cleansing before the ritual began. The Baron's incense was no match for Agnelli tomato sauce.

A bright-eyed preschooler with mother in tow, a pointed crepe-paper witch hat tottering on her head, rang the doorbell in quest of Hallowe'en treats. With all their Samhain preparations no-one had picked up candy—not even Sally whose two children were still in the country with their grandmother. A quick collection produced a handful of change and an unopened roll of mints which were accepted with a whispered "thank you." The coven stared sheepishly from one to another until Lise laughed aloud.

When the meal was done and it was time to rearrange the livingroom for the serious work of the evening, the question of the Baron's gift returned and could not be put off any longer.

"What shall I do with them?" Jessica asked, holding the candles at arm's length. She might respect Lise's perogatives, but that didn't make her like the candles.

"I'll take them," Lise said. The sun had already set but the Lammas Plague was darker than the night sky: darker and larger than it had seemed even the night before, or was it flowing closer to the apartment? Lise made her decision, setting the candles on the windowsills of the bedroom and the livingroom. If the Baron were against her he'd have found a more direct way of showing it.

"I wish you wouldn't," Maria interrupted.

"It's my decision," Lise replied, edging away from the window lest Maria notice what she had already determined; the Plague was not more than an arm's length from the windows.

Lise was the last of the twelve to ease into the tepid, salty water. A faint discoloration still remained on her cheek where Nigel had struck her; the scabs had fallen from her arms without leaving noticable scars. The line on her palm was still there but like the rest of the Otherworld devices it was powerless so long as the thoughts of Nigel remained alive within her. And they did—the screaming had begun again shortly after they ate and her body, if not her mind, was aroused.

She had set the Dragon's Blood incense in a small clay dish and lit it before she settled into the water. It blended pleasantly with the scent of the frankincense oil with which she anointed herself before dressing. When the bedroom was quiet, meaning that everyone else was dressed and waiting in the livingroom, she took the rich, red robe she had made for herself from the wardrobe.

Even dime-store paperbacks about witchcraft mentioned that a witch dressed in magickal clothing for Samhain. The Riverside grimoires were not so specific—it was assumed a High Coven priest or priestess knew what to wear to a ritual. The dark red cloth Lise draped over herself did not glitter or catch the candlelight; its embroideries, though lush, were done in subtle, matte shades yet she began to glow with a proper, Samhain richness.

Lise brushed her hair smooth down over her shoulders then braided strands of burgundy glass beads into it. The beads brought glints of dark fire to her face, as she had intended. She draped a necklace of dark, polished seeds around her neck and peered into the dim mirror. She was starting to look like a High Priestess though she didn't yet feel like one equal to the task of caging the Otherworld. She darkened and intensified her eyes with kohl until the open, friendly planes of her face had disappeared beneath brooding eyes. The High Priestess had finally emerged.

"Now you are Sybylla," she told the reflection. "You've got the power; you're going into that room and do what has to be done—"

Her image seemed to waver. Lise saw a nervous woman in faintly medieval attire and too much exotic make-up, then she saw the High Priestess again.

"You—no, I can make the magick work."

There were no stars above the Hudson River—the Plague hid them and the river as well. The livingroom was deathly quiet with eleven people not looking at the dark windows. There was more fear than power in the room.

"Let's get started," Lise announced, pulling the doors shut behind her.

The altar itself had been dressed by Sally and accorded precisely with the requirements Edith had set for them. Two candles were already burning beside the statue of the Goddess; the Guardian watchtowers had been placed just beyond the perimeter of the nine-foot circle.

Eyes moved from Lise to the ominiously dark windows and back again. She affected not to notice the stygian deep clinging to the glass. It wasn't easy. The velvet blackness was more pressing here than it had been in the bedroom.

She was about to ask to have the electric lights turned off when the bulb in the table-lamp exploded and the room plunged into candlelight. Gasps and stifled screams filled the room.

"Turn if off, anyway," Lise asked. "It's not a good idea to leave an open socket."

Neither the altar candles nor the Baron's gifts were reflected in the window panes. Indeed, without going closer to the windows and touching them it was impossible to be certain if the glass was still in place if the Plague had begun to ooze past the wardings.

They made a tight, anxious circle with Lise at the center kneeling before the Goddess. She inhaled, counted to ten, exhaled and felt the painful pounding of her heart ease a bit. Small bundles of bittersweet berries concealed the base of the statue. Lise stared at them and thought of autumn in Michigan—trick-or-treating through huge piles of leaves. Then, when she was relaxed, she picked up the silver sword for the first time and went to the unlit candle of the North.

"Hail and welcome, spirits of the watchtower of the North. Interweave your powers with ours on this sacred, dangerous night. Preserve with us the flow of life and death through this perilous rite."

She heard the swish of heavy cloth moving behind her as they all saluted the North. They turned in place and followed her to the East, the South and finally to the West where it took no imagination to see the Otherworld itself looming behind the watchtower.

"I believe in the power of the Wicca," Lise whispered to the darkness. "I believe in our power as Guardians. Our circle cannot be broken."

She held the image of the inviolable circle in her mind as she navigated around the circle with the ritual elements. The coven faced the altar as she moved behind them; they couldn't see the oozing fingers of Otherness coming down the back of the sofa. Lise managed to maintain a belief in herself that strengthened the thrice-made circle. Their sphere was solid and impervious to the Lammas Plague, though its tendrils snaked up the sides.

"Let us gather our thoughts before the invocation of the Goddess," she told the coven.

The disk of the Otherworld was invisible though the candles on the altar pulsed to its unseen spinning. The presence of that awful power all but drained her breath from her. They would reopen the Rift—though it had never been closed—consign human souls to pass through it then, with the abiding grace of the Goddess and the Guardians, the aberration would be sealed a new.

The circle was stocked with new witches experiencing the rite for the first time; as High Priestess she might have stopped and told them the purpose the ritual and recounted the history of the High Coven Samhain. Edith had suggested such an interlude if the situation warranted it, but Lise, who was also experiencing Samhain for the first time, was not sure enough of her stamina to indulge in windy lectures. The circle was not impervious to the aroma of the Otherworld, she and her witches were enveloped by terror; the ritual would have to move quickly if it were to succeed.

"Sister, Mother, Crone," Lise began, speaking only to the Goddess, "whichever face You show to us this night—You are always a part of this world—You are never Otherworldly. You understand our needs better than we do ourselves. You've stood by us in catastrophe."

She paused. The Goddess had not always stood by them. Perhaps the gods and goddesses had past their times and all this was just a hollow farce, however real the Rift might be. The human realms of life and death might indeed be ripe for plunder.

Lise shivered violently, shaking the thought from her mind. She would not question the power of the Goddess again. The statue might be just a statue but there were more than twelve mortals in the circle.

An urgent voice broke into her thoughts. "Lady Sybylla? The Western watchtower?" Rachel pointed across the circle.

The candleflame had shot up to a height of several inches, blazing mightily yet casting little light. The Lammas Plague encroached, cutting the flame in half with bands of darkness. The bands widened and the flame was gone.

"Should we relight it?" Rachel asked.

"No." The candles were at the perimeter of the circle; they could not be relit without violating the sphere of power Lise had created. The rite would have to survive the loss of the Western watchtower. "The circle will hold," Lise said aloud.

The darkness retreated and a tiny, bluish flame could be seen struggling for life in the wax-pool of the Western candle. Rachel sat down.

"On this most sacred and terrible night of Samhain
When the spheres are strained and bursting
And the fires of life and death burn brightest,
"We come together in our ancient, august ritual
With shouts and songs to fling apart
The drawn curtains of our lives and all else,

"To bid fond, sad parting to those who must now depart
And greet with joyous thoughts and song
Each spirit whose journey is now begun,
"With fear and trembling, yet stalwart in our duties—
EVOI! EVOI! EKO! EVOK!

They had agreed, in long hours of practice, that they would believe their power had to be combined to open the warding around the Rift and call forth the exchange of spirits. They would also believe it would take only one of them, surviving, reciting the words of closing to stop the process should it go awry. Lise told herself the coven wouldn't forget any of that as the yawning black disk of the Otherworld oscillated slowly above the altar.

The Lammas Plague was excited. It swirled just outside the sphere. The watchtower flames in all points had been obscured by Otherworld minions. The coven's instinct was to creep toward the altar, but the Otherworld itself waited there.

Steaming drops of dark liquid oozed steadily from the Rift. They hissed and stank when they struck the altar and then burned. The twelve witches linked arms and began a slow dance. Lise saw faces in the Otherworld blackness—Nigel mostly. Nigel as he had been when she loved him. There were other faces too. Plague victims—their faces too torn to be recognizable—but not the Baron. She saw Madame Odile and a handful of other blacks but not the Baron.

The disk had settled into a stable rotation, aligning itself so Lise could always see the abyssmal darkness as she moved. When they went to their knees to wait out the thousand heartbeats during which the exchange of souls would occur, the Rift disk froze in place in front of her as well.

"Save me, Lise," Nigel called to her.

He was a tiny figure deep within the disk. His form was purely human, except that it had no hands. The bloody stream from the stumps of his wrists flowed onto the Goddess and did not burn. Lise let go of Mark's arm and reached out to the disk.

"Don't!" he whispered and pulled her arm back.

The blood began to hiss and boiled clean of the statue. The Goddess could take care of Herself. They should not succumb to foolish temptation at this late time on Her behalf. Lise looked around her coven and saw the shadow of temptation on every face. The Otherworld had not singled her out this time. Maria whimpered and hid her face on Bob's shoulder but did not break the circle. Jessica shook with convulsions, but Jason and Sally restrained her. Eileen, on the far side of the circle, who had not seemed much affected by Rift-borne temptation, shrieked at the sight of Jessica's jerking, swelling limbs.

Eileen struck free of her partners and ran across the circle, brushing against the Rift itself as she went. Her eyes turned red and fiery, like the demon-cat's. Rachel tried to stop her as she careened out of the circle. The room was eeriely silent.

Lise had lost count of her heartbeats and now her heart pounded too fast for counting. Nigel was dragging himself through the stream of his blood. Everyone who remained in the circle was caught in no less terrifying visions. The High Priestess had held with tradition as best she could, but the Rift had to be closed before Nigel reached her.

"Great Goddess! Help us!" she exclaimed, hauling Mark to his feet beside her. "Abide with us as we seal this abomination."

Nigel's mutilated arm reached out of the Rift; his screams were far louder than their chant. Lise tensed and pulled away from him.

"Go back!" she whispered hoarsely.

The truncated limb probed the air and stretched out to her, she inhaled but dared not step backwards, out of the circle and into the buzzing maelstrom of the Plague.

"The moment comes—and is gone—" she began the closing chant and stopped suddenly as the bleeding stump adhered to her neck.

She would have bolted from the circle, if Rachel and Mark had let her, but they held her firmly between them. The disk began to pivot again as the coven tried to dance through the closing chant. Lise couldn't speak through her fear and revulsion but she thought the words and tried not to think about the thing caressing her neck. She closed her eyes and thought of Caer Maen.

Camulac's thoughts had wandered into the sunlight expanses of the summer moors but they came back at the tug of Lise's panic. Riverside's High Priestess felt herself in the safety of the Caer Maen warrens, looking at Lady Camulac in her half-moon crown. She was at Gretna too, though she didn't truly recognize the darkhaired woman who sat on a forbidding throne.

—If this is real; if this is you, please help me!—

Lady Camulac nodded and walked forward until Lise could see no more of her than her steel-blue eyes. She kissed Lise lightly and embraced her. Lise felt her breath being squeezed away.

—Edith!—Lise's thoughts poured into the ether.—Why? Where are you? What did I do wrong? Help me, please!—

The room spun violently, lurching sideways and knocking her off balance. She was tossed into realities she could not comprehend until her mind refused to accept anything more and surrounded itself with darkness of its own creation.

Caer Maen and Gretna bore down on her, squeezing her into nothingness. The Otherworld caught her in its breath and drew her into its everlasting cold. Though she had lost contact with her coven and reality, she had not lost consciousness and knew when she had passed through the Rift.

The husk of Anerien floated past her, breaking into ever smaller pieces as it whirled. He, at least, had been freed from torment, re-absorbed into the Summerland where he belonged.

Threads of Nigel's screams and agony wrapped around her, but not Nigel himself and though the part of him that was within her remained, he himself was gone—returned to the substance of the Otherworld yet beyond the torment of the Otherworld as well.

The winds shifted, reversing themselves, picking up speed until the cold was burning against her and she could discern nothing of her surroundings except the sense of falling. And the dread knowledge that she would eventually strike something.

"It's over," a voice whispered in her ear.

Lise believed it was. She had felt the shattering impact and now had no sense of her body at all.

"Lise, Lady Sybylla?"

Maria's voice—and her hand holding a glass of wine. Lise took the glass carefully, watching her fingers curl over the surface she could not feel. The only light in her livingroom came from hand-held candles, but it was enough to show her the faces of her coven and the clear air above the altar.

"We did it," Jason assured her, shaking her cold hand vigorously. "The Rift is gone."

So was the exquisite statue of the Goddess. A pile of glass shards covered the bittersweet berries. They saw her staring at it.

"It exploded as the Rift closed. We all blinked, when we looked again, the Goddess and the Rift were gone," Bob explained.

The livingroom was still dark and buzzing with the Plague beyond the circle, but already it was possible to see the valiant watchtower flames through the devolving cloud. It would not survive long without the Rift. Still, it was not safe to banish the circle. There was no sign of Eileen.

"I just don't know," her partner admitted. Of all of them, he was the palest, the most shaken but the reality of what happened—of the transformation of his companion, of her capture by the Plague had not yet become clear to him.

Lise sipped her wine too grateful to share another's grief just now. The air in the room continued to clear. Moonlight flooded the room. All that remained of the Plague was a layer of grey dust. Lise got to her feet and brushed the broken glass from her athame on the altar.

"Our gratitude and thanks for Your sacrifices," she whispered to the shards and extinguished the altar candles.

They held their hands above their heads and in weary unison chorused: "The Circle is Broken!" and held their breath.

When finally each had had to breathe and acknowledge that the Otherworld was indeed departed, they dispersed from the strict circle formation. Eileen had vanished. Not so much as a fiber of her robe remained, not a drop of blood.

Reluctantly Jessica felt the carpet where the missing woman had broken out of the circle.

"She's gone."

Her partner left almost at once with Jason, Sally and the other two from Sally's covens. Lise doubted any of them would return. She thought of the price they had paid, and coldly concluded the sacrifice had been justified.

"You did not force them," Jessica reminded her. "They came here knowing—if not believing. I do not blame myself that *my* struggles were more than she could bear."

Lise was not convinced. The psychic's eyes had always been haunted; a new burden of guilt would be easily hidden in them. Rachel and Mark took Jessica with them across the hall and into their home.

"I can't believe it's over," Maria said, making small gestures to rearrange the room.

"Don't bother, I can take care of everything tomorrow," Lise took the spent candles from the windowsills and set them on the table. "It isn't over—there's still next year and every year after that."

"We'll get stronger," Bob said, slapping her on the shoulder and not noticing that she winced. "We'll be going home now—if you'll be okay here?"

Lise nodded and stood alone in the livingroom while they changed. The clock had stopped when the bulb exploded; she'd left her watch in the bedroom. She went to the windows, hoping she could see a clock—she guessed it was past midnight. The world outside didn't know what had happened in her apartment, as it should not know. There were even people walking down the street below. A man stepped out of the shadows, almost deliberately, so she could see him in the moonlight. She thought of the policemen watching the apartment but this man had a top hat, cape and cane. He bowed up at her; she waved, knowing he could see.